Mercy at Midnight

Mercy at Midnight

Sylvia Bambola

Heritage Publishing House

IF
Bambola

ISBN: 0989970752
ISBN # 9780989970754

Library of Congress Control Number: 2016943195

Heritage Publishing House, Bradenton, Florida

Scriptures taken from Holy Bible, King James Version, Cambridge, 1769

For information:
Heritage Publishing House
1767 Lakewood Ranch Blvd.
Bradenton, FL 34211

ACKNOWLEDGMENTS

My family is always on the top of this list. Did I mention they were wonderful? A big "thank you" to my daughter, Gina, for her critique and invaluable input. Gina, I always appreciate your perspective and how you find those inconsistencies I fail to. And then I extend appreciation to my son, Cord. Where do I start? How do you say "thank you" to someone always willing to help no matter what time or day? Always willing to go the extra mile? Thank you for keeping my computer humming.

Next, I'd like to thank a precious woman of God, Gloria Smith. What eagle eyes! I won't embarrass myself my mentioning just how many grammar and spelling mistakes she found during her edit. What a gift you have, Gloria, and thank you for using it to help make *Mercy at Midnight* better.

And finally, a big "shout-out" to Miranda Lee, the very talented graphic artist who put together the cover. Miranda, I love your spirit of excellence and desire to make everything perfect.

Love and blessings to you all!

CHAPTER 1

Cynthia Wells hoped she wasn't going crazy.

She had always thought the scanning of obituaries a harmless pastime. Now, she wasn't so sure. And it wasn't because of her string of recent nightmares, either. Rather, it was due to the fact that lately, the names and particulars of the departed were sticking to her brain like her mother's dumplings used to stick to her stomach. Hazel Dowd, Charles Mactrell, Amelia Davis, Thomas Gates and a host of others—all strangers, all names off past obituaries —had taken up residence inside her head as though it were a hotel with plenty of vacancies.

She remembered who the grandmother of eight and great-grandmother of nine was, the World War II veteran, the buyer for Flossie's Mercantile, the pastor of the Beacon Mission. And that wasn't all. She knew, for instance, that Hazel Dowd was born in 1924, that Charles Mactrell was awarded the Silver Star, that Amelia Davis worked for Flossie's for thirty-five years, that Reverend Gates had been in ministry even longer. And considering that Cynthia had trouble remembering how long her own mother had worked for the legal team of Sly and Sly before retiring last year or whether her father had gotten two Purple Hearts in Vietnam or just one, this whole obituary thing was beginning to disturb her.

She folded the pages of the *Oberon Tribune*, ignoring the smudges of newsprint that covered the tips of her fingers, and placed the paper on top of the pile of other folded papers beside her bed. She supposed this obsession with the obituaries bothered her because it made her life smack of "imaginary friends"—if you could call a bunch of dead people that. Her mother called it something else.

Isolationism-the word she coined for Cynthia's self-imposed socially-Spartan lifestyle.

But who was her mother to talk? There were other ways to become inaccessible. You could party more than Paris Hilton and still be isolated, with emotions penned up, and left to starve. Her parents had mastered that one.

Still . . . both methods, her parents' and hers, resulted in a sort of self-destruction, like the end of a Mission Impossible tape where it goes up in smoke. But wasn't life, after all, a vapor? She had heard that somewhere. She tried not to brood over the obvious metaphors. Brooding came all too easy these days. It was silly to think of her life as a played-out tape when it was still on its first one-third of the reel. And her life, instead of smoke, was a block of concrete; a veritable bulwark of solid employment, solid finances, solid future. And though living could be rough, it was hardly "mission impossible." Besides, she thrived on the difficult. Everyone said so. She had even built her reputation on it.

Cynthia absently brushed her fingers against the blue and cream Jardin sheets, leaving behind a faint smudge along the top edge. She was *finally* sleepy and needed to push that roster of names in her head and all that nonsense about self-destructing tapes into the backroom of her mind.

And maybe, if she was lucky, she'd actually get some sleep.

A sudden blast of cold air slapped Cynthia's face just like when she opened that old GE refrigerator Mom kept in their well-lit garage to house chocolate pudding and Jell-O and other snacks, only this room was murky . . . dark as though she were looking through black gauze, and this blast of cold air made Cynthia's heart race. She stood still, tilting her face upward like a mouse sniffing for danger. Gradually, her eyes grew accustomed to looking through gauze and she was able to distinguish familiar shapes: the doll house in the corner, the rocking chair, the little clothes-tree whose branches resemble hands and . . . the faint outline of her new Holly Hobbie kitchen. She was still angry over this newest outrage—that of her little oven door hanging by a thread.

Julia wasn't supposed to touch it. But she'd never get punished for wrecking it. She never got punished for anything.

Oh, that cold air . . . so out of place in this warm, happy room. Where was it coming from? Cynthia sniffed the air again, then froze. Nearby, she heard the rustle of denim and smelled what must have been the entire contents of her new Blossom Eau de Toilette.

Julia!

Her arm shot out, but still she failed to clasp the fairy wisp that seemed just centimeters from the tips of her curled fingers.

She wanted to shout, "Stop!" but her tongue remained as slug-like as the time Miss Wilson asked her to recite the Pledge of Allegiance in front of the class. Her legs pumped furiously trying to get to the source of the cold before that wisp did. She was running with all her might but going nowhere. Her breath came in fits and starts as perspiration tickled the sides of her face. And her heart sounded like the pounding of surf in her ears.

"Stop!" she screamed, at last able to speak. A soft giggle answered. Finally, she seemed to make headway and moved toward the blast of cold air. Barely able to see, she ran with arms extended like a mad sleepwalker heading pell-mell toward a cliff. She made one final lunge

for the wisp, her fingers clawing air and nothing else, then heard the scraping and scratching of metal against wood, and one last giggle before it turned into a scream.

Cynthia shot up in bed. Her chest heaved beneath perspiration-soaked pajamas. A sharp, piercing noise bounced off the blue faux-finished walls. She covered her ears—her fingertips lost in the tangle of wet hair plastering her head—and rocked back and forth until realizing the sharp noise was her alarm clock. She lunged for the nightstand and slapped down the button.

Another nightmare.

The third this week.

She swung her legs around and let them dangle off the bed.

It must be the sleeping pills.

The thought evaporated when she remembered she'd skipped her pills last week and still had had two nightmares. She dropped her head to her chest and rotated it like that TV fitness instructor, the one with the great washboard-abs, had demonstrated.

Slowly, roll slowly.

She could almost hear his sexy, melodic voice. *First to the right, then to the left. Round and round, round and round.* It was supposed to ease the tension between her shoulders.

Another minute and she stopped rolling and rose from the bed, still feeling like someone was pinching the back of her neck. She stepped over the stacked copies of *The Oberon Tribune, Morning News* and *Oberon Times*—all folded to the obituary section. She tried not to think what Bernie would say if he found out she was an obituary-holic.

No wonder you have nightmares.

She shuffled to the bathroom vowing to toss the sleeping pills and try some melatonin from the health food store that someone in archives told her about yesterday. And she'd pick up some wholegrain bread and some of those organic vegetables, too. And maybe some of that tofu that looked like barf when you crumbled it up in a salad as Bernie's wife, Roberta—the health nut—did at her dinner parties.

"You've got to stop poisoning your body with junk food," Roberta kept telling her. Maybe Roberta was right. Two thirty-minute TV workouts a week and a half dozen TV dinners, and now, sleeping pills, didn't exactly qualify as a healthy lifestyle. Maybe if Cynthia lived healthier, the nightmares would stop, and those brooding fits of hers, too.

Okay, it was a visit to the health food store tonight, but now it was a quick shower and then a trip to Starbucks for some high-octane so she could start her engine before Bernie called, wondering where she was.

Cynthia waited in line, taking long, deep breaths in-out, in-out—Roberta's prescription for importing oxygen to all those oxygen-starved cells of hers. "Deep breaths, deep breaths," Roberta had instructed, as though it was a mantra. But this in-out in-out stuff wasn't working. Even now, after her shower and time spent on makeup and hair, all Cynthia longed for was a bed and five minutes of deep REM sleep. She once read that constant fatigue could be a sign of depression. And hadn't Bernie called her the Grim Reaper last week just because she refused to laugh at his corny jokes? But she was tired of pretending Bernie was funny. Though he was . . . sometimes. But most of his jokes were lame, so his Grim Reaper remark was hardly credible. Besides, she'd seen firsthand what a lifetime of pretending could do.

She pictured her mother—with eyes lifeless as brown buttons—sitting at one end of the family dinner table, politely spooning her vichyssoise and politely listening to Cynthia's father retell a story they had all heard a thousand times. Politeness had ruled their house for years, which meant never discussing things like death or dying or how a heart could be shredded as easily as tissue paper. And of course, allowing pain to rise from some secret inner pit to tear your eyes like common onion vapor was out of the question. No wonder she rarely ate with her parents. But she rarely ate with anyone, anymore. Eating alone had it own rewards, Cynthia thought, shuffling forward in line and stifling a yawn.

"So, Toby aced his math test?" the thin, pimple-faced kid behind the Starbucks counter said to the man in front of her as he finished making a latte.

"Yeah," returned the customer.

"That's great. I know you were worried. When I was his age I had trouble with math, too. He'll make out fine, you'll see."

"Hope you're right." The customer took his coffee and handed the employee a ten-dollar bill. "Keep the change."

"Thanks. You take care now, Mr. Potter. See you tomorrow."

Cynthia stepped up to the counter and smiled at the kid who had been making her café mochas for the last two years. "Double espresso."

He nodded, then headed for the espresso machine, never commenting that she wasn't getting her usual today or saying her name or passing along trivia or asking her questions. She knew he was going to Community College and that he had a girlfriend named Linda, all from overhearing his conversations with others. But he knew nothing about her.

She was struck by how few people really knew her—not Cynthia Wells the hotshot reporter, but just plain old Cynthia. And if she were to disappear, just drop off the face of the earth, there wouldn't be many who'd care.

She paid the kid, feeling peeved that her thoughts were jogging this morbid path. She had to get out of her funk.

And she really had to stop reading those obituaries.

"I'm scared. Real scared."

Stubby White watched his friend, Turtle, jam shaking hands into the pockets of his trousers, except one pocket was ripped and only a thumb caught, leaving the rest of his hand exposed and jerking like a hooked mackerel.

"They worked him over good, Stubby. You shoulda seen him."

"Yeah. I heard." Stubby swallowed hard, thinking of the description of splattered blood and pulpy flesh circulating through the hood.

Bad news traveled fast on Angus Avenue.

"I still can't believe Manny's dead. But it ain't good for us to be talkin' out here . . . in the open." Stubby glanced over his shoulder. "Somebody might hear." He inched toward the alley.

"They put him in a dumpster. You believe it?" Turtle's hacking made Stubby step backward. "In a dumpster. Like he was garbage or somethin'."

"I warned you. Didn't I warn you? Not to mess with that bunch? Didn't I say Snake was trouble?"

"You shoulda seen his face. You wouldn't a recognized him. They worked him over good." Turtle dropped his head, revealing the frayed rim of his baseball cap. "I can't take pain."

Stubby rubbed his aching hands together thinking that sooner or later pain got them all. The throbbing in his fingers reached all the way to his shoulders. But even if pain was to win out, a body didn't have to flirt with it, run towards it like it was Lila Stone sashaying down the middle of the projects in her low-cut red dress. Messing with Lila sent a body to the clinic for penicillin. That's what she had taught him. *You don't go lookin' for trouble.*

So what did Turtle and Manny expect? That they could go messin' around and not pay?

Stubby yanked Turtle's arm. "Pull yourself together. Everythin's gonna be fine. You gotta lay low for awhile, that's all."

"Easy for you to say. No one's lookin' for you."

"Turtle, this ain't doin' neither of us no good. You gotta leave. Make yourself disappear for awhile. These people got eyes everywhere. It ain't no good to be seen like this. And you're puttin' me on the spot, too." Stubby knew saying this was sure to reflect on his courage. But to Stubby's way of thinking, it wasn't a matter of courage, but of street justice. Why should he take penicillin for someone else's folly?

Turtle pulled a shaking hand from his pocket and held it out in front of Stubby. "Look. When was the last time you saw me this bad? You know I gotta shoot. After that . . . I'll do what you say and make myself scarce." He ran the hand over his dry, cracked lips, oblivious to the grime covering his fingers. "You got any cash? I need it bad."

"What about the stuff . . . you know . . . the stuff you and Manny . . . ?"

"Are you *crazy*? I can't go nowhere near it. Not after what they did to Manny. Suppose they're watchin' and find me with . . . ?" A coughing fit caused Turtle's shoulders to heave beneath his oversized shirt.

Stubby stood watching, feeling sorry for his friend, and feeling angry, too. *Why hadn't Turtle and Manny listened? Why had they gone and pulled that harebrained stunt?* "I can't help you this time, Turtle. I'm down to my last two quarters."

"Then an extra snowball, maybe?"

Stubby shook his head.

"*Anythin'?*"

Stubby fingered his back pocket and felt a bulge, along with a rising resentment. Years on these mean streets had taught him not to go expecting help from others, the kind of help others seemed so quick to expect from him. It was one of those irregularities of life discovered long ago, that two people could travel the same road without necessarily learning the same lesson.

"No. I got nothin'." He glanced backward to avoid Turtle's eyes. When he did, he saw two men crossing the street and heading toward them.

"You go on now, lay low 'till this thing blows over." Another glance caused perspiration to dot the top of Stubby's bald head and drip down onto the curly fringe of white hair that cupped his neck. He sighed with relief when the men walked by without a glance.

As he headed toward the Angus Avenue Hotel, the clomp-clomp of Turtle's boots echoed behind him. Let Turtle think him a coward. Cowards were made; not born. *It was livin' on the streets that did it.*

"It's not gonna blow over, Stubby. That's what I'm tryin' to tell you. I got this bad feelin' and can't shake it."

Stubby stopped, reached into his pocket and pulled out his quarters, then handed them to Turtle. *Two miserable quarters. What good were they, anyhow?* "No one can hole up like you when you put your mind to it. They don't call you Turtle for nothin'. You gotta do that now. Hole up where no one can find you."

Turtle blinked at the coins in his hand. "I didn't mean for you to give me your last . . . but I gotta take 'em. I wouldn't except I need 'em real bad. I don't feel right about it though." Turtle curled his fingers around the money.

"Don't make it a big deal. We're friends, remember?" Stubby guessed that's what it boiled down to. *Turtle was his friend.* That's why he'd help. That's why he'd stick his neck out if it came to that. "You go on, now," he said, heading for the crumbling steps of the hotel.

A large sign with bleached-out lettering and the Angus trademark—a giant **A** pierced by two lightning bolts suggesting both power and something fearful—sagged over the entrance. The soft breeze carried the smell of urine, along with the dust of the tired, antediluvian neighborhood, and the suffocating sense that here, as though sentenced by an unknown judge, walked life's banished.

"You stayin' the night?" Turtle asked, continuing to follow Stubby.

Stubby nodded without turning. He didn't want to look into his friend's pleading eyes that were sure to ask if he could share the room. "Paid this mornin', then I'm out, maybe go to Fourth Street."

"Stubby . . . ."

"Get some rest. I'm gonna use the day to think. I need that—time to get my mind around things. Maybe come up with a plan."

"Okay . . . sure . . . I guess that would be best. Me and Manny, we always liked it when you thought things through . . . for all of us. You'll come up with somethin'. You always do. The Idea Man, that's what Manny used to call you. The Idea Man. We could always count on you."

"Well, don't expect much! You really got yourself in a jam this time!" He didn't mean for his voice to snap like that, to lay it on so heavy—drive the point home like his father used to do with a snap of his belt. But he didn't like being the Idea Man, either. That felt too heavy for his shoulders.

As Stubby reached the door, Turtle doubled over in a coughing fit. Maybe he should let Turtle spend the night. The way Turtle was feeling, he'd be grateful for a spot on the floor. But when Stubby thought of the danger, he changed his mind.

"You go take care of that cough," he said in a low voice. "It ain't never gonna go away if you don't take care of it. I'll get in touch when I think it's safe." Turtle nodded, and Stubby thought it was to Turtle's credit that he took it like a man and just clomped across the street and down an alley without another word.

But he felt guilty. And that made him mad. What was he supposed to do? Ask Turtle to stay? With Snake's goons everywhere? He had to keep his distance. Just for awhile. Give himself time to think, time to work this out. Assuming it could be worked out. This was bad business. Turtle and Manny's stunt could end up getting then all killed. A person could get hurt just for butting into the wrong business. How many times had his father's fists fallen on Stubby for coming to the defense of his mother and brothers?

And with never a thanks from any of 'em. So who could blame a body for lookin' out for number one? And you couldn't make too many mistakes, neither, and live to tell about 'em.

He'd do what he could for Turtle. Try to come up with a plan. And stick his neck out only if he had to. He balled his hands into fists, wincing from the pain in his swollen joints. No question about it, pain would have its way, would own bits and pieces of them all 'til it became master. And when it did? What then?

A helpless old man on the street didn't last long.

Jonathan Holmes barely stirred when the old grandfather clock chimed. But it did bring him earthbound enough to smell the musty Parthia wool rug, feel his head soaked with perspiration, feel a tingle in his right hand where his head had been resting.

My soul pants for you, Lord, just as the deer pants for water.

He tried to continue praying, tried to rise heavenward again, but couldn't, so he just remained sprawled on the floor. *You know I want to do Your will.* He rolled onto his left side and began exercising his hand. *But I don't understand, Lord. Why change things now? When Your Spirit is beginning to stir the congregation?*

When the numbness in his hand turned to pins and needles, Jonathan pulled himself to his knees, then lingered a moment in hope of hearing an answer.

There was none.

"'Trust in the Lord with all thine heart and lean not unto thine own understanding; in all thy ways acknowledge Him and He shall direct thy path,'" he whispered the familiar verse, a verse he had felt the Lord tattoo on his heart more than once.

"Pastor Holmes? You in there?"

The voice and the impatient knocking brought Jonathan to his feet. He unlocked his office door without bothering to put on his shoes, which were taken off in anticipation of being on "holy ground".

"My . . . if you aren't the prayingest pastor I've ever known! 'Course I haven't known that many. After all, Pastor Sorensen was here twenty-five years. But if I tried, I could come up with a few names, and none of them, as far as I can remember, *ever* spent as much time in prayer as you."

Jonathan grinned at the church secretary and noticed that her gray, steel-wool-like hair smelled freshly permed. "Nice hairdo, Gertie."

Gertie's mouth curled into a rare smile. "I thought you should know—the new choir robes aren't in. They were supposed to be in our hands by Tuesday and here it is Thursday, and you know that we've already bundled up all the old robes, just like *you* asked, and shipped them off to that church in South Oberon. I know you were trying to be a good Christian, giving to the less fortunate and all, but seems you jumped the gun. A lot of people aren't going to take that lightly. They're still used to the way Pastor Sorensen ran things, and he never jumped the gun. 'Course, he had a lot more years to learn the ropes."

Jonathan sighed and wondered if he'd ever get used to all the minutiae that made him feel, so often, like he was running a business instead of tending a flock. And that feeling didn't sit well. He couldn't imagine Smith Wigglesworth, "the apostle of faith" or Jack Coe, "the man of reckless faith" ever bogged down with such details; not that he compared himself to them, but he did, with all his heart, want to be used of God like they had been. And he desperately wanted to see revival come to Christ Church. Other pastors, with more experience, had confided in him that bothersome details and endless busyness could shrivel one's spiritual life, suck the fervor and passion right out of it; faster than you could recite the one-hundred and seventeenth Psalm. But he supposed there was a lesson in all of it—all the minutiae, the nagging details. Such things could be used of God like pruning shears, trimming, as it were, the tendrils of impatience and perhaps a budding branch of spiritual pride. "So, when will the garments of praise be here?"

Gertie Eldridge wrinkled her nose. "I called the trucking company and the entire shipment is lost. Vanished into thin air! They're trying to track it down. But nothing will happen by Sunday, that's for sure. The choir's meeting tonight for practice. What am I supposed to tell them? I'll have to leave a note, explain this whole thing and . . . ."

"Why don't I break the news?"

Gertie Eldridge relaxed her nose. "You plan on being here tonight? Don't you *ever* go home?"

"I am home." Jonathan felt the words stick in his throat.

"Well, it would help if you addressed the choir. Maybe you could explain everything, tell them you miscalculated. They'll take it better if it comes from you."

Jonathan nodded, trying to ignore the sorrow that pressed heavily on his chest. "When all is said and done, they're not the garments of praise that matter, Gertie."

"I'll have you know the choir takes their robes seriously."

"Of course they do. But the thing is they'll manage to sing just fine without them. At least for one more week."

The church secretary worked her eyebrows into a knot. "Maybe . . . except I can tell you it's going to be hard for the congregation to concentrate on the singing if their choir looks like a bunch of wildflowers, dressed every which way, instead of in their smart matching robes. It's unsettling. I can't remember it ever happening here. Not once."

Jonathan walked over to the huge mahogany desk and placed his hand on the leather executive's chair. A Greek lexicon lay open on the desktop and his eyes rested on the word "pepoithesis"—reliance, confidence, *trust*. He just couldn't get away from that word. "Trust in the Lord, Gertie. It'll all work out." But he was saying that as much to himself as to his secretary. "He has a plan. He always has a plan."

"Well . . . I suppose. But people are going to be disappointed. They were looking forward to the new robes. Took a long time to decide about the double strip around the collar and wrists. It's the extra touches, you know, that make a church stand out, sort of gives it a signature. And that's important for a church like ours. After all, Christ Church is a landmark. One of the first built here in North Oberon. It goes way back, and so do most of the families. But you wouldn't know about that. Being an outsider and all. Although I suppose with your Aunt Adel heading the Ladies Auxiliary for the past twenty-five years, you're not a real outsider. And I did hear that you once lived in the area, awhile ago, so that counts for something. *I suppose.* Still, you don't act like one of us. But come to think of it, your Aunt Adel's a bit strange, too."

Jonathan pulled out the chair that squeaked on its rollers, and sat down. "Revival, Gertie. That's what Christ Church needs. Choir robes are fine, but they can't replace the *fire* of God."

"Sometimes I worry about you, Pastor." The small, spry woman picked at her hair as she backpedaled toward the door. "You work too hard. Here from sunrise to sunset and beyond. Pastor Sorensen, God rest his soul, never kept such hours. It's not healthy. And come to think of it, he never talked about the fire of God, either."

CHAPTER 2

Cynthia Wells took a swig of her cold double espresso, then placed the tall paper cup next to a bulky ceramic mug inscribed with the words, **Stakeout Queen**—a Christmas gift from Bernie. Fatigue slid down some inner tunnel of her body along with the mouthful of espresso. She was grateful it was already noon. It seemed wrong to wish for the hours to gallop by as if they were horses in a race. That implied a wasteful mentality which didn't ring true. She well understood that each passing hour represented a withdrawal from some invisible account—the kind where no deposits could ever be made.

Still, she found it hard to rouse herself, and sat cradling her face with one hand and drawing stick figures with the other. Only one word was scrawled on her entire page.

Manny.

Even the noise and high energy of the newsroom failed to revive or inspire. It just annoyed. Phones rang and people shouted over each other. In one corner, two reporters argued over politics or sports, Cynthia couldn't tell which. In another corner, three more reporters clustered near a nineteen-inch wall-mounted Toshiba watching CNN.

She was glad to be in this predominately male club, still amazed she had been invited and still amazed how little women's lib had penetrated the inner sanctum of the *Oberon Tribune*. But her

17

"invitation" had been a mixed blessing, necessitating that she work harder than the other reporters and accepting the fact that Bernie always expected more from her than say Bob, or Howard or Ray.

Cynthia scrunched lower in her chair trying to tune it all out, and wished Bernie would make good on his promise to provide those five-foot-high sound-proof partitions around each desk instead of leaving it like a haphazard warehouse of men, women, desks, computers, phones, and various other tools of the trade. She squinted at her stickmen. Drawing them helped her think. She started a second row, avoiding eye contact with the small plaque on her desk framing Benjamin Franklin's words: *Time lost is never found again.*

"Is this what I pay my number one door-knocker to do? You want to learn art, go to night school."

Cynthia's long, slender fingers continued marching an army of stick figures across the page. She didn't glance up at the rotund city editor. She already knew, without looking, that he had a smile on his face, that his shirt was only partially tucked in, that under close scrutiny, traces of powdered sugar would be found dusting his bottom lip from this morning's Krispy Kreme orgy.

She bent lower over her well-appointed metal desk, causing a patch of shiny, blonde hair to fall across her forehead, obscuring the frown on her face, a frown she'd been wearing since leaving Starbucks this morning. "I'm thinking," she finally said.

"Good for you, Wells. But how about translating it into some work? You haven't given me anything worth a nickel this week. It looks like all you've attended to are your nails."

Cynthia glanced at her French manicure and tried not to show her irritation as Bernie Hobbs pushed aside her neat stack of manila folders—folders that had taken two hours to organize—and settled his plump posterior on her desk.

"Just wanted you to know your little ditty on waste at the state capitol doesn't have teeth."

"You printing it?"

"Not on your tintype. Not even as an off-lead, unless you go for the jugular. I want to see blood. You know it's got to bleed for it to lead. You've collected good, solid facts, but your piece doesn't deliver."

Bernie bent closer as though about to impart what he considered a worthy punch line. His face was knotted and serious, but funny, too, with that powdered sugar outlining his bottom lip. Cynthia's high opinion of him forced her to stifle a giggle. But she almost came unglued when he rose up on his haunches and squared back his shoulders as though preparing to recite a key passage from Macbeth. Sheer will power enabled her to keep a straight face.

"You didn't deliver," Bernie repeated. "You failed to tie the facts into a firm rope-bridge over which your readers can navigate to the correct conclusion. Instead, you gave me tip-toe-through-the-tulips, and the prize is what? A little wading pond? Hardly substantial enough to wash the stench of this scandal away. And hardly Wells-quality."

Cynthia colored the "a" in Manny with blue ink. *Dear sweet Bernie.* She tried not to react when he thumped her page of stickmen with his index finger. *Dear sweet irritating Bernie.*

"There's your problem. *These* are the only men in your life. Everyone needs a little fun, Wells, a little romance. Otherwise, burnout. That's what's happening here. Too much nose-to-the-grindstone and not enough time to recharge your battery. Rewrite that piece, then find yourself a man. And that's an order! And not that clod, Steve, either. The two of you have no future and you know it!"

Cynthia twirled her Papermate between her fingers and gazed at her boss—a generous man of excesses whose body confessed his sins to the world while her own sins remained hidden. How could such a man understand someone like her? She had always aspired to become a Bob Woodward or Carl Bernstein—uncovering Watergate-like scandals— but ever since the nightmares, she'd been feeling more like a Mary Shelley—obsessed with bringing back the dead. "Okay, I'll give you blood. I'll bleed the state dry, if that's what you want, but forget the man part. I'm not interested just now."

"Oh, no? Then who's this Manny?"

"A dead guy."

Bernie let out an exasperated hiss. "What is it with you and dead people? You have a fixation or something? Should I start worrying?"

Dear sweet Bernie. Ever willing to charge to her rescue like a big brother, extending his hand of friendship—and she only able to brush his fingertips. She wanted to tell Bernie about her dreams. She wanted to tell him about the nightmares that made her wake up in a cold sweat, made her hear giggles and screams. It would be nice to tell someone, to get it out in the open. Maybe it would even make them stop. But habit was a bully that kept one from straying into unfamiliar territory. And that's where she'd be, in unfamiliar territory. Because after years of keeping things to herself, locking them up in the cupboard of her heart, she found it hard to share with others.

Even someone as dear as Bernie.

"No need to worry. I'm okay. Not like this guy." Cynthia circled Manny's name, then tapped it with one of her manicured nails hoping Bernie would allow her to change the subject. "Steve tells me they found this guy three days ago in a dumpster—a homeless drug addict. Now who would want to murder some poor homeless guy?

Nobody's claimed the body. Or made inquiries. Can you imagine? Not one person. It's sad."

She removed the pen from Manny's name, brought it back to her row of stickmen and began drawing. "Ever wonder what it would be like to die and have nobody care?"

"No. Once you're dead what difference does it make? But you're wondering, aren't you? I swear, Wells, you're getting more morbid by the day. I'm warning you, you start dressing in black and you'll find a pink slip on your desk faster than you can say, 'Chernobyl'. What's going on with you, anyway? Maybe you should see a shrink." Bernie pushed himself off the desk. "You've got me worried. There, I said it, okay? You've become disconnected. You don't date. You don't even go out with your friends anymore. It's just you and your job. You've got no way of blowing off steam. It's killing your edge. And if you don't stop it, you'll wake up one morning and find that all you can write are a few lines for Hallmark."

Cynthia tossed her pen in what she hoped was a cavalier manner for Bernie's sake. No point in letting him see how deeply this issue disturbed her. But she'd have to toss more than a pen, she'd have to toss a bone, too. Give him something so he didn't worry, something that was true without really getting to the heart of it. "When a person's occupation is to always dig for dirt, it makes that person . . . well, not like other people very much, you know? It sort of turns that person off to the human race."

"Well, get turned back on!"

Cynthia eyed her pudgy boss as he walked away. Bernie had been in the newspaper business a long time and knew a scam when he heard one, or at least a partial scam. But he was letting her get away with it. At least, for now.

"Find a man, Wells. Have a little fling. Get your edge back," he said over his shoulder.

"Too late, Bernie. You're already taken." And without understanding why, she suddenly felt as empty as one of her stick men.

Stubby lay in bed, his mind balled in a knot of thoughts about Turtle. He should be napping. Not tossing and turning and racking his brain. Five more days before he got his Social Security check; which meant four nights on the street. He'd have to sleep most of the day and night, stored it up like his mom used to store up groceries after cashing her welfare check—maybe get him a reserve to drawn on.

A cockroach brushed his skin. He watched it scurry across the healed tracks of his inner arm before snatching it. Then he held it between a thumb and forefinger, which looked like tips of a black Magic Marker, and watched it pedal air. It was God's creature. They were all God's creatures, no matter how disgusting. Only some creatures didn't have much use. Didn't deserve consideration. He hesitated, then squeezed until he heard a crunch. Then he flicked the carcass across the room and wiped the ooze from his fingers onto his dirty jeans. At least he wasn't as lowly as that cockroach. Only problem was, the older he got, the harder it was to remember it.

The sagging mattress seemed to swallow his limbs as he tried forgetting that lump of cocaine in his back pocket. He tried forgetting his guilt, too, over lying to Turtle. What was he supposed to do? There wasn't enough for the two of them. His small stash, wrapped in a paper towel, suddenly felt like a mountain, as temptation rose. *No. Not now.* If he used now, there'd be no sleep. Still, the familiar temptation continued to rise. Cocaine would help him forget that pain in his fingers; help him forget this dingy room; help him forget the mean streets he called home; help him forget who he was and maybe help him see how things might have been—could have been if not for all those bad breaks.

He laid there, flat on his back, his arms and legs like putty. But his mind flipped this way and that until it settled on a decision: he'd use his C-dust later. The decision gave him comfort, like one of the hymns he used to sing at the mission, promising peace and heaven. Yeah, later he'd let his C-dust bring him peace, take him to Paradise, at least a Paradise of sorts. He was glad it wasn't a snowball. He'd never be able to put that off. He touched the bend of his arm. There was nothing like cocaine and heroin together. But he wasn't doing anymore of that. If only Turtle would stop. He thought of Manny. *Why didn't he listen? Why did he go messin' with jojee and snowball? And why had he gotten mixed up with that crowd?*

And now there was Turtle to worry about.

Stubby turned on his side facing the dirty plaster wall. Holes, the size of golf balls, formed an abstract. He wondered if someone hadn't dug out the plaster and eaten it. Once, he was so hungry he ate some and got sick, but that was in another hotel. And that was long ago. His Social Security checks kept him from wanting to try anything like that now.

At least most of the time.

He changed positions, and when he did, body odor wafted through the air. He never used to notice how bad he smelled, but lately he'd been noticing it, and thinking it reminded him of something *dead.*

He pictured the cockroach. Wasn't the world trying to squeeze him, too? Just squeeze him 'til there was nothing left? He didn't know how much longer he could last before he was crushed and flicked against some wall.

Shame covered him, then filled every pore as though his body was a rag sopping up grease. He was a loser. Had never been nothing else. Wouldn't be either, though he had tried. God knows he had tried. But his life had been one long list of bad breaks; bad breaks that crowded him like a vicious gang, a vicious army. Those breaks had been too strong for him, an overwhelming force that had beaten him down. Though once . . . just once . . . he had thought his luck had changed, that he had run the gauntlet and come out the other side, but then that kid went and died.

No use thinking about it. There were already too many bums on Angus Avenue who liked telling everyone what they could have been. But he had come close . . . he was sure of it . . . close to beating the odds, close to making something out of himself, and sometimes he'd let himself imagine what life would have been like if that kid hadn't died. And never once did he imagine himself in this crummy hotel room, on this crummy street.

Pain shot through Stubby's hands as he balled his fingers. Life was nothing more than a crap shoot. There were them that were lucky and them that weren't. And no one every called him "lucky". No matter how hard he tried, all he kept rolling was snake-eyes. So why bother hanging on?

Why didn't he just do everyone a favor and die?

He closed his eyes and Manny's face flashed in front of him, like it was on the big screen of that cheap movie house around the corner where they showed skin flicks. *Manny.* He didn't want to think about him. The bed jiggled as he thrashed around.

Heaps of garbage form a mound:
Stinkin', torn, foul.
Human flesh by the pound . . . .

He had to turn off that mind of his—stop thinking about Manny or Turtle. Stop composing those silly poems. He drew his knees into a fetal position and rocked back and forth like he used to do after his father finished wallopin' him with the strap.

Go to sleep. Just go to sleep.

"Stubby." Turtle's voice rolled around in Stubby's brain like a bowling ball, knocking over all hopes of sleep. It was the way Turtle had said it, like Turtle had wrapped all the longing of a lifetime around Stubby's name, and somehow made him responsible. *"We could always count on you."* Well, maybe Stubby didn't want to be counted on. Maybe he was tired of always being the one who had to come up with the ideas.

He squinted back tears. A man on the street had no business having friends. He pictured Manny in the dumpster. What were Manny's last minutes like? From how everyone described the body, Manny had to be glad when death came. And now Turtle might be next. But what was Stubby supposed to do? Hadn't he warned Turtle? And Manny, too? But the thing was done and couldn't be undone. He was no miracle worker. He wasn't God. What did Turtle want from him anyway? But even as Stubby lay curled in a ball, he knew he'd try to come up with a plan. Turtle was the best friend he had—now the only friend since Manny ended up in the dumpster.

Slowly, Stubby rolled off the bed and onto his knees. He knew he was a jerk for doing it. What was the use? He wiped his eyes with the back of his hand, trailing a smudge of dirt and tears. It was clear what the Almighty thought of him. God had wasted no time in trashing Stubby's prayers for Manny. Put them right in the garbage where they belonged. But he thought it mean of God to place Manny right alongside them.

Stubby bowed his head and folded his hands like he'd seen the old ladies at Saint Luke's do—the ones that always wore black, and lit candles, and fingered rosary beads. Maybe his technique had been wrong. He'd been watching those ladies since the mission closed. Been going to St. Luke's even though it was a good hike—almost five blocks—mostly when it was raining and he needed someplace dry to rest his aching bones. And after all his watching, he got to thinking that maybe the last time he had prayed he hadn't approached the Almighty with the proper respect. So here he was, on his knees, like an old woman, with his hands folded, willing to try again. Maybe this time the Almighty would lean over in that big, golden throne of His, look down, and take notice of poor, old Stubby White. Maybe this time, Stubby's prayers would be answered.

And if God didn't answer?

Stubby shook his head. He didn't know how much longer he could hang on. Maybe he'd just give up and stop trying altogether.

He balled his hands into fists even though it brought a fresh wave of pain. He had to get this right. It might be the last chance he had of getting it right. He closed his eyes and dropped his head against his chest. "Please God, I can't go on like this no more. I'm a mess. My life's a mess. I got nothin' to keep me goin'. If you don't help me, I don't know what I'm gonna do. Please, God, You just gotta help me and . . . Turtle."

Jonathan Holmes stood in back of the sanctuary listening to the choir. "'All to Jesus I surrender.'" His heart soared. *Oh, the tender persistence of God.*

"I give up, Lord. I surrender," Jonathan whispered. What else could he do? He had been wrestling with the Master for two weeks. But even as he stood there, Jonathan felt a tiny pocket of resistance, a little Alamo raising its battle flag. He tried to identify it. Ambition? He didn't think so. Pride? No . . . well . . . it could be. Hadn't he felt a bit of pride over being chosen to pastor this prestigious old church even though it was whispered that it was as dead as a doornail? And hadn't he, just the other day, when a new tenant in his building asked him what he did for a living, told her he was a pastor, then punctuated it with *at Christ Church*? And what about last week when he had tilted back in his leather office chair and admired the rich paneled walls, the expensive crown molding, the beautiful new Pella Bow window, and flirted with vanity by thinking how both strange and marvelous it was that God had brought the poor boy back as a man, to preside over the office of the wealthiest church in North Oberon?

So, was he guilty of pride? It seemed likely. But now what he was feeling most wasn't so much puffy as painful—like a tearing—as if something was being ripped away; a feeling he had experienced only one other time when he had walked away from the woman he loved. And now, like then, it left him with a profound sense of loss.

He smiled as his Aunt Adel waved from the back row of the choir. From this distance, she looked like his mother, with her broad shoulders, and standing a head taller than the men. He watched as she sprang from her place, after the choir director called a break, and headed toward him.

"Jonathan, I've got your dinner all packaged up in the car. Remind me to give it to you before you leave." She squeezed him between long, strong arms.

He breathed in the scent of eighty-dollars-an-ounce perfume when he kissed her on the cheek. Ever since he was old enough to remember, his aunt wore expensive perfume and clothes, drove luxury cars. Not like his mother, who got her clothes from thrift stores and paid for them with jar change she managed to save from using grocery store coupons. "Thanks for thinking of me," Jonathan said, meaning every word.

"Oh, dearest love, who else do I have to think about? Besides, how could I ever face your mother, in the hereafter, if I let you waste away? Her last words to me were, 'Adel, help the Lord take care of my son.'"

Jonathan looked away, ashamed of his feeble faith, a feebleness exposed while he was lying prone on the Parthia rug. The Lord had always provided. Never once had He let Jonathan down.

So how could Jonathan doubt Him now?

"Gertie's been on the phone all afternoon blabbing to everyone about the choir robes. Some of the folks are upset. But most of them are taking it in stride. I think your sermons are starting to penetrate. There'll be no riots, and no tarring-and-feathering, either. I'm thankful it didn't happen last year or even six months ago. God is doing a work here." Aunt Adel threaded her jeweled-studded hand through Jonathan's muscular arm. "For ten years, I've been praying for revival to fall on this church, and I never doubted that God would do it, but what I didn't know was that he'd use my very own nephew as His instrument."

Jonathan felt his muscles tighten. So did Aunt Adel.

"What's wrong, Dearest?"

Aunt Adel's gentian blue eyes, so like his mother's, brimmed with love and made Jonathan's insides twist. There was no way around it. He had to tell her, even though he knew she'd be sick with disappointment. "Aunt Adel . . . ."

"Pastor Jonathan! What's this I hear about the choir robes?"

Jonathan spun around and watched the choir director, a tall, thin man with a bulbous nose walk up to him. The director's razor tongue and temper were legendary. Jonathan braced himself. "I promised Gertie I'd come tonight and break the news, but it seems everyone already knows."

In a flash, Aunt Adel lept between Jonathan and the director. Her brows were knotted, her eyes laser-focused. But her mouth, which was curled upward from years of perpetually smiling, betrayed a sweetness of temperament that was impossible to hide. Even so, from past experience, Jonathan understood that at times like this, it was best not to get in his aunt's way.

"You and the Finance Committee have been haggling over those robes for six months," his aunt said sharply. "And if I recall, it was you, Mr. Director, who stopped the whole shebang for almost two of those months while the factory sent color swatches just so you could be sure you were getting the right shade of blue. With that track record, I don't think you should be worrying about waiting a few more days until we get this straightened out. Do you?"

"Put your gun back in its holster, Adel. No one's going to lynch your boy here. I just wanted to make sure Gertie had it straight. Is it true, Pastor? Will the choir be singing in their regular clothes this Sunday?"

Jonathan nodded.

"Well . . . okay then. I'll tell everyone it'll be another week or more before we'll be in proper attire. And if they don't like it, they can take it up with me."

When the director walked away, Aunt Adel squeezed Jonathan's arm. "See. God *is* changing this church."

"Yes," Jonathan said, feeling his courage drain from him like water from a leaky bucket. *More than you know.* But he'd wait to tell his aunt about it until tomorrow . . . or maybe the next day or . . . .

CHAPTER 3

S tubby pulled the crumpled paper towel from his back pocket. All day he had tossed and turned, racking his brain 'til
the idea came, making him tingle and float like he was high on
C-dust. And making him feel smart, too—something as rare as
clean fingernails.

Tucson.

Tucson was their salvation. His and Turtle's. He was sure Turtle
would see it that way, too. But there was no going 'til Stubby got his
next Social Security check. Turtle would just have to wait it out, and
Stubby right along with him.

With a sigh—a blend of satisfaction and weariness—Stubby
unfolded the crinkled edges of the towel. No sense in fighting
any longer. It cost him an extra night at the hotel, but what did it
matter? His room was a dump, hardly better than the alley. He'd
let C-dust carry him off to a better place, let it free his mind, let
himself be taken on its white powdery wings and soar with the
eagles like superman, up, up, up in the sky where he could do
anything, be anything . . . anything but a nearly crippled, old
loser.

"Tell me it's not true. I want to hear it from your own lips." Aunt Adel pressed long, slender fingers against the soft puffy skin under her eyes, blotting her tears.

Jonathan continued packing in silence, placing his *Strong's Concordance* atop his Greek lexicon and three Bibles, then closed the top of the cardboard box. He never had found the words or will to tell Adel, and now felt a coward's regret.

He pushed strands of blond hair from his eyes and avoided his aunt's gaze. Boxes were everywhere, and piles of books and folders formed little stacks along the perimeter of the room. His eyes rested on the sizable portrait of Pastor Sorensen who, from his lofty position on the wall opposite the desk, surveyed his former domain through metal-rimmed glasses. For the first time since stepping into this office, Jonathan was certain the old pastor was displeased. There were other times—when purchasing new hymnals and choir robes even though the old ones were still good, just so he could donate the used ones to that small, poor church in South Oberon; when instituting the all-night prayer vigils on Fridays; when convincing the Finance Committee to divert money from the more than ample decoration and renovation fund to the new missionary efforts he and Andrew Combs had begun—that Jonathan was certain he detected a slight hint of disapproval on the old pastor's oil-painted face. But today, disapproval seemed to pour in angry waves through those hard, blue eyes that followed Jonathan around the room. Still, it was easier to accept Sorensen's displeasure than his aunt's.

"Tell me it's not true," Aunt Adel repeated, fidgeting in the small armchair by the side of the desk.

"You see me packing, so you know it is. Besides, you knew it when you came in. I saw it in your eyes. I'm just sorry you didn't hear it from me first."

"But *why*, dearest love? Why now? You saw the church Sunday. In spite of no choir robes, it was packed all the way back to the Swenson pew, and that hasn't happened in at least three years, and then only on Easter. God is getting ready to do a work here, Jonathan. A mighty work. Much prayer has gone up for this. A handful of my Auxiliary Ladies and I have prayed our knees flat. If you don't believe me, you should see me in pantyhose. They sag right where my kneecaps used to be."

Jonathan stuffed a batch of sermons into a manila folder, hating the fact he was putting his aunt through this. "God is well aware of your knees. And yes, I know revival's coming."

"Then all the more reason you should be here. You've worked so hard this past year. I've never seen anyone work harder. Now, I'm going to have to listen to Gertie Eldridge go around saying 'I told you so'." Adel pulled a monogrammed hankie from her purse.

Any minute Jonathan was going to need one, too. He had never given himself over so completely to the workings of the Holy Spirit as he had while at Christ Church. It was a bitter business to have to leave it now.

"She's getting used to you, you know—Gertie is. I heard her say the other day, when she didn't know I was listening, that she'd make a fine pastor out of you yet. That's as close as she'll ever come to admitting I was right to recommend you."

Jonathan walked over to his aunt's chair and ran his hand along her prominent square cheek that spoke of strength and character, and watched wisps of gray hair fall across his fingers. "Recommend? I don't think recommend is the right word. I believe 'shove down everyone's throat' would be more accurate."

"It's not like they had a string of other candidates. And yes, I did use my influence to press for you. And nobody made much of a fuss after I stressed you'd just be the temporary pastor."

"And that's the key word, isn't it? *Temporary.*"

"But I had hoped . . . I had so hoped . . . ." Aunt Adel dabbed her eyes with the hankie. "Oh, Jonathan, you're such a wonderful pastor and I know you've come to love these people, and what's more, they've come to love you, too. So how can you leave them? Before you see the fruits of your labor?"

Jonathan felt the familiar churning. After all his prayers, it was still hard to let go. He hoped that fact wasn't written on his face. "The Lord is directing me elsewhere."

"And where is that?"

Jonathan removed his hand from his aunt's cheek knowing what was coming. "I don't know."

She gasped as if his words were blows. "Please tell me you're not serious?"

"Andrew will do an admirable job. He's been involved with me from the beginning, on everything. I've discussed this with him, and the changeover will be seamless. He'll be a fine replacement until the Search Committee can locate, then vote in a new pastor."

Aunt Adel leaned forward in her chair. "Andrew Combs is a good man, and has been an admirable assistant pastor, and his wife is a precious lady, but he's half the man you are."

"You're talking with you heart, not your head. And my last official act here will be to implore you to be his ally—to implore you to help him as much as you can—to keep the Body united. For years, Christ Church has been a Laodicea, neither hot nor cold. But now . . . now that's all about to change. So you must do everything you can to keep it on track. To see that the work of the Holy Spirit is not hindered."

Aunt Adel twisted her handkerchief, making it resemble a rope. "When revival comes, and it will, everyone will credit Andrew. They'll forget about all your hard work, your prayers."

Jonathan felt that pocket of resistance grow stronger as cannons rolled up to strategic positions along his Alamo wall, could feel his heart twist and crack, releasing an ooze of self-pity. He had never worked harder in his life. And now the Lord was asking him to pass the mantle of authority over to someone else . . . before he could see the fruits. And aside from disappointing his aunt, that was the part that stung the most, the part that cut deep into his core.

Before he could see the fruits.

It was a lot easier talking about—preaching about—doing the will of God, no matter the cost. But paying the price—that was another matter.

"When revival comes," he said softly, trying to corral his feelings, "the credit will go to the Holy Spirit, where it belongs."

His aunt's broad, square shoulders heaved as she slumped backward in her chair. She gazed at the ceiling as though listening to silent instructions from on high, then absently released her white monogrammed handkerchief. Jonathan watched it flutter to her lap like a flag of surrender.

"Oh, dearest love . . . I had such hopes . . . I had so wanted you to be the one . . . ."

"I know." Jonathan squeezed her shoulder. "Forgive me?"

"Forgive you? For obeying the Lord? How can I even answer that without sounding presumptuous? No, you must obey God, of course. But, He's given you no clue? No hint of what He wants?"

Jonathan shook his head.

"Then you'll be needing prayer cover. My ladies and I will see to it."

Jonathan turned to an empty box on the floor and began filling it so he couldn't see the hard, disapproving eyes of Pastor Sorensen or the hurt, tear-filled eyes of his aunt. "We'll both need prayer."

"How's that?"

"Gertie Eldridge. You know what she's going to be like when she hears the news."

Aunt Adel chuckled. "Yes, you'd better cover me in prayer, too."

Cynthia's lower back screamed in protest as she sat rigid in the wooden chair opposite Bernie's desk. The chair had been an issue between them from her first day on the job six years ago when she made the mistake of telling Bernie he needed to buy a new one. Now, it seemed like Bernie kept it as a matter of principle, as though reminding her that *he* was the boss, a fact he often accused her of forgetting, and which, Cynthia believed, he secretly feared was not always the case.

In vain, she tried to get comfortable by shifting her weight from one side to the next. All the while Bernie's sausage fingers flipped through the pages she had handed him late yesterday afternoon— the rewrite of her government waste story. She knew he'd prefer to take the pages home to read rather than waiting to read them off the composition system or computer network this morning. And she could tell by his face he was pleased.

"This is more like it!" Bernie said, smacking his lips as if he had just eaten a Krispy Kreme. "Guaranteed to shake up those bureaucrats at the state capitol. They don't call our business the 'fourth branch of government' for nothing. It's a good watchdog piece, Cynthia. Good for circulation, too."

Cynthia smiled. Bernie always worried about circulation. "Glad you like it. You running it tomorrow?" When Bernie nodded, she rose, anxious to relieve her back of its torture. "Okay, guess that wraps it up. I think I'll take the rest of the day off." She was exhausted. The melatonin from the health food store hadn't helped. And the nightmares . . . they were worse than ever. She hadn't had a good night's sleep in days. She planned on taking a few sleeping pills and going to bed early. But when her hand brushed against the hard chair, she added, "If you don't mind, that is."

Bernie tilted back then plopped his feet on the desk. "Since when did you start worrying if I minded what you did?"

"I'll be in bright and early tomorrow."

"You could take a few days off, you know. I don't have an assignment for you and the *Trib's* not going to fall apart if you're not here. Besides, those bags under your eyes are not terribly attractive."

"Tomorrow, Bernie, I'll be at my desk." She heard him sigh.

"You got something you're working on?"

Cynthia shrugged. "Nothing special." As city editor, Bernie handed out the assignments, but he was always open to suggestions. Still, she wasn't ready to tell him what was on her mind. Bernie would get upset and accuse her of being morbid. And the way she felt right now, he would be right.

As soon as Stubby rounded the corner of Angus Avenue and Fourth he saw her. There was nothing that made him feel as good as seeing Miss Emily passing out sandwiches. It was her permanence, her always being at the mission, and now on the street in front of it, that gave him a fleeting sense of stability, a knowing that the world hadn't slipped off its axis and gone careening into outer space, forever lost, and him with it. Here on this street, even those dirty, gnarled fingers of his could touch the pure hand of kindness. For one minute, life made sense. And for one minute, fear didn't eat at him.

"Hey there, Miss Emily." Stubby wiped his hands on his pants— the closest he'd come to any kind of personal hygiene today, "I'll take the house special."

Miss Emily smiled, not one strand of white hair out of place. She held a baggie-wrapped bologna sandwich between small, pink fingers that boasted of short, well-manicured nails. "I've got one here just the way you like it, with lots of butter."

When she handed it to him, Stubby smelled the scent of lavender and wondered how anything could smell this good on these mean streets.

"I wasn't sure you were coming today. I figured you'd have your check by now."

"Ain't cashed it yet. Got it too late. Gonna do that tomorrow, so don't expect me here. Gotta let some of them others, who ain't got any ways and means, get a chance to sample your good home cookin'."

Miss Emily's laughter floated like flower petals on the warm, humid air. Then she frowned. "You don't look good today, Stubby. I don't even want to ask what you've been doing because I can guess. But don't think that'll stop me. I've been asking Jesus to clean you up, and I'll continue to ask. That's His specialty you know, cleaning people up. And you know I'm qualified to speak on that subject."

Stubby thought of his empty back pocket and how he had been drugging for the past four days, and getting the money by going up-town and panhandling. "No denyin' it, Jesus did you good. But some folks have used up all their chances, Miss Emily, and I'm one of 'em." He wasn't proud of what he had been doing but he wasn't one to put on airs either, trying to make people think better of him than they should. Besides, he was sure Miss Emily knew the worst. He was still a little chalked up, and Miss Emily could always tell if someone was high. "I'm sure I used up all my chances," he repeated, then smiled in spite of himself when he saw that familiar twinkle in her eyes.

"You don't believe that, Stubby. Because if you did, you wouldn't be standing here on this street with me. I know you've had your ups and downs, like a man riding an elevator but never going anywhere.

Still, you wait and see. One of these days you're going to give in to Jesus. Then look out! He'll get you off that elevator and fill you with so much life you'll never be the same. Resurrection day's coming, Stubby. Like Lazarus, you'll be walking out of your tomb."

Stubby took a bite of his sandwich and looked at the building behind Miss Emily. "Maybe Jesus would do better to put some life back into that."

Miss Emily turned to face the empty Beacon Mission that was locked up tighter than a vault. "He will, in His own good time."

"It looks kinda sad, all closed up like that. Still don't understand why God let it happen. Reverend Gates was a good man."

"God's ways are higher than our ways, Stubby. His ways are not like our ways at all."

Stubby shrugged. "I ain't sure I can buy into that kinda thinkin'. Makes no sense to use that to account for all the miserable things that happen to people. But I can still picture him, you know—Reverend Gates at the bottom of them cellar stairs. His head all bloody, his body twisted. Don't understand how it could happen. He walked them stairs a million times."

Miss Emily nodded.

"I never told you this, but I ain't convinced it was an accident." Stubby squinted at Miss Emily and when he saw her expression hadn't changed, that she didn't look at him like he had two heads, he decided to say what was on his mind, what had been wedged in his brain, like a splinter, for months. "You can say what you want, but I think someone pushed him; that someone wanted him dead." He looked again at Miss Emily's face, studying it like you would a map for signs, and though she was smiling, her eyes told him that she believed it, too.

CHAPTER 4

Afour-year old girl died yesterday. Carrie Ann Dietch. Pneumonia, the obituary said, though it wasn't the season for such illnesses. And that made Cynthia suspect that Carrie Ann had a history of asthma or bronchitis or some other respiratory aliment that made even the simple things of life, difficult. Cynthia was surprised that the obituary mentioned the cause of death since most didn't. She also supposed that laying it out in the open like that, filling in the blank of everyone's question of *what happened*—sure to be asked again and again—was a matter of self-defense on the part of the parents. At least at the funeral they would be spared the need to give an explanation.

A small mercy.

Cynthia slouched on the floral couch, her pj's crumpled and moist with perspiration. It was three in the afternoon and she had yet to rouse herself. What was the point? Too late to follow her plans now—shopping for new art supplies at Creativity Plus, which closed at two on Sundays, then treating herself to a mocha frappuccino with a double portion of whipped cream at Starbucks—a treat she didn't deserve, since treats, to her mind, implied a reward for accomplishments. Instead, she supposed she'd continue doing what she had done all day, blow around like a wind chime and cry buckets of tears.

What would Bernie say if he saw her now?

He had called this morning to invite her to dinner, an invitation she refused. Then his wife, Roberta, called two hours later trying to get her to change her mind. Cynthia pictured Bernie's sweet face twisted with confusion. He never could figure her out. She felt tears well up then run down her cheeks. Lately, she had trouble figuring herself out. And those annoying emotional lows were getting to her. It wasn't her period so she couldn't blame it on hormones—not that she had problems of that kind to begin with. But it would be nice to put her finger on something; to point to something tangible like an unplugged phone and say, "There it is. There's the problem. That's why I'm not working, why I'm not connected."

Tears dripped from her chin onto her pajama top, making small wet marks near her neck. No denying it, something was going on inside her, churning deep like a washing machine agitator, disquieting her whole system. And though she didn't want to admit it, though she had fought admitting it even up to this very second, she actually did know what it was. And that was the problem. Sometimes knowing the reason for a thing was worse than not knowing. Once you knew, you couldn't play with it anymore, shape it to your liking, or blame it on someone or something else.

You couldn't pretend.

With a languid motion and a sigh, the kind one makes after too much crying, Cynthia reached for the folded *Oberon Times* on the coffee table and began to reread the obituary of Carrie Ann Dietch.

"It was standing room only! You pray for a thing and believe God for it, but when it happens, well, it takes you a little by surprise.

But Jonathan, revival has come to Christ Church! I wish you'd been there to see it."

Jonathan stood in his cramped kitchen, fighting the urge to throw his phone into the air out of sheer joy. "God is in the mountain-moving business, Aunt Adel. Just shows you that nothing's impossible for Him, not Christ Church or . . . hidden pockets of resistance." Jonathan's Alamo had been reduced to near rubble over the past several weeks, though a small footing remained.

"Well, I didn't see too many people resisting. When the power of God fell, it was incredible. People were on their knees, crying like babies and confessing their sins. And some folks who hadn't talked to each other for years were suddenly hugging and kissing. And after the service, nobody wanted to go home. They just hung around the altar—not wanting to leave what everyone knew had become holy ground. Oh, Jonathan, we could have the beginnings of another Azusa Street on our hands!"

Jonathan's eyes misted. It was said that during that revival the presence of God was felt even on the street around the building. Daily, thousands of people from all over the country poured into the former Methodist church on the dead-end street—a church that had been converted into a horse stable before William Seymour acquired it in 1906.

Could Christ Church become another Azusa?

"I'm overwhelmed with joy, Aunt Adel."

"Well, dearest love, that's as it should be since you played such a large part. I wish you'd come next Sunday and see it for yourself. You may not be pastor anymore, but nothing says you can't fellowship with us."

"You know that's not possible. I've told you how important it was that I make a clean break." Jonathan slipped a crusty fork into the dishwasher, happy that his aunt couldn't see the condition of his kitchen, of his whole apartment for that matter. He hadn't cleaned in days. Prayer had kept him too busy, and the apartment looked like someone had detonated a case of C4. "Andrew Combs needs to establish his headship at the church, and my presence would make it difficult. People, because they're used to it, would seek me out instead of Andrew, and that's counter productive. You know in your heart I'm right."

There was a long pause and Jonathan knew his aunt was thinking, in that customary way of hers, of how to say what was on her mind without being unkind. He pictured her face contorting with indignation, anger, sadness, and compassion, all at once. His mother had been like that—ever ready to speak her mind, but never wanting to be unkind, and he had always admired her propensity toward mercy.

"I suppose there's no point in arguing the matter. You can be as stubborn as a rash when you've made up your mind about something."

"Leave me in God's hands, Aunt Adel. I'm safe there."

"I *have*, Dearest. I've put you in His hands at least a hundred times since you've left Christ Church."

"And yanked me back a hundred times." Jonathan heard what sounded like kitchen cabinets and drawers slamming. When pot-banging was added, Jonathan knew his aunt was more than displeased.

"Just tell me this; have you been out at all?"

"No." His aunt's ensuing silence told Jonathan she was close to losing her temper.

"Jonathan, this-has-got-to-stop," she said, running her words together like an auctioneer at an estate sale. "You've-been-cooped-up-in-that-apartment-for-the-last-month!"

"I've been busy . . . praying."

"For Christ Church?"

"Yes . . . but when you told me revival had fallen, I felt God's release. Now I can seek Him for myself. Get the direction I need." Excitement curled around Jonathan's nerves, making them tingle. Would God send him to another church in North Oberon or pull him out-of-state? It would be nice if he could stay close to Adel. He was the only family she had left, and she wasn't getting any younger. Ever since his mother died five years ago, his aunt had been there for him and he'd like to be there for her, too, when the time came.

"You still haven't a clue what the Lord wants you to do?"

"No."

"You know your Uncle Douglas left me more money than I can spend in a lifetime. I'd hate to think of you without electricity and eating cold beans for dinner. Do you . . . have you . . . enough money?"

Jonathan's neck muscles tightened as he tossed an empty can of Dinty Moore Stew into the garbage. His years of poverty had stayed with him, like a threatening cloud over his head. It was one of two things he feared. The other was falling in love with someone like Lydia. But he had turned both over to the Lord. Even so, he couldn't shake the fear.

Perfect love casts out fear.

Did that mean God's perfect love had yet to be fully installed within him? Or did it mean Jonathan had yet to learn how to walk in that love?

"Will you be okay? Money-wise, I mean?" his aunt repeated.

"I've few expenses and enough in the bank to keep me going for awhile." It was true. Jonathan never spent all he earned, but had made it a habit every week to set money aside. A cushion, he called it. But in some deeper sense he always wondered if his "cushion" didn't reveal a lack of trust in God. He countered that by telling himself Scripture also called one to be a good steward, and part of that stewardship involved saving. "I'm fine, Aunt Adel." He wondered why there was a strain in his voice. "Please don't worry."

A new round of pot-banging drifted over the phone. "Gertie Eldridge is telling everyone you've had a nervous breakdown. She said she saw it coming—in your work habits and strange talk. It makes my blood boil; knowing that what happened this Sunday is largely due to your faithful year-long intercession and . . . ."

"You and your Ladies Auxiliary have been interceding for Christ Church for ten years. And you know it's 'not by might nor by power.' No one can take credit for a sovereign move of God. And since when have you taken what Gertie says, seriously?"

"Since she's been speaking ill of you."

No mistaking it, Jonathan heard the catch in his aunt's voice and knew tears weren't far behind. He shoved a pile of dirty dishes aside and leaned against the white Formica countertop where splotches of dried gravy made it look like a child's finger-painting. He swiped at it with a sponge. When he did, the worn, leather Bible tucked in the corner caught his eye.

Lord, why does following you have to bring pain to those we love?

"The worst part is that everyone knows how Gertie is, and still they listen. A few people actually asked me if what you have was serious, and will you recover? Can you believe it? How could people pay attention to Gertie's foolish talk after knowing you? After knowing what you've done for Christ Church?"

Jonathan heard his aunt sniffle, then blow her nose. "Aunt Adel, please don't cry."

"I know I'm being silly . . . and self-indulgent. Your Uncle Douglas always did say I cried at the drop of a hat. Don't pay any attention. I'll work through this."

Jonathan drilled his fingertips against the Formica. He never could stand when his mother cried either—and she had done a lot of that during the final year of his father's illness. "Why don't we go to the Beef & Brew? I'll treat us to a couple of big juicy prime ribs. And we can wash the whole thing down with coffee and a slice of their famous cheesecake."

"I'm not in the mood."

"You wanted me to get out more. Think of it as a favor. You'd be helping me."

"Don't try to handle me, Jonathan. I'm too upset. I know I shouldn't be, but Gertie has a way of pushing my buttons."

"All the more reason we should go. It looks like we both could use an outing. What do you say?"

"I don't know . . . ."

"*C'mon.*"

"Well . . . if it's that important to you . . . I suppose so . . . but how about we make it The Cattleman instead?"

Jonathan picked up a bowl and scraped out crusted leftover stew. "You know the steaks are better at the Beef & Brew." He placed the bowl in the dishwasher without rinsing.

"Yes, but Gertie goes to The Cattleman on Sundays, along with half the church since she's made it the trendy thing to do. If they see you, talk to you, maybe it'll stop all this gossip."

He could just about hear his aunt's mind shifting, then idling in a low, silky purr like his first car—the old, green Plymouth he had tagged "Hot Wheels". He closed the dishwasher, then picked up his Bible and carried it into the living room. With one easy motion, he plopped down on the faded, russet-colored couch and stretched out his long, muscular legs. He felt responsible that this thing with Gertie had mushroomed so large in his aunt's life—a Dagon with arms and legs. Jonathan knew all about idols. How things like cars or girls or lettermen's jackets or financial security or the opinion of others could take the center stage of one's life. Well, he'd have to help his aunt cut off those arms and legs, let her Dagon tumble to the ground where he belonged. "I'm sorry, Aunt Adel. It's the Beef & Brew or nothing."

"*Oooh* . . . honestly! Sometimes you're as stubborn as your mother. I don't like speaking ill of the dead, but your mother was one of the most stubborn people I know. There were many who swore she was half mule, and you couldn't disprove it by me."

"Aunt Adel . . . ."

"You could be gracious and give in and let your old aunt maybe get some peace out of it. Maybe get a little satisfaction from seeing the look on Gertie's face . . . but no. Stubborn. Just plain stubborn."

Jonathan removed the Bible from his lap and placed it on the coffee table, next to a brown banana peel and a half-eaten sandwich on a plate. "What time do you want me to pick you up?"

"It's still the Beef and Brew?"

"Yes."

"All right . . . but that means you'll have to give in on this next point. *I'm* paying."

Jonathan glanced at the cheese sandwich which was supposed to be dinner. The cheese was hard and discolored around the edges. Under normal conditions it would have seen the inside of a garbage pail. But last week, he had started cutting back, had started economizing on his meals, and eating things he normally would trash. Growing up he had learned that thriftiness was preferable to hunger.

"Okay, you're on," he said, surprised by how much the prospect of eating a two-inch prime rib with all the trimmings, pleased him. Aunt Adel was right. It *would* be good to get out.

Jonathan hung his keys on the peg beneath the kitchen light switch, then walked into the small living room and settled on the couch. He had that contented feeling one gets after eating a good meal. His prime rib had been superb. So had his sides of sautéed mushrooms, baked potato and asparagus with hollandaise. He couldn't remember enjoying a meal more. His visit with his aunt was also enjoyable, even though she was pensive, tense and spent most of the evening scanning faces—obviously in the hope that Gertie Eldridge or one of the deacons would show up, find Jonathan's mind soundly intact, and vindicate her.

For the most part Jonathan had retained his good humor about the whole thing and had kept the conversation light by rehashing happy childhood memories, peppered with a string of pastor-jokes as fillers. By evening's end there was a discernable difference in his aunt, evidenced by the fact she began laughing at his jokes. Still, he had sensed her need for prayer and had made a mental note to be more diligent on that score. Throughout the evening he had sensed something else, too—the Lord had a word for him.

Now, with great anticipation, Jonathan picked up his Bible from the coffee table and propped an extra pillow behind his back. He would stay with it all night if he had to. And if God hadn't given him anything by morning, he'd continue praying—non-stop, grabbing bits and pieces of sleep only when absolutely needed. He had prayed like that for an entire week before God answered him about coming to Christ Church.

Excitement mounted. He wondered if his next assignment would be half as rewarding as Christ Church. He closed his eyes, preparing himself to alternately praise and pray so that when he sat quietly before the Lord his ears would be open to hear what the Spirit was saying. But he didn't have to wait long. No sooner had he placed the Bible on his lap then he heard the familiar still, small voice.

Do not eat, do not wash, do not change your clothes for three days.

Cynthia stepped out of the shower and walked to the vanity, trailing wet footprints over the ceramic tile floor. She toweled off with stiff, angry motions, leaving behind red blotches and more than one area tender to the touch. She shouldn't have invited Steve over. His all-to-eager response confirmed what she already knew—their evening would be as predictable as tonight's TV lineup. He'd bring a half-pepperoni, half-mushroom pizza, greet her with an infuriatingly sly smile and kiss on the cheek, deposit the pizza along with all his hardware—the Glock, the handcuffs, his gold detective's shield—on the kitchen table, then go to the refrigerator and pull out a Heineken. Their conversation would be superficial, since he didn't like talking about his work and she didn't like talking about hers. Instead, they'd talk about the weather or their cars or the ongoing construction in their neighborhoods. He'd have three Heinekens; one with each of his three slices of pepperoni pizza. She'd have two glasses of Merlot and one slice of mushroom. Then they'd end up in her bed.

She shouldn't have invited him.

It wasn't fair to use him just because she had wandered the apartment all day crying like a diva in a silent film. Had she expected him to assure her she was alright by reinforcing the familiar, the predictable—to assure her she was not having a meltdown of some kind? Was indulging in food, wine and sex supposed to prove she still had a grip on the reigns of that bucking bronco that had become her life?

Yes, all of the above, but now it seemed worn, and made Cynthia feel guilty. How could she use Steve like that? And her guilt made her angry.

She was so sick and tired of feeling guilty!

Guilty over Steve, guilty over being a woman on a man's newspaper, guilty over not seeing enough of her mom and dad or anyone else for that matter, guilty over . . . Julia.

Well, at least she could trim off one guilty layer by ending it with Steve, telling him they were through. They had never been much of an item anyway, so he wouldn't be hurt. Then she'd plunge herself into her work. It had always been her salvation. She'd forget about all this nonsense. Get her mind on other things. Get her nose out of the obituaries and onto the trail of a good story.

Yes, that's what she'd do. And she'd start by telling Steve it was over . . . first thing in the morning.

CHAPTER 5

Jonathan stared into the mirror, hardly recognizing the image that stared back. Clumps of greasy hair stuck out in all directions. His crumpled shirt and pants looked more like grimy rags than clothing. And his breath smelled like dirty socks. When he ran his tongue across his teeth he felt plaque clinging like Elmer's glue.

He pulled out a paper cup from his bathroom dispenser and filled it with water. He swished the water around in his mouth then held it for a minute wondering if this counted as "washing"—which God had forbidden him to do.

He quickly spit it out. When he did, he smelled body odor seeping through his shirt. He had never felt so disgusting—had never looked so disgusting. The dark stubble on his face looked like charcoal smudges. But the worst part was the hunger. The Lord had called him on many fasts, but never had Jonathan felt so ravenous, so crazed from want of food.

He ran his fingers through his hair, trying to both settle it down and take his mind off of a stomach that seemed to twist and turn and gnaw until his nerves were raw. His hands shook as they combed. How could he be this hungry after only three days?

He looked at his watch. Five more hours before he could eat . . . and wash. For two and a half days he had prayed—pleaded with God for more direction. And now that it came, Jonathan was sorry he had been so persistent. He had trouble believing the instructions. He was to walk the streets as he was. And the Lord had confirmed it.

Three times.

Even now, Jonathan would have asked for a fourth if he dared. But to ask again, when God had been so clear, would be an act of disobedience.

But what if someone saw him? How could this bring honor and glory to his precious Savior? How could walking around dirty and smelly bring anything but scorn? *Lean not, lean not.* That's all he was getting. And that was the hard part, that was the temptation— wanting to slip into his own understanding, trying to figure it all out, trying to complete in the flesh what had begun in the Spirit.

He flicked off the bathroom light and went into the kitchen to retrieve his keys. There was nothing more he could do to improve his appearance, not if he wanted to continue in obedience. His one hope was that God wouldn't keep him on the streets too long.

Out of the corner of his eye he saw his hunter green jacket draped over a kitchen chair. As he reached for it, Jonathan felt a check in his spirit. Surely, God wouldn't mind him wearing a jacket to keep warm? If he had to stay out late, he'd need it. Evenings could be chilly. He put it on and zipped it to his neck. When he passed the small mirror in the hall and saw that the jacket made him appear a little fresher, he felt relieved. But there was still his hair and face, not to mention his mouth and body odor.

He rummaged around trying to find his baseball cap. After ten minutes, the pull of the Lord grew too strong and he gave up. With a sigh, he took fifty dollars from his dresser drawer and shoved them into his pocket. Then he walked out the apartment and headed for his car.

For over an hour, Jonathan drove aimlessly around until he found himself on the outskirts of North Oberon. He pulled into a parking garage and started walking.

Where was he going?

He felt like a fool. But then wasn't he supposed to be a fool for Christ? To obey? To trust? No matter what? He had given his life to the Lord when he was five and was no stranger to His ways. So why was this different? Because . . . of the pain in his Aunt Adel's voice, because of the idle talk about the stability of his mind.

Was he losing his mind?

Was Ezekiel losing his mind when he lay on his left side for three-hundred and ninety consecutive days, then turned over and lay on his right side for another forty days at God's command? Was Hosea losing his mind when he obeyed God and married a prostitute? Was Isaiah losing his mind when he walked naked and barefoot in the streets for three years because God told him to? But he was no Ezekiel, Hosea or Isaiah. He was just an ordinary servant of God. He prayed as he walked down the street hoping to see the revealed will of God etched on some storefront, or blazing across the sky. Finally, he stopped praying and just walked.

By the time Jonathan noticed the change in the neighborhood, he was already deep into South Oberon and approaching Skid Row. Buildings peeled their paint, and many store signs were torn off or barely readable. Empty bottles and unidentifiable refuse littered the sidewalk. Here and there sheets of newspaper, blown by the wind, pressed against the battered buildings like bandages over sores. When Jonathan passed the Angus Avenue Hotel, he smelled urine. Two men stood on the hotel steps passing a bottle. In an alley, a woman was throwing up. He heard the clanking of freight cars in the distance; smelled the smoke pouring from the stacks of the Angus Glass Works; tasted the grime of two decades of South Oberon poverty, and shuddered.

God, why am I here?

Jonathan quickened his pace, heading west. He raised no eyebrows or interest as he walked. He could have been one of them, the way he looked and smelled. Only his cotton jacket gave him any air of respectability.

He stopped when he saw a woman pull a half eaten sandwich from the garbage pail and hand it to her child. He was surprised he didn't feel revulsion; surprised to feel his hunger so voracious that he, too, would willingly eat from the garbage if his fast were up. He probed for the money in his pocket and pulled out everything except a ten, then walked over to the woman and handed it to her.

"What you expectin' for this, Mister?" she said, holding the bills in her hand.

Jonathan looked down at the small child clinging to the woman's tattered skirt. Under the dirt and layers of clothing, and with the short matted hair, he couldn't tell if the child was male or female. But he saw a sore, the size of a quarter, along with a half dozen smaller sores covering the child's scalp.

"I said, what you want for this?"

"Nothing. It's for you and the child."

"You don't look like one of those do-gooders. You don't smell like one neither." Her harsh tone and apparent lack of gratitude startled him. She folded the money and stuffed it between the layers of her clothing. "But I ain't gonna ask you again. I'm just gonna take it."

Jonathan nodded and backed away, feeling a sudden urge to flee. "God . . . God bless you."

The woman laughed, revealing a missing bottom tooth and two chipped uppers. "You a Bible thumper?"

Jonathan nodded.

"Well, it don't look like it's done you much good."

"I'm sorry I can't help more," he said walking away, his skin feeling like it was crawling with ants.

Before he went a block, Jonathan felt an anguish of soul. Why hadn't he ministered to that woman and her child? Why hadn't he spoken words of life? Why hadn't he tried to introduce that woman to the Savior, the Provider, the Father, the Husband?

What was wrong with him?

His heart was still heavy when he came upon an area buzzing with activity. Men loitered in groups on the sidewalk; others streamed through the double-doorway of a building; a building which appeared surprisingly well maintained. Jonathan stopped and read the sign: Angus Avenue Men's Shelter.

He was glad these homeless men had such a nice facility. Even so, he didn't want to spend time here. It wasn't the kind of neighborhood he wanted to be in after dark. Already, the angle of the sun told him he should head for his car. And it would take all his remaining strength to get there. He still couldn't understand why God had brought him here.

What do you want me to do, Lord?

He was horrified at the answer, which came like a shot and hit him in the chest like Tommy Sullivan's fast ball in his high school all-star play-offs.

Eat, bathe and spend the night here.

The tone was firm and one familiar to Jonathan. It was a tone that left no room for argument. Still, Jonathan persisted. *Why, Lord?* He listened a moment, but only heard the chatter of men and the scraping of feet as more and more homeless scurried to the shelter.

With a heavy heart, Jonathan entered the building. The fine impression he had formed while on the outside evaporated when he stepped inside. Metal bunk beds—so close together a person could barely pass between them—filled a room that resembled a barracks. A burly man, with a snake tattoo on his arm, held a clipboard and barred his way.

"Name and bed number?"

"Jonathan Holmes. And I don't have a bed. I've never been here before."

The man ran his thumb down the clipboard. "You're in luck. Got one bed left. Number one thirty nine, a lower."

"Thank you." The phrase was insincere. He wasn't thankful at all. He had hoped there wouldn't be a spare bed and that he could just walk out that big double door and head home, exonerated from the Lord's directive. Instead, Jonathan turned toward the maze of bunks but stopped when he felt strong fingers grip his arm.

"Not so fast. First the paperwork." The man with the snake tattoo handed his clipboard to an assistant. "Follow me."

As Jonathan did, he tried ignoring the swarm of male bodies shuffling stiff-legged like his grandfather used to do, the one who had died from Alzheimer's.

And then there was the smell.

It made him want to gag. How could men live here? Sleep here? Eat here?

When his guide ushered him into a tiny office, Jonathan was relieved to be away from the sea of bodies. How close had he come to being homeless himself while growing up? He couldn't count the times he'd heard his mother praying for the Lord to provide their rent money. And the sight of his mother on her knees before the fifteenth of every month, when the landlord would knock on the door, was a memory that harassed him still. He should have helped his mother more—gotten a part time job instead of playing baseball.

But he had needed that baseball scholarship. . . .

"Are you employed?" The man retrieved papers from one of the piles that covered every inch of the desk, then plucked a pen from a mug stained yellow around the rim. "Well?"

"No."

"How long you been unemployed?" The tattooed man sat down and in spite of the fact that there was an empty chair nearby, made no suggestion, either by word or gesture, that Jonathan should take it, so Jonathan remained standing. "How long unemployed?" the man repeated.

"One month."

"How long you been homeless?"

"I'm not homeless."

The man's jaw twitched. "So why are you here?"

"I . . . that is, God sent me."

The man's eyes narrowed. "Any physical or mental handicaps?"

"No." Jonathan watched the man check the "yes" box.

"Any problems with drugs or alcohol?"

"No."

"Job training?"

"I'm a minister, a pastor." Again Jonathan saw the jaw twitch.

"Education?"

"Seminary graduate."

"Wait here." The man left the room, and for the second time since entering the shelter, Jonathan felt a budding hope that he won't be allowed to stay. That hope was dashed when the man returned carrying bedding.

"Dinner in half an hour. They'll announce it over the loud-speaker. When you're done eating, go to the reading room and see the social worker for your intake interview."

Jonathan nodded. He had no idea what an intake interview was. He should have asked but was too numb. His senses were on overload, no longer able to absorb everything: the sights, the noise, the smell, the instructions. He clutched his bedding and stumbled toward the direction of his cot, wading through a sea of men not subject to any discernable tide, a sea that bumped and shoved him as he went. When he found bed 139, he staked out his territory by spreading the white sheets over the stained mattress. Over that, he spread out the thin, tan blanket. He tried fluffing the flimsy pillow then gave up and placed it at the head of the bed.

A glance at his watch told Jonathan his fast was over. First he'd wash, then try to rest a few minutes before dinner—seek the Lord for direction. Was he here to minister to someone? *But there were so many*. What exactly was he to do?

He asked the closest person where the rest room was, but the man just mumbled incoherently, so Jonathan wandered in the direction of the greatest activity. It took him a full ten minutes to traverse the fifty feet to the men's room, and when he stepped in, Jonathan's first inclination was to step right back out. Men, some carrying toilet articles, others empty handed, were lined eight-deep in front of ten white porcelain sinks. Off to the side were six urinals, and six toilets without doors—all of them in use. At the far wall ten shower stalls, minus curtains, were filled to capacity. The total lack of privacy was appalling.

Jonathan took his place behind a man who looked like he was high. He watched him sway and bump against the man in front of him who became annoyed and began shoving back. For a minute, it looked like a fight would break out, but then it just fizzled into a shouting match. Language, the likes of which Jonathan had not heard since high school, passed like volleys between the men, but nobody paid attention.

How had these people gotten used to living like this?

When it was Jonathan's turn, he stepped up to the sink and turned on the water. He couldn't remember water feeling this wonderful. He stood holding his hands under the tap, letting water lap fingers and palms. When he heard what sounded like impatient shuffling behind him, he reached for the soap dispenser, and pumped. Nothing came out. He looked around to see if he could spot one that was full.

"Don't bother. They're all empty this time of day."

Jonathan turned to the voice behind him. A man, surprisingly clean, stood holding a towel and bar of soap.

"You're new. I can always spot the newbies. But you'll learn the ropes soon enough. Tomorrow morning, they'll hand out a bunch of stuff at the toiletry station. You can get soap there, and toothpaste."

Jonathan's face reddened. He was sure his breath was beyond nasty and bent his head so his mouth opened away from the man. "Thanks."

"They'll give you other things too, if you want—shampoo, razor blades, shaving cream. It's not easy, but you'll learn how to keep clean."

Jonathan nodded before returning to the sink, then pulled a paper towel from the dispenser. He wet it and used it to scrub his face and neck.

"They start handing the toiletries out around 5:30 but I'd get there earlier if I were you. The station closes at six, and the line gets long. Those at the end don't make it before the window shuts."

Jonathan pushed up the sleeves of his hunter green jacket. "Thanks. I'll do that." He ran the wet paper over his arms, wrists and hands, then pulled several more sheets from the dispenser and dried himself. He turned one last time to the man behind him and smiled, then left the room.

Before he could get to his bunk, the loudspeaker blurted that dinner was being served, and Jonathan found himself carried by a swell of bodies into a twelve-hundred-square-foot room filled with long rectangular tables and chairs. At the far end, a massive metal serving counter held steaming chafing dishes.

Jonathan shoved his hands into his pockets to keep them from shaking, and tried ignoring the painful rumble in his stomach. The smell of food now overpowered the smell of dirty men. It was agony standing in line.

What if the food was gone before he got there?

He looked around at the nameless men and wondered if they felt that way, too. But God would bring him through this, and in due time reveal the meaning of it all.

It surprised Jonathan how fast he consumed his portion of beef stew, biscuits and butter, chocolate pudding and coffee. Throughout his meal he had not spoken a word to anyone. He paused only long enough to give silent thanks, then inhaled his food. When he finished, he went for seconds and returned with a plate more heaping than the first. The depth of his hunger was still vivid and real—surely supernaturally induced.

But God never wasted anything. Perhaps this training was in preparation for a new church ministry, an outreach to the poor and homeless. Jonathan had failed to install such a ministry at Christ Church. The closest thing he had done was to send old hymnals, choir robes and the like to a small church in South Oberon. In the face of what he was seeing now, Jonathan realized it had not been enough. Not nearly enough. God had opened his eyes, enabled him to recognize areas of neglect, areas essential to a properly rounded church. And he was grateful. When he got his new church, he wouldn't omit them again.

With renewed vigor and enthusiasm, Jonathan made his way back to his bunk. There was no point in going to the reading room to see the social worker and fill out any more forms. Tomorrow, he'd go home. Of that he was certain.

He sat on the mattress and pulled off his shoes, then tucked them under his bed. Next, he unzipped his jacket and took it off, then in an uncharacteristic manner, folded it neatly and placed it next to his pillow. He slipped between the covers. He was exhausted and closed his eyes, trying to ignore the noise of men talking, of feet scraping the floor, of the loudspeaker blaring announcements or instructions, of the clanking from the kitchen, of the TV blaring, and of all the other strange noises that worked his nerves.

But movement by his bunk caused Jonathan to open his eyes. The lights still glared overhead making it easy to see the two men sharing a needle and shooting something into their arms. Jonathan turned around. On the other side of him, a man wept and mumbled to himself. Jonathan rose on his elbow, praying that God would give him a word of comfort to share. When the man hissed at him, Jonathan laid back down. Everything around him was soiled, damaged, scarred. It was overwhelming, and Jonathan found himself praying. He was still praying when the lights went off.

Stubby crept along the shadows of the building, looking from side to side. He didn't like being on Angus Avenue this time of night, but how else was he going get to The Gorge without being seen? He had checked Turtle's other hideouts and this was the last one.

A car approached and Stubby hugged the building until it passed. His heart pounded against the small flashlight in his shirt pocket. He was too old for this. The night air was already aggravating the arthritis in his hands. They throbbed even when he held them still. If Turtle wasn't at The Gorge, he'd give up. There was no place else to look. But if Turtle was there, he'd tell him the plan. Lots of men, who traveled to warmer states during winter, said they liked the Tucson shelter. Things could be different there. They'd stay a few months 'til things calmed down. Or . . . if they wanted, they could stay for good. Start over. He liked that idea, of starting over. Maybe he could get his life together in Tucson.

He had already priced bus tickets, and would have more than enough from his Social Security check to pay for them.

Another car approached, then slowed. Stubby darted into the alley and held his breath. *He was outta his mind to be here.* But he had to get to Turtle before they did. After Manny, Stubby had hoped things would blow over, that they'd forget about Turtle or maybe just rough him up a bit and leave it at that. But Turtle was right. Word on the street was this thing wouldn't be going away. And word was that Stubby might be in bad straits, too, being Turtle's friend and all. Once trouble came, it was like the flu, and had a way of infecting everyone nearby.

That's just how it was.

Stubby inched out of the alley. In front of him, the Angus Glass Works slouched like a giant beast behind barbed wire, its nostrils not spewing clouds of smoke, but lacy tendrils, as it lay asleep. He darted from shadow to shadow until he stood at the edge of The Gorge. He looked down, unable to see anything but darkness. One false step and he'd drop fifty feet onto a pile of rubble. He'd have to use his flashlight. But using it was a problem, too—he'd be easy to spot.

He was crazy to be here.

He listened for any sound, then pulled the flashlight from his pocket and turned it on. A beam of light sliced the darkness and danced at his feet like a giant firefly. He looked around nervously. He might as well have taken out an ad in the paper and let everyone know he was coming.

He took a step and tapped the ground with his shoe to make sure he was on solid footing before releasing his full weight. He did this over and over. It was tough going downhill and having to cover ground inch by inch. But if he didn't, he'd get hurt. Finally, his luck ran out and his foot slipped between two chunks of concrete. He felt a burning pain around his ankle where concrete tore skin. He pried his foot free then checked it. It was bleeding but not broken.

He'd have to take it slower. The Gorge was deep and dangerous— an abandoned excavation site that was supposed to boast of a twenty-story business complex and boasted instead of concrete chunks, rusted Lally columns, twisted metal, and broken glass.

He had one more mishap—a fall onto a patch of glass where one of the shards cut his left hand. By the time he stood at the mouth of an enormous pipe he was sore and out of breath.

"Turtle." No answer. "Turtle! It's Stubby." Still no answer.

He entered the pipe and scanned the interior with his flashlight. The far end of the pipe was jammed against earth, which formed a wall and made the pipe look like a large round room in which he could stand upright. Toward the earthen wall, a pile of blankets formed a bed, and stacked nearby were assorted rags, a rusted Coleman stove, a large flashlight, cans of peaches and other fruit, a stack of old magazines, and various drug paraphernalia. But Turtle was nowhere in sight.

Stubby limped toward the bed. He'd wait.

Jonathan awoke to the loudspeaker announcing breakfast. It took him a full minute to remember where he was. He rolled onto his side and pushed himself up. When he did, a noxious odor floated from his shirt. It wasn't subtle anymore or discernable only when he moved a certain way. He was now nose-pinching foul. He greeted the Lord in prayer, then made his way to the toiletry station. It was closed.

Jonathan stood a moment watching men, in various levels of disarray, swarm into the dining room. He headed for the lavatory. Only a handful of men were there. He'd wash and leave without breakfast. The mirror told him just how big the task of clean-up was going to be. His stubble was more than just a dark shadow now. It looked like something alive, with a mind of its own, jutting in different directions. His hair was a mess too, sticking up in greasy spikes all over his head. And then there was his mouth. It smelled like a cesspool, while his clothes looked like dingy rags.

He turned on the faucet, then pushed the soap dispenser and was rewarded with a squeaky sound and nothing else. He didn't bother trying any of the others but just splashed his face with water, then rinsed his mouth. Finally, he wet his hair, slicking down the spikes. When he was finished, he studied his reflection in the mirror. Someone resembling a drug dealer in a police movie stared back. He felt horror and shame as he darted out the bathroom door.

It was easy getting back to his bed. The swarm of humanity had already migrated to the dining room. He'd retrieve his jacket and leave. No need to stay any longer. He had already felt God's release. Later, after a hot shower, shave, and some breakfast, Jonathan would review what he had learned here.

But before he even reached bed 139, Jonathan saw that his jacket was no longer next to the pillow. He pulled off his sheets and shook them. He checked the floor then looked under the bed. Panic gripped him. How could he walk the streets without that thin shield of respectability? He looked around trying to spot anyone with the contraband but without success. He then scouted around the other beds hoping to see it on the floor. After awhile, he gave up and walked out the big double door.

Jonathan moved east on Angus Avenue all the while praying that God would be merciful and not let anyone he knew see him like this. He laughed when he realized no one he knew frequented Skid Row. Until yesterday, he had not seen it himself. He felt an overwhelming sense of shame. Why hadn't he been here before? Why hadn't his church done more for these people?

He passed the Angus Avenue Hotel and looked for that woman with her child. If he found her, he'd give her his remaining ten dollars and worry about how to get his car out of the parking garage, later. As his eyes searched, he stepped into a puddle of vomit. For a moment, he thought he was going to heave what was left of last night's dinner. He tried scraping his shoes on the curb but all his scraping couldn't leave the stench behind. Now the smell of vomit mingled with the other odors that floated from him.

He walked another five blocks, thinking only of getting his car and going home. It wouldn't be soon enough to suit him. He stopped at the corner of Angus and Fourth, puzzled. Where was he? He didn't recognize a thing. Had he missed his turn? He was about to backtrack when he felt the pull of the Lord and groaned.

Not now, Lord, please not now. Just let me get home.

But the pull was too strong, like that of an undercurrent gripping his ankles and towing him into deeper waters. He found himself walking up Fourth. A building to the left caught his eye—a four-story brick structure, attractive, well kept and free of graffiti. Mounted on the roof and rising several feet into the air, was a huge, white wooden cross with the word JESUS written across it. Under the cross hung a sign, BEACON MISSION.

Jonathan stood gazing upward, feeling both puzzled and alarmed. And when he moved to the alcove beneath the wooden canopy, his heart thumped wildly, though he didn't know why. He stared at the front door, feeling like a man on the edge of a cliff. A glass-enclosed sign, made up of little black letters that could be changed, hung to the right. "For the wages of sin is death; but the gift of God is eternal life through Jesus Christ our Lord." He wondered how many tired, homeless souls had come to this door seeking refuge and found eternal life instead. He turned the knob but the door wouldn't open. Next, he peered into a window and saw it was dark inside. That's when he felt the edge of that cliff give way. That's when he knew.

"Lord, this has to be a mistake." His palms began to sweat even as his mouth became a desert. How many times had he told God, "Here I am, send me"? He had meant it, each and every time. He was willing to go to any church, large or small, to a church in any part of the country, to a church in any country for that matter.

But this wasn't a church.

He stood waiting, hoping that a new word would come. Finally, he hung his head in submission. "Lord, I feel sorry for these people, but I don't love them. If you want me to do this, You'll have to change my heart."

Jonathan was now on the right street heading for the parking garage. His feet flew over the pavement. Soon he'd be home. After his shower, he'd have time to pray, ask God for another confirmation. Perhaps he had misunderstood. The thought added wings to his feet. Yes, there was a chance he had misunderstood.

"*Pastor Holmes? Is that you?*"

Jonathan turned to the sound of the voice and saw a car slowing beside him. The passenger window was open and Jonathan's breath caught when he recognized the driver. "Oh . . . hello, Gertie."

"Is everything alright?"

"Yes, of course." Jonathan tried smoothing his shirt.

"You look . . . poorly."

"I'm fine. Just had a . . . long night."

"You don't look fine. You look like something the cat dragged in." The car had stopped and Gertie leaned towards the passenger window. For a moment Jonathan was afraid she was going to get out. "My husband's Uncle Alistair used to have long nights, too. That's when he used to drink and go on week-long binges. Come to think of it, Pastor, he looked a lot like you do now."

"What brings you to this neighborhood?" Jonathan deliberately remained several feet away. One good whiff and Gertie would be off on her tangent again.

"Sissy Wheeler just donated two brand new coffee urns to Christ Church. Said the coffee out of the old ones tasted like someone was laying asphalt on her tongue. I was for throwing them out, but Pastor Combs insisted they still had a lot of life left and that we should donate them to that little church here in South Oberon. Seems you got us started in the donating business and now Pastor Combs wants to give everything we can't use, away. I swear, all the garbage has to go through his office before it's allowed to be put in the dumpster!" Gertie laughed. "Well, not really, but it sure feels that way.

"Anyhow, Pastor Combs asked me to call the church and see if they could use the urns, and of course they said 'yes'. Then he asked me to deliver them, but I said not on your life. I don't do South Oberon. You think I want my hubcaps stolen? I'll have you know these hubcaps cost three hundred dollars apiece! Then Pastor Combs said it wasn't really in South Oberon, but more on the border of North Oberon. Then he showed me on the map and well, what could I say? I've always been a pushover. 'Just let Gertie do it.' That's what everybody says. So here I am." She jerked her chin to the side. "It's just ahead, down that street on the left."

From where he stood, Jonathan could see the giant, silver urns sitting in the backseat like two tin men. "Well, don't let me hold you up." He backed further away just as the wind kicked up behind him and blew in Gertie's direction, making her face wrinkle.

"Pastor, if you don't mind me saying, you can't sweep problems under a rug. Uncle Alistair tried that for years and ruined his liver. You're young, yet. You have time to change. But you need to get a grip. I'm not clergy so I'm not qualified, otherwise I'd offer to help you myself. And Pastor Sorensen never had an ounce of trouble so I can't even share any of his remedies. The only thing I can say is that Pastor Sorensen was never interested in changing things like you are. Never tried stirring things up, either. He was content with things as they were, so were the deacons—all like-minded godly men. Why, the church practically ran itself! 'Course I can't prove it, but I believe that's how come Pastor Sorensen died peacefully in his sleep. Just slipped away one night—like it was a reward of sorts. There's a lot to be said for letting things be." Gertie looked at her watch. "Time's flying. Can I drop you anywhere?"

"No, thank you."

The look of relief on Gertie's face was unmistakable. "Okay, then. I'll be going. And I'll be praying for you, Pastor. I'll pray that God helps you get a grip on your life."

CHAPTER 6

The sirens and cavalcade of squad cars made Stubby sprint the entire block as he followed them from the Angus Avenue Hotel to what the inhabitants of Skid Row called the Industrial Strip. Going from east to west, the Strip consisted of the Angus Glass Works, The Gorge, the freight station, and Nationwide Distributors—with their half dozen warehouses that looked like neatly aligned loaves of bread. It was all that was left of the Angus Empire in South Oberon.

Stubby lurked in the shadows of Nationwide Distributors, in their lot of ready-for-shipment containers. From here, he had a clear view of the freight yard. He watched the police drive stakes into the ground, then wind their yellow tape until a huge section of the yard was cordoned off. Most of the activity centered around a disconnected freight car sitting on a dead-end track.

Turtle never showed up at The Gorge. Now, Stubby waited for some clue, some sign to confirm what he already knew.

Turtle was never coming back.

A crowd had gathered, and when Stubby saw two uniformed cops begin to question everyone, he pressed closer to the side of the warehouse. First Manny, now . . . . He brushed his eyes with the back of his hand, trying to ignore the sick, lonely feeling in his chest.

They'd come for him next, though he never had no part in it. Justice rented no rooms on Angus Avenue, not the kind you read about in books, anyhow. The best thing for him to do was hop the first bus to Tucson and kiss this whole sorry neighborhood goodbye.

He pictured Turtle with his dirty, over-sized shirt, ripped pants, hacking cough and shaking hands, and how Turtle had clomped away in his old boots without looking back. Turtle would have liked Tucson. And that hot, dry air would have done his lungs good—maybe cleared up that cough. Stubby kicked the dirt with his sneaker. *Well . . . at least Turtle didn't have to scratch and scrape no more.* It hardly seemed worth all the scratching and scraping it took to make it through a day. Maybe that's how Turtle had felt, and Manny, too. Else, why would they pull that stunt unless they figured they had nothing to lose? Though when Stubby remembered that scared look on Turtle's face he knew in his heart Turtle hadn't been ready to cash in his chips.

Stubby leaned against the corrugated wall of the warehouse thinking that maybe Tucson wasn't such a good idea after all. Why bother? Word was, this crowd could find anybody, no matter where they went. And if they didn't get Stubby, then the hunger would, or TB, or cold or . . . .

Stubby pulled away from the wall, turned and headed for the Angus Avenue Hotel. *No, there weren't no point in goin' to Tucson. He could see that now. Better to forget it and just get high—maybe go back to snowballs.* Nothing made him feel better than cocaine and heroin. He'd get a stash, then hole up in his room 'til his Social Security ran out. Let them come for him if they wanted. It didn't matter. He was tired of trying; tired of thinking life would get better. It was all useless. There was no God, at least not One Who was interested in answering Stubby's prayers.

Cynthia pressed against the tape as she watched the swarm of uniformed and plain-clothes police. "Steve, what's going on?"

A tall, redhead extracted himself from the crowd and walked over to where she stood. His shield was clipped to his belt and under his blue suit she saw the bulge of his Glock. The smile on his face told her he was pleased to see her, a surprise since she had given him the boot.

"Uniform division called us. They found a John Doe in one of the cars. Ident's just arrived."

Cynthia knew Steve was referring to the Identification Section or Major Crime Scene Unit that was there to collect fingerprints and other evidence as well as take photos. Part of the uniform division was now busy controlling the scene by keeping unauthorized personnel out of the way; the other part was busy isolating witnesses.

"Sorry, but I can't let you through. The ME still has to certify that our John Doe's dead. And Ident's dusting for prints and casting tire tracks."

Cynthia looked past Detective Steve Bradley and watched as men combed the freight yard. "Can you tell me anything?"

"Only that a white male, between fifty and sixty, has been beaten to death—a brutal, methodical beating by someone who enjoyed it."

"Can you do better on the age—narrow it a bit?"

"The guy was homeless. It's hard to tell with them. I've seen twenty-year-old homeless druggies look forty."

"So . . . he was homeless and a drug user?" She scribbled some notes on her pad. "Anything else?"

"Don't waste your time. This is not your kind of story. Go hang out at City Hall."

Cynthia tapped her pad and frowned. Steve, during those rare times when he talked about his work, only gave bare details as if to spare her the "dirt" of his trade, never connecting the fact that her trade was dirty, too, that politicians committed their own share of homicides and robberies by assassinating their opponent's reputations or scamming taxpayer money. And he didn't know, nor would he understand, about her growing obsession with the dead. "I go where my instincts lead me and right now they're leading me here."

Steve squared his shoulders. "You want to dig around for a story that's not there, be my guest."

"I take it you're not going to spend much time on this."

Steve's wide brow pinched over algae-green eyes. Cynthia knew that look. Pure business. "One of the reasons I like you is because you're not a bleeding heart. So I'm assuming you're seeing something I'm not."

"Doesn't it seem strange that three people, in a matter of a few blocks, have all died from unnatural causes within two months?"

Steve shrugged. "I count two. The guy in the dumpster and now this one."

"What about that pastor at the Beacon Mission?"

Steve laughed, a condescending sort of laugh, as though he found himself in the unpleasant position of lecturing a child. "Stick to uncovering government waste. Homicide's obviously not your thing. That pastor's death was accidental. The old guy slipped, and that was that. As for the rest . . . this is Skid Row, Cynthia, not exactly the healthiest part of town. People here die all the time for all sorts of reasons."

"Maybe. But I still count three strange deaths within two months and I don't like those odds."

Steve leaned over the tape and stuck his face within inches of Cynthia's. She could tell by the look in his eyes and by that Clark-Gable-kind-of-smirk that business was over. "Tell you what. I'll give you everything I have on these cases over dinner."

Cynthia shook her head. "We're no good for each other." She meant every word. His line of work left him not liking people much, either. And two such disconnected souls could never create a connection. "I just want to be friends. And friends don't use their friends." She meant that, too. She was through using him, though he hardly seemed to appreciate it. "I've explained all this already."

"You did. But I told you I don't mind being used. In fact, I *like* it." He brushed her forehead with his fingers. "Don't be so quick to give up on us. We understand each other. We're a lot alike, you and I."

"Perhaps that's why they say opposites attract."

"Oh, Jonathan, it's horrible! Gertie's been telling everyone how you've sunk into some sort of abyss that includes mental illness, drunkenness and depravation all rolled into one. She says she knows all about these things because of some uncle of hers. She's been entertaining people for hours with her descriptions of your hair and clothes, your face. She even had the audacity to tell everyone you smelled to high heavens. I'm telling you, Jonathan, I've been on my knees three times today, praying for God to lift my bad temper and forgive my desire to wash her mouth out with soap. But I'm still so angry!"

Jonathan used his shoulder to cup the phone against his ear while he opened the refrigerator and pulled out a gallon of milk. Nothing he put in his mouth these days escaped his appreciation.

"Jonathan, did you hear what I said?"

"It's partially true. But only partially, and of course there's a good explanation." The silence on the other end of the phone was deafening. He filled his glass then described his Skid Row experience.

"So, God is sending you to work with the homeless?"

"Yes, Aunt Adel, I believe He is." He wondered if his voice sounded as agitated as his emotions. The possibility of being surrounded by poverty again had created such anxiety over the past forty-eight hours that he couldn't help but see it as a red flag. Had his years of struggling and working two jobs to get a degree been motivated more by a desire to leave behind an impoverished lifestyle rather than a desire to serve God? That possibility pricked him like a bee sting.

"Did you really smell like vomit?"

"That, and other things." He heard his aunt laugh, but the laugh was strained. "I'm sorry for all the embarrassment I'm causing. I just don't know any other way . . . ."

"Don't be silly, Jonathan. There is no other way. You have to obey and I . . . well, I'll have to learn to deal with Gertie's wagging tongue aside from wanting to lather it with Lava soap."

"I wish I could do something to make this easier for you."

"Obviously it's not meant to be easy or God would have made it so. But I must tell you that ever since you left Christ Church, I've been seeing myself more clearly. And I see that I'm not nearly as far down that road of sanctification as I thought I was."

Jonathan eyed his prayer journal on the counter. He had not written a word in it since his return from Skid Row. "Neither am I Aunt Adel. Neither am I."

Cynthia walked down Angus Avenue clutching her purse and feeling foolish. As a veteran investigator, she knew better than to come to South Oberon carrying an alligator bag. But she had been in a hurry and overlooked the obvious. Even her expensive high heels betrayed her with their click-click-click along the uneven pavement, a sound as strange and out-of-place here as a woodpecker tapping a telephone pole in New York City.

"Hey chickie, chickie," came a voice out of nowhere. "Come look what I got."

Cynthia spotted a grimy man hovering by an alley. He looked in his thirties. She remembered Steve's words about not being able to tell a homeless person's age and decided he could just as well be twenty. He held a pack of cigarettes. Cynthia wondered if it wasn't full of drugs.

"You lookin' for something special? I got it," came the voice again.

Cynthia quickened her pace, each footfall creating a cacophony of noise which seemed to grow louder. Eyes watched her from the shadows, sizing her up. She was a stranger, a trespasser who had wandered into a hostile land. She skirted a man sprawled unconscious across the sidewalk, then darted passed two drunks sipping from bottles in paper bags. Cynthia avoided looking their way, but couldn't avoid the pleading stares of the two approaching women.

"You have a little something you can spare? It's for the kids," one of them said, glancing at the children that appeared like miniature bookends on either side of her.

Cynthia tried to discern if the women were high. When she decided no, she opened her purse and pulled out two tens then gave one to each of them.

"Thank you. That's most generous," the same woman said, smiling.

"I wonder if you could help me? I'm trying to find out about that man who was killed the other day. The one the police found in the freight car."

The woman drew her children closer. "Yes, I heard about it. Don't know anything, though, except that his name was Turtle. I'm new around here." She turned to her companion. "Anything you can add?"

The second woman shook her head. "Sorry."

Cynthia watched them walk away, half expecting to see them stop by the man with the cigarette pack and relieve themselves of their newfound wealth, but they passed him without a glance.

At least they hadn't made a fool of her. Still, she was getting nowhere. She had made a tactical error. Her attire—a black pantsuit and two-inch-high Nine West heels, not to mention the three hundred dollar black alligator bag—was all wrong and had created a barrier between her and everyone she encountered. She wouldn't get her story looking like this. Maybe things would be different at the shelter.

As she walked up to the Angus Avenue Men's Shelter, she hoped she'd be more successful. When she pulled the door and it wouldn't open, she tried the bell.

A man with a snake tattooed on his upper left arm opened the door and looked at her as though he had never seen a woman before. He gave her the once-over before settling his attention on her purse. "Read the sign, lady. This is a men's shelter."

"I'm Cynthia Wells. I called and made an appointment with a Mr. Jake Stone."

"*You're* that reporter lady?"

Cynthia forced a smile. "Guilty on both counts."

"Well, I'm Jake." He opened the door wider to let her in. "We can talk in my office."

As Cynthia followed him she scanned the place, noticing that it smelled disgusting, that the beds were claustrophobically close, and that the shelter was deserted. She decided to zero in on her last observation.

"Where is everyone?" She took the chair indicated, opposite a desk piled with papers so high they obscured the middle of Jake's chest when he sat.

"No one's allowed in until five, except for those who have jobs. Otherwise, you'd have some of 'em lying around all day, not even looking for work."

"Do most of them work?"

Jake shook his head. "Not those with drug or mental problems. But some of the others, they manage to find jobs here and there. Some even steady. You said you wanted information? What sort of article are you doing? I mean, what angle are you looking for? It'll help if we just stick to the facts you need, 'cause I don't have much time. We open in an hour and I got things to finish up."

"Actually, I was thinking of doing a piece on the two men who died recently, Manny and Turtle. I was hoping you knew them and could give me some background."

Jake's jaw tightened. "We've got a hundred and fifty beds in this place. I don't get to know all the men who use them. I don't even get to know half of 'em. Here today, gone tomorrow. There's only a certain amount of time they can stay, you know."

"What's the limit?"

"Depends on what the social worker says. If the guy needs psychiatric treatment as an outpatient, the stay is longer. If he's got a drug problem and he wants rehabilitation, then it depends on how soon he can get into rehab, how long the rehab program is, if he has to be hospitalized, things like that. Then there are programs for guys who want jobs. You see the problem?"

"So, you don't know or remember if Manny or Turtle ever came to your facility?"

"Nope."

"What about your records?" Cynthia pointed to the desk. "Looks like you've got a heap of paperwork on these people. Can you check your files?"

Jake compressed his lips, making them look as thin as knife blades. "Like I said, I don't have much time. When you called and said you wanted to come, I thought it was because you wanted to see the facilities, get a few facts, like what they cook in the kitchen, the number of beds. You know—the usual. But if you're gonna get specific and want a lot of stuff that needs looking up, we'll have to reschedule."

Cynthia crossed her legs and settled back in her chair, then pulled her cell phone from her purse. "Excuse me for a second." She punched in numbers.

"Who you calling?"

"First, Department of Social Services, then HUD, then if I have to, the Oberon police. One of their detectives is a good friend."

"What for?"

"To find out why I can't get access to records in a public facility."

"Just hang up, okay?" Jake's teeth made grinding sounds. "You don't need to play hardball. Just because you're some hotshot reporter doesn't mean that everyone's got to bow and scrape when you want something." He opened one of the file cabinets. "You got a last name?"

Cynthia shook her head. Steve, despite more effort than she cared to give him credit for, had been unable to come up with anything more than first names. "No. No last names."

Jake banged the drawer shut. "You can go ahead and make that call, now, 'cause I'm not going through all my files looking for someone's first name. In case you don't know it, lady, these records are filed under *last* names."

Cynthia slipped her phone back into her purse and rose from her chair. "In that case, I'm sorry I took up your time." And without waiting for him to escort her out, Cynthia exited the building.

There was only so much you could squeeze from a block of granite.

Jonathan sat clean and crisp in his blue twill suit. It was one of two suits he owned. He picked it rather than his seersucker because he thought it made him look older than his twenty-nine years.

"So, you want to reopen the Beacon Mission?"

Jonathan inclined his head, producing a nod devoid of enthusiasm. He still believed God had made a mistake by calling him to something he was so unsuited for.

If Charles Angus guessed Jonathan's reluctance, he didn't show it. Instead, he sat behind his desk, large and imposing in his expensive leather chair, holding a five-inch Ashton between his fingers. He brought it slowly to his lips, took a puff then blew smoke rings into the air. Jonathan was certain Charles Angus never wasted anything, including a cigar. It was obvious that he was treating Jonathan to a bit of theater—featuring Charles Angus as Capitalist Extraordinaire.

"Why do you want to open it?" Angus finally said.

"Because I believe it's the Lord's will."

Angus returned the cigar to his mouth and after making the end glow, removed it. "Did He tell you this Himself? The Lord, I mean?" His polite tone partially cushioned the sneer in his voice.

Again Jonathan nodded.

Angus placed his Ashton in a long marble ashtray, his face a kaleidoscope of humor, peevishness, stoicism and amiability. Jonathan was certain that Charles Angus had taken years to perfect it in order to confuse an opponent. And for Jonathan, it was working.

"What did He say?"

"Don't eat, wash or change my clothes for three days." Jonathan thought he heard Angus chuckle. No use. The man wasn't going to believe a word he said. Why throw pearls before a swine? Still, he'd opt for the truth; do his best for the Lord. Try not to let Him down. "After that, God led me to the men's shelter, and then to the Beacon Mission. That's when I knew."

Charles Angus picked up his cigar and rolled it between his thumb and forefinger. "I'm not going to toy with you, Jonathan." His eyes never left the cigar. "You don't mind if I call you Jonathan, do you?" Without waiting for an answer, he continued. "You seem sincere enough. Though I'm uncomfortable with the thought of God actually speaking to someone, but never mind that. Still, you've been honest and direct instead of giving me some pat line about wanting to help the poor. You've got guts and I like that. And I guess that God can talk to a preacher if He wants. I mean, after all you're transacting business for Him. A good Chairman of the Board will communicate with his corporate officers from time to time. See, that's what I understand, business."

Jonathan glanced at the small Picasso hanging on the wall behind the mammoth cherry desk. "Everyone knows how astute you are in that arena."

Charles Angus laughed, but Jonathan could tell the compliment pleased him. "No denying the Angus family has been lucky. That's what it takes, that and brains and hard work. But you can't do it without luck—being at the right place at the right time. Timing is everything . . . knowing when to quit something and begin something else. My father saw that it was getting too hard to make money in the manufacturing of clothing, shoes and glassware. U.S. companies that didn't move their manufacturing to developing nations could no longer compete. But computer software, PCs, e-commerce—that was the wave of the future. And anyone in that line stood to make a bundle."

Jonathan nodded. The Angus family had exerted their influence in the affairs of Oberon for years. Even now, the Angus Empire, headquartered in North Oberon, took up an entire block to house their new dot com businesses and software companies.

"But we Anguses have always felt strongly about giving back. Even though we got rid of most of our manufacturing plants, we never closed our glass factory or distribution company. We knew there was a need for low-skilled jobs in South Oberon, so we left them. And that's why when Reverend Gates came to me fifteen years ago and asked me to build him a mission so he and the good Lord could minister to the homeless, I did it."

Charles Angus took another puff of his cigar, then filled the office with smoke. "And ever since Reverend Gates had that unfortunate accident, I've been waiting for someone like you to come along so I could reopen it. You have a dollar?"

Jonathan dug into his pocket and pulled out a bill.

Charles Angus reached over and took it. "Okay. The place is yours. You've just paid one year's rent. Any problems, repairs, etcetera you call my assistant, Bill Rivers. But the rest of it, the food, the programs, and the like are all up to you. From time to time, Bill will contact you for updates—just to see how things are going. You'll find he's very interested in the mission and will make a good ally. I know Reverend Gates found him so. But don't worry, he won't interfere. The running of the place is all yours. You call the shots. So . . . if you don't mind his phone calls, and if the rent is to your liking, I think we have a deal."

Jonathan looked at the man, speechless. God had made it easy. *Too easy.*

"You'll probably get volunteers to fill most of your positions, but you'll still need some steady, reliable staff. I know that's how Reverend Gates worked it. There's one person I'd call if I were you, because she knows more about the running of the mission and that neighborhood than anyone." Charles Angus checked his Rolodex and scribbled something on a piece of paper, then handed it to Jonathan. "She can help you get the mission back on its feet. She'll know the food and clothing stores that made regular contributions in the past, and she has plenty of street contacts."

Jonathan read the name on the paper: Miss Emily. Underneath, was her phone number. "Does the young lady have a last name?"

Angus laughed. "If she does, I don't know it. But you could ask Bill. He might. By the way, the young lady is . . . seventy." Jonathan shrank in his seat and watched Charles Angus blow another smoke ring. "Surely God didn't tell you it would *all* be easy."

When Cynthia walked into the Department of Social Services she felt her head begin to pound. People were everywhere, in lines or walking from one office to another. Others sat waiting in rows of white plastic chairs. She wore her press badge in clear view, hoping it would act as a shield and protect her from being shuffled from person to person like she had been when she tried making an appointment over the phone. That ended by her hanging up in frustration. So instead of making an appointment, she had come cold, ready to seize any opportunity.

She was not, however, without a rudimentary plan, and ducked down a hall that sprouted small, bland cubbyholes like tomatoes along a stem—offices belonging to the caseworkers. She darted into the first open door. A young, pretty woman, not much past college age, sat typing furiously on her computer keyboard.

"Hi there." Cynthia walked up to the desk and pointed to her badge. "I called to tell everyone I was coming." She was not above bending the truth. "I'm Cynthia Wells, reporter for the *Oberon Tribune*."

The young woman smiled. There was warmth in that smile, and at once Cynthia felt those familiar juices well up, oiling her gears, preparing her for action. She had gotten a live one—an idealistic newcomer who was going to make her mark on the world by righting wrongs and kissing booboos—a perfect source of information.

"I'm working on a piece for the *Trib* and wanted to interview a few of you here at Social Services." Cynthia didn't even stammer over the lie. She had yet to clear this story idea with Bernie. She had decided not to tell him until she was sure there *was* a story. "Mind if I ask a few questions?"

The pretty woman shook her head. "I liked your Nanny Scam article. It saved my sister a ton of legwork. Your government waste story was good, too." A look of panic suddenly etched her face. "What kind of piece are you doing now? Nothing about . . . this office?"

"Oh, no. Something on the homeless."

The woman relaxed. "I'm glad someone's taking notice. Ever since they began gentrifying the blighted neighborhoods and stripping them of inexpensive housing we've had a mass exodus from Skid Row and South Oberon into areas that have never seen the homeless before. Now, they're everywhere. And that's got people upset. They don't like seeing them so . . . up close and personal, you know? I'm surprised there's been no interest in doing a story before."

Cynthia scribbled on her pad for the benefit of the social worker. She was deep into her role now—a seasoned actor who knew how to improvise. "What I'm looking for is more of a personal angle. Maybe a case history or two."

"Oh, I don't think I can give you access to my case files, not without permission. It's never come up before, but I'm sure I couldn't take it upon myself to violate a client's privacy."

"The cases I'm interested in involve two men who are dead."

"Well, that's different, I guess. But I still can't help you. When a client dies, that file is market closed and then removed."

"You mean erased from your computer?"

The young woman laughed. "Maybe other Social Service offices have paperless files, but here we still have a hard copy on every client." She pointed to the row of metal cabinets behind her. "Those drawers are jammed."

Cynthia leaned over the desk. "Look, I'm going to level with you. The story I'm working on is more of a human-interest piece than investigative. I want to track a couple of men, find out what went wrong, what caused them both to became homeless and eventually die on Skid Row. I think that way people will understand the devastation of homelessness, what it can do to a life. You see where I'm going?"

"Oh, yes. And it's a great idea. You can't imagine how hopeless many of these people are. You have about a third hooked on drugs or alcohol, another third with mental and physical disabilities, and the rest are those who try to work, but either can't find steady employment or they find jobs that pay too little to keep a roof over their heads. The saddest cases are the women. Most of them are battered and have run away, usually with children they can't support. A lot of them won't even come to Social Services for fear their children will be taken away and . . . ."

"My slant's going to be on two men—homeless men who have died recently."

The young woman nodded. "Right. That'll work."

"The problem is I'm having trouble getting background information. That's why I'm here. I assume they've passed through the paper mill of Social Services at least once, and if so, that you still have a record."

"Well, it's possible. What are their names?"

"Manny and Turtle. I don't have last names." Cynthia watched the young woman work her face like a corkscrew.

"Yeah, I heard about them being found dead like that—you know, cafeteria talk. A lot of time our work spills over into lunch hour. We discuss our cases or some unusual things we've heard or seen. It's hard to get away from it. Although sometimes I feel it's a bit much. A person needs a break from a job like ours. But it's a shame about those two—ending up dead like that. The streets are tough. These people have to take a lot. I don't know how any of them survive."

"Were either of them your client?"

"No . . . I'd remember someone called Turtle—though I doubt it was his real name."

"Maybe you could ask around. See if you can come up with the caseworker who handled one or both of them. Any information would be appreciated." Cynthia pulled a card from her purse and handed it to the woman. "Here's the number where you can reach me. Is there anything else you can tell me? Anything you may have heard about these two men?"

"No . . . well . . . nothing important."

"I'd like to hear anything you have. You never know where even a minor detail can lead."

"Well . . . right after that man, Turtle, died, I was talking to one of my clients and he said what a shame it was and that Turtle was a nice enough guy when he wasn't so high."

"You couldn't tell me this client's name, could you?" Cynthia smiled sweetly. She was pushing it now, but her audacity had worked before, gotten her important facts on other stories. In her six years as a reporter, Cynthia had discovered that most people loved to tell what they know and could be squeezed with little effort. "Could you let me have this client's name?" she repeated, slouching over the desk trying to take on the look of a long-time friend. She wasn't beyond feigning friendship, either. The young woman shook her head, which mildly irritated Cynthia.

"Okay. Maybe you can tell me how your client came to know Turtle?"

"Yes, he said that several months ago they bunked next to each other at the shelter."

"The shelter?"

"The Angus Avenue Men's Shelter."

Jonathan was getting ready to put the final touches on the oversized hamburger he had made when the phone rang. He was exhausted from the long day and considered not answering, until Caller ID revealed it was his aunt. He picked it up more out of habit than anything else.

"Don't be angry with me, Jonathan, but I've started praying that God would send you a wife."

Jonathan placed an onion on the cutting board and pulled a serrated knife from the drawer. "Does this have anything to do with Gertie Eldridge telling everyone I smelled like vomit?"

"Well . . . in a way. Gertie did mention that men with wives don't act so irrationally. She said that's what straightened out her husband's Uncle Alistair. I know most of what Gertie says is drivel, but on this point, at least, she makes sense. I never told you, but your Uncle Douglas was a little strange, too, before I married him."

"You think a wife will keep me from acting crazy?" How could he be angry with his aunt or with Gertie for that matter? From an outsider's point of view he *had* been acting crazy. But so had many devout men of God, men like Evan Roberts, the Welsh revivalist, with his fiery sermons, his prayers of healing and deliverance.

But come to think of it, didn't Evan Roberts have a nervous breakdown?

"So you believe a wife will keep me from acting crazy?" he repeated.

"I didn't say you were acting crazy. But I think a wife will help you carry the load that God is asking you to carry. God gave Adam a helper, remember? It was God who said 'it's not good for man to be alone.' And that's what you need, Jonathan. You're nearly thirty and you need help."

"Thanks, Aunt Adel."

"Dearest love, you know I didn't mean it that way."

Jonathan chuckled as he sliced the onion and slapped it on his burger. "So maybe that's why God sent a new woman into my life today, someone who's going to assist me at the mission."

"Well, for heaven's sake, who is it?"

"Miss Emily."

"Rather provincial of you. I'm all for you showing your young lady respect, but I think that's carrying it a bit too far. I hope you don't expect me to call her 'miss'?"

"I haven't met her yet, but we spoke on the phone and hit it off right away."

"Oh Dearest, tell me all about it!"

"I don't know what she looks like but she has a kind voice and seems very committed to the homeless."

"Oh perfect, perfect. See how quickly God can work? How old is she?

"Seventy." Jonathan heard the phone go dead.

CHAPTER 7

Panic clutched Stubby's throat as he rounded the corner of Fourth. He scanned the long sidewalks, first one side of the street then the other. The grip on his throat tightened. It was rough and choking, like his father's when he'd tell him to "listen up". He leaned against the building and shook his head trying to dislodge what felt like cotton wadding inside his skull. Then he tried to "listen up"; take stock of what he saw. And what he saw, or rather what he didn't, brought on a fresh wave of panic.

Miss Emily was nowhere in sight.

Had he come too early? Or too late? He had no idea of time, only a vague sense that it should be noon. He pressed one palm against his forehead. He was still high, but not so high he didn't know how easy it was to get confused.

That had to be it. He had gotten his time messed up. He'd come later to see Miss Emily and get a sandwich. After drugging for days and eating nothing except what he'd found in the pails, he needed something decent if he wanted to keep up his strength; if he wanted to keep from getting sick.

He let his hand slide off his forehead and down the length of his dirty shirt. That's when he noticed the throbbing—not from his arthritis but from the cut he had gotten at The Gorge. He wiped his hand on his jeans, then looked at it.

His palm was red with pus oozing down his fingers.

He knew someone who had lost his arm this way—clear up to the elbow. He had to get it fixed before it was too late. But not at the clinic. Too many questions and too much paperwork. He had hoped Miss Emily would tend it. Now, he didn't know what to do.

He was about to leave when someone came sauntering out of the Beacon Mission.

Weren't possible.

If the mission had opened, he'd have heard. When a second person came out, Stubby staggered over the sidewalk and entered. And there was Miss Emily, humming *Amazing Grace* and washing down the long stainless steel counter that separated the main room from the swinging kitchen doors, her white hair and face shining like an angel.

It was the sight of her and the sound of her voice that pried the hands of panic from his throat. He was safe here. And slowly, like the barely discernable legs of a moth, a feeling of security crawled from his cotton-wadding brain and moved down his chest. That's when the corner, where a dozen folding chairs ringed the lectern Reverend Gates had used for preaching, seemed to beckon him as if the Reverend's words, the only kind words Stubby had heard on these mean streets, still hung in the air like fruit waiting to be plucked. He stumbled toward the lectern, knocking over a chair.

"Stubby! Praise be! I heard you were drugging again, but I didn't believe it. Not for one second. Come here where I can get a good look at you."

Without wanting to, Stubby reversed course and moved toward the counter, keeping his head bent, his eyes directed at anything but Miss Emily; certain he looked every inch the cockroach.

"You look up at me, now. Let me see your eyes. They'll tell me everything I need to know."

Reluctantly, Stubby lifted his head and looked at Miss Emily's kind, smiling face.

"Oh, Stubby, now why did you go and do that? Start up with heroin again? You had it licked. I've been asking Jesus to get on your case. To wring you out like a rag and leave nothing of that old desire, that old life in you. I suppose He'll just have to do some more wringing."

Stubby brushed a dirt-caked hand over his hair—the little tuffs of white that formed a ring around his bald dome—as though trying to spruce up a bit before Miss Emily found cause for further disappointment. "Save your prayers for the more deservin'. I told you there were some beyond helpin'. Some who don't deserve the consideration of the Almighty. I'll just settle for one of them sandwiches." When he held out his hand, Miss Emily gasped.

"Goodness! Your hand's as big as a baseball mitt!" She grabbed his wrist. "And look at that nasty infection! That cut's oozing all down your palm."

"I was hopin' you could doctor it."

She studied him. "How long since you've eaten?"

"Don't know. Things blur . . . maybe two days. Maybe three."

"I suppose you've used up all your money?"

Stubby hung his head. "You hear about Turtle?"

"I heard. I suppose that's why you're in this state. But no sense in fussing at you. Not in your condition. Not when you need food and tending. We're not set up, yet, but I did bring some sandwiches. And I've got one of my deluxes—a double-decker bologna and cheese. But first you wash up. You look like a chimney sweep. After you eat, I'll look at that hand."

Stubby hurried into the bathroom and with his good hand pumped the soap dispenser. Then he turned on the faucet and lathered his hands, arms, and face. He ignored the pain from his cut;

ignored the fact that every time he touched it or moved his fingers the pain made him grind his teeth. And then there was the pain in his joints. He ignored that, too.

He watched small, foaming bubbles fill the sink then float around his head. He felt as light as one of them, as light as though he had just gunned another snowball. Miss Emily always made him feel good.

When he returned, Miss Emily had his place set with a tall glass of milk, a sandwich on a paper plate and a white, folded napkin. She gestured for him to sit, then took the opposite seat. When he picked up his sandwich, she gave him a stern look.

"Don't you think you should thank the Lord first?"

Stubby dropped his head and mumbled a quick "thanks," then shoved the sandwich into his mouth. "I can't believe the mission's open," he said between bites. "Who's runnin' the show?"

"A nice, young pastor. Jonathan Holmes. We opened yesterday to clean the place and connect with our old contacts; have them send food and clothes. In another day or two, we should be ready for business."

"So, they sent a young one this time." Stubby narrowed his eyes. "Let's hope he knows how to walk down them stairs better than Reverend Gates."

Miss Emily shrugged off his innuendo. "Pastor Jonathan doesn't seem to know much about places like Fourth Street. I don't think he's ever worked at a mission."

Stubby swallowed his last bite, then wiped his mouth with the back of his good hand. "Lots of luck." He grinned when Miss Emily handed him the napkin, but instead of using it, he just held it in his hand.

"Of course, he could make a real go of it if he had proper help. Grady—you remember him—the maintenance man who worked for Reverend Gates? Well, he has disappeared. No one's seen him in weeks. And we need to get someone quickly because Pastor Jonathan's as green as kale." Miss Emily leaned over. "So . . . what I've been thinking is that you're just the one who could break him in."

"Me?" Stubby pushed away from the table, making a scraping sound with his chair. "Take a good look, Miss Emily. My nose is runnin', my hands sweatin'. I ain't in no shape to help anyone. Beside, Reverend Gates never allowed dopers to work the place. What makes you think the new kid will?"

"That's the whole point, isn't it? You wouldn't be using anymore. You'd clean yourself up. The job pays minimum wage, but you'd get free room and board. Think of what that would mean. Three squares a day and a roof over your head, plus a little extra pocket money. Combine that with your Social Security and you can live very well. Maybe even help someone else once in awhile. Not to mention Pastor Jonathan. A person as wet behind the ears as he is needs someone like you."

Stubby rested his oozing hand on his thigh. He was coming down fast, judging by how much pain he was feeling in his hand and fingers. It was driving him mad. He couldn't wait to get high again just to make it go away.

"What do you say?"

"No use talkin' about it 'cause it's never gonna happen. I ain't no good, not to myself, not to nobody. You know what I'm gonna do soon as I get outta here? I'm gonna panhandle. And if I don't get enough money that way, I'll steal it off some drunk in the alley or outta some old lady's purse. 'Cause if I don't get a G-shot soon, I'm gonna be in real trouble. Now, what do you think of that?"

Miss Emily took Stubby's good hand and held it so gently Stubby swore it was being cradled by butterfly wings. And as she did, he smelled baby powder and lavender, and wondered if it was strong enough to cover the stink of his shame.

"Suppose you get your little dose of drugs to hold off withdrawal, what then?" She released his hand as if giving him more freedom to ponder the question. "What about tomorrow and the next day, and the day after that? Nothing's going to bring Manny back, or Turtle, either. Jesus is patient, but how many times do you expect Him to come knocking at your door? How much longer do you plan on keeping Him waiting? Chances like this don't come around everyday. This job can set you for life. Make you useful and give you a reason to get up in the morning. Are you going to throw it away because you need a G-shot? Like I said, after you get it, then what?"

Stubby stared at Miss Emily's clean, pink nails, then at his own blackened fingers that hurt so bad he could hardly sleep nights unless he was doped up. "There ain't no 'then what'," he said. "There's only *now*."

"Aren't you tired of scratching and scraping just to keep high? Don't you know Jesus has something better for you?"

Stubby wrapped the napkin around his oozing cut. "Miss Emily, your Jesus has nothin' for me."

"Don't be too sure," came a stranger's voice.

Stubby looked up. A tall, handsome man with broad shoulders and straw-blond hair stood next to the table. There was a smile on his face and his green eyes glowed, just like Miss Emily's, as though plugged into some inner power pack. No matter how hard he tried, Stubby couldn't tear himself away from those eyes.

"Miss Emily thinks Jesus has a plan for your life. I think so, too," the stranger said.

"And you bein' who, exactly?" But Stubby instinctively knew it was the young pastor. A renewed panic gripped him, and a fear so great it made him want to bolt from his chair and race out the door.

Any minute now this tall, strong man would tell him to "listen up" in a way Reverend Gates never could. Then there'd be nothing Stubby could do but obey. "Who are you?" Stubby repeated, glaring at the man, hoping his glare was menacing enough to make him back off.

Instead, the man winked at Miss Emily and extended his hand. "I'm that young, inexperienced pastor who could use your help. Jonathan Holmes is my name." Jonathan continued holding his hand extended, but after a few moments of awkward silence, with Stubby remaining rigid in his chair and not moving, he dropped his arm.

"You don't look like no preacher I ever saw." Stubby hoped he sounded as disagreeable as he felt. He was coming down fast, and feeling sicker by the minute—too sick to listen to any preaching. "With your build I figured you for a Marine. Or maybe a prize-fighter. I once knew a prizefighter about your size. But never no preacher, that's for sure."

Jonathan smiled, a warm, tender smile that drew Stubby like a heater in winter. "As Miss Emily said, I could use you. You don't have to answer now. Take some time and think it over."

"No need. Won't do no good. My mind's made up." *Why did the pastor keep starin' at him like that—like he was somethin' special?* "Besides, I do drugs." That should clench it.

Instead of recoiling or looking disappointed, Pastor Jonathan slid a chair closer to Stubby and sat down. "Why don't you and I pray about this?"

"You mean now? Together?" The panic was fierce now, raging like a bull with no place to go. When Jonathan didn't answer, Stubby shrugged. "I been prayed over lots of times. Never did nothin'." The tender love in the pastor's eyes made Stubby swallow hard, made him continue sitting in his chair instead of getting up and running out, made him nod his head and add, "But I guess you could pray if you want. Just don't go thinkin' I'm gonna change my mind about workin' here. Like I told Miss Emily, I got problems to iron out. I ain't much good to no one right now, maybe never will be." It was still there, that love, shining through those green eyes and pinning Stubby in his chair.

"Let's see what Jesus has to say about this, okay?" Jonathan said.

"He's heard the gospel a hundred times, Pastor," Miss Emily said. "It's just a matter of him opening up his heart."

Jonathan rearranged his muscular frame, then stretched out his legs right under Stubby's chair as though preparing to stay as long as it took to wear Stubby down.

Stubby glanced at the front door, wondering if it was too late to run.

"Well, if what Miss Emily said is true, then Jesus is no stranger. You already know about Him; enough to understand that He's kind and loving and wants only what's best for you."

"I heard a lot of preachin' on the matter."

"But you don't believe it?"

"I want to. I do." Sweat beaded Stubby's neck, right under his hair line. Then his thumb began twitching like one of those Mexican jumping beans an old sailor once showed him.

"Why not ask Jesus to take control of your life right now? Let Him show you what He can do? Let Him help you with those problems you spoke about," Jonathan said.

Stubby shrugged, unconvinced. "I been prayin'. Don't go thinkin' I don't pray, that I never asked God for help because I have. But it ain't done no good. He never listens."

"I'm sure you've prayed and that you were sincere when you did, but have you ever *specifically* asked Jesus to forgive you for all your sins and to take control of your life?"

Stubby didn't like that word, "specifically". It felt too much like a choke-hold, fastening him in place with no wiggle room. "Well . . . not exactly."

"He can help you. He *wants* to help you."

"Yeah, that's what everyone keeps tellin' me."

"Maybe it's time you listened."

Stubby's throat caught. *He knew it! He just knew this guy was gonna tell him to "listen up".* And now Stubby couldn't do a thing except sit there like a girl and take it. It was those eyes; those glowing green eyes that kept him pinned, then pulled words out of his mouth.

"Well . . . I haven't been doin' such a good job at helpin' myself. I . . . suppose it wouldn't hurt none to ask Jesus. If He can do better and wants to try, I guess that'll be okay with me."

That seemed to please the young pastor because his smile deepened. "Of course, in order for Jesus to help you, you'd have to give Him your life—turn it over to His care."

Stubby squirmed in his chair. He was stuck now, too late to run, and he was tired, bone tired, and feeling lousy. Getting up would take effort. Much easier to go along, just say what was expected. It would make the pastor happy. Miss Emily, too. And get them off his back. He saw no harm in that.

"It's not much of a life . . . I ain't much," he said, looking down at his injured hand, at the napkin soaked with pus. "And I don't have much. If Jesus wants someone like me, okay, I won't argue." When Stubby saw Jonathan's eyes tear he added, "But just in case He don't, want me I mean, don't say I didn't warn you."

Jonathan rubbed his chin, his eyes ablaze as though a sudden thought sparked a fire within him. "Don't you know that Jesus promises He'll never leave you or forsake you? That He loves you with an everlasting love? And that He'll stick closer than a brother?

You'd want someone like that, wouldn't you, taking charge of your life, leading you, directing you, helping you through the rough spots?"

"Well, sure . . . ."

"It wouldn't be a hardship giving someone like that control, would it? Obeying what He said, trying to do everything to please Him?"

"No . . . I guess not." *Why didn't the pastor just pray and get it done with?*

"And it would be a comfort, wouldn't it, to know that after your days are finished here, that you'd know just where you were going, that you'd know Jesus had prepared a place for you in heaven—because He promised in His Word He would? Now, that would be something to look forward to, wouldn't it?"

"Even a man with half a brain would like a deal like that."

"So, if all that's true, what's stopping you from asking Jesus to come into your life right now? To take control?"

Stubby settled back in his chair, wondering why the pastor's words made him feel high, why they made heat rush through his body and stir up something deep inside and almost forgotten—a kind of hope so battered and fragile it had to limp, rather than run, to the surface. But it made him smile. "Can't think of one thing."

Jonathan placed an arm around Stubby's shoulder. "Of course on the other hand you have to mean it. You have to really want Him. It's not something you'd do in a casual way. That would be insulting. When the God of all glory offers us freedom, forgiveness, wholeness and heaven all in the same breath, it wouldn't be right to be flippant about the offer."

Stubby paled as a new kind of fear gripped him, one he couldn't identify. "Yes, sir, I . . . see your point. And I wouldn't want to do nothin' like that. Like I said, I ain't much. Maybe I was too hasty . . . maybe we should forget this whole thing." No sooner were the words out then a deep disappointment overwhelmed him as if he had just stomped on his last chance for happiness. It made his heart ache. "But . . . that is . . . if you think God wants me, would want someone like me, then I'd like to go ahead and get the thing done." The words seemed to come out of nowhere, yet felt so right.

"You're exactly the kind of person God wants."

Stubby felt Miss Emily's hands on his back, right next to Jonathan's, heard their voices praise the Lord, saw the hairs of his arms rise, tasted the salty tears that ran down his cheeks and into the corners of his mouth. Then, as though a lifetime of sorrows weighed him down like sacks of cement, he bowed his head. "Jesus, I'm a miserable sinner. Can't seem to do nothin' right. Please forgive me. Right now I ain't got a friend in the world, and I ain't much the way I am. But this preacher says You want me. I don't know if that's true 'cause not even my mama wanted me. But if You do, if this is for real, you can have me." And he meant every word.

Cynthia sat in Bernie Hobbs's office hoping he wouldn't notice that her makeup was heavier than usual. If he did, he'd know it concealed something—like those dark circles under her eyes. Then he'd try to force an explanation. How could she explain all those nights of sleep deprivation?

Would the nightmares never end?

Now, if Bernie would just provide the cure, albeit unwittingly, by approving her proposal. She desperately needed to immerse herself in a story. Fix her mind on something other than vapor.

"I don't like it," Bernie bellowed with authority, but even so Cynthia detected the sweetness that coated his words like honey glaze. "This whole scheme of yours sounds too dangerous. If I thought there was something to your hunch, I'd say maybe the risk was warranted, but this story has no legs."

Sweetness or not, it wasn't what Cynthia wanted to hear. "You've always said I had the nose of an aardvark, that I could burrow under anything and find a story. I'm telling you there's something here."

"If it is, it's well hidden."

Cynthia watched Bernie mutilate a paper clip, twisting it into the shape of a pretzel. A good sign. It meant he was considering the idea. "But these people will only talk to their own. To get the story I've got to go undercover."

Bernie tossed the paper clip into the pail next to his feet and leaned his elbows on the desk. "Why this sudden obsession with the homeless? I hope you're not planning a sob-sister piece. Your readers won't stand for it. They've come to expect solid, gritty reporting not hearts and flowers."

"You'll get grit, I promise, or I won't do the piece."

"You know how dangerous it is for a woman on the street?"

"I plan to make myself as unattractive as possible."

"That won't make any difference. A bag lady's an easy target for . . . for all kinds of predators. Have you thought this through?"

Cynthia nodded. "I've thought of nothing else. I want this, Bernie. *Please*. Let me do it." She was sure this kind of harsh assignment that required her to leave her comfort zone and forced her into an unfamiliar and hostile environment would serve as shock therapy, bring her back to her old self, make her shed this obsession with the dead and dying and hopefully . . . end her nightmares. She leaned back in her chair wondering if she looked as desperate as she felt.

Bernie muttered something under his breath then cupped his baby-pink cheeks in his hands and sighed. "How much time would you need?"

"Three weeks."

"I'll give you one."

"Two."

"All right, you've got it—against my better judgment. But I want you phoning in every day."

"Done," Cynthia replied, able to keep the elation from her voice by concentrating on the pain in her back. It had gone into spasms from the hard seat. "Bernie, you need to do something about this chair."

"You come back with a great story and I'll buy a new one just for you."

Jonathan wiped his hand on his jeans, then pushed strands of blond hair away from his eyes. Every muscle in his body ached. Not since his college days had he worked this hard, physically.

"Looks like you're not going to get another thing in here," Miss Emily said, bustling into the pantry. "You've been stocking all morning and there are several cases you haven't even touched."

"That was generous of the S&S Market."

Miss Emily's eyebrows arched. "*Generous*? It's the biggest delivery S&S has ever made to the mission." She moved closer to Jonathan. "We've also received a sizable delivery from Everyday Ladies Wear. And wait till you see what Jolson's Men Shop sent. I started sifting through it—a whole crate of slacks and shirts, marked 'irregular' and another two crates of belts, shoes, socks, underwear, plus assorted sweaters and sweatshirts. Henry Jolson told me this stuff had been on the sales rack too long and needed culling. But Jonathan, I didn't see one tag reflecting a discount. I don't believe this stuff came from the sales rack at all. And I bet he wrote 'irregular' on that crate himself, so we wouldn't know just how generous he was."

"Yes . . . it's amazing. All morning I've gotten calls from other merchants wishing us well and promising to help in the future, some even financially. I'm overwhelmed, and a little . . . ashamed."

"Ashamed?" Miss Emily squinted at Jonathan. "Oh . . . you were doubting the Lord, is that it? Well, you might be young and inexperienced, but as sure as God made little green apples, He's going to see you through. Next thing you know, He'll start sending you staff. You got your first last night."

Jonathan laughed. "Stubby? You think he'll stay?"

Miss Emily nodded.

"Well, you know him better than I do."

"And others will come, too. You'll see. And there will be miracles happening here. God's going to send revival. People are going to be saved, healed, delivered. He's going to do a new thing at this mission. Yes, sir, He's going to gather up those precious souls on the sidewalks and alleys all around here, just like a mother hen gathers her chicks."

"I hope you're right."

"I am. And you know how I know? Because He's already given you the *anointing*. I saw it last night, and knew. And that surprised me a little."

"Because I'm young and inexperienced?"

Miss Emily's blue eyes twinkled. "No. Because your heart isn't in it, yet. But it will be. You wait and see. You may not love this place and these people, now, not like you should, not like God wants you to, but you will."

Cynthia sat at her Chippendale desk staring at the two cards in front of her. Her birthday had snuck up on her. *She couldn't believe*

she was thirty. She hadn't even thought about it until she got the cards. She had read them three times. *Two cards.* How had her life shrunk to this? She reopened one. Love Bernie. Then the other. Love Mom. Bernie Hobbs and Mom. Were they the only people in the world who remembered her—who cared if she was alive and well and growing older? She felt depressed. Not even Steve sent a card. But what could she expect?

You can't dump a guy then expect him to remember your birthday.

Already, the morning was gone and she had nothing done. Her new assignment had created a whopper of a "to-do" list, one of which was going to the thrift shop and getting half a dozen "bag-lady" outfits. If only she could get herself going instead of reading and rereading those two silly cards and brooding. Still . . . a person shouldn't be alone on her birthday. It smacked of deficiency. Mom or Bernie would be happy to spend time with her, but she was the one who didn't want to. And of course calling Steve was out of the question, though she was embarrassed that she had picked up the phone twice and hung up.

She rose from her desk, with cards in hand, walked several feet then plopped on the couch.

What was her problem?

She had begged Bernie for this assignment. Now that she had it, she couldn't get herself going. She supposed it was because she had gotten little sleep last night thanks to the same nightmare. But having the nightmare twice in one night was a first. That had rattled her. She needed a good rest. Maybe she should take the day off. After all, a birthday only came once a year. It might be the perfect prescription for what ailed her. But what would she do with it? Go to the movies? Read? Watch TV and eat chocolate? Sleep?

She scanned the living room as though looking for a clue. Navy blue walls with seven-inch white molding across the top and bottom made her think of a safe, cozy nest. A red and white floral couch and loveseat filled the center of the room, along with a walnut end table and coffee table—both with carved cabriole legs and brass feet. An antique walnut bookcase hugged the back wall and her Chippendale desk faced the single French door through which she could see the sun outline the branches of a large maple, several dozen azaleas and a small flower garden.

Her gaze lingered on the view outside the French door.

Outside.

It was becoming a chore to go anywhere. Maybe Bernie was right. Maybe she was burnt out. Maybe she shouldn't have pressed so hard for this story, even though she still thought it was the right thing to do—maybe the only thing, considering her other therapeutic options—sleeping pills or a psychiatrist. She took a deep breath and smelled lemon oil and pine. She loved her clean, tidy apartment. Now, she was leaving it for two weeks to go to God knows where.

As a bag lady.

She hoped going out into the world as someone else would help her face her dark secret once and for all, see it from a new perspective, maybe lay it to rest.

Forever.

But if that were her sole reason for wanting this assignment she would have felt guilty for conning sweet, lovable Bernie like that. The fact remained she was still a reporter; still knew a story when she saw one. And she still cared; cared that some agencies used illegal aliens as nannies; cared when state officials took trips to Vegas or LA or Bali and charged it to the taxpayers.

She wondered how long she could go on caring. Because the more she cared, the less she liked what she saw, and the less she wanted to be part of the world. Still, she couldn't just lay on a couch for the rest of her life. Unless, of course, she followed her mom's advice and "secured a husband." But from what Cynthia had seen, there wasn't much in that department that interested her, either.

She forced herself to rise, then went to the kitchen. On the table, spread out over a vinyl drop cloth, was her latest project—a 15 X 10 inch painting of wildflowers in a white porcelain vase. Cynthia touched it. The second coat of oil-based varnish was still tacky. *Perfect.* It was ready for the cracking varnish. With a clean, soft brush she began applying a thin, even coat of cracking. In thirty minutes, if no cracks appeared, she'd use a hair dryer to heat the surface and force the cracks. Then after a few hours she'd mix some turpentine and burnt umber and rub the blend over the surface then use a toothbrush to spatter the painting with the same mixture. If it still wasn't antique looking enough, she'd work a little raw umber into the crevices. Yes, this was what she was going to do with the rest of her day—her birthday—shut out the world and her problems just a little longer.

She moved her brush in long even strokes, and then, in a near whisper, began to sing. "Happy birthday to me, happy birthday to me, happy birthday to . . . Cynthia . . . happy birthday to me."

When Stubby awoke, he was surprised to find himself in a clean bed with sheets that smelled like the fresh air at that "Fresh Air Camp" the Oberon Housing Authority had sent him to a zillion years ago that was supposed to help inner-city kids at-risk. He inhaled deeply, enjoying the smell.

Where was he?

He blinked away the sleepy haze and saw that the room was large, with a single bed, nightstand, dresser, desk and chair, along with a stuffed recliner in the far right corner. To the left was an alcove with a toilet and sink. The walls were freshly-painted beige, and while the tan industrial carpet on the floor wasn't new, it was clean and far from threadbare.

For a moment, Stubby wondered if he was dead and in some holding room waiting for his entrance interview into . . . where? Judging by the luxury around him, he was sure it had to be heaven.

He had already been to hell.

He ran his fingers down his chest, feeling concave ribs. *Okay, so he was flesh and still livin'.* When he sat up, he felt so refreshed, as if he had been sleeping for a week. He rose, walked to the window, and looked out. Across the street was Reggie's Pawn Shop and Fourth Street Liquors.

The mission. He was at the mission.

Bits and pieces of last night began coming back, like a black and white newsreel that jerked from frame to frame. He had prayed with that nice, young pastor. He remembered crying and feeling kinda strange . . . but kinda wonderful, too.

Without thinking, he ran his left hand through the greasy fringe cupping his neck, then stopped.

It didn't hurt.

He held his hand in front of him. No swelling, no redness, no pus; just a pink scar where the cut used to be.

What happened?

He made a fist, first one hand, then the other. He did this over and over again. The joint pain was gone, too. He couldn't believe it. He couldn't get over how good his hands felt, how good *he* felt.

He walked to the dresser and looked into the mirror. His eyes weren't tearing, his pupils weren't dilated. He ran his hands over his arms, then his forehead. No fever, no perspiration. And instead of wanting to puke, he wanted to eat, in fact he was starving. What's more, he felt no muscle cramps, no agitation, no restlessness.

And he wasn't scared.

He held up his hand again, making sure it really was healed, and then realized he had no craving, not an ounce of craving for a snowball and any other drug. He walked back to his bed and sat down. Something important had happened. He closed his eyes and tried to concentrate. When it all came back, he began to laugh, then cry. Stubby had heard about this from ex-street people who talked about a Divine Appointment but he never expected, never in a million years expected it to happen to him. But it could be nothing else. It was the only thing that made sense. Somehow, he had met with God.

He jumped to his feet and skipped around the room like a kid, then sank to his knees.

God had answered his prayer.

But He had done much more. Stubby felt a peace he'd never felt before, felt a well-being and acceptance he'd never felt before, felt a love he'd never felt before. It was like he was a new person. A different person. And the joy! He'd never felt such joy.

God hadn't rejected him.

Stubby felt like his heart was ready to burst, that it couldn't contain all the joy and love bubbling up inside it and would just split open like some overripe melon.

How could God love a bum like him?

He could hardly believe it. But there was no denying it, either. Not anymore. Not after God had healed him. Not after God had filled him with peace and love and joy. Stubby went from his knees to lying prone on the floor, his face touching the industrial carpet. "Thank you, God. Thank you. I ain't never gonna forget You for this. All the days of my life I'll remember, I'll remember what you did. And whatever you want from me, you got it."

"How's your Miss Emily doing?"

Jonathan lay sprawled on the couch, Miss Emily's deluxe bologna and cheese in one hand, the cordless in the other. "Would you believe she's already fixing me meals?"

Aunt Adel laughed. "Sorry I hung up on you the other day. I wasn't in the best of moods. Guess I let Gertie get to me. Forgive me?"

Jonathan swallowed the bite of sandwich he had been nursing. "Nothing to forgive. I was the one who baited you. But speaking of Gertie, how is she?"

"Don't ask. She has put you on the prayer chain—said she and the other prayer warriors will pray you right out of that pit of degradation you're in."

Jonathan forced a chuckled. "She means well."

"I'll not comment. I'm trying to be more charitable. Been feeling too much like a noisy gong lately. Anyway . . . why do you sound so exhausted?"

"Because I *am*. I've been lifting and hauling and cleaning all day. You wouldn't believe how dirty the place was or how much work it takes to get a mission the size of Beacon ready for business. We open tomorrow."

"God's moving fast."

"Lightning speed, Aunt Adel, lightning speed. Last night we had our first conversion. A man named Stubby White. He's going to stay and work at the mission. He's street smart and knows the people here. I think he'll be a great asset."

"A homeless man?"

"Yes, and a drug addict or rather ex-drug addict because last night God healed him—healed his body and took away his addiction, just like that. It was incredible. I've never seen anything like it."

"I know what you mean, Dearest. It's been happening in our Sunday services. Lives are being changed though maybe not as dramatically as your Mr. White's. But people are being touched right here at Christ Church. Pastor Combs is doing a fine job. God is using him mightily."

"We both knew that would be the case. Didn't we? And it doesn't matter which yielded vessel the Lord uses, does it?"

"No. Only . . . ."

"Only what?"

"Only I wish Gertie Eldridge understood that. She claims revival only came because you left. That the Lord had to clean house before He could do anything significant at Christ Church."

Jonathan closed his eyes. "I'm exhausted, Aunt Adel."

"Okay, Dearest. Good night then. Keep me posted on the happenings at the mission."

After Jonathan hung up, he rolled off the couch, bologna sandwich and all, and began praying for Gertie Eldridge.

CHAPTER 8

Perspiration soaked Cynthia's ski cap as she walked down the street. She pictured her hair looking like Plaster of Paris. Perhaps she should take off the cap. No, better not. She was determined to look the part, now that she had roused herself out of the apartment and onto the streets. She certainly felt the part, all tired and sweaty and dirty and layered in mismatched clothing—four layers in all. Enough clothes to make her look thirty pounds heavier and make her perspire like one of those out-of-shape joggers she passed every morning on the way to Starbucks.

Already she felt dehydrated. She needed water or maybe one of those sports drinks. The problem was she couldn't pull her money out, not here in front of everyone. Maybe she'd get into the spirit of things and try panhandling. She needed practice if she was going to be convincing as a bag lady. A lot was riding on her success in scooping this story, a success, as far as she was concerned, which included more than seeing her piece in print. Somewhere on these streets, she had to find peace. Had to get her life back. Had to . . . bury the past.

The bulky layers of clothes made her gait graceless; made it look like a shuffle, which Cynthia thought served her purpose well. As she walked, she tried making eye contact with a friendly face, but no one looked at her.

Was she invisible?

"Hey buddy," she said to a nicely dressed passerby with short cropped hair, "can you spare a dime?" She stifled a smile over using that old cliché. To her surprise, he brushed by without a word. Other people followed, streaking like comets to some unknown destination. Then, a promising sight—a young couple holding hands. Idealism usually resided in the young. She stepped in their path. "I could use anything you can spare," she said, but she had stepped too close because the man thrust himself between Cynthia and his companion like a barrier.

"Get away," he snarled, "or I'll call the cops." Then he grabbed his companion and fled.

Cynthia felt silly for allowing her feelings to be hurt, but they were. Maybe it was because she was used to intimidating people as Cynthia Wells the reporter. It was obvious that here she was Cynthia Wells, the nobody; and it felt odd, unpleasant, even. Still . . . the man could have been kinder. Suppose she had really needed help?

"Neanderthal," she mumbled under her breath, then continued walking toward South Oberon.

She was sweltering now. Perspiration dripped down her face and onto the sidewalk. Drip. Drip. Drip. Like an IV plugged into the vein of these streets. She turned, half expecting to see the sidewalk awash. All she saw was the wall of people to the right and left with a space in the middle where she had just passed, a space opened to her as though she were a leper. It made her feel isolated and alone.

You asked for this assignment. You wanted shock therapy. Remember?

Hope budded anew when she saw an elderly woman coming towards her. Maybe compassion was about to meet her. But the woman walked by without a glance, turning only after she passed.

"Why don't you get a job? You look young enough."

Cynthia opened her mouth to say something sassy but nothing came out. Perhaps because the woman reminded her of her mother—gray-haired, thin, and nicely dressed; and under different circumstances, probably a decent sort. But why had she been so uncharitable? Fear? Fear of a lone homeless female? Or was it because Cynthia didn't look like someone you needed to be nice to? Didn't look like someone who could give you back anything for your trouble?

She gave up trying to make eye contact and concentrated on the surroundings. Without benefit of sign or marker, Cynthia knew she had crossed from North to South Oberon. The curbs weren't Belgium block but concrete, and the huge flowerpots, spaced every ten feet, had disappeared. The stores were different, too. Pawn shops and consignment depots dominated. And all the shop windows exhibited big "bargain" and "sale" signs, and with their merchandise of clothes, shoes, toys and whatnot looking more like they had been thrown into the display window rather than staged.

A wave of dizziness forced Cynthia to stop and lean against the wall of a small grocery. She needed to hydrate. A Gatorade or Sprite, or maybe just a bottle of water. No more putting it off. She'd have to chance going for her money. She reached into the third layer of her clothing, probed the pocket of the shirt where she had hidden her cash then pulled out a twenty. She was about to enter the store when suddenly three teenagers—the size of Hulk Hogan, their heads covered with red bandannas—surrounded her. She tried slipping through the grocery store door but one of them barred her way.

"You must be new here, otherwise you'd know this sidewalk belongs to us. To the Salamanders." He pointed to a picture of a reptile tattooed around his wrist. Cynthia guessed he was the ringleader. "And since it belongs to us, you gotta pay a toll to use it. See?" With that, he snatched the bill from her hand.

Cynthia held her breath. *Jackrollers*—young people who prey on the homeless. Hopefully, they'd take the twenty and leave.

"This ain't much," said the ringleader. "What else you got?"

Cynthia shook her head.

"You better answer when the *Man* asks you a question," the one behind her said.

"Maybe she ain't got no tongue," said another, making everyone laugh, the kind you hear when boys get ready to pull wings off flies.

"Or maybe she's got no respect for us," said the ringleader. "Maybe what she needs is a lesson in manners." The ringleader jerked his head in some secret signal and Cynthia found her feet dangling in mid air. Then the three teens carried her into the nearby alley. She squirmed and kicked and wiggled with all her might, but she was like a toy in their hands. And for the first time in her life, she wished she were a man. They put her down next to two garbage pails.

"Now, we can do this nice like or we can do it hard. You call it," said the ringleader.

Cynthia backed away, trying to catch her breath. Her heart pounded like a gong while dark scenarios raced through her mind. What where they going to do? Rape her? Kill her? She balled her hands into fists and stuck them out in front of her.

The ringleader laughed and shoved her hard against the wall, causing Cynthia's head to bounce against the brick. Even with the wool hat to buffer the blow, Cynthia felt a sharp pain behind her right ear and thought she was going to pass out. As she tried steadying herself, two of the teens pressed against her, pinning her to the wall. The third was all over her, running his hands up and down her body. Within seconds, he discovered her phone; a few seconds later—the rest of her money.

"That's it," said the one who frisked her. "That's all she's got. For a minute I thought she was a cop."

The ringleader studied her, taking his time, allowing his eyes to linger here and there, letting her know by this unhurried action that he was in control; that he had the power to keep her or let her go, to harm her or not. Through it all, Cynthia barely breathed, barely managed to keep her chin from quivering with fear, barely kept her eyes dry of tears. Using every ounce of inner fortitude she could muster, she managed to hold his gaze, to follow his every move. Her years as a reporter had taught her the value of eye contact.

"Well, whoever she is, she's got spunk," the leader said. "I gotta give her that."

"She might be kinda pretty under all that dirt and clothes," said one of the gang. "Too bad she smells like a toilet. We could've had ourselves a little fun."

The ringleader gave her a final once-over, then shook his head. "No . . . leave her be. She's got guts. I like that." He nudged the others to move out. "Thanks for the phone and money. You can use our sidewalk, now." Then all three laughed and disappeared around the corner.

Cynthia remained propped against the wall, unable to move until nausea overwhelmed her, making her bend over and retch, though nothing came out. Her head felt like someone was using it as a drum, beating, beating. She tucked her fingers under her cap and touched the spot behind her ear. It was wet. When she pulled them out they were covered in blood. The sight brought on a fresh wave of dry heaves, and with them, dizziness.

Oh God, don't let me faint. Not here, not now.

She pressed against the wall, afraid to leave, afraid to stay. What if they came back and found her? What if she left and passed out on the street? That gang was sure to be close by. *What would they do?* The thought made her heave all over again. Finally, she pushed herself off the wall and staggered out of the alley.

"I've been mugged!" she said, in a squeaky voice to the first passersby, holding up bloody fingers as proof. No one looked. "I was mugged," she repeated over and over like a wind-up doll. But she was invisible. No one saw, no one heard. She felt violated, dirty, angry, terrified . . . *insignificant.*

She stumbled along the sidewalk for three blocks pleading with people to look, to listen, to help, until she spotted a policeman standing on a corner. If only she could make it that far. Her head felt like it was ready to crack open; her vision was blurred, distorted. "Help me, officer, please help me," she said, even before reaching him. "I've been mugged." She walked the last few feet under his gaze, then leaned against the graffiti-covered mailbox. "Help me please."

"You can't sleep it off here, lady. You'll have to be on your way."

"You don't understand. I've been *mugged.*" Cynthia held up her bloody fingers. "See, they mugged me, in the alley." She pointed in the direction behind her and noticed the policeman was no longer looking.

"Move along, now."

"But I . . . need help. Won't you help me?"

The policeman rested his hand on his belt and glanced her way. "Go one mile straight ahead, make a left onto Angus Avenue, then go another block and make another left. They'll help you there, at the mission. You're in luck. They just opened today."

"You don't understand . . . ."

"Go sleep it off, lady. Everything will look better in the morning." The officer turned his back. "Off with you, now. You can't stay here."

How she managed it, Cynthia didn't know. But there she was, standing under a huge wooden cross and a sign that said, Beacon

Mission. If she could just get some water, maybe a little food, and something to put on her cut. She had to get her strength back, then plan what to do next.

When she put her hand on the door, her eyes caught sight of the large glass encased bulletin board. "For the wages of sin is death; but the gift of God is eternal life through Jesus Christ our Lord." What she knew about Jesus was learned when a friend invited her to a two-week Vacation Bible School ages ago, and didn't boil down to much. But she did know that somehow He was made to carry a heavy load—too heavy for one man, she always thought, because she understood about burdens. But as far as Jesus being a gift from God, one thing she had learned from her job, and now walking down Skid Row, was that there wasn't one person deserving of any gift from God.

She hesitated, then entered the mission. Music filled the place, making it vibrate while a cluster of people, all men, sat in folding chairs, singing. Her overwhelming urge was to backtrack but she was too weak. Instead, she took an empty chair in the last row, then slumped down when the good-looking man behind the lectern glanced her way.

"You've just missed our Bible study," he said. "We've been talking about how God is our great shield and buckler."

As if that was supposed to mean something to her.

All eyes turned and looked at her, and for the first time that morning, Cynthia didn't feel invisible. She burst into tears. "I was mugged," she said sobbing, feeling both foolish and angry at herself, as though she were some cry-baby who had come running in with scraped knees. She had asked for this assignment. She knew how tough it was going to be. Now, she had to suck it up, get a grip. Even so, she continued crying.

"There, there, everything's going to be all right." An elderly woman came from out of nowhere and locked onto Cynthia's arm.

"Let's have a look." The woman tucked her hand under Cynthia's chin and lifted it, and Cynthia found herself looking into twinkling blue eyes that exuded so much love it made her shiver.

"You've got quite a bump," said the woman, after gently pulling off Cynthia's cap and pressing her fingertips behind Cynthia's right ear. "It could use tending. Get me that first aid kit, would you, Stubby?" A short, balding man popped from his chair and disappeared down the hall. Others had also gotten to their feet and gathered around Cynthia, craning their necks to see what was wrong, and smiling shy, reassuring smiles.

Even the good-looking man had left his lectern and now stood over her. "What is it, Miss Emily? Anything serious?"

"Luckily she was wearing her cap, though for the life of me I can't understand why anyone would wear wool this time of year." She gave Cynthia a curious look. "Someone bring a glass of lemonade. Looks like our guest has sweated out all her juices. She's dripping wet."

By now, Cynthia had stopped crying and was feeling embarrassed by all the attention. What must these people think of her? "I didn't mean to interrupt. I'm just shaken. I don't want to be a bother. I'm fine, now."

Someone handed Cynthia the lemonade which she took and gulped down. By the time she was finished, the first aid kit was in Miss Emily's hands.

"Maybe Stubby should run her to the clinic," the good-looking man said. "If she was . . . roughed up, a doctor should check for internal injuries."

"No, it wasn't anything like that. Really." Yes, wimp, with a capital W, that's what they all thought. She could see it in the young man's eyes that looked so concerned it unsettled her. "I'm sorry. I didn't mean to make so much of it. They . . . those boys . . . just pushed me into a wall and I hit my head. Nothing else. Now, I feel stupid for making a fuss, for . . . crying."

"Did you report it to the police?" the young man asked.

"Yes . . . no. I tried."

"By the way, this is Pastor Holmes," said the elderly woman with the kind eyes. "But he likes to be called Jonathan, and I'm Miss Emily." She pulled a wet wipe from a dispenser and began cleaning Cynthia's cut. "Looks deep. Might need a few stitches. After I finish, Stubby can walk her to the clinic."

"No." Cynthia said, sitting upright. She had to take charge. Get a grip. She wasn't the first person to be mugged and wouldn't be the last. "No clinic." That was sure to blow her cover. Besides, she didn't want Bernie getting wind of what happened. Not yet, anyway, not before she had a chance to do some poking around, because Bernie was sure to pull her out at the first sign of danger. "Couldn't you just put a Band-Aid on it?"

Miss Emily cupped Cynthia's chin and smiled. "Sure, dear. If that's what you want. I've got a little butterfly here. That may hold it closed until it starts healing. But you'll have to keep it clean or there'll be an infection." When Miss Emily let go, she looked Cynthia up and down. "We must have something in the storeroom that fits you. Something fresh and clean. You can wash your things in the basement laundry when you're feeling up to it."

"Right. And she can use one of the staff showers. No one will bother her there," Jonathan added.

Cynthia avoided looking at the pastor who, as far as she was concerned, appeared too young and trouble-free to be taken seriously as the head of a mission, and watched Miss Emily rip open a package of waterproof bandages.

"After your shower, I'll do it right," Miss Emily said, applying one over her cut. "Are you staying the night?"

"I hadn't thought about it." The prospect seemed at once intriguing. What better way to get her story? And . . . it would be safe. After the Salamander incident, she wasn't ready to brave the streets at night. Somewhere between now and the morning, she'd find her nerve again and start doing what she had came here to do. But right now . . . okay, call her a wimp.

She looked from face to face, hardly able to take in the kindness and acceptance she saw. She was one of them, now. They'd trust her, might even open up and give her information when she asked. That was good. It was one reason to be grateful for her encounter with the Salamanders. Unwittingly, they had opened the door of Skid Row for her. "I suppose I'll stay if you have a place for me. Of course I can't pay you or anything."

Miss Emily snapped the first aid kit shut then looked at Jonathan. "I've been meaning to ask you if I could hire someone for the kitchen. I could use an extra pair of hands. We're not full, yet, but when we are, it's going to take a lot more than me to cook three meals a day."

Jonathan nodded. "Sure. Get whomever you need. But does . . ." he turned toward Cynthia, "What's your name?"

She wished he wouldn't look that way. The trust on his face made her feel dirty, like her veins were the pipeline for the municipal sewer. "Cynthia," she said, looking past him to Miss Emily. Was that how all con men felt after fleecing one of the more gullible types like a widow or . . . pastor. "My name's Cynthia," she repeated.

Jonathan tapped the back of her chair. "Well, Miss Emily, the question is, does Cynthia want to work here?"

Miss Emily pulled Cynthia to her feet. "Can you cook?"

"Well . . . I . . . ."

With one swoop, she tucked Cynthia under the crook of her arm and led her down the hall. "You don't take drugs do you? Because we have strict rules about that."

Cynthia was sure Miss Emily was leading her to the room where all the clothes were stored, but on another level Cynthia had a vague sense she was being led into something more than she had bargained for. "No, no drugs."

"That's what I thought. You don't have any of the usual signs. The job pays minimum wage, and comes with room and board. We'll also throw in a few outfits." Miss Emily smiled a funny, knowing little smile, then looked back at Jonathan. "She's perfect. Just what I want."

Cynthia placed her new jeans and shirt, bra and panties, on the small shelf outside the shower stall, then turned on the water. While she waited for it to heat, she stared at the wide wall-to-wall mirror over the sinks. A grotesque creature stared back—with a matted head of blonde hair. Blood streaked her neck and right cheek. And dirt, the dirt she had applied as part of her disguise, was smudged all over her face. She looked, smelled and felt the part of a homeless nobody. And yet . . . these people had taken her in, had opened their collective arms and accepted her just as she was. They had even offered her a job. It was more than she had bargained for. It was more than she had imagined. It was almost more than her conscience could bear.

Never in her life had she felt such acceptance.

CHAPTER 9

I will give you every place where you set your foot.
Jonathan awoke mouthing those words. He showered and dressed with them. Drove his car with them. Now, standing in front of the Beacon Mission, he understood what God was inviting him to do—to claim the mission, to take possession in His name. It would be both an act of faith and an act of war.

Where to start? He looked around at the deserted street. Barely sunrise but already the sun was brilliant and made the neighborhood glow. Shafts of light, like fingers, tickled the rotund storefronts and for a brief moment seemed to make them smile. It made Jonathan smile, too. It was as though God was showing Jonathan His promise, His assurance that a future Fourth Street could be a place of beauty instead of ashes, a place where the garment of praise could replace the spirit of heaviness.

Jonathan passed Reggie's Pawn Shop, crossed the street and headed toward the mission. Then he paced the perimeter of the building, calling it "holy ground" and rebuking the devourer. He moved left, around the cracked concrete and into the narrow alley, then stopped where the back of the building butted another. He turned and retraced his steps, crossing in front of the building, then down the alley to the right, repeating, as he went, the prayers, praise, the rebuking.

The right alley was wider, cluttered with garbage and untouched by sunlight, making it dark, foreboding, with sinister shadows dancing along the wall. Jonathan sensed that the physical reality mirrored a spiritual one.

"Lord, I'm so inadequate." The words made a hollow sound in the breeze, though it came from a heavy heart. "I want to be Your servant; to obey You in everything, only . . . help me. I can't do it alone." He had not wanted this. He had not asked for this. God would have to see him through.

I will give you every place where you set your foot.

Jonathan dropped to the ground beside the pails, oblivious to the stench, the sharp pebbles digging into his knees, the dark shadows. "Yes, Lord, for Your glory, for Your kingdom." And in that moment, Jonathan felt as if a shaft of light, as powerful and penetrating as a laser, punched a hole in some darkness deep within him.

Cynthia fumbled the potato peeler, nearly nicking her index finger. She glanced at Miss Emily, hoping she had not seen the near miss, but the old woman's face was an open book with the word "puzzled" written across it. Well, Cynthia was puzzled, too. She had never had such a good night's sleep. And not one nightmare, either. And she felt . . . what? Happy? Yes. But something else, something she had not felt in a long time—a sense of peace. How was that possible in this cul-de-sac of down-and-outers? She should feel out of place. She didn't belong and yet . . . .

"I've never seen anyone more transformed in my life," Miss Emily said, beating a dozen eggs with a fork in perfect rhythm, and with a sense of pride, Cynthia thought.

But what was the point in mastering scrambled eggs?

"Yes, totally transformed. Yesterday you looked one way and today, today you look another. Today, you look beautiful."

Cynthia felt her cheeks burn. "It's the new clothes."

"No, the truth is you *are* beautiful. And I never would have thought it the first time I saw you."

Cynthia's eyebrows formed a V.

"Now, don't tell me no one's ever called you beautiful before?"

Cynthia shrugged and pressed the peeler too hard, slicing off a chunk of potato. Her sister, Julia, was the beauty. Everyone said so. At least they used to, even years after the accident. People said lots of things about Julia, how she would have grown up to be a heartbreaker, a man killer, with her looks. Or a famous movie star with her handprints preserved on the sidewalk of Groman's Chinese Theater. Or perhaps a supermodel with her face on the cover of *Glamour* and *Vogue* or *Mademoiselle*. She was that pretty, though now, in retrospect, saying such things about a four-year-old seemed inappropriate, perverse even. And it was odd how no one ever said Julia was willful or spoiled or catered to like a duchess, or that she had no respect for property. Especially other people's. Nobody ever said things like that. But why speak ill of the dead? Let Julia be enshrined, like a relic, in people's minds—forever the "Little Beauty." Cynthia had always thought it odd that most people rarely called Julia by name but rather the "Little Beauty" as though she were part of a doll collection—The Fantasy Adventure Doll, the Forever Friendz Doll. *The Little Beauty Doll.*

"There are lots of reasons why a girl can't see herself." Miss Emily's fork tapped against the metal bowl in a steady click-click-click, as she beat the eggs, her eyes fixed on Cynthia. "Maybe she had a father who wished she were a boy, or maybe she's too busy exhibiting her brains. Lots of maybes. But one thing's for certain, you can't peel potatoes to save your life." Miss Emily added the eggs to a larger bowl of other beaten eggs. "The other certain thing is you're not homeless."

The potato squirted out of Cynthia's hand. "What . . . makes you say that?"

"Looks like there'll be slim pickings in the home fries department this morning."

Cynthia put the peeler down and faced Miss Emily. "What makes you think I'm not homeless?"

"Well, for one thing, your nails. No polish, but they're manicured. And for another, I lived on the streets for twenty years and I know a street person when I see one."

"Then why did you offer me a job? Why did you ask me to stay?"

"I figured anyone pretending to be homeless had to have a mighty good reason."

Cynthia picked up the peeler and worked another potato. "You sound like you know who I am." She held her breath.

"Oh, I do. I do. You're a little lamb, lost among the wolves. A precious little lamb that Jesus is just itching to gather up in His arms."

Cynthia's sigh of relief came out like a hiccup. Good. Her cover was not completely blown. "You won't say anything? Tell anyone, will you?"

"No, dear, I won't even tell them you can't cook. Let's let them find that out all by themselves."

Stubby swept up the last of the dust balls around the lectern, then turned his attention to setting up the breakfast chairs. He couldn't remember when he felt this good—strong as a bull, like a man half his age, like someone who had never poisoned himself with drugs or alcohol. He still couldn't get over God wanting someone like him; couldn't get over the love he felt, even now, as though the mighty arms had nothing better to do than wrap themselves around him. But it scared him, too. *What if God made a mistake? Poured out His grace on the wrong guy, thinkin' it was somebody else?* But even if He had, and ended up dumping Stubby back into the garbage heap where He found him, there was no turning back. Not now. Not after seeing the goodness of God first hand.

Stubby glanced at the clock. The men's floors weren't even a third full, and the women's less than that. But not for long. Word traveled fast on the street. By week's end, the place would be packed. And now, people would be coming for breakfast and he wanted to be ready. He pictured Miss Emily with her snow-white hair and rose-petal mouth that was always smiling. Still, when it came to her kitchen, she could be hard as a drill sergeant, insisting things being just so, and on time.

Stubby positioned the metal chairs around the tables, enjoying the chatter that filtered between the swinging double kitchen doors along with the sound of frying bacon. Yes, Miss Emily could be hard, but he liked the idea of making everything shine, making everything come together as it should, knowing it would give her pleasure. Maybe he couldn't preach the love of Jesus like Pastor Jonathan, but he could show that love by what he did for Miss Emily and others. This was no flunky job he had here. Not like all those other jobs he had had sweeping up people's dirt. No, this was different. He knew that, as though he had new eyes that could see beneath the surface of a thing. God had entrusted him with this work; had given him, Stubby Nobody White, the privilege of helping out in a place where lives would be touched and changed for the better. The thought made his lips curl, made him spend extra time fussing with the chairs until they were aligned just so.

Then he focused on the stainless steel serving counter. The silverware bins needed refilling, so did the napkin dispensers. After that, a ton of plates needed to be brought from the kitchen. He began by stacking the plates.

"Well, look who's here!"

Stubby turned toward the voice. Panic gripped him when he recognized the taller of the two men entering the mission.

"Guess the runt thought hiding with the Bible thumpers would keep him safe, as if we couldn't find him, as if we couldn't put our hands on him anytime we wanted."

The man Stubby didn't know, laughed. "Yeah. Turtle and Manny thought they could hide, too."

Stubby peeled two heavy ceramic plates off the pile on the counter. Once, he saw someone bust open a guy's head with them. "Look, don't go makin' trouble now. The pastor's been workin' real hard to get things goin' again. Why don't you two just go and leave us be?" His eyes went to the tall man's waist, searching for the blade he knew would be there, then watched as the man fingered the sheathed, hunting knife. "Ain't no weapons allowed in here."

"People say I can skin a man faster than a seasoned hunter can skin a deer. 'Course I never seen a deer skinned so it's hard for me to say."

"Shut up, Skinner!" The second man moved between Skinner and Stubby, as though he were breaking up a fight. "How this goes down is up to you. For my part, I like things easy. Not like Skinner, here. He likes the rough stuff. But if you don't want what happened to your friends to happen to you, you need to cooperate. That's all, just cooperate."

Stubby raised a plate. If he flipped it just so it would hit the man square in the middle of his forehead. That should stop him long enough for Stubby to get the other plate off at Skinner's throat.

"Now me and Skinner here, we want the stuff or the money. Don't matter which. But we gotta get one or the other. If not, it won't go down easy. We can't let everyone who has a mind to, run off with our property. Word would get out. People would start thinking we were soft. Then what would happen to business? You see how it is? But we want to be reasonable, don't we Skinner?" Skinner grunted like a hog. "You just give us what's ours so we don't have to make no examples."

"Can't give you somethin' I ain't got."

Skinner pushed his friend aside. "Let me take him to the alley."

"Here or in the alley, it's gonna be the same." Stubby glanced at the ceiling as if hoping to see the Almighty come down like the shield and buckler Pastor Jonathan had talked about in his last Bible study. "I ain't got nothin' of yours. I wasn't in on it with Manny and Turtle."

"Maybe you were and maybe you weren't." Skinner unsnapped the sheath of his knife. "But there's just one way I can know for sure and that's if I have at you."

Stubby waved one of the heavy, white plates in the air. He knew this moment would come. Knew it ever since Turtle was found in that freight car. Now that it had, he wasn't as scared as he thought he'd be. "You fellas get outta here!"

Skinner laughed. "Who's gonna make us? You, old man?"

"I will."

The two men turned. Over Skinner's shoulder, Stubby saw Jonathan's tall, muscular frame coming through the front door.

"And who might you be?" Skinner said.

"The new pastor." Jonathan walked toward them, a good-natured grin on his face which made Stubby inclined to smile, too, until he saw Jonathan hold out his hand to the two men in friendship. That was the easiest way to stick a guy—grab him by the arm and plunge the belly.

This new pastor couldn't be that stupid, could he? Oh God, You gotta help him.

Just then, Miss Emily and Cynthia bustled through the swinging kitchen doors, chattering like magpies and carrying steaming dishes which they placed on the stainless steel counter.

"Morning Pastor," Miss Emily said, almost as if she were singing, unaware of what was happening. "Stubby, call everyone to breakfast, will you? It seems no one has gotten down the system, yet. I guess they think they're living at the Waldorf and can get their meals anytime they want."

Stubby stood motionless, clutching the plates. Maybe he should let them drop. That would snap Jonathan out of his stupor and make him lower his arm. Even so, Stubby didn't move, not even his eyes, which were riveted on the intruders, not until Jonathan dropped his arm and Skinner unhanded his knife.

"Who's that?" Skinner said, jerking his head in the direction of the two women. "Not the old crow, the young one in jeans."

"A worker," Stubby said, feeling nervous for Cynthia.

"If you're joining us for breakfast, you'll have to surrender your weapons," Jonathan said, moving in a semicircle until he was positioned behind Skinner.

Maybe this young pastor weren't so naive after all. It looked like he was getting ready for a tackle. Stubby tightened his grip on the plates, and moved closer. He'd be ready when Jonathan was.

Skinner's eyes widened when he realized what was happening, and for a second his hand moved toward his knife again, then stopped. "We didn't come for food." He squinted at Stubby. "But we'll be back. You haven't seen the last of us."

Stubby watched the two men walk out the door. Then he glanced at the ceiling. He couldn't see it, but he was sure the shield really was there, big like the wooden door of the mission and just as strong, hanging right over him and Jonathan both.

"What was that all about?" Cynthia said, after the two men left.

"Nothin' you need to be worryin' your head about, Miss Cynthia," Stubby answered. "Just some ruffians." The short, balding man smiled as he walked over. "But don't you go worryin' none. I'm here and I'll protect you."

"Well, thanks . . . ."

"Gregory White. That's my name if you're askin', but people call me Stubby. Seems like we ain't been properly introduced, though it was me who got you that first aid kit, last night. Glad Miss Emily was able to tend your cut and that you'll be with us awhile."

Cynthia's heart thumped. "Well, thanks Stubby. And call me Cynthia, just Cynthia. No need for the Miss."

"You got a last name?"

"Cynthia's good enough." She turned and headed for the kitchen, her insides shaking. Was it possible? After all these years? No, it couldn't be. But why did her insides shake, so? Twisting and turning and quivering. Her instincts, Bernie called them. She had always been able to trust her instincts, and right now they were screaming. Miss Emily, who had followed her, saw it, too, how Cynthia's hand shook; how she wiped the same spot on the counter over and over with her towel; how she kept moving from the counter to the stove and back again like a toy on a track.

"Don't worry," Miss Emily said, hovering like a brooding hen. "People like Skinner are no match for Jesus."

Skinner? As if that stranger could bring her to this state.

No. It was that little balding man. *Stubby White.*

"People just call me Stubby."

And he had said it with delight as if his name was something that pleased him and sure to please everyone else. But it hadn't pleased her. It had frightened her. She had not heard that name in twenty-five years and had thought . . . believed . . . hoped she'd never hear it again.

But two people can have the same name.

And he looked nothing like that other Stubby. At least not that she remembered. But that name. And the way he had said it . . . just like years ago. *"My nickname's Stubby. Just call me Stubby."*

She snapped the wet dishtowel over her shoulder and grabbed two bowls filled with little pads of butter encased in peel-top plastic, then headed for the stainless steel serving counter. The swinging kitchen doors whooshed behind her.

Get a grip, Wells. Stop letting your imagination run amuck.

She willed her hands to stop shaking as she placed the bowls on the counter.

Okay, good. Breathe. Breathe. Regain control. Then start plying your skills and find out if this is the same guy.

She should be able to do that. She was, after all, a reporter.

That night Cynthia had another nightmare. The worst yet, because it was in color and she could see the red blood splattered on the concrete patio, and Julia lying there, dead, the window screen beside her. And when Cynthia woke up, her first instinct was to run from the mission as fast as she could. Instead, she cried, then washed her face.

"You've got competition, Bernie. If that raise doesn't come through soon I might quit and start a whole new career." Cynthia stood in the mission foyer, cupping the mouthpiece of the payphone and speaking in a low tone. It had taken her the better part of the morning to free herself from that Technicolor nightmare. And only when she was sure her voice was firm and wouldn't betray her, did she make her call to Bernie. Even so, she felt distracted and knew it wasn't because of the steady stream of people entering and leaving the mission.

"What are you talking about Wells? What competition? And why haven't you phoned in? You're supposed to call every day. Remember?"

"I know . . . sorry about that but it's been . . . difficult. I can't always get away and . . . ."

"Stop conning me, Wells. I hate when you try to con me, though most of the time I ignore it. But it ticks me off. And I think you should know that. Okay?"

"Okay." *Dear sweet, Bernie.* He must have been really worried. "I'm sorry."

"Fine. Just call when you're supposed to. Okay? Now . . . what's this about a new career? Did one of the other papers offer you a job?"

"Not another paper, Bernie, the Beacon Mission. They hired me as their cook, rather as the cook's assistant." Bernie howled so loud she had to pull the phone away.

"How did that happen? You can't even boil water!" The laughter was still in his voice.

"I know. I think they felt sorry for me."

"Well, whatever the reason, you did good. You've established a cover. So, what have you found out? Got anything that even resembles a story?"

"Not yet, but I'm keeping my ears open."

The operator cut in asking for more money and Cynthia picked up a few of the coins she had lined up on the little metal shelf in the phone booth and dropped them into the slot.

"Why aren't you using that expensive cell phone you made the *Trib* pay for?" Bernie said when the last coin went down.

"Because I don't have it."

"What do you mean you don't have it? You wouldn't leave it home . . . not when you're undercover. So that means . . . . Don't tell me you've lost it?"

"Well . . . ."

"How am I going to explain *that* to the front office? You know they're looking at every penny we spend these days. I don't believe it, Wells. The thing was brand-new!"

"It's a year old, Bernie, and I didn't lose it. It was stolen . . . when I got mugged." She said the last part in a near whisper hoping Bernie wouldn't catch it. But he did.

"*Mugged*? You gotta be kidding!" He waited a second. "You're not. For heaven's sake, didn't I tell you it was dangerous? I ought to have my head examined for letting you talk me into this. *You* ought to have your head examined."

"Go ahead, do the 'I told you so'."

"I just did. And I will again if there's one more mishap. You weren't hurt, were you?" Cynthia heard the worry in Bernie's voice which he tried covering with a gruff, "and of course you reported it to the police?"

Dear sweet Bernie.

"No, I'm not hurt. As for the rest, let's just skip it. But next time I call, I'm calling collect. I had to borrow two dollars from Miss Emily and . . . ."

"Miss Emily? What are we, back in grade school?"

"and I'm on a tight budget. Minimum wage doesn't go far."

"You mean they got your phone *and* your money?"

"Yup." Cynthia heard air pass between Bernie's lips and frowned. She knew what was coming.

"You need a man, Wells, to take you out of this rat race before the rubber band snaps. Roberta wants to fix you up with her cousin, Harvey, you know—the accountant. She said he'd be a good change after your cop friend. Roberta says Harvey's already bought a ring and is just waiting for the right girl to come along so he can give it to her. 'Course I told her you might not be ready for that."

Cynthia's insides twisted. She'd never be ready for *that* until she picked herself up from that blood-splattered patio. Why was so much of her still lying on that terrace where Julia had fallen, refusing to get up and leave? Oh, how she wanted to get up and leave!

"So, should I tell Roberta to call Harvey?"

Cynthia placed her free hand on the phone cradle for a quick disconnect. "Gotta go. It's prayer time."

"Prayer time? Now you're really starting to scare me."

"Miss Emily wants me to go, says it'll do me good."

"There you go with that Miss Emily again. What's going on over there?"

"Listen, regarding Harvey, just tell Roberta 'thanks but no thanks'."

"I'm not telling Roberta anything. You think about it. After this assignment, you might want to party with someone."

"Bye, Bernie."

"Wait! One more thing. Someone from the Department of Social Services called. She left several messages on your office machine and when you didn't call back, she called me. She wouldn't give her name, but said you'd know who it was. She wants you to call her. Said it was important."

"You have her number?"

"Yeah, just a minute." Cynthia heard the phone bump against the desk, then some papers rustling, then more fumbling, then finally, "It's her home number. She wants you to call her there and not the office."

Bernie rattled off the number which Cynthia committed to memory. "Thanks. I'll call you in a few days."

"Tomorrow. You'll call me tomorrow."

Jonathan stood behind the lectern scanning the twenty souls seated on folding chairs. Their faces resembled worn leather pouches, with deep wrinkles grooving the areas around their eyes and mouths, across their foreheads and down their cheeks. It was hard to tell the young from the old because even the ones he knew were young, looked old.

He noticed the woman with her child, the same ones he had seen eating from the garbage pail the first time he had come to Angus Avenue. Even from this distance, he could see that the child's head was still scabbed. If the woman recognized him, she gave no indication. But she had attended all his Bible studies, and even came up, at the last one, when he gave the altar call. Since his arrival, she was the first woman to receive Christ at Beacon Mission.

Jonathan looked at the only other woman present, and wondered if he had been right in letting Miss Emily hire her. The new employee, Cynthia, seemed out of place. He detected a hint of sadness, suffering even, hidden behind her eyes that oozed through when she didn't think anyone was watching. But her shiny, blonde hair and flawless complexion spoke of a pampered life. Even now, in her jeans and with her hair pulled into a ponytail, she looked more like someone attending a college lecture than a homeless woman trying to learn how to survive. All in all, he found her clean, flawless beauty, distracting.

And he hadn't been distracted by a woman since Lydia.

"We haven't got everything up and running yet," he said, taking a deep breath. "Our schedules are not fully established, but generally speaking, we'll have prayer every morning around this time, followed by Bible study. Also, beginning tomorrow, I'll be available for individual counseling in my office. And if you don't want counseling but just want to talk, that's okay, too. We also have a bulletin board where employment opportunities will be posted. There're a few things already for you to look at. Also posted will be phone numbers of various agencies that can help with some of your specific needs.

"Most of you know that I've departed from Reverend Gates' practice of only housing men. While the second and third floors are still for the men, our fourth floor is now for women." Jonathan looked at the mother with her child. "So if you know of anyone who could use a place to stay, we still have rooms available. Of course Reverend Gates' rule about no weapons or drugs on the premises, still stands. Anyone caught with either will be required to leave.

"I must confess, this is the first time I've worked at a mission and I've a lot to learn. For that reason, I'd like you all to keep me in prayer. Pray that God will help me, and teach me, and guide me. I can't emphasize how much I covet your prayers."

He hadn't meant right this second, but the group took him literally and at once closed their eyes and bowed their heads. He listened to the sound of mumbling as some composed their prayers out loud. He watched as others mouthed them silently. And as he dropped his own head, he could feel love begin to take hold of his heart. It was as if a seed had sprouted and pushed through crusty soil. This was his little flock, and like a shepherd, he didn't want any harm to come to them. He wanted to gather them up in his arms and carry them until they were safely deposited into the arms of the greatest Shepherd of all.

Cynthia crept into Jonathan's office, closed the door and turned on the light. Then she walked to the desk, picked up the phone and dialed.

"Hello, this is Cynthia Wells. I got your message." She kept her voice low. The small hand of the Bulova on the desk pointed to eleven. Everyone had gone upstairs for the night and Pastor Holmes had gone home. That left the first floor of the mission deserted except for Miss Emily and Stubby White. "Sorry for the late hour, but you wanted me to call you at home and this is the first chance I've had."

"That's okay," A drowsy voice answered. "I won't have trouble getting back to sleep. The minute my head hits the pillow, I'll be out."

"Bernie Hobbs said you had some information."

"Your editor was *so* very nice. I didn't want to bother him, but when I couldn't get you . . . I didn't expect a big important person like him to be that nice. He spent a lot of time with me on the phone and didn't rush me, you know?"

Cynthia glanced anxiously at the door. "So what did you want to tell me?"

"I shouldn't be talking to you, but I like your work. Your writing has integrity, you know? And I'm not snitching or anything. Just repeating what I heard. It's not the kind of information that could get anyone into trouble. If it was, I don't think I could do it."

"I understand." Cynthia fingered a pile of papers on Jonathan's desk. "Just give me what you have."

"It's probably nothing. My friends tell me I have an overactive imagination. I'm an Agatha Christie fan. I've read *The ABC Murders* five times. I think I'm in love with Hercule Poirot. He's such a kind, sensitive man . . . a real gentleman. Guys today hardly know the meaning of that word, you know?"

"Yes, I know." Cynthia absently read the first paper on the pile in front of her. It was a copy of the building lease. "So, what did you want to tell me?"

"Well, I found out who handled both of those men you asked about. It was the same caseworker for each of them, a real nice guy, too. Close to retirement age. Lost his wife last year and, well . . . that was sad. But anyway, I talked to him and told him you were interested in knowing more about those two who were killed, and he said he'd try to get as much information as possible."

Cynthia tore a page off a note pad and picked up a pen. "Okay, shoot. What did he get?"

"I don't know. He told me he'd go through his files and make some phone calls to the drug rehab center—both of these guys were on drugs—then he'd call the shelters in town and any place else he could think of. He was excited about helping you. He liked the angle of the story. He said it would be good to track two men like this and see what happened to them and why. So I expected to get some great information, instead . . . well, he up and quit. Just like that! I went to his office one morning to see how he was progressing and he was gone. I couldn't believe it! Someone told me he took early retirement. But that surprised me because he once told me how much he loved his job and that he didn't know what he would have done after his wife died if he didn't have this place to come to every morning and if he didn't have other people to worry about.

143

He and his wife never had kids, so I guess he considered his cases, family, you know?"

Cynthia shifted on her feet. "What's the name of this caseworker? I'll try to call him and see what happened." She heard a sigh on the other end of the line.

"I guess I shouldn't have done this, and you can't tell anyone, because I know I crossed the line and could get into trouble at work, but I tracked him down. Once, he had mentioned where he lived and I looked in the phone book under his last name and called every one of them. There weren't that many, just eight in his area, but I called each one and spoke to seven of them. When I called the eighth, I got the answering machine and knew by the voice it was the right number. A few nights ago, I stopped at his house after work and there was a big "For Sale" sign in front. The lady next door was out walking her dog, a little black terrier. I don't like dogs, do you? Especially little ones. They're too yappy. But I guess this one was sort of cute."

Cynthia began drawing stick men on the paper.

"Anyway, we got to talking and she told me that Andy, that's the name of the caseworker, had put his house in the hands of a realtor and left town. He didn't even pack his things! The neighbor said that once the house was sold, Andy would have a moving company come and clean everything out. I thought it was kinda bizarre. So did the neighbor. She said Andy had lived in that house with his wife for over thirty-five years. He worked at the Department for forty, ever since getting out of college. He was really sweet and a hard worker, but no one would ever call him spontaneous. Don't you think this is strange? I think it's strange and I wanted to tell you, that's all. I hope you don't think my friends are right. About my overactive imagination, I mean."

"No." Cynthia put her pen down.

"What do you think it means? You think Andy quit because he wanted to retire?"

"I don't know. People addicted to routine and the familiar don't usually up and do something this sudden or drastic. On the other hand, maybe Andy got tired of being predictable. Maybe he's in a resort somewhere having a good time. But just in case, do me a favor and keep your eyes and ears open. I appreciate all you've done so far. And don't worry. I won't tell a soul."

"Well, okay. I can do that. And if I learn anything, I'll let you know. Sorry I couldn't give you better information. But you can call me . . . any time . . . if you need help or anything, just as long as I don't have to violate a client's privacy. You know I couldn't do that."

"I know, and thanks again." Cynthia hung up the phone and crumpled up the paper full of stick men. Then she began reading the mission lease.

"Are you and Miss Emily engaged, yet?"

"Aunt Adel? Do you know what time it is?"

"You rarely go to bed before twelve, so that gives me thirty minutes. I've been thinking about you all day. How are you, Dearest?"

"Tired." Jonathan pushed the *Tribune* off his lap and began unlacing his sneakers.

"I bet you just got home."

"About twenty minutes ago. On the way here I was thinking maybe I should give up my apartment. Half of the mission's first floor is nothing but private bedrooms for the staff. If I move in I could use my rent money to pay wages. So far I have three employees. They're just getting minimum wage, but it adds up." Jonathan heard his aunt groan. "What's wrong?"

"Gertie said you'd be doing that. She cited the scripture about the prodigal son and how he went and lived with the pigs. She said you could feel sorry for a penned hog, but you didn't have to get into the pen and go rooting around with it. She said it was okay to help the less fortunate, but that you didn't have to live with them. Gertie said that would be the first sign to watch for."

"The first sign of what?" Jonathan kicked off his sneakers and stretched out on the couch. His body ached and he hoped his aunt wouldn't keep him long, though he didn't want to be rude by rushing her.

"Suppose I were to pay everyone's salary at the mission."

"Out of the question."

"Jonathan, I know it's easier to see the speck in someone else's eye than the beam in your own, but right now I'm seeing that speck in your eye and it's called pride. You're just like your mother in that regard. Maybe if she hadn't been so prideful she'd still be with us today."

"Aunt Adel . . . ."

"Don't Aunt Adel, me. You know what I'm talking about. Your mother worked herself to death, taking care of your sick father all those years and working two jobs; and me, with more money than Midas. You know how many times I tried to help her?"

"You know how mom was. She believed in hard work and never took a handout from anyone." He didn't know why, but this conversation irked him. Maybe because part of him had yet to understand why his mother refused Aunt Adel's help. It would have made life easier . . . for all of them. "You know how mom was," he repeated.

"Pride. Let's call it by its right name. You know I loved my sister, but you also know what the Bible says, 'pride goes before destruction.' Ruth just didn't know how to accept a helping hand. That was her speck, and now I'm seeing it in you."

"Aunt Adel, it's not like you to be critical." Was it wrong to try to do things on your own? Already he noticed how some of the homeless were so unwilling to do for themselves, and wondered if his mother hadn't been right in trying to handle things herself, and to teach him that as well. On the other hand, pride was as sinful as sloth.

"I know I'm hurting you when I talk about your mother. I know how much you loved her. And she was a good mother and deserved that love. She was also a wonderful sister."

"Then let her rest in peace. Mom was a gracious and kind woman who tried to teach me the value of hard work, and the only thing she loved more than her family was the Lord." But hadn't lack during his grade school years been the catalyst for erecting idols in high school and beyond? What about his Hot Wheels? His varsity jacket? What about . . . Lydia, the beautiful woman who had little interest in the things of God?

"Even people who love the Lord can have leaven, you know. Besides, don't you think that the Lord uses other people as His hands of blessing?"

"Yes"

"Then what's the problem?"

Jonathan's insides churned as he recalled those lean years. Had they jaded him? Had they twisted him so that pride had gotten the upper hand and he couldn't accept a gift? Maybe his form *had* become misshapen, maybe that was the very reason God had brought him to Beacon Mission. "All right," he said. "You can pay the salaries. But just until enough cash contributions start coming in which may be soon since we've already gotten a few checks from local merchants."

"Then you'll stay in your apartment?"

"No. And that's the speck you'll have to get out of your own eye."

"What speck?"

"Gertie Eldridge."

CHAPTER 10

Cynthia was not assigned the potatoes this morning. Instead, Miss Emily had given her the job of beating eggs and turning bacon. She seemed more skilled at these, and was pleased at the thought of actually being useful. From her place at the griddle, Cynthia watched coarse potato skins fall effortlessly onto a paper towel as Miss Emily worked the peeler.

"What makes you so good at that?"

"Practice." Miss Emily grabbed another potato—the third in less than a minute.

Cynthia's feelings of envy surprised her. But everything about Miss Emily seemed to inspire envy in Cynthia: her smile, her friendliness, her composure, her way with people . . . her proficiency in peeling potatoes. And there weren't many people Cynthia envied.

So why this admiration for someone who had spent half her life on the streets or working in a soup kitchen?

Cynthia stabbed the sizzling bacon with her fork, annoyed by her feelings.

"Good morning, everyone!"

The sight of a smiling Jonathan Holmes with his face partially obscured by hair hanging over one eye made Cynthia smile in spite of herself. She knew the first thing he'd reach for was a mug and he did, then helped himself to a cup of coffee from the giant one-hundred-cup urn. "Care to join me?" he said, raising his brimming mug.

Cynthia nodded, then glanced at Miss Emily. "How about you?"

"I still have an hour before breakfast has to be served. I guess I can indulge."

"Make that four," said Stubby, entering the kitchen with a mop and pail and perspiration slicking down the white fringe of hair around his collar. "Finished the bathroom floors." He deposited the mop and pail in the corner before joining the group. "I guess that oughta earn me a cup."

Mugs clattered as they all fetched and filled them, then formed a semi-circle. Cynthia used the time to size up Stubby. With each sip of coffee she swept him with her eyes. Nothing jolted her memory. Nothing was familiar. Not his looks, not the way he moved. It couldn't be the same man she had briefly known as a child

"Tell Cynthia how you came to the mission, Stubby, and what happened to you," Miss Emily said, winking at the balding man.

Stubby hesitated, and Cynthia saw the vestiges of a shy childhood flicker across his face. Then he pushed away from the counter and straightened to full height. "Divine Appointment." His smile seemed to come up all the way from his toes. "That's what it was. Divine Appointment. Ever hear of it?" He looked straight at Cynthia, making her almost choke on her coffee.

"No, can't say that I have."

"Well, that's when God plans everythin', fits all the pieces together so He can meet with you. And when He's done, you ain't the same. Ain't the same at all."

Miss Emily filled in by telling Cynthia about Stubby's healing and deliverance. A good story, Cynthia had to admit, as stories go. But how much was fact and how much fiction? Their faces conveyed sincerity but even sincere people could be fooled, could mix up their facts or assign a wrong explanation. "I guess miracles can happen," she said, "It's just that I've never seen one."

"Your being here is a miracle, don't you think?" Jonathan said, a bit too eagerly to suit Cynthia. "You could have been killed instead of mugged. You could have come after Miss Emily hired someone else. Any number of scenarios could have taken place. But you're here, and I think for a Divine purpose."

Well, that cut it. It was her nose for a story and not God that brought her here. That, plus her need to get a grip on her life, to be served a heaping dose of reality so she'd snap out of her funk. Why were these people trying to making something big out of it? Something noble and mystical and wonderful? It ticked her off. It also made her ashamed of her duplicity; ashamed of how she had wormed her way into the mission and their lives. "You know nothing about me. I could be anyone. A thief, a liar, a murderer . . . anyone. If you'd seen as many scams as I have, you wouldn't be so trusting, so ready to believe a . . . ."

"Goodness gracious, child! How old are you?" Miss Emily said.

"Thirty." Cynthia avoided her eyes.

"Thirty and so tired of life? You think we haven't seen our share of the kind of rottenness this world can dish out? Ask Stubby here. He could write a book. And me—I've seen more misery in seventy years than most three people see in that time combined. And what about Jonathan? This may be his first time heading a mission, but he's a pastor and I'm sure he's had a bellyful of seeing what people can do to each other. Compared to us, you're a baby. We live in a sinful world, Cynthia, and there's only one remedy, and that's Jesus."

Cynthia slumped against the counter, allowing the smell of bacon and coffee, of fried onions, and toast to comfort her. If only there was a tonic for life's hurts and not that snake oil the world passed out. Could Miss Emily be right? Could Jesus be the answer? They all seemed so sincere, so genuine, making her dishonesty the more odious. "Maybe if you knew who I was you wouldn't be so trusting," Cynthia repeated.

Suddenly, Cynthia found herself enfolded in soft arms and the scent of lavender. "We love you, dear," Miss Emily said, holding her close. "We love you no matter who you are, and so does Jesus."

Over Miss Emily's shoulder, Cynthia caught sight of Stubby smiling at her and wondered just how long that love would last if they ever found out her secret.

"Reverend Holmes? Bill Rivers from Angus Enterprises."

"Oh, yes, hello, Mr. Rivers. But you can drop the Reverend. Just plain Jonathan will do."

"Okay, Reverend, whatever you say. Just wanted to touch base. See how things were shaping up at the mission."

"It's going well." Jonathan noticed that Bill Rivers had not offered him the use of *his* first name. "The response from the community has been overwhelming. I've never seen such generosity."

"That's what Reverend Gates used to say. Of course there are some who'd credit it to P.T. Barnum's jaded saying that 'there's a sucker born every minute.'"

Jonathan cringed. "I hope you're not that cynical."

"Oh, I'm cynical, for sure." His words came out heavy as stones. "But not in that way."

Jonathan picked up the gray marble paperweight that Aunt Adel had given him as a gift with Psalm 118:24 written in gold letters, and turned it over in his hand. "Was there anything in particular you wanted, Mr. Rivers?"

"Well . . . no . . . not exactly." There was a long pause. "I imagine you're pretty full by now."

"About two-thirds in the men's floors. Less in the women's."

"*Women's?* I . . . didn't know you were taking in women."

"I decided to do that when I learned women and children were the fastest growing group of homeless. Did you know that last year alone . . . ?"

"But doesn't that leave less space for the men? I mean . . . under Reverend Gates, the mission was just for men. I don't know why you'd go and change that."

Jonathan replaced the paperweight, then hooked the toe of his right shoe behind one of the rollers of his executive's chair and stretched out his other leg as he prayed for patience. This *was* the day the Lord had made and the very reason he didn't want to waste it on useless dialogue. "I believe I explained the reason, Mr. Rivers. And it's just one floor. The second and third floors are still devoted to the men."

"But there was no mention of this when you met with Mr. Angus. I don't believe you outlined any plan to house women."

"Mr. Angus gave me the impression that I was in charge when it came to the running of the mission. Was that a mistaken impression?"

"No . . . of course not. You *are* in charge. Total charge. I'm just surprised, that's all. But no matter. You still have two floors for men. I don't suppose you're planning to change that? Maybe give the women another floor?"

"Not at this time."

"Does that mean you may do so at some point?"

Jonathan shifted his weight. Patience was a fruit of the Spirit that was quickly withering on his tree. What did Rivers want? And why didn't he just come out with it? "I plan on being flexible; change only when change is needed."

"That's good, I suppose. Well, okay, it was nice chatting with you. I'll keep in touch." Then the phone went dead.

Jonathan held the receiver, letting it drone in his ear before placing it on the hook.

Now what was that all about?

When the tall, thin man entered the mission, Stubby nearly dropped his tray of biscuits. He managed to place it on the counter, then scanned the room to see who else was here, who else could be counted on in case there was trouble. Jonathan stood talking in the corner with a woman Stubby had never seen before. And a guy he knew from way back was sitting at a table eating breakfast. Maybe he'd help. Sorta chancy though. Still, that made three, counting Stubby. And three should be enough to take Skinner and his knife.

With a flash of inspiration, Stubby pushed the biscuits from the tray onto the stainless steel counter, then held the tray against his chest. "We told you yesterday, we didn't want no trouble." He walked toward Skinner.

"What are you supposed to be, the tin man?" Skinner eyed the tray with a smirk. "That won't do any good. If I wanted a piece of you, I'd get it, no matter what you put between us."

"Why are you here? I already told you I ain't got nothin' of yours."

"I came for breakfast. Any law against that? I thought this place was open to everyone."

Stubby frowned. He could see the bulge beneath Skinner's jacket. "No weapons allowed." He pointed to Skinner's handcrafted leather belt that he knew secured a large sheath. "Either you leave or I gotta take that."

"Don't try little man or you'll be eating steel."

"I see you're back." Jonathan had slipped alongside Skinner, unnoticed.

"Yeah. But I'm not getting much of a welcome. I thought you Bible thumpers believed in loving your neighbor."

"We do." Jonathan squared his muscular shoulders like a fighter just before answering a challenge.

The motion wasn't lost on Skinner and his jaw clenched. "Then how come this runt keeps trying to kick me out?"

"I told him he could stay if he were to give up his weapon," Stubby said, keeping his eyes fixed on Skinner.

The heel of Skinner's boot made a scraping sound as he shifted his weight. It was obvious he was using the time to size up the situation and consider his options. Finally, he laughed, then opened his coat to reveal an empty sheath. "Is this how you treat someone down on his luck, someone who's just looking for a hot meal and bed?"

Jonathan's eyes strayed to Skinner's handcrafted leather belt, then his handcrafted boots. Stubby hoped that Jonathan would see their quality, a quality no down-and-outer could afford.

"We can't give you a bed, but you're welcome to eat all you want of the hot breakfast," Jonathan said.

There were still ten empty beds on the men's floors and that meant Jonathan wasn't going to let Skinner stay in any of them. Stubby sighed with relief, then removed the tray from his chest and walked away. He knew, without looking, that Jonathan followed. He didn't say a word until they entered the kitchen. "Thank you, Pastor, for not lettin' Skinner stay. I appreciate that."

"Stubby, when a man of your experience senses trouble, I'd be a fool not to pay attention. I didn't question you yesterday, but now that Skinner's back, don't you think you should tell me who he is and what he wants?"

"He's a killer," Stubby said, without hesitation.

"Who's a killer?" Miss Emily put down her oven mitts and walked over. Cynthia remained standing behind her, her green eyes large with questions.

"Now, don't go gettin' upset, ladies. But you gotta know this, especially you, Miss Cynthia; yesterday, this creep, Skinner, the one with the big scar on his face, was askin' about you. He's a no good, scum-suckin' bottom dweller . . . ." Stubby stopped when he saw Miss Emily's jaw move back and forth like a horse straining at the bit. "Okay, let's just say he's a bad egg, a *real* bad egg, and leave it at that. But you need to keep clear of him, Miss Cynthia. No tellin' what he's got on his mind."

"Maybe we should call the police," Jonathan said.

"And tell 'em what?"

Jonathan shrugged. "You got me there, Stubby. All I know is that Skinner seems bent on making trouble, but you still haven't told me why he's here. What does he want?"

Jonathan's voice was low, controlled, and Stubby guessed he was trying not to panic the ladies.

"Don't know." Stubby said, feeling three pair of eyes bore into him like diamond-tipped drills. "I *don't*." The way Jonathan shook his head told Stubby he hadn't been convincing.

"We're the staff, the four of us," Jonathan said, in his serious preacher-tone. "That's all there is. We have to work together, and we have to trust one another. People are counting on us, people like you were, Stubby, and Cynthia, here, people with problems. For some, this is the end of the line, and if nothing changes they're going to quit. You know better than anybody, Stubby, how fragile they are. But Beacon Mission has the answer and maybe some of them will find it. I want them to have that chance. And I won't let anything come along and steal it from them. So, if there's danger or a threat of danger to this mission, I need to know about it."

Stubby's face reddened all the way up and over his bald head. It was that guilty stain of someone caught in a lie. Now, there was nothing left to do but tell the truth. "A while back, my two friends got killed. Sometimes street people ain't particular in how they get cash and that could mean anythin' from panhandlin' to stealin' and sellin' drugs. My friends, they got involved in drugs . . . and a bad crowd. And they did somethin' stupid. I guess there are some who figure I was in on it, too, and Skinner was sent to find out. The people he works for want them drugs back or their street value in cash. Thing is, I ain't got a clue where Manny and Turtle stashed 'em. They never told me and I never asked. No way I wanted to know."

Stubby watched Cynthia's nostrils flare, watched her eyes cloud then clear. He recognized that look, a cross between revulsion and curiosity, between loathing and wonder. He'd seen it often enough on his mother's face when his father staggered through their apartment door and she'd try to guess how much of the welfare check he had left after getting his drugs and if he was going to share those drugs with her.

"Did you say your friend's name was Turtle?" Cynthia said, as though not hearing the part about danger that Stubby had tried so hard to convey.

"Yeah. You knew him?"

Cynthia shook her head. "I heard about him on the street. I'm sorry. I didn't know he was your friend."

"Then Skinner's a drug dealer?" Jonathan asked.

"He deals." Stubby shifted his weight, feeling burdened by how he had brought danger to the mission—to all those here. If he hadn't come, Skinner wouldn't have either. "He deals," Stubby repeated. "But mostly he's a trouble-shooter." *Might as well tell 'em the worst. If Jonathan asked him to leave, so be it.* "He does special work for them who operate the drug rings—like makin' people disappear or end up in dumpsters."

Jonathan looked worried. "Okay, so he's dangerous, but what makes you think Cynthia has anything to be concerned about?"

Stubby frowned. "Because he noticed her. And Skinner ain't the kind you want noticin' you. So you all, especially Miss Cynthia here, need to watch out. He's killed before. And he's the kind that likes it. He don't need no reason. Okay?"

"She's killed before." Cynthia turned to the voice behind her. The face was shadowed and she couldn't make it out, but it was a man, judging by the deep tone. And short. And he was pointing at her. Cynthia tried putting distance between her and the stranger but her feet had turned to lead, too heavy to pick up. "She's killed before," he repeated. It took every ounce of strength to raise one leg and slide it forward. Then she raised the other. The exertion made her breathing come hard, made sweat trickle along the sides of her ears. She couldn't keep this up. The strain was too great. She had moved less than a foot. But she had to get away. She couldn't stay here with him. Her heart pounded, then fluttered against her chest. She had to escape. With her last ounce of strength, she flung her body forward . . . .

Cynthia awoke with a jerk and found herself dangling off the side of the bed. Her sweat-drenched pajamas stuck to her chest which quivered like a frightened bird's. She remained sprawled half on, half off the bed. There was no rush. It would be a long night. The clock on her nightstand told her it was 2:00 am, and she had no intention of going back to sleep.

Cleaning had always given Cynthia pleasure. She supposed it had something to do with a desire to create a perfect world—sanitary and neat and free of spoilers. Clorox took care of mold in the shower. Scrub Free removed soap scum. Lysol was great for kitchen grease. Windex removed smudges from windows and mirrors. All simple solutions for life's messes. It was a comfort to know there were areas still under her control.

Miss Emily, after discovering this propensity, assigned Cynthia the task of scrubbing the appliances, counters and tables. Now, kitchen duties weren't as stressful. Cynthia no longer had to worry about burning the eggs or cutting away too much of the potatoes. She no longer had to compete with Miss Emily.

Yes, cleaning was her thing. Something that gave her pleasure.

Except today.

Cynthia guessed it was because she was still brooding over her nightmare. And then there was Skinner. His eyes had been on her ever since she started wiping down the tables and chairs. They were still on her the last time she glanced his way. And this was the second day in a row he had come to the mission and just sat, watching her. Or was her imagination working overtime?

She didn't think so.

And he looked weird, sitting like that at one of the tables—the only person left, his hands folded in front of him—staring like a battered tomcat stalking prey.

For the most part she had ignored him but each completed job brought her closer to where he sat. Sooner or later, she'd have to clean his table. She glanced at Jonathan not twenty feet away, talking to two men, and took comfort in his proximity. Even Stubby left his chores in other parts of the building to come and check on her, though he tried not to be obvious about it. His last pretext—bringing in a single folding chair and setting it up near the lectern—almost made her laugh. It was clear that Stubby had a soft center, a tender nature, though considering that she still thought he might be a ghost from her past, his presence was hardly a comfort.

But Skinner was another matter. She saw that meanness had set up residency long ago just by the way he'd smirk when one of the older occupants walked by limping or wheezing as though seeing someone suffering from an infirmity pleased him.

Maybe if she wasn't such a diehard reporter, Skinner would have frightened her more, revolted her even. But the truth was, while he made her uneasy, she was studying him as much as he was her. Stubby said there was a connection between him and the two dead, homeless men. He was also afraid of Skinner, though Skinner was the type that could frighten anyone. But already she had come to trust Stubby's judgment when it came to matters of the street. Based on that, she knew she needed to be careful.

When there were no other tables left to wash, Cynthia approached Skinner. Miss Emily's instructions were to avoid all contact; to return to the kitchen if there was a problem. But no one had anticipated that Skinner would still be seated two hours after breakfast was over. If she asked Miss Emily to come now and clean this last table it would look strange, arouse Skinner's suspicions.

And then there was the story.

She owed it to Bernie and herself to nail it down, to chase all possible leads.

"I need to clean up." Cynthia hoisted the bucket of sudsy water onto the table top.

"Who are you, lady?"

"Miss Emily's assistant."

"No, I mean *who* are you? Why are you here?"

Cynthia felt his steel, gray eyes, sharp as any blade, pierce her courage.

Keep your cool, Wells. Just keep your cool.

"I told you, Miss Emily's assistant. And I need to clean the table. All the tables have to be washed down before lunch. In case you haven't noticed, this is the last one. So I'd appreciate you moving. You can sit at any of the other tables or in one of the folding chairs by the lectern."

"Someone told me there was a woman, a reporter lady, snooping around asking questions."

Cynthia's breath caught as she squirted disinfectant over the tabletop. She pulled a rag from the bucket and squeezed it. "Do I look like a reporter?"

"I was told to look out for this busy-body."

"By whom?"

"By someone dangerous."

Cynthia dropped her wet rag onto the table, ignoring that it caused water to splatter across the front of her white tank top. While she washed the area on both sides of Skinner, she could feel his eyes on her. Her survival instincts told her to flee. Her reporter instincts kept her rooted in place.

"You that reporter lady? You sure match the description."

"How many times do I have to tell you I'm Miss Emily's *assistant?*" She couldn't let him bully her or let him think she was afraid. She swiped her rag in front of him and tried to look peeved. "Gimme a break here. You looking to get me fired? It's not much of a job but it pays minimum wage, plus three squares a day and a cot."

"You trying to tell me you're homeless?"

"That's right. I'm a homeless woman who caught a break."

"Sure you are lady." Skinner's mouth curved into a sickly arch. It took Cynthia a minute to realize he was smiling. "And I'm Peter Pan."

Jonathan ran his finger down the manual of the South Oberon Coalition for the Homeless and stopped by the phone number of The Center for Day Care. "You sure you don't want me to call?"

The woman in front of him clutched her child and shook her head. "I won't leave her with strangers. She's fragile. She'd been through a lot. I gotta know who she's gonna be with. I gotta know I can trust 'em." With one hand the woman stroked the scab-encrusted head of the little child. "Why haven't you got a Day Care here?"

"We've just reopened. Maybe in time we can provide that service but for now . . . ."

"Then how you expect me to take this job?" The woman poked the ad resting on Jonathan's desk. "I'd be glad to pack at the glass factory, but I got no place for my Daisy. And without a job, how am I gonna support us?" The woman made a fist. "You just like the rest. I can see it in your eyes. You're thinkin' I'm lazy. That I want a hand-out. But I ain't afraid of hard work. And I can work with the best of 'em, but I ain't gonna put my Daisy into the care of people I don't know. I've heard stories of what happens in places like that. Daisy's been through enough. I ain't gonna let nobody hurt her again."

Jonathan watched the woman wipe her eyes. She looked cleaner than the first time he saw her—Miss Emily had given her clothes from the storeroom. But the child still had sores on her head, sores that looked close to becoming infected. "What about your husband? Can't you get him to pay child support?"

The woman snorted with laughter. "The only thing I'll get from him will be more busted teeth. And Daisy . . . he nearly killed her, just for wettin' the bed. She wets sometimes, 'cause she's scared, scared from all the fightin' and shoutin' in the house." The woman ran her thumb down Daisy's cheek. "She's startin' to get better. Don't wet as much, not since we been here. I don't know what I woulda done without this here mission. There's not many places women and children can go. None that's safe, anyhow. I gotta thank God. I know He's the one Who brought us here."

Jonathan rubbed the cleft of his chin longing for the wisdom of Solomon. The burden he felt for this woman was terrible and heavy, tugging at his heart and nearly breaking it in two. He couldn't have been more pained if she was his sister. But then, she was his sister, wasn't she? And more, too. She was one of God's lambs He had entrusted to Jonathan.

What should he do?

"I been readin' Daisy scriptures every night. I think that's one of the things that's been helpin' her. I know it's been helpin' me. Sometimes I don't understand what I'm readin'. But I read anyway. I'm believin' the Lord will get me to understand it, little by little."

Jonathan felt a sudden stirring as he silently prayed for guidance, then he smiled a big toothy smile. "You know you never told me your name." He felt as light as air.

"Effie." The woman looked confused.

"Well, Effie, how would you like to work here? To be one of the staff? It doesn't pay much, but you and Daisy could move to the first floor where the rooms are larger, so that'll give you more space."

Effie's mouth dropped. "This ain't no joke, is it? I mean, you're serious. Right? 'Cause I sure would like that. Yes, I sure would. This way I could take care of Daisy, keep an eye on her. 'Course I wouldn't let nothin' interfere with my work. I'd work real hard. Give you your money's worth, that's for sure. You wouldn't be sorry. But what kind of work is it? You being a preacher and all, I know it's gotta be honest, decent work. What you want me to do?"

Jonathan tilted back in his chair thinking that when God allowed you to participate in His solutions, those were the best of times, times you'd remember for years to come. "You'll be heading our new Day Care Center. You'll supervise and care for the children, and once a day, for about half an hour or so, you'll read them Bible stories. We'll have to get you a children's Bible, with lots of pictures, and maybe some wooden toys like Noah's Ark and ABC blocks, and maybe some balls and puzzles. Things like that. What do you say?"

Effie brought her hands to her face and began to sob. Normally, Jonathan would have been concerned when a woman cried in his office. But today, he stared at his marble paperweight and whispered praises to God. He had been a pastor long enough to know the sound of joy when he heard it.

After Jonathan and Stubby unloaded the produce and other supplies that S&S Market had delivered, changed a flat on the mission pickup truck, and broke up a fight between two drunk men, Jonathan decided to take a break, and headed for the kitchen. He felt unexpected pleasure at seeing Cynthia. He watched her a moment as she scrubbed the giant coffee urn, then felt nervous when he realized Miss Emily was nowhere in sight. He had never been alone with Cynthia before.

"Looks like I'm too late for coffee," he said, staying in spite of his better judgment.

Wisps of blonde hair, that had escaped the scrunchie holding Cynthia's ponytail, swirled around her face. "I can put another pot on after I'm finished here. Or, there's some iced tea in the fridge if you want."

Jonathan opened the door of the gleaming commercial refrigerator and pulled out a large plastic container. "Tea's fine."

"What was all that commotion I heard?"

"Stubby and I broke up a fight."

"No need to ask if it was between guys." Cynthia buffed the urn with a clean towel. "Not to sound sexist but what makes guys need to settle their arguments with fists? When women fight, the tongue is their weapon of choice."

Jonathan studied Cynthia, the contour of her chin, her full red lips, her long sweeping eyelashes that dropped like a curtain when she didn't want to let anyone in. He felt a stirring he hadn't felt in a long time and that added to his discomfort. Still, he remained in place. She was beginning to open up more. Maybe that meant soon she'd open up to the Lord. Jonathan was surprised at how much that mattered to him. And the trouble was he didn't know what he wanted most—for Cynthia to open up to *him* or to God.

"And speaking of women, I met our newest employee and her daughter."

Cynthia's use of the word "our" produced another jolt of pleasure in Jonathan.

"I've never seen anyone so happy. That was nice of you."

"The mission needed a Day Care and she fills the need," he said, happy that Cynthia faced the urn and couldn't see the red blotches along the sides of his nose that he knew were there, that always appeared whenever he was embarrassed.

"Is it like you thought it would be? Working at the mission?"

Her question took him by surprise. It was innocent enough, but it had the tone and directness of an experienced interviewer. He filled his glass with tea. "Well, I expected it to be hard, but it's harder, much harder. But it's also more rewarding. And humbling."

"*Humbling?*"

"I always knew the Lord had to be in a thing before any real good could come of it. But I've never felt so helpless before. No matter what I do, it'll never be enough to make a difference in these people's lives. They're so damaged, so needy. Only the Lord can mend what's broken here."

Cynthia placed her towel on the counter and faced him. "You really care about these people, don't you?"

"I care."

"But don't you find them . . . disappointing? People in general, I mean."

"Sure, people can be disappointing. That's why I try not to expect too much. That's why I try keeping my eyes on the Lord. Only Jesus is perfect, Cynthia." He could see by the jut of her chin he had struck a nerve.

"I guess you have to say things like that, being a preacher. But you have to know that kind of talk has no relevance in the real world."

"Then what does?"

"Hard work. Self-sufficiency."

Jonathan looked at the shining, stainless steel coffee urn. "I believe in hard work, too. I was raised on it. You're a hard worker. I can see that. I wish that more of those who came here were willing to work half as hard. But it's still not enough. All the hard work in the world can't change a heart or make a sinner feel clean again, or fill the void of an empty soul."

Cynthia's face clouded. "Back to your Jesus again?"

Jonathan nodded. "Has anyone ever talked to you about Him?"

"Once, at Vacation Bible School years ago."

"So what happened?"

"My sister died."

Jonathan put down his glass. "I'm sorry. I know how hard it can be to lose someone you love."

"You ever lose someone close?"

Jonathan nodded and thought of his father who had been an invalid for years and his mother who worked two jobs to keep a roof over their heads. In a way, he had lost them both long before they died. "I know how hard it is," he repeated, and was surprised by the anger on her face.

"Why do you preachers do that?—say it's hard, say you understand the cruelties of life, then in the next breath talk about a God of love and mercy and how *He's* in control of everything? It seems hypocritical." Cynthia grabbed the dishtowel and ran it over the counter top.

Should he tell Cynthia about his childhood? Should he share his own hurts and disappointments with her? Or would that put him on dangerous ground? That's how he and Lydia started, by him sharing about his dad and her listening. Jonathan picked up his glass and drained it. No, best not to go down that path. Already, he was much too drawn to her.

And that was a problem.

"Bernie, my instincts were right! There's something going on here, but I can't tell you about it now because I don't know enough. But good news; I've connected with someone who knew those two murdered men." Cynthia heard a yawn on the other end of the phone.

"What happened to calling me collect, while it's *daylight*?"

"Sorry, Bernie, but it gets crazy around here. The phone booth is right by the front door. Impossible to talk with people parading in and out. I had to find an alternative."

"But you didn't find one that suits me. It's past my bedtime. *Way* past. And you know how cranky I get without my mandatory eight hours. You need to find a better time to communicate."

"There *isn't* a better time, Bernie. It's just too nuts here. But next time I could call the office and just leave a message on your machine for the morning."

"Suppose I have questions? Or want to give advice?"

"You can't have it both ways. I'm the one out here trying to scratch for a story while you're snoring in bed."

"I don't snore, and I'd be careful how you talk to me, Wells. The Newspaper Association just came out with their latest prognostication and the trend doesn't look good. Advertising is down, cost of newsprint is up and the Internet is scooping newspapers like crazy. You know what that means. Layoffs."

"Whining doesn't become you."

"You know that here at the *Trib*, bootlickers have the edge. I'd be nice if I were you."

Cynthia giggled. "Come on, Bernie, you know that profit margins for most newspapers are still higher than most other industries. And you and I both know that during the dot com boom, newspapers received the lion's share of advertising dollars. There still should be plenty in the till to cover any lean times."

"Maybe so, but shareholders have become accustomed to large profits forcing newspapers to bleed themselves in order to maintain them."

"You being pressured, Bernie?"

"Well . . . ."

"Okay, I'll be nice, just because I want to make your life easier and because I'm feeling generous. Now, let me tell you what I've got: this story involves drugs."

"Oh, c'mon Wells, we already knew those two dead men were drug users. Tell me something I *don't* know."

"I can't. Yet. But I'm on it and when I'm finished, I'm expecting a Pulitzer or a raise, either one."

"I'd shoot for the Pulitzer. You'll have a better chance."

Cynthia pushed away from Jonathan's desk and craned her neck towards the door. "I think I hear someone. Gotta go."

"Where are you?"

"In the pastor's office."

"And he doesn't know, right? That's just great. Now you're going to go and tick off someone who's in good with God. Really counter productive, Wells."

Cynthia laughed before she could cover her mouth. She was sure she heard footsteps. "Bye, Bernie."

"Call me tomorrow . . . anytime."

Cynthia hung up and crept toward the door. She pressed her ear against it, listening for a sound. When she was sure all was quiet, she opened the door and almost jumped out of her skin when she saw a man standing in front of her. It took a minute to recognize him.

"Stubby! You scared the wits out of me!"

"I heard a noise. Sometimes people steal things, you know, for drugs and stuff, and I didn't want no one takin' from Pastor Jonathan."

Cynthia eyed Stubby. She had to get to know him better; had to get the silly notion that she knew him way-back-when out of her head. Then there was her story. She needed information for that, too. Bernie was always telling her honey drew more flies than vinegar. Maybe now was the time to try a little of that honey.

In one fluid motion, Cynthia threw up her hands and twirled around. "I'm clean. See. No contraband." Then she leaned closer to Stubby. "I was making a phone call. Guess I should have asked first." When she saw the suspicious look on his face she grabbed his arm and headed down the hall. "Come on, let's have a sandwich." She felt Stubby's resistance and stopped.

"Ah . . . you makin' this sandwich, Miss Cynthia? 'Cause if you are, no offense, I'll pass."

"No one, not even I, can mess up a sandwich." Cynthia's grip tightened as she resumed her trek toward the kitchen with Stubby in tow. "Trust me. You'll love it."

"Miss Emily don't like it when someone goes messin' in her kitchen."

Cynthia continued leading him down the hall and through the kitchen door. This was her chance and she wasn't about to let it slip away. Before the sun came up she wanted to know Stubby White.

When they reached the mammoth, stainless steel refrigerator she released him. Then without a word she flipped on the kitchen light, opened the fridge and pulled out a turkey carcass and loaf of bread. Good. There was still white meat left. She cut a few slices and slapped them between two pieces of rye, then handed the creation to Stubby.

"Ah . . . hows about a little mayo, and some salt, and maybe a piece of lettuce?"

Cynthia sighed. What did he want? Gourmet? She rummaged through the refrigerator thinking how a few weeks ago he would have been content with just the rye. It showed how quickly a person's expectations could change. She found the requested items and added them to the sandwich, then watched Stubby take a bite. "Pretty good, huh?" Stubby just kept eating. When he finished she handed him a napkin. "You've never gotten over being hungry, have you?"

"You never get over hunger. Not the kind that makes your stomach lay flat against your spine. I been that way lots of times. Always figured that's how death would get me, unless the drugs got me first. Some say when you been hungry long enough you ain't got no appetite no more and just throw up when you try eatin'. Don't know if that's true. Never got that bad. I could always find somethin' in the pail, somethin' someone else didn't want. You'd be surprised what a person's willin' to eat when he's hungry."

"What happened to you?" Cynthia's chest tightened. No use putting it off. She couldn't squander this chance. "I mean . . . how did you get on the streets?"

Stubby brushed crumbs off his shirt and onto the floor. "Sometimes I write poetry. Did I tell you? Nothin' good. Just stuff that means somethin' to me. Stuff that helps me remember I ain't no cockroach. Maybe I'll write you a poem one of these days."

"Okay, if you don't want to talk about it, we don't have to." She held her breath. *Don't clam up now. Please don't clam up.*

"You confuse me, Miss Cynthia. You're suspicious and don't make friends easy, just like a street person. But you meddle, which is out of character. I still ain't figured you out."

Cynthia snatched a Bartlett pear from the refrigerator and began nibbling on it. *Come on, you're the professional. Get him to talk.* But she couldn't think of one thing to say.

"And you don't act like you ever gone hungry, neither," Stubby continued.

Great Wells, now he's interviewing you. "Maybe someday I'll tell you my life's story."

"Not tonight?"

Cynthia shook her head. "I'd rather hear yours."

"I don't like talkin' about myself." He seemed embarrassed.

Think, Wells, think. Don't lose him now. Say something to make him talk. "Don't I get something for fixing you the sandwich?" She forced a smile. *Lame, very lame.*

"Well, you been nice—and I appreciate the sandwich, and I guess it would pass the time. So, okay, let's see . . . the day I was born was the tenth anniversary of the Hindenburg goin' up in flames. I guess it shoulda been a warnin' of what was comin'; of how my life was gonna crash and burn. 'Course I didn't know about the Hindenburg until I was in junior high, and by then it was too late. I was heated up and ready to explode. My family—my mom, dad and both brothers—all used drugs. I swore I was never gonna touch the stuff. But I did. It gets holda you, you know?—when you're hurtin' or lonely. I joined a gang. They all used. It was cool. It made you a big man. You felt like somebody. Then I started usin' more and more, until it weren't just to get through them rough times, or to make me feel like I was somebody. It was everyday. You tell yourself you can quit anytime you want. Then one day, you wake up and know it ain't true. You know that this thing's got you by the throat and it ain't never gonna let go."

"Were you ever married?" Cynthia watched Stubby's eyes glaze over.

"I had a girl once. Real special, too. But she left me. Long time ago. She couldn't stand the lyin' and stealin', and the drugs. She saw I was never gonna amount to nothin'. It weren't her fault. I gave her grief. Didn't treat her right. Drugs do that. They make you crazy. Make you a different person than you wanna be. In a way I guess it was just as well—that she left me, I mean—'cause I never wanted kids. I told her so, too. Guess that's what finally cut it between us, 'cause she did want 'em. But I told her I didn't want to bring no kid into the world if he had to grow up like me. On welfare. Watchin' my parents druggin'. One of my brothers went to prison for sellin' drugs. The other was killed in a liquor store robbery."

"I don't know what to say except that I'm sorry." But Cynthia didn't feel sorry enough to stop pressing. And she knew she'd go the distance—push him right to the wall if she had to. "I guess it's hard to overcome something like that. I suppose it would be difficult, almost impossible to get into any real profession. Did you . . . ah . . . were you able to get work? Anything steady, I mean? Something that you liked, maybe something in construction, or as a handyman? You seem like you would have made a good handyman."

Stubby scratched the top of his bald head and smiled. "If I didn't know better, I'd say you was interviewin' me."

"Am I overstepping?" Her heart pounded. *Don't stop now, Stubby! Not before telling me what I need to know!* "I didn't mean to overstep," she said, when he remained silent.

"Just who are you, Miss Cynthia?"

"I'm . . . I'm somebody who lost her way."

"You think you gonna find it here at the mission?"

When Cynthia tossed the half eaten pear into the garbage she saw the dismay on Stubby's face over her wastefulness. She turned and picked up a dishtowel and began wiping the spotless counters.

"You want me to trust you and tell you about myself, but you don't trust nobody."

"I was just trying to be friendly. That's all. I'm sorry if I offended you." She dropped the towel on the counter and started to walk out. *She blew it!* How could she have been so stupid? Why did she have to come off sounding like Barbara Walters on 60 Minutes? Who knew when he'd open up again?

"Hows about I fix you a *real* sandwich?"

That stopped her in her tracks. She studied Stubby's face and saw kindness and intelligence, and felt guilty as she walked over to him. *Should she tell him she was a reporter? Tell him her name? Ask him point blank if he ever installed a casement window on Spring Terrace in North Oberon twenty-five years ago for someone named Wells?* She struggled with those questions for a full five minutes, the time it took Stubby to make a turkey and grilled cheese. He handed it to her on a plate as though it was one of the crown jewels. She waited another few minutes for it to cool, then took a bite. She had never tasted anything so delicious. Neither she nor Stubby said a word while she devoured it. When she finished, he handed her a napkin. There was something about sharing a meal that bonded people.

"Thanks." She found herself squeezing his hand. She couldn't go on like this. She had to tell him. And if it turned out badly, if it turned out that Stubby was *that* Stubby, she'd just have to deal with the fallout. It was better than letting things continue. "You're right, you know. I am asking you to trust me, without trusting you. So I'd like to tell you who I am and why I'm here." She groaned when he shook his head. She just couldn't let it go like that, with a shake of the head, not now when she had gotten up her courage. "I'd really like to tell you, Stubby."

Again Stubby shook his head. "It'll keep for another night. Tonight I'm gonna tell you about me."

Then the moment passed. And Cynthia knew she had lost her opportunity and wondered if she'd ever get another as she listened to Stubby tell her about his life growing up in the Projects. Of the poverty and deprivation. Of the countless young lives that were cut short by violence or drugs. Of life as a gang member. Of his own efforts at self destruction. Of his wasted school years. Of how he met and fell in love with his girlfriend, then abused her until she left him. Of the wasted years in and out of rehab and the welfare system. Of his clean years when he had kicked drugs, of his employment as a custodian and his basement apartments where he saved every penny he could until he had enough for a down payment on a used truck, a truck that would launch him in his own handyman business, a truck that would be his passport to a real life, a life where he could be somebody. Then he told her how his business grew. How his reputation for doing a fine job grew until he had more work than he could handle. The first time he had to turn work away was the happiest day of his life because he knew he had beaten the odds, that he wasn't going to be a loser all his life. He told her how he had even started thinking of buying a little place, nothing fancy but all his. And then he told her how everything came crashing down after *that terrible accident and a little girl died.* Of his slide back into addiction. Of his life on the streets and the utter hopelessness of those years.

And when he was finished Cynthia wanted to cry, wanted to tell him how sorry she was for everything, how sorry she was that he had fallen through society's cracks, that he had lived his life in waste and want. But most of all, she wanted to tell him how sorry she was that he had not been able to have that normal life he had worked so hard to achieve. And she wanted to tell him it was because of her.

All because of her.

She was the one who had stolen his dream, ripped it right out from under him because she was a coward. And then she wanted to ask his forgiveness, wanted to drop to her knees and *beg* his forgiveness. But she didn't because the moment had already passed. It had passed long before he shared his story, long before she came to Beacon Mission, and even before the coroner had removed Julia's body from the patio in the large back yard of a Victoria on Spring Terrace. It had passed right after she first heard metal scrape and scratch against wood, when the fairy-like vapor sailed out into the cold, crisp air with a giggle, then a scream.

She brought her dish to the sink and scrubbed it. The only thing for her to do now was to get her story about Manny and Turtle and leave as quickly as possible. Leave and forget this man named Stubby White. And as she scrubbed, she wondered how many sleeping pills, how many men like Steve Bradley bringing pizzas and drinking beers and ending up in her bed she'd need to help her forget. "You haven't mentioned Manny or Turtle. How did you meet them?" Stubby's sad, beleaguered face made her stomach feel like it was churning cement.

"They was my friends," he said, his voice sounding old. "I just wish they had come to Jesus before they died."

No mercy, Cynthia. Go for the jugular. It's too late about the other thing. Get the story. That's what's important now. The story. Then get out of here. "What were they like?"

"What in the world are you two doing?"

Cynthia turned to see Miss Emily, hair standing straight up like Dracula's bride, and wrapped in a pink terrycloth robe, her arms folded across her chest. She looked so out of her neat-as-a-pin character that Cynthia almost laughed.

Almost.

"Thanks for the sandwich, Miss Cynthia," Stubby said, in a hushed voice as he bolted out the door.

"I repeat, what were you two doing in my kitchen?"

"Getting to know each other." Cynthia eased past Miss Emily as gingerly as if she were easing past razor wire.

"And eating me out of house and home, I bet?"

"We tried."

"Well, next time invite me to the party, will you?"

"Sure thing." Cynthia laughed a hollow, empty laugh, then disappeared into her room.

"Aunt Adel, did I wake you?"

"Of course you did, Jonathan," returned a sleepy voice. "It's almost midnight."

"I'm sorry. It's just that I've been wrestling with something. It's about a woman . . . . "

"Ooooh! Well, you tell your aunt Adel all about her."

Jonathan nearly tripped over his untied sneaker as he paced. "It's not what you think. I've got a burden for one of the women at the mission, and I'd like you and the Ladies Auxiliary to pray for her."

"Oh. Of course, Dearest. What's her name?"

"Cynthia. I don't know her last name."

"How old is she? *Ninety?*"

"No, thirty."

"Ooooh! Well, what do you want me to pray about?"

"She's homeless—"

"Oh."

"I'd like you to agree with me for her salvation, and deliverance and guidance and . . . ."

"That's quite a petition."

"And protection. I keep sensing that she needs protection."

"Fine. You can count on us. How? I mean, why is she homeless?"

"I don't know. She's hard working, smart . . . seems to have a lot on the ball. It's a puzzle."

"Is she pretty?"

"Pretty? Well . . . yes . . . very."

"Ooooh! And she's hard working and smart? Well, well. Let's pray this lady into the kingdom and back onto her feet, and then we'll see what we shall see."

"Aunt Adel, your mind is going in the wrong direction here. I sense this woman is in real trouble. Let's keep focused on the issues I mentioned."

"You pray the way you're led and I'll pray the way I'm led."

Jonathan stood behind the lectern gazing at the people around him. A good crowd. Some new faces. His eyes rested on Cynthia. He had asked Miss Emily to make certain that Cynthia started coming to the Bible studies. The urgency from last night had not diminished.

"Luke 11 is a familiar story about a person who, at midnight, goes to his friend's house to borrow three loaves of bread because an unexpected guest has arrived and he had no bread to give him." Jonathan tried hard to keep his eyes from roaming back to Cynthia but they went there anyway.

"The first thing that struck me was that this person went to borrow bread. And since Jesus is the Bread of Life, it's reasonable to say that he was looking for spiritual food for his unexpected visitor. Now, who would visit someone at midnight? No one, unless . . . you were hurting or in trouble or searching for answers to some pretty important questions. The Bible also tells us this visitor was "in his journey." We're all "in our journey" and that journey through life can be bumpy, and sometimes there are collisions and breakdowns and all sorts of road hazards that drive us to a door at midnight. And how sad to get there only to find our friend has no 'food' to give us. No answers, no help, no hope because the Bread of Life isn't there.

"I believe it's no accident that you're all here today. You've all come, in a sense, looking for mercy at midnight, and we . . . . "

With a pang, Jonathan watched Cynthia get up and leave the room.

Cynthia slapped mayonnaise on one slice of bread, then another, then another until she had ten slices lined up in front of her. What was the matter with her? Why had she walked out like that before Jonathan finished his study?

Because he was making you nervous, Wells, that's why.

She couldn't remember the last time she felt so tense around a guy. Grade school? And what a laugh that after all these years, it took a preacher to make her feel that way again. He was just too maddeningly sincere. And she hadn't seen sincerity in a long time. Years.

Cynthia peeled back the plastic wrap and began dealing out bologna slices, like cards, depositing three on every piece of bread. Then she slapped mayonnaise on more slices of bread. She just couldn't fit another problem into her life right now. She was still reeling over Stubby. She had tossed and turned most of the night and when she did sleep, she had had her usual nightmare. No surprise there. The best thing for her to do was to get her story and get out of here before this whole Stubby thing broke wide open.

If he ever found out who she was . . . .

And now this morning, when she was hoping for a little peace, a little time to collect herself, Miss Emily insisted she go to the Bible study. And instead of just vegging out she actually listened, then she began watching *him*. Watching the way he swiped at the strands of blond hair that kept falling over his left eye. Watching the way he'd turn a page with his thumb and index finger. Watching the way his broad, muscular shoulders would tilt back whenever he was about to stress a point.

And he was watching her, too. Though not in the usual way men watched her. His glances suggested religious zeal and . . . sincerity. Back to sincerity again. And her, the mistress of deception. *Dear Miss Emily and . . . Stubby.* She had deceived them all. What would they think of her when they found out? She hoped she'd be long gone before that happened.

She paired the bread and found she had made an extra top. She shoved it to the side.

The thing that puzzled her, that really got her goat, was that Jonathan had been around long enough to see mangled humanity at its worst and still he liked people. It wasn't natural. In fact, it was downright unnatural.

She spread mayonnaise on more slices of bread, all the while trying to ignore Miss Emily's humming. Probably some Gospel tune. Nobody had a right to be *that* happy. What was wrong with Miss Emily anyway? Singing and humming and doing those little skipping moves with her feet? She glanced over and saw the white-haired woman putting the last minute touches on the chicken soup. The smell was enough to drive anyone crazy. Everything that woman cooked was delicious. Even Miss Emily's bologna sandwiches tasted better than Cynthia's. She wondered if those hungry men and women who'd be coming for lunch would notice. Somehow she couldn't imagine any of them refusing to eat because *she* had made the sandwiches.

You never get over real hunger.

That's what Stubby had said. Now, why was she thinking about *him* again? She had to get him out of her mind. Forget him. There was no point in rehashing the past. Somehow she had to find a way to let it go. Still, even now she couldn't stop thinking about how easy her life had been compared to his. And how much her selfishness, her weakness had cost him. What was a person to do, with a secret like hers? Was there no remedy? No forgiveness? Was she doomed to have nightmares the rest of her life?

Or was there really mercy at midnight?

CHAPTER 11

Jonathan opened the last of the boxes and sighed. No way was he going to get all this stuff in here. Eighty percent of his belongings were already in storage, and these remaining possessions still seemed to overwhelm the available space—the proverbial attempt to stuff a hundred pounds of belongings into a ten pound bag.

His biggest concern was finding room for all his books: three Bibles—an Amplified, NIV and King James—a concordance, two expository dictionaries, a Greek lexicon, two books on archaeology in the land of the Bible, and one hymnal. All his seminary textbooks were packed away along with his Watchman Nees and Andrew Murrays and books by a dozen other favorite authors. He had brought just the bare essentials.

The space would take getting used to. It made his former apartment, of four small rooms, seem large and open by comparison. Now, all he had to call his own was a single bed, a nightstand, a desk and chair, a four-drawer dresser, a small stuffed recliner, a closet for his clothes, and an alcove where there was a sink and toilet that smelled of Pine-Sol.

But thank God for small conveniences.

At least he'd have some privacy. But showering would be another matter. The men's showers were down the hall, the women's in the opposite direction. But he shouldn't complain. It was for staff.

Which meant that for now, only he and Stubby would be using them.

Foxes have holes and the birds of the air have nests, but the Son of Man hath not where to lay his head.

He sighed again, feeling like a spoiled child. Oh, how much work God still had to do in him! His heart was more like a tea cup than the well of love it should be. It still made him angry when an able-bodied homeless person was unwilling to even look for a job. Didn't Scripture say 'if a man will not work, he shall not eat'? How was he to reconcile that with the mandate to love unconditionally? He knew it was wrong to judge. He had never walked in their shoes. But he couldn't help how he felt.

Oh, God, make me more like You.

Cynthia jammed her pay into her jean's pocket and gave Miss Emily a kiss on her soft, wrinkled cheek. "I've never been so happy about a payday in my life!"

"God knows you've earned it. Don't think I haven't noticed the little extras you do. Cutting up my vegetables so I don't have to, and leaving them in the refrigerator for the next day. Putting my spices in alphabetical order. And the other night, you spent an hour of your own time organizing all those bottom cabinets. That's why I asked Jonathan to slip in a little bonus."

Cynthia's mouth dropped. "You shouldn't have. He's on a tight budget."

"Well, bless my soul, the girl's starting to care about us here at the mission."

Cynthia gave Miss Emily's arm a squeeze. "I need a few hours this morning. Just dock me, okay? I'll be back before lunch. I've finished kneading all the dough for the bread and made a ton of egg salad."

"Where are you going?"

"To the drug store and Christian bookstore."

Miss Emily's eyes narrowed. "What are you up to?"

"None of your business. Just tell me how old Effie's little girl is."

"Effie said she's four."

"What kind of books do four-year olds like?"

Miss Emily stopped mixing the tuna salad. "You'll have to ask someone at the bookstore." Her eyes narrowed again. "Are you planning to blow all your pay?"

"Maybe."

"Then you should know Effie has two more in Day Care. They just started yesterday. A brother and sister. The boy's two, the little girl's three."

"Now, what makes you think I'd be interested in knowing that?"

Miss Emily washed her hands at the sink causing the scent of lavender to fill the kitchen. "Because I can read you like a book."

Cynthia saw the twinkle in Miss Emily's eyes as she blew her a kiss. "Okay. I'll take care of it."

"You be careful, with all that cash on you. You hear? This neighborhood's not safe."

"Then you'll just have to ask your Jesus to protect me, won't you?"

Miss Emily wiped her hands on a towel. "What's all this about?"

"I thought you could read me like a book."

"I can. I just want to know if you can read yourself."

"Okay . . . it's about mothers who have to work and have to leave their children, even though it breaks their hearts."

Miss Emily smiled. "I see. Yes, indeed. I see."

"You think you know it all, don't you?"

Miss Emily nodded.

"Then tell me this, why doesn't my egg salad look anything like yours?" She laughed as she watched Miss Emily scurry to the refrigerator and pull out a huge, stainless steel bowl.

"Goodness gracious, what is it?"

Cynthia was still laughing when she darted out the front door.

Cynthia walked the mile to the nearest bus stop, then hopped the first bus that would take her another three miles to the outskirts of the Projects. When she disembarked she wasted no time in finding the drug store where she spent an hour picking out crayons, coloring books, puzzles, two Baby-Cry-and-Wet dolls, baby shampoo, a tube of Triple Antibiotic Ointment, and a little girl's brush and comb set with three fake pearls imbedded in each pink plastic handle. Then she hurried to the Christian bookstore where she spent another hour picking out nine books, three for each of the children, and a painted wooden Noah's Ark, complete with ten different pairs of animals. Just the thing a two-year old boy might like.

She looked at the wall clock behind the register. In twenty minutes Miss Emily would be serving lunch. Cynthia had one more stop to make before she caught the bus back. She was cutting it close. As she paid the clerk, she noticed the wooden plaque hanging beneath the clock. In bright letters it said: *Jesus Loves You.* Well, Jesus might love her but Miss Emily wouldn't if she were late. She pictured the mob scene that was lunch. She'd have to rush. She grabbed her bundles and raced out the store.

She had seen a little grocery a few blocks from the bus stop and headed towards it. Within minutes she had gathered everything she needed. Now, her hands were loaded, clutching three bags apiece.

She struggled through the door, then stopped to redistribute the weight. She was finishing just as three teens, wearing red bandanas, came up to her. She recognized two of them as the ones who stole her money and phone. She hoped they wouldn't recognized her, too.

"Hey, girl. What you got in them bags?" One teen pushed against her. It was the one Cynthia had thought was the ringleader last time.

She closed her eyes. *If you love me Jesus, please get me out of this.*

"Hey. I'm talkin' to you. What you got there?"

Cynthia opened her eyes. *At least he didn't recognize her.* "Toys, for the kids at the mission."

"You from the mission?" said the one Cynthia had never seen before. He was younger than the others and seemed less threatening. On his wrist was a tattoo of a salamander. "You from the mission?" he repeated.

"Yes. I work there as a cook."

"You don't look like no cook," said the leader.

Cynthia met his eyes. "I'm late and can't afford to lose my job." She tried to press through but the ringleader clamped her arm with a hand the size of Miss Emily's favorite potholder.

"Who are the toys for?" the younger one said.

"I told you. For some kids at the mission."

"Do they got names?"

"I know the name of one of them—Daisy."

The young boy's face twitched, then he nudged the leader. "Let her go, man. She's late for work. It ain't right interferin' with a workin' girl."

Cynthia and the ringleader faced off for what seemed like minutes, then he released her. "Go on, get outta here."

Cynthia tightened the grip on her bags and hurried away. When she turned the corner and could no longer hear their voices, she stopped, braced herself against the side of the building and tried to catch her breath.

Maybe Jesus really did love her.

Cynthia was grateful for Miss Emily's forbearance. Fifteen minutes late, and Miss Emily never said a word or gave her one dirty look.

She owed her.

Cynthia went through the whole lunch madness before she was able to calm down or get the Salamanders out of her mind. The gang situation in South Oberon was horrendous. She tucked away the idea of doing a future story on it. *What else could she do but write about it?* Gangs, poverty, drugs, welfare, poor education, mental illness, homelessness—all spokes on the same wheel. The problems seemed insurmountable. What could anyone do that would make a difference?

She thought of Jonathan and Miss Emily. How could they love a God that allowed this? He was cruel. And hadn't she experienced that cruelty first hand? She pictured Julia lying on the concrete patio.

But . . . what of Stubby?

Hadn't this same God shown kindness to him; a man written off by society? But chances are God had nothing to do with that. Chances are Stubby was ready to change and he changed.

You don't believe that for a second, Wells.

After the last dish was placed in the giant conveyor dishwasher, Cynthia slipped into her room and retrieved the toys and books. Then she headed for the Day Care Center—an unused staff bedroom that had been emptied and refitted with a few folding chairs and a blackboard. The blackboard and chalk, plus a few soft rubber balls were the only items available for play. It was the place where Effie spent her days with her daughter, and now two other children.

She pushed thoughts of God out of her mind. These were His problems, too big for her to take on. All she could do was small, insignificant things. Plunk a few drops into the empty well.

"Hey, Effie. How are you?" Cynthia said, opening the door.

Effie turned from the blackboard where she had been printing the ABCs in large, poorly formed letters, and smiled. "The little ones are playin' real nice with them balls, and Daisy here can say her letters up to E."

"That's wonderful, Daisy. Before you know it, you'll be reading." The child ducked her scab-covered head behind her mother's skirt. "I have a few things for you," Cynthia said, handing Effie four of the five bags. She watched Effie's eyes brighten then mist as she pulled out one thing after the other.

"Miss Emily kept tellin' me Jesus would provide. I knew Pastor Jonathan was strapped and couldn't spare money just now to get the Day Care up to speed but I never thought God would be usin' you to do it. I don't know what to say, 'cept God bless you." She fell on Cynthia's neck and hugged her until the children began pressing in.

They squealed and jumped up and down when Effie showed them the new toys. Then they picked out a few things and took them to a corner to enjoy. Cynthia was sure that, in time, they would share and play together.

The one thing she was learning here at the mission was that everything took time.

Cynthia opened the last bag and pulled out the shampoo and ointment, and went over the druggist's instructions with Effie. Then she handed her the little pearl-handled comb and brush. For a moment Effie seemed on the verge of tears. Then she clutched the items to her chest and looked at Cynthia with a mother's expression that said it all.

Cynthia smiled as she closed the door behind her. She couldn't remember feeling this satisfied over anything. Not even after finishing a great article.

If Bernie could see me now!

The thought made her laugh out loud.

"Glad you're in such good spirits, Miss Cynthia."

Cynthia turned and saw Stubby walking towards her with something in his hand. His clothes were neat and clean, and there was a spring to his step.

"I wanted to thank you for makin' me that sandwich last night and for listenin' to all my troubles. 'Course now that I'm a new creature in Christ, my troubles are startin' to fall away. Some of 'em, anyhow. But I wanted to thank you. For bein' my friend." He handed her a piece of paper. "I wrote this for you." Then he walked away.

Cynthia unfolded the page and began reading:

Father's heart is big and round
Like a ball, like the earth—solid ground
A hidin' place to go when you're scared
when you ain't sure
'Cause it's large enough and pure.

Father's heart is big and round
And full of tears,
Like the ocean that splashes and pounds
Out a sad love song
Of things that coulda been
Of kids lost and not found.
Who's gonna wipe the tears

From eyes that watch through painful years
As kids play in slop, with swine,
Covered with dirt and grease and grime?

Father's heart is big and round
Like a bubble or the O in a happy sound
When sinful kids come homeward bound.
Quick! Grab robe and royal ring, He shouts,
And cow on spit,
To make a bash fit
For a king.
But ain't for king this all is done,
It's for a lowly son, not worthy of the name,
Who, on account of love has been forgiven his stain.
What kind of love is this?
That waits and waits and waits,
Watchin' in silent agony?
How wonderful that all this love
Is there for you and me!

Father's heart is big and round.

Cynthia folded the paper as she walked to her room. Only after locking the door, did she allow what she had read to sink in. She thought about it a long time. She thought about the mission, the poverty she had seen, the ruined lives, the young gang members, the battered women with their children, the drug use, the mental illness, the jobless, the homeless . . . and little girls who watch their sisters die. And after she did, she dropped her face into her hands and wept.

Cynthia slipped into the kitchen, feeling guilty for not watching the time. "Are the tables done?"

Miss Emily shook her head and continued cubing a giant slab of beef for stew.

Cynthia grabbed a bucket, squirted some liquid cleaner into it and filled the rest with water. "I'm on it." She pulled a clean rag from the drawer and threw it across her shoulder. As she passed Miss Emily, she squeezed her arm. "Sorry I haven't been much help today."

"How did the kids like their things?" Miss Emily's eyes twinkled.

"They loved them. They're having fun with them right now, but not half as much fun as I had giving them."

"Some things are more important than cleaning a kitchen."

"Yes . . . I know."

"If that's so, then it was time well spent."

"You're a dear, you know that?" Cynthia whispered.

"Now, don't go thinking you can soft-soap me. I'm still docking your pay for this morning *and* this afternoon."

Cynthia nodded. "I'd be disappointed if you didn't."

The first thing Cynthia saw was Skinner sitting at one of the tables with his hands folded in front of him. Why was he here? *Again.* It could only mean trouble . . . trouble for the mission, and she was beginning to take that personally.

This time she made no pretense. She walked up to him and plopped her bucket on the table. "Why are you sitting here?"

"I'm waiting for dinner."

"Dinner's not for another four hours."

Skinner's nostrils flared. "So I'm early. Any law against it?"

"No." Cynthia slopped water all over the table. "It's your time. You can waste it any way you like." Some of the water reached Skinner and dribbled over the edge forcing him to push away.

"That's unfriendly. You don't wanna be unfriendly to me."

"I'm not trying to be unfriendly. I'm trying to do my job and you keep getting in the way."

Skinner frowned and fingered the angry, red scar that veined his cheek. "Where's that little runt? I haven't seen him since I got here."

"If you're talking about Stubby, he's busy. And what have you got against him, anyway? Why don't you stop trying to scare him and just leave him alone?"

Skinner reached for Cynthia. "Has he gone and shot off his big mouth?" His fingers clamped around her wrist like handcuffs. "You listen here, girlie, you use any of what that little runt told you and it'll be the last story you ever write."

Cynthia pulled away. "Stubby didn't tell me anything. And I don't know what story you're talking about."

"I've done some checking. I know who you are, and all I gotta say is that nannies and politicians play nicer than we do." Skinner rose to his feet then kicked over his chair. "You're outta your league, girlie. And if you're not careful, someone's gonna separate you from your good health."

"What did he say, Miss Cynthia?" Stubby's breathing was hard from running across the room.

"Nothing much." Cynthia watched Skinner walk out the front door "He was just mad because I spilled water on him." She avoided Stubby's eyes and wished he'd stop being so nice. She couldn't stand that, him being so nice.

"Is that why he kicked over the chair?"

Cynthia shrugged.

"Next time he comes, you stay far away. You hear?"

Cynthia nodded and without thinking, gave Stubby a hug. When she did, she smelled the hint of aftershave. "I loved your poem."

"You *did*?"

"Yes."

Stubby beamed like the neon above Reggie's Pawn Shop. "Well, I appreciate that. I sure do." Then it faded. "But Miss Cynthia, I ain't kiddin' about Skinner. You got to stay clear. He likes to hurt people. And it don't matter if it's a woman, neither."

Cynthia looked into Stubby's worried face, trying to decide if she should ask him what it was that Skinner didn't want her to find out. Then decided against it. Pressing too hard would only make Stubby suspicious. "Next time he comes I'll avoid him like the plague."

"You promise?"

Cynthia nodded.

The neon-like beam returned to Stubby's face. "My mind's been troubled over you and I been gettin' scared every time that front door opened. But now you've gone and given me your word, and I know I can trust what you say."

Cynthia opened her mouth as if to speak then closed it and walked away all the while wondering just how elastic her conscience was going to get.

"You want to do *what*?"

"Make a birthday cake for Jonathan."

"But child, you can't cook."

"I can read and follow directions." Cynthia held up a box of yellow cake mix. "There are only three steps listed on the back and I think I can manage that."

Miss Emily chuckled. "I didn't mean to be insulting. But what about the icing?"

Cynthia pulled a can of ready-to-use chocolate icing from the plastic bag in her hand.

"What else do you have in there?"

Cynthia placed the mix and icing on the counter, them dove back into the bag and came out with a pack of candles, paper noise-makers and happy birthday plates and napkins.

"My, my. You have been busy. You must have precious little of that pay left."

"I have enough to get me through until next week." Cynthia ignored the look of doubt on Miss Emily's face. "So, what do you say? Can I make the cake and then later tonight, when things calm down, we can all wish Jonathan a happy birthday?"

"You mean, like have a little party?"

Cynthia began arranging and rearranging the party supplies. "I thought it would be nice."

Miss Emily picked up the package of plates and turned them over in her hand. "I like the colors—red and blue. Sort of patriotic, too. Makes you feel like celebrating." She put them back on the counter, then covered Cynthia's hand with hers. "You're a strange one. You're a loner and don't like people much yet you do something like this. Sometimes you remind me of me before I got saved. Except I used drugs and alcohol to deal with my loneliness. You use work."

Cynthia's long lashes shaded her eyes. "Perhaps . . . I do. But it's only because I don't like people much. They're . . . disappointing."

"I know, child. But that's because you have your eyes on the wrong things. They should be on Jesus. And you need to understand that people are just like you. They're all looking for someone to love them in spite of their defects and failings. And when you begin to understand that, it won't be as hard as you think to like people. You like us well enough, don't you?"

Cynthia's eyes misted as she nodded.

"Well, go ahead, then. Make that cake. I'll even take a chance and have a piece."

Cynthia laughed.

"But the thing that has me puzzled is how in the world did you know it was Jonathan's birthday?"

Cynthia felt her face flush. "One night I, well, I saw it on the lease agreement that Jonathan had filled out. His date of birth was one of the entries. He's thirty today."

Miss Emily frowned. "But that was on his desk."

"I know."

"So what where you doing in his office?"

Cynthia took a deep breath. "Using the phone."

Miss Emily nodded. "People have grown to love you around here. I hope you'll keep that in mind when you do what you have to do."

"I would never hurt any of you or the mission."

"Sometimes, child, people get hurt whether you try to hurt them or not."

When Cynthia opened the door of the Day Care Center, she found Effie sitting on a blanket with the children reading *Boy with a Sling*. She waited for Effie to finish before joining the group. She could see by the smiling faces that no one had tired of the new playthings.

"I just wanted to tell you that after dinner and cleanup, we're going to have a birthday cake for Jonathan in the kitchen." Cynthia helped Effie to her feet. "I hope you and Daisy will come."

"It's Pastor's birthday? Well, sure we'll come. Only . . . I can't afford to bring no gift or nothin'."

"Just bring yourself, and Daisy of course." Cynthia's smile faded when she noticed worry lines creep across Effie's forehead. "What's wrong?"

Effie gazed at the children playing at the other end of the room. "Nothin'. Nothin' you need to worry your head about."

Cynthia placed her hand on Effie's shoulder. "Jonathan said we're staff and need to stick together, help each other. So tell me, what is it?"

"Well . . . when you said birthday, it made me think of my son. His birthday's next week."

"I didn't know you had a son."

Effie ushered Cynthia out into the hall. "Daisy misses her brother somethin' fierce. She don't miss her daddy, but her brother . . . they were just like that." Effie crossed two fingers. "I try not to say much about him in front of her."

"Where is he?"

"He's gonna be fourteen next week. He thinks he's a man, but he's just a boy. A hurt, scared little boy. And angry. He's got a lot of anger. You don't grow up with violence in your home without gettin' angry."

Effie pointed to the empty space where a front tooth should be. "The day my husband did this was the last time I saw my son. Jeff tried to defend me, and my husband nearly killed him. Jeff said he wouldn't live another day under his father's roof."

"How long ago was that?"

"Three months. I worry about him. I worry myself sick. I know he's out there takin' on the world, tryin' to lick it like he did his daddy. But now that I know Jesus, I wish I could tell him about another Daddy, a Father who loves him, cares for him. He needs hope. He don't have no hope. That's what gets 'em, you know. A boy needs hope or he don't grow right. If a tree gets battered enough by a storm it gets all gnarled and twisted. That's what happened to Jeff. He's all twisted up."

"I'm sorry, Effie. I had no idea. I can't imagine what you're going through. It must be hard not knowing where he is."

"Oh, I know where he is. That's why it hurts so bad. That's what makes me worry so much. If I could just get to him, see him, tell him I'm alright, and give him a chance to see what Jesus has done for me—a job, a roof over my head and Daisy—to give him hope. I gotta show him there's hope."

"I wish I could help."

"You . . . mean it? Those ain't just fancy, full-of-air words? Are they?"

"I mean it," Cynthia returned, though the words stuck a bit in her throat. *What was she getting herself into?*

"See, the thing is you're smarter than me, Cynthia. And you know how to get things done. I seen how you operate. You're a real doer."

"I guess . . . ."

"Maybe you could ask around, send out some feelers."

The pleading look on Effie's face made Cynthia avert her eyes. "I could try. Just tell me where you think he is."

"With the Salamanders."

"Blow out the candles and cut the cake, Jonathan."

Jonathan Holmes put down the paper noisemaker and stared at all the excited faces. They had just finished singing happy birthday and no matter how hard he tried, he couldn't wipe away the silly grin he knew was on his face. He paused a moment to inhale the sweet yeasty aroma that hovered over the kitchen like a canopy. He still couldn't figure out how they knew it was his birthday. He had been quiet about it, not wanting anyone to feel they had to fuss. It also surprised and pleased him that it was *Cynthia* who had baked the cake.

Miss Emily handed him a knife. "Come on now, blow, then cut six pieces. And make them *small,* at least until we know what we're getting ourselves into." Her eyes twinkled with humor when she looked at Cynthia.

Jonathan noticed that the cake leaned to one side, and hoped it wouldn't flop over before he blew out the candles. His first attempt ended up as a soft puff extinguishing only one of thirty. He grinned then lowered his head and tried again. Ten more went out. At this rate he'd layer the cake with spittle.

"Ah . . . Cynthia, you want to help me out?" If she blew and the cake toppled, he wouldn't feel so bad.

A chorus of "nos" filled the room.

Even so, Cynthia slipped alongside him. "If it falls, no one will blame you," she said in a whisper.

Jonathan smiled. This time he'd make an end of it, one way or the other. He blew with all his might and was gratified to see all the candles go out and the cake still standing. Then he cringed when he noticed a big dent in the icing where his chin had landed like a hang glider. As he brought his head up, he smelled chocolate, felt it sticky and wet on his face. The first person to laugh was Cynthia, then Miss Emily. Then everyone, including him.

Cynthia picked up one of the birthday napkins and wiped his chin.

"Thanks for baking the cake." He was surprised to feel his heart thump. "That was thoughtful."

"You've been working hard. I figured a little celebration would be nice."

He smiled, then began cutting the pieces. With each cut, the cake leaned further to one side. After the last one, the top layer slid off, making a soft landing on the counter. Without a word, Cynthia scooped it up with a paper plate.

"Talk about perfect timing." She winked at him.

He was grateful for her good nature, grateful for the cake and this small circle of friends to share it with, and for the first time, he was grateful that God had sent him here.

"But how did you know it was my birthday?"

Cynthia shot a furtive glance at Miss Emily. "Let's just say I came across it by accident."

"Boy this cake is great!" Stubby said, carving another slice. The large crumb on his bottom lip was all that was left of his first piece.

As Cynthia looked down at her collapsing masterpiece, her apparent vulnerability pricked Jonathan's heart. It wasn't the God-kind of prick, but the kind a man feels for a woman when he is overcome with a desire to protect her. He had a sudden urge to whisper in her ear—to tell her he was here for her.

"Happy birthday, Pastor, and good night, Cynthia," Effie said, mercifully squelching that urge. "Daisy's tired. And I wanna wash her hair and use some of the salve you got her."

Jonathan watched Daisy hug Cynthia around the knees, then scamper off behind her mother. "Looks like you've made a friend."

Cynthia's eyes followed Daisy as she disappeared through the doorway. "I'm beginning to understand how important your work is and why you love these people."

"When I see God touch lives like theirs, it makes the other disappointments easier to bear." Jonathan's hand rested on Cynthia's arm causing that former urge to return.

This time it was Stubby to the rescue. "Well, I'll be sayin' my goodnights, too. I'm gonna take this piece and eat in my room." He held up a plate containing a mammoth chunk of yellow cake. "Gonna write Pastor Jonathan a birthday poem. You won't mind gettin' it a day late, will you?"

Jonathan shook his head.

"It's been a long day. Guess I'll turn in, too." Cynthia said, leaving her spot in order to cover the remaining cake with plastic wrap.

Jonathan didn't think she looked tired at all then realized it was because he didn't want her to go. "Thank you for making my birthday special."

"It was just a packaged mix."

"It was much more. You brought us all together tonight, Cynthia, and made us feel like family. That's important in a place like this."

"Well, I'm glad it pleased you."

"It did, very much." And when he looked into her eyes, he realized for the first time just how incredibly drawn he was to her—the first woman since Lydia. *What was wrong with him?* Hadn't he learned anything from Lydia? A pretty face, a sweet disposition, a deep vulnerability—all bait on a hook he seemed too eager to swallow. He was playing with dynamite. He couldn't let this happen. History was *not* going to repeat itself.

"I've been thinking about that sermon of yours—mercy at midnight," she said softly.

"And?"

"And, I've been thinking about it. Happy birthday, Jonathan."

Long after she left, Jonathan stood in the silent kitchen thinking that maybe Aunt Adel's prayers for Cynthia were being answered. Then he began wondering what exactly his aunt was praying for.

Jonathan played the two messages on his cell; both of them from his aunt, then dialed the familiar number.

"Hi, Aunt Adel. Just returning your call."

"Jonathan, Dearest! Happy, happy birthday. I wish you could have gotten away from the mission this evening. I so wanted to cook you something delicious and make you a great big cake."

"I know and I appreciate it. But like I said this morning the whole moving-in process took me away from my other duties and I needed to catch up."

"Well . . . I forgive you. Just as long as you let me cook you one of my classic dinners. Let's say—this weekend?"

"We'll see."

"You're being difficult, Dearest, but I love you anyway. Are you all moved in?"

"No." Jonathan pushed a stack of clothes off his bed and sat down. Then he peeled off his shoes and sank into the bed.

"I can have my cleaning lady come tomorrow and organize your whole apartment. She's a treasure and will do wonders with . . . ."

"Aunt Adel, I'm in one room." He thought he heard his aunt gulp.

"Okay, she could arrange your room."

Jonathan laughed. "What would I do without you?"

"Then she can come?"

"Of course not. And I want you to stop worrying about me. Everything's fine. Believe it or not, I even had a birthday cake today."

"*Really?* Who made it?"

"Cynthia," he said in a lowered voice.

"Cynthia? The keep-this-woman-in-prayer Cynthia?"

"Yes, and I hope you are."

"My ladies and I are on it. But Jonathan . . . it's the strangest thing. Every time I pray for her I picture a seesaw and I can't tell which way she's going to go. It doesn't make sense I know, but I feel such an excitement in my spirit and also . . . ."

"What?"

"A sense of dread."

Cynthia dried herself, wrapped her wet hair in a towel, then slipped on her robe. She was getting used to the community showers and no longer had to make two trips back and forth to her room to retrieve forgotten items. She now kept her shampoo and other toiletries organized in a plastic shower caddy, much like she did in her college days. And her routine of cleaning the kitchen after dinner, then showering before she settled into her room at night was almost beginning to feel comfortable. By the time it did, it would probably be time to go home.

She was sure Bernie wouldn't give her an extension. Not unless she handed him something he could sink his teeth into. Right now, she had nothing. Stubby was the key. But she couldn't press him too hard. In fact, pressing him at all didn't sit right with her anymore. He had written her a poem. Called her *friend*. Street people didn't make friends easily. And neither did she for that matter. It surprised her that she wanted to be his friend, too. But how could she? Sooner or later he'd find out who she was. How would he feel then? Disappointed?

Betrayed was more like it. And she couldn't bear the thought.

She picked up the plastic caddy and shut the bathroom light behind her. The hall was dark, with one small plug-in nightlight at each end for illumination. All was quiet. Everyone had gone to bed or settled in their rooms for the night. She wasn't used to that. She was usually the first to disappear behind closed doors, then had to endure the chatter and noise in the hall for another hour.

She walked toward her room, wondering if she should call Bernie. *What for?* She had nothing new to tell him. Let him lecture her tomorrow. It was late. She was beat. All she wanted was to lie down and unwind. The day had been long, and full of emotional ups and downs: the shopping, the encounter with the Salamanders, the excitement of giving out the presents, the birthday party, Jonathan.

Jonathan.

He was a pastor and that alone would be a turn-off, but for some reason she wasn't turned off at all. When she looked at him, she saw a man—a handsome, kind, loving, *desirable* man.

None of that, Wells. Pastors didn't go slipping in and out of women's beds.

When she opened the door to her room she was surprised it was dark. She was sure she had left her desk lamp on. She closed the door then groped for the light switch. As her fingers felt along the wall, she heard a noise behind her. Before she could say, "Who's there," someone grabbed her. She felt a rope snap across her throat, felt it tighten until she could hardly breathe. She tore at it with her free hand, choking, gasping for air. The rope continued to tighten. *And the pain.* She had never felt pain like that. She wondered if this was how death felt.

She tried to cry out, but couldn't. Then she realized she was still holding the shower caddy. She swung it at the body behind her, heard it crack as it connected. But the rope, the ever tightening rope, didn't slacken. She knew it was a matter of seconds before unconsciousness. With all her remaining strength, she spun around taking the intruder with her, then pushed backward, slamming him hard against the door. She heard the sound of wood cracking, then a far away voice calling out, "Miss Cynthia, what's happenin'? Are you okay?"

Then nothing.

When Cynthia opened her eyes she found herself on the floor and Stubby White kneeling beside her.

"Are you okay, Miss Cynthia? Can you talk?"

Her door was open and barely hanging on its hinges. She saw movement in the hall and Miss Emily and Effie standing in the doorway. Then Jonathan entered, breathing heavily.

"Did you catch him, Pastor?" Stubby asked.

"No. I ran as far as the Angus Avenue Hotel, then lost him. How is she?"

Stubby leaned closer to Cynthia. "Her eyes are open, but she ain't talkin'."

Cynthia listened to musical beeps as Jonathan punched numbers on his cell. She tried to say something, but no sound came out. She closed her eyes while Jonathan spoke to the police. When she opened them, he was kneeling beside her, opposite Stubby. She flinched when his fingers brushed her throat.

"That's a nasty rope burn, Pastor," Stubby said.

Jonathan smiled down at Cynthia, but she could see the worry on his face. "I think Stubby saved your life."

Cynthia nodded and felt pain. She wondered if her neck was broken, then realized she wouldn't have been able to nod if it were. Maybe it was just her larynx. Maybe the intruder had crushed it with that rope. She tried to speak and heard her voice come out a croak.

"Don't talk, not until a doctor examines you." Jonathan pulled the spread off the bed and covered her. She was shaking now. "An ambulance is on the way, so are the police."

"Fruit," Cynthia croaked in a whisper. "He smelled like fruit."

Cynthia lay strapped to a gurney watching a sea of people stream by. She was in the hallway outside her door. Her room had become a crime scene and already two cops were collecting evidence. When she saw Detective Steve Bradley coming down the hall she closed her eyes and groaned.

"What the . . . I don't believe it!"

Cynthia opened her eyes.

"*You're* my 10-5? Are you crazy, Cynthia? Are you plain out of your head crazy? Because if you're here doing what I think you're doing, then you are certifiable."

"Ease up detective. It's hard for her to talk. I don't know what kind of trouble she's gotten into in the past, but since she's been here I can vouch for her."

"And who are you?"

"Pastor Holmes."

Cynthia watched Stubby, Miss Emily, and Effie gather around her like a shield. She caught Steve's eye and sent out a silent plea. It worked, because he just shook his head and walked away.

"Don't worry. This will all be sorted out." Jonathan ran his thumb down Cynthia's cheek. "First, we'll get you to a hospital and have a doctor check you out. Then you'll have to help the police find the person who did this. But don't worry about anything. Whatever trouble you're in, we'll stand by you."

CHAPTER 12

Cynthia walked into the Beacon Mission feeling like she had been run over by a Mack Truck. She had not slept a wink. Impossible when being examined by three doctors, then having to answer a hundred questions for the police—a process made longer since she could hardly talk and had to handwrite all her answers on a small chalkboard.

The doctors had ordered bed rest, and she planned to obey *after* one last thing. She glanced around the large room. A sizable crowd loitered near the long, stainless steel counter waiting for lunch—which was late. Already, several men pushed and shoved each other as though that would speed things up. Cynthia felt sorry for Miss Emily. For a crowd this size, lunch was difficult to do alone. Miss Emily's Jesus would have to help her today, because she couldn't.

Cynthia tried slipping past a dozen men she recognized but they spotted her and bombarded her with well-wishes. Several gave her hugs. Everyone talked at once. They had all heard about the attempt on her life.

Then suddenly there was Jonathan, his face a kaleidoscope of surprise, pleasure and concern. He greeted her with an unexpected hug. "What are you doing out of bed? And what are you doing *here*? I can't believe the hospital released you."

"They discharged me with orders to go home and rest." Cynthia's throat still felt like she had swallowed gravel.

"Well, then, you better." He guided her to the hall then toward the staff bedrooms. "When you're up to it, we'll have to talk."

She gave him an anxious glance. "About what?"

"Those weren't empty words when I said I—we at the mission—would stand by you." They stopped in front of a door that wasn't hers. "Miss Emily made up the bed in here. The police still have your room roped off and the door hasn't been fixed. Detective Bradley said you could have it back by tomorrow." It was evident that Jonathan wanted to say more. His square jaw clenched and unclenched.

Tell him the truth.

She owed him that—to let him know she wasn't in any trouble and didn't need his help.

"Detective Bradley seemed angry. It's obvious he knows you. But whatever trouble you're in, you won't face it alone. I haven't much money, but if you think you need a lawyer, I know someone who would lend me the funds."

Cynthia blinked back her surprise. "You'd . . . do that for me?"

Jonathan nodded.

"But *why*? You don't even know me." Cynthia felt anger well-up, felt her defenses rev into high gear like a racing car in the Indy-500. Before this was over, they were all going to be disappointed. And there was nothing she could do about it. "You have no idea who I am. Maybe if you knew, you wouldn't like me very much," she said in a croak and watched Jonathan flinch.

"Don't strain your voice. We can talk tomorrow. Just tell me now if you think I should borrow the money. If you need a lawyer, it's best we get him sooner rather than later."

"No lawyer."

Jonathan appeared relieved.

"But thank you, anyway." She placed her hand on the knob and turned. Her throat felt like it was on fire. She couldn't deal with this now—not the truth, not Jonathan's kindness. She had to get away, by herself, and think. Even so, she had to know one thing. "You haven't told me why. Why the offer?"

"Because God instructed me to meet your needs. Whatever came up."

"You're kidding!"

"You're not here by accident, Cynthia. No matter what you think."

Something in Jonathan's look, in his soft, green eyes that brimmed with compassion, stoked her anger even more. "You have no idea why I'm here. And when you find out, let's see if you're still singing the same tune." She slammed the door behind her.

None of Cynthia's belongings were in the room. They were still sealed off behind the police tape. But Miss Emily had brought in a few items: a clean nightgown and robe which Cynthia recognized as Miss Emily's, a drinking cup, a toiletry kit—the kind Miss Emily handed out each morning to those who needed them. She even included a small writing pad and Bic pen. Cynthia looked at the bed with longing. One second on it and she'd be out like a light. But first things first.

She scribbled a note then headed for Stubby's room and slipped it under the door. Within seconds she was back, lying down. Now all she had to do was wait.

She closed her eyes.

Cynthia awoke to the sound of steady tapping. She covered her head with the pillow. "Go away," she croaked.

"Miss Cynthia, you in there?"

She opened her eyes. The room was dark and strange.

"Miss Cynthia! You there?"

She forced herself up, then flicked on the light. Her feet felt like concrete as she lumbered to the door and unlocked it.

"I . . . was just gettin' ready to knock again." Stubby's fist was raised in the air.

She gestured with her head for him to enter and watched him tiptoe into the room as though trying not to wake a sleeper, then settle in the small recliner.

"I got your note. It said you wanted to see me. But you shouldn't be doin' any talkin'. You gotta protect your voice. So we're gonna make this quick. Okay?"

Cynthia nodded and sat on the edge of the bed.

"Everybody's talkin'. They ain't figured out why someone would go after you. 'Course I thought of Skinner right away. But he'd have used a knife." He studied her. "You okay?"

She took a deep breath. "Stubby . . . last night I realized I was in over my head. And I need answers."

Stubby scratched his head. "What answers, Miss Cynthia?"

"I need to know two things. First, what is Skinner afraid you're going to tell me? And then I need to hear about Turtle and Manny." Cynthia saw fear cloud Stubby's eyes.

"Why you want to know, Miss Cynthia? You thinkin' there's some connection between this and what happened to you?"

"Maybe."

"Well, okay, then. Sure, I'll tell you, if you think it'll help."

Her throat throbbed. She shouldn't be talking. The doctor had given her strict orders. But she had to get this out. "Before you start, there's something I must tell you. And I hope you won't be mad at me."

"You shouldn't be strainin' your voice, Miss Cynthia. And I could never be mad at you."

"Try to remember that." She leaned over, attempting to erase the distance between them. The recliner was a few feet away, too far to take Stubby's hand and hold it like a friend bearing bad news. "I'm a reporter. I've been working undercover on a story involving Turtle and Manny. I wanted you to know that before you got started."

Grief twisted Stubby's face, making the corner of his mouth turn down, and his forehead droop. "A *reporter*? You mean you ain't one of us?"

Cynthia shook her head.

"A reporter," Stubby repeated. "Then . . . then you bein' here was just somethin' you had to do—just a job. Then we mean nothin' to you. We ain't any of us a friend. And that means all I am to you is just a . . . snitch, a stoolie. Someone you had to be nice to so you'd get what you wanted."

"No Stubby, it's not like that at all."

"I trusted you. It ain't easy for someone like me to trust." He looked at her with weepy eyes. "I *trusted* you. I thought we were *friends.*"

"I never wanted to hurt you." Every word pained her throat but she couldn't stop now. She had to make Stubby understand. "It was just an assignment. I never expected to get involved. To come to love all of you and this mission. I'm sorry, Stubby."

Stubby shrugged and picked up the pad and pen and handed them to Cynthia. "Here, you'll be needin' this. Ain't reporters supposed to take notes?"

"All of you are always talking about forgiveness. Why can't you extend some of that now, to *me*?" She bit her lip. If he couldn't forgive her about this how was he ever going to forgive her about her sister? All the more she hoped he'd never find out.

Stubby rose to his feet. "You shoulda been honest. I woulda helped you."

"No you wouldn't. You street people don't talk to anyone but your own. I tried it already and I know." Cynthia slipped off the bed and onto her knees. "Forgive me?"

"Now, Miss Cynthia, stop that! Get off the floor. It ain't proper."

"I'm not budging, Stubby, until you say you forgive me. And I can be stubborn when I want."

"Just how long you plannin' on stayin' like that?"

"All night if I have to."

"This is just plain silly."

Cynthia nodded and watched Stubby cover his mouth to hide a smile.

"Come on, Miss Cynthia. Get up. Just get up. I forgive you. Okay?"

Cynthia rose and walked to where Stubby stood, then threw her arms around him. "Thank you."

"Now, Miss Cynthia, you needn't get all mushy. Stop that before I start blubberin' like a baby."

"Just one more thing. Please don't tell the others who I am. Let me tell them when I'm ready.'"

Stubby nodded.

Cynthia returned to the bed and sat down. "Okay. Let's go. Tell me about your friends and what happened to them."

Stubby rubbed his chin. "We best begin with Manny. I met him five years ago. He was passed out in the alley next to the Angus Avenue Hotel and some kid in a red bandanna was robbin' him. The Salamanders don't come to Angus Avenue much. Ain't their turf. But sometimes, one or another of 'em tries fleecin' the drunks in the alley. They don't get much—pocket change—but it's easy money, like takin' candy from a baby.

"Anyway this kid was cleanin' Manny out and I happened along at a time I was sick and tired of takin' everyone's guff. I guess you could say I was itchin' for a fight and I started in on the kid. Funny thing, these tough gang types ain't so tough when they gotta fight someone alone. He cut and run before I even landed three good punches. After that, I guess I felt responsible for Manny. Don't know why, but I stayed with him all night. Next mornin', when he woke, I told him what happened. From then on, we made it a habit of watchin' each other's backs. He was a good friend. More than once, he saved me from gettin' my lumps."

Cynthia had been writing on her pad and stopped. "I'm sorry, Stubby. About you losing such a good friend."

Stubby shrugged. "Yeah, well . . . it happens. A lot. On the street. Usually, sickness gets 'em. Or they move on and you never see 'em again. A friend's a rare thing. You know?"

Cynthia swallowed what felt like a golf ball. "I'm beginning to see that."

"A year after I met Manny, Turtle showed up. I can't remember the first time I saw him, 'cause he just sorta started showin' up wherever we—Manny and me—were. It was like he was our shadow. Like he had adopted us or somethin'. Later, when we got to be friends, he told us how he had watched us, studied us for a long time before pickin' us out. People called us the Three Stooges, but we didn't care. They were just jealous 'cause we had each other, someone we could count on. You know?"

"Yes . . . I think I do." Cynthia looked up from her pad. "How did Manny die?"

"Don't know exactly, just that he ended up in a dumpster, dead. But I can tell you why—drugs. Manny and Turtle, they got in with

Jake's crowd." Stubby rose and began pacing. "Jake, the guy who runs the Angus Avenue Men's Shelter, he's a mean dude. Nobody crosses him and lives to brag on it."

"I met with a Jake at the Shelter, a Jake Stone. You can't mean him?"

"Yep. That's the guy. Jake the Snake."

"He said he never heard of Manny or Turtle, and he was pretty convincing. He wasn't that helpful, either." Cynthia cleared her throat. "Now, I know why."

"Jake's been runnin' drugs out of the shelter for years. He's the neighborhood supplier. Some say organized crime's backin' him. It could be. All I know is someone's payin' off the right people. He's never been touched. Not once."

Cynthia put down her pen and rubbed her hands together. It felt like the strain in her throat had traveled down her entire body. She felt tired, sore and something else, too.

Outraged.

She had seen so many scams, written about so much abuse and corruption that the feeling surprised her. Maybe she wasn't as hard-boiled as she thought. When she picked up her pen, Stubby resumed his narrative.

"Jake uses people like Turtle and Manny, people who got habits to support, and gets 'em to act like mules and run drugs to the crack houses. Pays 'em in drugs, mostly, but sometimes a little cash, too. Cops don't normally check the bags of street people. It's like he's got an army of cockroaches scurryin' all over the city for him."

Cynthia rubbed her throbbing forehead. "Did Jake have your friends killed?"

"Can't think of nobody else. One day Manny and Turtle came up with this harebrained scheme and wanted me to go in on it. But like I told you, Jake and his crowd are mean. I heard about people who crossed 'em—the stories would curl your hair. I told 'em no way, count me out. I tried talkin' 'em out of it, too." Stubby quit pacing and sat down. "I tried."

"What did they do?"

"They switched a load of crack with perp."

"Perp?"

"Fake crack made of bakin' soda and candle wax. They thought because the crack houses got so much traffic, the perp would be used up before anyone was the wiser. And they never thought it could be traced to a specific delivery. I told 'em that was stupid thinkin', that they were sure to get caught. I told 'em Jake had to have a quality control system, had to mark the deliveries somehow, 'cause that's what I woulda done. Sure enough, I was right, 'cause it didn't take Jake long to figure out who pulled the switch."

"What did your friends do with the crack?'

"Hid it. They said after things cooled down, they'd sell it off, little by little. They said it would keep us all in pocket change for a year. I wanted no part of it, the drugs or money, and told 'em so. I told 'em I didn't want to know nothin' about it, neither. That way, when Jake and his boys showed up, I couldn't talk. Manny and Turtle laughed. They said come winter when my money ran out between checks and I wanted to stay in a nice warm room at the Angus Avenue Hotel, I'd be singin' a different tune. Three days after they done it, Manny was dead. A week later, Turtle."

Cynthia began drawing stick men around the edges of the pad. "Stubby, do you think they'll come for you, too?"

Stubby frowned. "Manny and Turtle muled Jake's drugs for years. I ain't never been part of that. They know I had nothin' to do with it. Only . . . ."

"Only what?"

"They think I know where their stuff is. That Manny or Turtle told me. That's why Skinner keeps showin' up."

"What happens to you if I try to expose Jake, and print this story?"

"They'll know I talked and come for me."

"Even if we can get enough evidence on Jake and send him to jail?"

"They'll still come. And Miss Cynthia . . . they'll come for you, too . . . again."

Cynthia paced the floor and wondered what time it was. She had been walking the floor since Stubby left. It had to be late because she heard all the usual noise in the hall—Miss Emily's gay chatter, Effie coaxing Daisy to get ready for bed, Jonathan's heavy footsteps and cheery "good-nights," and even Stubby's low masculine voice, which, tonight, sounded grumpy to Cynthia's ears.

What was she going to do? If she believed in God, she'd ask Him. She smiled at the thought. Who else could she ask? Bernie? She knew what he'd say. Bernie always opted for the jugular. *But what about Stubby? What would happen to him?*

Cynthia sat down on the bed. She was worn out from all the pacing. She propped her pillow against the wall and sank into it. She'd have to tell Bernie. She owed him that. And if he told her to go with the story, she would. But she'd speak to Steve Bradley; see what he could do about protecting Stubby, protecting the mission.

She rested against the pillow listening for the last of the hall noise to die down. When it did she couldn't bring herself to get up. *Fear.* She could taste it. Stubby's disclosure made her realize there was much to fear. She chided herself for not wanting to unlock her door, for not wanting to go into the dark hallway and into an even darker office to call Bernie. She swallowed and the pain in her throat reminded her that her fear was justified.

You can't lay here all night.

She forced her body to rise, forced her legs to walk across the room, then out the door. Her stomach churned all the way to Jonathan's office. She closed the door, then flicked on the light and went to the desk. She picked up the phone and punched in Bernie's number, all the while listening for any sounds in the hall.

"Bernie . . . ."

"Where in blue blazes are you! I've been calling your apartment for hours. The doctor told you to rest."

"I'm at the mission . . . and how did you find out about . . . ."

"Steve Bradley. He called to chew me out. Said I had a cash register for a head and all I thought about was selling papers. How are you?"

"Glad to be alive." Cynthia picked up the paperweight on the desk and read the inscription. *This is the day the Lord has made; we will rejoice and be glad in it.*

"Mind telling me why you haven't bothered to call? Why you didn't let me know what happened?"

"I didn't want you to pull me off the story." Cynthia hoped her croaking voice didn't remind Bernie how close she had come to never speaking to him again. "Not until I did some more checking."

"You sound awful. Should you be using your voice like this?"

"No."

"Then you'd better hang up . . . but first tell me, did you? Did you do your checking?"

Cynthia put down the paperweight. "Yes. And now I'm not sure I want to stay on the story."

"I've never known you to quit something once you started. So either you found nothing or you're scared. Which is it?"

"A little of both. Other people could get hurt. It's not just my neck I'm thinking about."

"Okay, Wells. You've got something, and sore throat or not, I want to hear it."

"Drugs are being distributed from the Angus Avenue Men's Shelter and they're using homeless men to do it."

"Well, dip me in printer's ink! If your nose still isn't one of the best in the business! Okay, you've got a story; now explain why you don't want to go with it."

"I don't have any proof."

"I'd say the attempt on your life means you're getting close. I could put Jones and Bodkins on it. They're both gorillas and a lot harder to hassle. They could do the rest of the legwork. It would still be your story, with a sidebar for each of them. It's the best of both worlds. We could keep you out of harms way and still get the scoop."

"That'll only solve part of the problem. What about my source? What happens to Stubby? They'll kill him, Bernie. They already killed his two friends for stealing from them. And unless there's some way we can protect Stubby, I'm not sure I want to go ahead with this."

"This isn't the iron maiden I've come to know and love. Since when do we provide protection for our sources?"

"I was planning to talk to Steve. If he can't help, I thought we could work something out. Have Bodkins go undercover, be Stubby's bodyguard. And while he's doing it, he could dig around for more information."

"There's no way Bodkins would ever convince anyone he's down and out. He's got too much ego, and he's too healthy looking.

But Jones might pull it off. I could send him tomorrow, do an even exchange. You come out, and he'll go in."

Cynthia felt her stomach knot. *Leave tomorrow?* She hadn't counted on that. Neither had she counted on feeling sad at the prospect.

"Earth to Wells. Where are you?"

"Okay . . . send Jones. I'll see you in the office tomorrow morning, and then I'll give you everything I have. I'm trusting you, Bernie, to make it clear to Jones that his first priority is to protect Stubby."

"Get serious, Wells. I can't tell a reporter his main job is babysitting. You let me handle him. You just be here, tomorrow. Early."

"Good night, Bernie."

"Right. Take care of that throat. And Wells . . . I'm glad you're okay. *Really* glad."

"Yeah . . . I love you, too. But that doesn't mean I'm going to date your wife's cousin."

When Cynthia hung up, there was a smile on her face but it faded when she heard a scratching sound outside the door. She picked up the paperweight and watched in horror as the door opened.

"I hope you're not planning to use that on me?"

Cynthia lowered her arm. "I'm still a little jumpy."

"Small wonder with what you went through last night." Miss Emily walked over to Cynthia and hugged her. "I heard you were back and came by earlier but you must have been sleeping because you didn't answer my knock."

"I didn't wake up until it was dark."

"You can move back to your room. The police pulled off their tape late this afternoon and Stubby fixed the door." Miss Emily draped her arm around Cynthia's shoulder. "I'm glad to see you're alright. I've been praying, asking God for healing, and for Him to keep His ministering angels as a hedge of protection around you. It wouldn't do to have something happen to you before you got to meet my beautiful Jesus."

"I could use your prayers. Thank you."

"If there's something special you want me to pray about, I'd do that, too."

Cynthia remained silent.

"I see you've been making more of your calls. Is your business almost done?"

Cynthia tried to read Miss Emily's face, but couldn't. "I'm . . . not sure."

Miss Emily slipped her arm through Cynthia's. "You must be starving. Come in the kitchen and I'll heat up some soup. It'll do your throat good. Besides, I think it's time you and I had a little talk."

Cynthia watched Miss Emily buzz around the kitchen and envied how much at home she seemed. Or was it that Miss Emily made everyplace seem like home? Cynthia took a deep breath.

What was she going to tell her?

The truth, for starters. There was no way she could dodge that bullet any longer. But she didn't have the same sinking feeling, that feeling she had had just before telling Stubby. Cynthia suspected it was because Miss Emily probably knew her secret. At least some of it.

"You know, by the time I was your age I already had three miscarriages. Then two more after that. That's when I started drinking." Miss

Emily poured the steaming soup into a mug and brought it to Cynthia. "The drugging came later, after my husband left me. It wasn't his fault. My loneliness was like a giant vacuum that had already sucked everything out of him. He had tried for years to give me what I needed. But that was like expecting a glass of water to fill up a ditch. It can't be done."

Cynthia blew on the soup trying to cool it off, then gave up and placed it on the counter. "You want to know about my past, is that it? All the sordid details?"

"I already know about your past. It's the future I'm concerned about."

"I must confess that's the thing I find irritating about you. Your insinuation, your supposing that you know me."

Miss Emily smiled. "But I do. The truth is, all I have to do is look in the mirror and I see you. Because . . . I *was* you. You've got a hole as big as mine was, right smack dab in your center, and nothing you do will fill it. You can find a good man to be your husband, you can have lots of pretty, pink babies, but your hunger will eat them alive. Only Jesus can fix what ails you."

Cynthia fingered her mug. "Is this what you wanted to discuss?"

"Nothing's ever going to change the past. You can't go *back*. But Daddy God has a lap for you, child. And He's just waiting for you to crawl up on it. If you try crawling on other laps, like I did, you're going to be miserable all your life."

Cynthia took a chance and sipped her soup. It soothed her throat going down. When she looked up, Miss Emily was standing by the sink, just staring at her. "I've hurt people . . . ruined their lives. There's no lap big enough to cure that."

"Life's hard, child. No getting around it. But you have a choice here. Either you continue down the path you're going or change directions."

Cynthia took another sip. "This is delicious, Miss Emily. One of the things I'm going to miss when I leave is your good cooking."

"You'll be leaving soon, I expect."

"Tomorrow."

"Then you have all you need for that article you're writing?"

"How did . . . ?"

"That was your first mistake. You assumed street people don't read; that they're not aware of what's going on in the world. And I guess that's partly true. But I've been reading your articles for years. I liked them, too."

Cynthia frowned and shook her head. "There's no picture next to my column."

"I saw your interview on Channel 11's local news just after your Nanny Scam story. Then when you got here and cleaned yourself up, I recognized you right away. Except I think you're prettier in person."

"Does Jonathan know?"

"Would it matter?"

Cynthia thought of Jonathan's offer to help. *Had he known all along?* "Yes . . . I think it would."

Miss Emily gave her a queer look and shook her head. "I never told anyone, though I was tempted to tell Stubby. He's vulnerable and trying hard to trust again. But when I prayed about it, I got a distinct command to keep my mouth shut. I guess God wanted you and Stubby to work things out for yourselves."

"Thank you for that." Cynthia placed her mug on the counter and walked over to Miss Emily. "We managed to get everything straightened out. Well, not everything. I guess some things can never be reconciled. But I hope you and I . . . that we can keep in touch. I'd hate to lose your frien . . . ."

Miss Emily's arms encircled her. "I know, child. Me, too."

Cynthia awoke to shouts and the noise of feet running down the hall. She jumped out of bed and grabbed her robe, then sprinted out the door. The first person she saw was Jonathan Holmes. He flew past her, heading for his office, his face ashen.

"What's the matter?" she said, running after him.

"Stubby!" His fingers frantically punched numbers.

"What *happened?*"

Jonathan ignored her, and spoke rapidly into the phone. When Cynthia got the gist of what was going on, she headed for the men's bathroom. Miss Emily and Effie were standing by the entrance, clutching each other. Cynthia streaked passed them and through the doorway. She stopped when she saw Stubby lying face up on the floor. His eyes were rolled back, and next to him was a tourniquet and empty syringe.

She knelt down and felt for a pulse, then put her hand in front of his nostrils to check his breath. Nothing. Already his nails and lips were blue. She pinched his nose and began CPR. She worked at a frantic pace until she felt a hand on her shoulder.

"I'll take over."

Cynthia looked up at Jonathan's drawn face, then moved so he could take her place. Her mind was racing. What happened? The needle . . . the tourniquet . . . . Stubby wouldn't go back on drugs. He just wouldn't. But a voice in her head nagged, *drug addicts do it all the time. They get cleaned up, then fall back down.*

She watched Jonathan work feverishly. It couldn't end like this. Stubby couldn't die, not like this, not on a cold bathroom floor. And what about Divine Appointment? Hadn't Stubby said God had healed him? And he believed it with all his being. No, it just wasn't possible that Stubby went back to drugging. So what happened? Only one answer came to mind. If Stubby didn't inject himself then someone else did.

That meant someone had tried to kill him.

Cynthia watched Detective Steve Bradley and his men mull around the hall. She had thrown on a pair of jeans and T-shirt and stood in a spot where she could see all the action. She was determined to stay at her post, to see this thing through, at least until they stabilized Stubby and moved him to the waiting ambulance. It made her angry the way Miss Emily and Effie had left—Miss Emily to her kitchen and Effie to Daisy. She was sure Jonathan would leave too, as soon as he had answered all of Steve's questions.

Maybe they don't have your guilty conscience.

Cynthia jerked her head and tried pushing that thought aside, tried pretending it didn't keep popping up like a Jack-in-the-Box she couldn't restrain. *Was Stubby dying because of her?* She had ruined his life once. Was she doing it again? Did this happen because he had told her about Jake and the drugs?

She leaned against the wall and closed her eyes. How was she ever going to deal with all this?

"Enough excitement for you?"

Cynthia opened her eyes and looked into the tired, angry face of Detective Steve Bradley. Just beyond him stood Jonathan, a concerned look on his face, and hanging back a bit as though waiting to see if she needed him.

"He didn't overdose, Steve."

"Why don't you let the SOPD determine that?"

"I'm telling you—look for signs of a struggle, bruises, lacerations. Someone wanted him dead."

"If you have pertinent information, you better not hold out. Otherwise, back off."

"I only have what Stubby told me, that drugs are being run out of the Angus Avenue Men's Shelter. And that a man, Jake Stone, runs both the shelter and the drug operation."

"That's hearsay. Do you have anything concrete?"

Cynthia shook her head. "You know I'm not a bleeding heart. And you know my instincts are good."

Steve leaned close to Cynthia and twirled a strand of her hair around his finger. "Your instincts are good in certain areas. In others, they stink; otherwise you'd still be going out with me."

"Will you at least check out Stone?"

Steve shrugged and released her hair. "Okay, for old-time's sake."

"And I get the story—an exclusive," she said, lowering her voice.

"You know I can't give you that," he whispered in her ear. "But I'll see you get our press releases a full half hour before anyone else. And . . . if you're really nice, I'll give you tons of off-the-record stuff."

Cynthia laughed and pushed Steve away. When she did, she caught sight of Jonathan's face, and watched it change as understanding washed over him.

Then he walked away.

Cynthia's ear was numb from pressing the phone against it. She had asked Jonathan if she could use his office phone and he had consented without waiting for the explanation she was so anxious to give. That was twenty minutes ago and she was still on the phone with Bernie discussing the morning events, and running out of arguments.

"Bernie, you've got to let me stay."

"Not on your life! Let Steve handle it from here. You can still do your story. Maybe make it a series, break it into two or three parts. And we'll scoop the other papers. But that's where it ends. Forget Jones and Bodkins. And most of all, forget you. Go home, and I mean back to your apartment in North Oberon. I'm giving you a vacation day, then tomorrow I want you at your terminal pounding out a Pulitzer. I want the first part to be an exposé on the homeless, give the usual stats, detail the trends, what's new, what's old. In Part Two, you'll put a face on it. Here's where you talk about the guy who someone tried to kill this morning, and his two friends. Then if Steve gets lucky and finds anything on this Stone character, we'll do a Part Three."

"Bernie, for your information the man who nearly died has a name. And he was my friend."

"Sorry. I know this assignment bit you in ways you hadn't expected. All the more to pull back and let Steve handle it. The best thing you can do for your friend now is to come in tomorrow and write a masterpiece."

"I just wish I could shake the thought that someone tried to kill Stubby because of me." Cynthia sank lower in the desk chair. "Because of this story."

"You didn't mess up this guy's life and you didn't make him live on the street, so don't go beating yourself up. Just try to bring some good out of it. Am I getting through to you, Wells?"

What would Bernie think if he knew the truth?

"You know what street people say? 'You can't spell bum without *u* in it.'"

Cynthia looked around her room for the last time. She didn't know why she had that feeling she always got when she left a hotel and was certain she'd forgotten something, because this time she was leaving everything behind. After the paramedics wheeled Stubby out, she had showered and put on clean jeans and a T-shirt. Then she had taken Stubby's poem from her night stand and shoved it in her pocket. All the rest—the robe and nightgown Miss Emily had loaned her, the assorted clothes she had taken from the stockroom, the four layers of clothes she had come to the mission in, and her sheets and towels—she had hauled to the basement and run through the washers and dryers. Now, they sat folded in piles on her bed.

Sadness pierced her. Why had she let everyone get so close? She took a deep breath.

She'd get over it.

She'd go back to her apartment, tuck herself into a familiar routine, get involved in another story. In a few weeks, life would return to normal and she'd forget . . . and so would they.

But did she really want to go back to normal?

She walked to the entrance of her room, turned and looked one last time, then closed the door behind her. She had said her "goodbyes" to Miss Emily, but she still needed to say them to Effie and . . . Jonathan.

Especially Jonathan.

He must feel like she had played him for a sap. She certainly reinforced the image of the hardboiled reporter.

Nice going, Wells.

When Cynthia opened the door to Effie's Day Care, she could see Effie was up to her eyeballs. One of the kids was crying, another was throwing up. And Daisy was hanging onto Effie for dear life.

"These kids are sick. I think they got fevers," Effie said, looking desperate.

"Anything I can do?" Cynthia watched Effie spread blankets on the floor and herd her little patients onto them. When Effie shook her head Cynthia decided to say her 'good-bye' in a note. Then she headed for Jonathan's office.

She rapped on the door. No answer. When she opened it she was disappointed to see the room empty. *Another "good-bye" note, Wells?*

She headed toward the kitchen and straight for Miss Emily. "Where's Jonathan?"

"He left."

"He left the mission?"

Miss Emily nodded. "He said he had errands to do."

Cynthia frowned. "That doesn't sound right. He knew I was leaving and . . . ."

"And what? You expected him to give you a going away party?"

"It's not like you to be sarcastic."

"Not everything's about you, child. If you had seen the look on his face when he left, you'd know the man was troubled. Right now, he has the weight of this mission on his shoulders. Strange things are going on here. Makes me think of Reverend Graves—what happened to him—things you know nothing about. And you're not the only one who cares about Stubby, you know. My guess is that Jonathan needed to be alone with the Lord."

Cynthia watched Miss Emily plunge her hands in dishwater, watched her scrub and rinse, then scrub some more. Cynthia had been wrong this morning for criticizing Miss Emily. It was obvious she was greatly troubled over Stubby. It was equally obvious that her kitchen, her pots and pans, her paring knives and cutting boards were all therapy.

"I'm sorry. For a reporter, I can be slow at getting the picture. Tell him 'good-bye' for me, will you?"

Miss Emily grabbed a dishtowel and dried her hands. "Haven't you learned anything? After people have opened their hearts to you, you have to give them their proper due."

"Fine . . . I'll say goodbye to him myself."

Cynthia rushed down the street to where the cabbie said he would meet her. She had called three cab companies and none of them would drive to Skid Row. She had one more block to go, and quickened her pace. As she passed a graffiti-covered mailbox, Cynthia saw a policeman walking his beat and recognized him as the one she had gone to for help after the mugging. She could hardly believe that was only two weeks ago.

It seemed like a lifetime.

She slowed down. After a moment's hesitation, she approached the cop. "Excuse me, officer, could you tell me where the City-Wide cab stand is?"

The officer smiled. "Sure, Miss. Just up one block and left. You'll see their orange sign about twenty yards in."

Cynthia stared into his eyes and returned his smile. "Thank you."

He responded with a slight gesture as though tipping his hat. *She wasn't invisible anymore.*

Jonathan Holmes strolled the perimeter of the glass factory, heading toward The Gorge. He had been walking up and down the industrial strip hoping to put his troubled mind to rest, hoping to connect with the Prince of Peace. But peace eluded him.

Something was very wrong at the mission. First, the attempt on Cynthia's life, then Stubby's overdose. It was as if an evil hand had ripped through God's hedge of protection.

But how?

The mission was God's. Jonathan was just the caretaker. He had given everything to the Lord, entrusted all to His mighty hand of provision and protection. Had he failed God in some way? Allowed the enemy to come in like a flood? And if so, where was God's promised standard?

At the edge of The Gorge, Jonathan dropped to his knees. People's lives were being changed at the mission. Just yesterday, two men fresh off the street accepted Christ after only a little encouragement from Jonathan. And the day before that four rough men, who cursed like longshoremen, were slain in the Spirit. And then there was the little girl with the clubfoot who was healed. All signs and wonders pointing to a new move of God. It just couldn't end now.

Oh, God, if the mission closes again, where will these people go? How will they come to know you?

Faces of homeless men Jonathan had gotten to know paraded before him. *Lord, please keep this mission open. I'll do whatever it takes, whatever you ask of me.* He closed his eyes and when he did, he pictured Cynthia. Bitterness filled his heart. She had used him— made a fool of him. She had made fools of them all.

"I know I'm to be a fool for Christ. But does that mean I must be a fool for everyone else, too?" Jonathan got off his knees and sat in the dirt.

I'll do whatever it takes, whatever you ask of me.

His words taunted him like a challenge. Would he meet it? He dropped his head into his hands, felt the warmth of his breath caress his face as though it were a caress from God Himself. What did it matter what Cynthia did? He wasn't in a position to judge or condemn her.

He lifted his head and gazed at the pit of rubble nearby. In the short time he had been at Beacon Mission he had seen more shattered lives, more broken dreams than in all his years combined. God had sent him to help people out of their own pit. Instead, he was sitting here whining about his bruised ego. "I'll be a fool in any way you want, Lord. Only, use me at the mission. Make the mission safe again, so people won't be afraid to come. Help the police get to the bottom of what's going on. And about Cynthia—I know she's hurting and needs You. She doesn't even understand how much she needs you. And . . . I forgive her. I don't know why she deceived me . . . deceived all of us at the mission, but I forgive her. And Lord . . . please forgive me, too."

Cynthia lounged on her floral couch studying the Waterford crystal paperweight that sparkled like an ice sculpture on her desk. It kept no papers at bay because they were all in color-coded folders and filed away in a bedroom cabinet. Aside from the paperweight, the only things on her desk were a six-inch solid brass table clock and a 5x7 Waterford Crystal picture frame containing a photo of Hawaii's Diamond Head which served as a reminder that this was a place she had promised herself she'd visit someday.

From where she sat, Cynthia could see a thin layer of dust coat the desk top, and was surprised she felt no compulsion to clean it.

Two weeks ago, it would have driven her crazy.

So, what was she going to do with herself for the rest of the day? Nap? Her throat still ached and she could use the rest. But she was too tense, too restless to sleep. Maybe she'd start that tortoiseshelling project she had wanted to do. It would transform her bathroom mirror. She could do the clear scumble and turpentine glaze today, then add the raw sienna tomorrow. If she did a process every day, she might finish in two weeks.

Two weeks.

About how long she had stayed at the mission.

She tapped her fingers on the sofa arm. Then stopped. Tortoiseshelling was the last thing she felt like doing. A nap. That made more sense. Bernie was expecting his Pulitzer-award-winning article tomorrow and she had better not disappoint. She looked at her desk clock. 2:30. Miss Emily was just finishing lunch clean up and about to start cooking dinner. Cynthia closed her eyes. That's what she wanted to do. Help Miss Emily make dinner—that and see Stubby's smiling face one more time.

Instead, she sat listening to the silence.

CHAPTER 13

Cynthia's fingers flew over the keyboard.

"Good to see you back," someone said, passing by.

"Thanks," she mumbled without looking up. People had been stopping by her desk all morning, asking questions, wishing her well, and making her feel they were pleased she had not ended up with a rope around her neck—dead. But all this warmth and sentiment had kept her from finishing her story. She slid lower in her chair as though that would make her harder to see, and tuned out the clamor and bustle that filled the newsroom.

She squinted at her monitor. Wiggly lines—like thin red worms—scoring dozens of words, told her Spell-Check was getting a workout. She didn't stop to correct. That would dam up the thoughts streaming from her mind and out her fingers like a geyser. Her fingers moved faster and faster in a mad effort to keep up. Then, in a Mozart-like finale, they crashed against the midnight-black keys and stopped.

"Don't tell me you've got Part One done already?"

Cynthia looked up in time to see Bernie Hobbs push her organized pile of notes aside and fill the spot with his ample bottom.

"So? You finished Part One?" he repeated.

"Just the draft."

"Let me see."

"Not yet. Needs more work."

Bernie looked at his watch. "Guess that day off did you good. I've never seen you work so fast."

"I gave it a lot of thought yesterday and organized everything in my head."

"Then you didn't rest?"

Cynthia straightened and watched Bernie's face cloud. "If you must know, I sat on my sofa for three hours—thinking."

"Thinking? You mean preparing for the article?"

"I mean *thinking*. About things. That kind of thinking."

Bernie hopped off the desk. "Roberta wants you to come over tomorrow night, and she won't take no for an answer."

"When someone you know almost dies, might still die, it makes you think. One minute you're here, the next you could be gone. It's unnerving."

"Cousin Harvey's coming for dinner and Roberta needs you to round things out."

"I keep picturing Stubby on that cold bathroom floor. How weird is that?"

"You coming, Wells?"

"You know, outside of the people at the mission, you're the only friend I have. I think that's sad, don't you?"

"Yeah, and that's what I'm talking about. You need to get out more. Socialize. Come for dinner tomorrow and get to know Cousin Harvey."

Cynthia folded her arms across her chest. "Tomorrow?"

"Yes. Can I tell Roberta you'll be there?"

Cynthia shook her head.

"Why not? You've just been complaining that you have no friends. You've got to make the effort, Wells."

"Nope. Not tomorrow. I have a date."

Bernie's face lit up in genuine delight. "No kidding? With who?"

"A preacher. And don't say another word. Not one word."

Cynthia's hand trembled as she dialed. Dinner would be over at the mission and things would be calming down. She held her breath and listened to the phone ring a half dozen times. Finally, Cynthia heard Miss Emily's familiar voice and found herself both relieved and disappointed.

"Miss Emily, it's Cynthia. How are you?"

"Missing you, child. Missing you. Lots of people have been asking about you. It seems you didn't say your proper goodbyes to anyone. Effie was really hurt."

"I know . . . that's why I'm calling. I thought I'd catch Jonathan. He's usually not busy this time of night and . . . I thought I'd try to explain."

"Aha. I'd say that was a good idea. And Effie? Are you planning to explain to her, too?"

"I thought I'd write a note. Maybe send a little something along for Daisy."

"Rather cowardly, but I suppose it's better than nothing. I was hoping you had came away with more. I've been praying for Jesus to break down those barriers you've erected. You're like a battleship, with all that armor plating."

"What's wrong with a letter?"

"Distance—a lot of tidy clean space without hugs or . . . tears. Paper and ink are poor substitutes, Cynthia."

Cynthia slumped against the pile of pillows on her bed. "Habits aren't easy to break."

"Almost impossible if you try doing it alone. That's what took Stubby so long to learn. Just don't wait till you're his age for this to sink in, okay?"

"How *is* Stubby?"

"Hanging by a thread. He needs all our prayers, now. So please pray because nothing is impossible for Jesus."

"I haven't prayed since I was five."

"Well, you have to start, because Stubby needs you."

"All right, if you think it might help, but I can't imagine God will bother to listen."

"You just do the asking and let God decide about the listening part."

Cynthia chuckled. "Miss Emily, you should have been a reporter. You're pushy enough."

"Good night, dear. I've got to finish shutting down the kitchen. You come visit us, okay?"

"Wait! What about Jonathan? I need to speak to him."

"Oh, he had an emergency. That's why he bounced his calls here, to the kitchen. He's expecting S&S to phone, and asked me to take it. He's shut up in his office behind closed doors—counseling a man who threatened to kill himself. The man's been living here two weeks now—a real quiet type—and all of a sudden, just like that, he went berserk. But that happens in a place like this. I'll tell Jonathan you called."

"Okay. And tell him he can ring me back no matter how late it is. I'll be up."

Cynthia covered the kitchen table with an industrial strength drop cloth, then carried the 3x2 foot mirror from the bathroom and placed it on top of the cloth. She knew it was crazy to start this project now—it was nearly eleven.

After she gathered her supplies, she mixed equal parts of scumble and turpentine and began glazing the mirror frame. She didn't know why she was so nervous. Maybe because she still hoped Jonathan would call.

How silly.

All she wanted to do was explain why she had come to the mission. She was sure he'd understand. And she wanted to do her explaining in person. Because contrary to what Miss Emily said, Cynthia didn't want the advantage of distance.

Not this time.

She couldn't forget the look on Jonathan's face as he watched her and Steve talk, as he understood she was a fraud and not homeless. And she had seen something else, something in his eyes—a look of humiliation that made her cringe. How like a fool he must have felt as he stood there remembering his offer to pay her legal fees. She had really made a mess of things. But this time she wasn't going to walk away, not without making it right.

She jumped when the phone rang, wiped her hands on a rag, then grabbed the cordless.

"Hello, Cynthia? It's Jonathan."

Cynthia detected weariness in his voice. His emergency must have drained him.

"Sorry I missed your call, but I was tied up."

"Yes, Miss Emily told me about it. Everything okay?"

"For now. I think. But it's hard to tell. The man is troubled . . . but there was something else . . . something I couldn't put my finger on. I'll have to pray about it. Anyway, what can I do for you?"

"Forgive me—forgive me for deceiving you."

"Well . . . sure. I've already done that."

"You *have*? I'm so . . . glad. Thank you. Still, I'd like a chance to explain, to tell you why I came to the mission in the first place. I know how busy you are but I had hoped you'd have dinner with me tomorrow night. I know a great steak place. And a neutral setting will make explanations easier."

"I don't know . . . ."

"Besides, I told my boss I had a date tomorrow night. Don't make a liar out of me." Cynthia listened to the stony silence on the other end. "You there?" She finally heard a soft chuckle.

"I don't date older women."

"Well, I don't date preachers. But this one time we can make an exception. What do you say?"

"Let me see what my schedule looks like tomorrow. I'll tell you by noon if I can make it. I'll let you know one way or the other . . . by noon."

"Okay."

"Was your boss imposing himself . . . making advances, I mean? Is that why you told him you had a date?"

Cynthia laughed. "No. He was trying to impose his wife's cousin. I had to think fast."

"Well, I'm glad you thought of me. I'll call you tomorrow. Good night, Cynthia."

When Cynthia hung up, she felt a foolish grin crawl across her face.

By twelve ten, Cynthia had filled two entire pages with stick men. By twelve twenty, she was glaring at the phone, daring it to ring.

"Are you in la-la land again, Wells?"

Cynthia ignored Bernie Hobbs as he pushed aside her four-pound Webster's New World College Dictionary which boasted right on the front cover that it was "the official dictionary of the Associated Press and America's Leading Newspapers."

"You're drawing stick men again, and that worries me."

"Go away. I'm thinking."

"Is that a way to talk to your boss? Even though you just finished writing one of the best pieces I've read in a long time—don't think your job is secure. Around here it's always 'what have you done for me lately?'"

Cynthia spun around in her chair, momentarily forgetting the phone. "You liked it?"

"It's good, Wells, and you know it. You've got plenty of facts and statistics, and still don't put the reader to sleep. And your seven point conclusion on homelessness is, well . . . I have to give it to you . . . inspired."

"Any surprises?"

Bernie shrugged. "Most of the causes were obvious: inferior education in poverty areas, mental illness, physical disabilities, addictions, insufficient low income housing, the decline of manufacturing jobs that pay enough to support a household. But the most startling were your stats on how much both the breakdown of the family and the welfare institution contribute to the problem. The increase in number of young people and mothers with children at shelters is staggering."

Cynthia pictured Effie with her damaged teeth. "Most of them have been battered for years and can't take it anymore."

"And what's this? Fifty percent, *fifty percent* of the homeless heads of households grew up in welfare families?"

"A sobering testimony that a lifetime of welfare promotes a cycle of dependency."

Bernie nodded. "Maybe another time I'll have you do a piece on our welfare system."

Cynthia swiveled around so she could face the phone. She looked at it a moment and sighed. *He wasn't going to call. He wasn't even going to have the decency to let her know he was standing her up.*

"I'm running this as a news feature. Just make sure Part Two is as good."

Cynthia picked up her pen and drew more stick men. "I've already started working on it."

"Really? Then where is it? Certainly not in front of you."

"It's in my head. It's all in my head."

"Then start getting it out of there and onto something I can read. By the way . . . Roberta's disappointed you can't make it tonight. I hope your preacher's worth missing out on her famous bouillabaisse and her infamous cousin."

"Infamous? Since when has Harvey become infamous?"

"Since he used the wrong overhead rates and messed up the second quarter and caused his company's stock to go down forty-two cents."

Cynthia giggled. "Poor Harvey."

"But I didn't tell Roberta it's a preacher keeping you from us tonight. She'd never believe it."

"It's not that kind of date. I owe him this courtesy. He was . . . they were all good to me at the mission." Cynthia looked down at her page of stick men to avoid looking at the smug expression she knew was on Bernie's face.

"Oil and vinegar don't mix. Remember that."

Cynthia opened her mouth to say something but the phone rang and she lunged for it. When she recognized the voice, her eyes drifted to her desk clock. *He was half an hour late but who was counting?*

"Cynthia, if you still want to meet me, I can make it."

"Great. How about seven at the Beef and Brew?"

"I'll be there with my appetite."

"This is my treat. So no show of force when the bill comes, okay?"

"In that case I'll be there with my *large* appetite."

Cynthia left the office early and headed downtown to the South Oberon Hospital. For the last two days she had called to check on Stubby, and each time she was told he was still in ICU . . . still critical. Today, a call wouldn't do. She needed to see for herself.

She parked and entered the lobby, then asked a silver-haired receptionist, in a pink-striped uniform, directions to ICU.

As Cynthia made her way there, her courage began to slip. What would Stubby look like? Full of tubes? Hooked up to all kinds of machines? She stopped and for a second considered turning around.

You going to send him a note, too, Wells? Maybe a get-well card?

She shook her head and tried picking up one foot. It felt rooted to the floor.

"May I help you?"

Cynthia turned to face a perky nurse with freckles. "I'm looking for Stubby White."

"You a relative?"

Cynthia didn't answer.

"This is ICU. Only family members allowed."

"Stubby doesn't have any family. I though I might . . . that is . . . I . . . ."

"Come to think of it you do look a lot like him. A granddaughter, I bet."

Cynthia smiled. "How clever of you to see the resemblance."

"I'll give you five minutes."

Cynthia nodded. "How is he?"

The nurse did a thumbs-down as she directed Cynthia to Stubby's room. That helped prepare her.

But not quite.

Tubing, carrying fluids in and out of his body, looked like a maze of miniature translucent tunnels. A respirator, that sounded irritating to Cynthia's ears, forced air into Stubby's lungs. Another machine monitored his heart. The room had that nauseating hospital smell and Cynthia thought she was going to gag. She looked down at Stubby's face. It was gray and rubbery-looking—like a death mask. She thought of her sister, and turned away.

She stood gazing at the floor, then slowing her eyes lifted. With a shy, awkward movement, she stretched out her hand and touched Stubby's—all purple and swollen from the IV. She sucked air to keep from crying. Stubby had lived a hard life, and now, just when things seemed like they were coming together for him, just when it seemed like he was turning the corner . . . this had to happen. It was so unfair. She pulled the nearby chair closer to the bed and leaned over until she could whisper in his ear.

It was now or never. This could be her last chance.

Her fingers brushed Stubby's veiny hand. "This is so hard to say. And I'm scared, Stubby. I'm so scared to tell you because I know this time forgiveness is impossible. And it breaks my heart because . . . I . . . love you."

Her fingers shook as she placed her hand on his. "You're my *friend*. And I don't have many. Yet all I do is disappoint you. And I'm going to disappoint you again." Her voice broke as tears rolled down her cheeks and dripped onto his hospital gown. "But I have to tell you. If I don't, this thing, this secret, this horrible secret is going to explode inside me. And it's important for you to know. You need to know it wasn't you. It wasn't you who killed Julia. It was *me*. And all this time I've let you take the blame."

"Sorry, you'll have to go now. I need to suction him." It was the cute, freckled-face nurse. "But you can come again another time. I'll put you on the 'family' list. You won't have any trouble getting in."

Cynthia released Stubby's hand and looked at his gray, rubbery face and wondered if there would be another time.

Jonathan Holmes had spent every spare moment of the day in prayer. His spirit was troubled and he didn't know why. Since counseling the suicidal Willie Tanner, Jonathan felt an uneasiness that wouldn't go away. He had asked the Lord to show him the cause, but all he got was *Trust Me*.

Something wasn't right about Tanner, something Jonathan couldn't put his finger on. He wished the Lord would just spell it out like He sometimes did. That was easier than trusting. Trusting made his carnal man rise up and balk. No matter how many times Jonathan had tried putting him to death, burying him and living totally by the Spirit, it was these "Trust Me" times that showed Jonathan how very much alive that man still was.

Even this meeting tonight with Cynthia had Jonathan worried. He had not felt a check in his spirit when he asked the Lord for direction. Still . . . he was concerned. He had the same weaknesses and foibles as any other man. Was he foolish to put himself in this situation? To meet with a woman who didn't know God? Who showed little interest in knowing Him? To meet with a woman he found incredibly attractive? Who made his stomach queasy and his breath catch?

He prayed again for direction, then got the familiar command. *Trust Me.*

Jonathan thought he'd clean his desk before getting ready to meet Cynthia. When the phone rang, he quickly picked it up thinking perhaps she was calling to cancel. The deep voice at the other end told Jonathan he was wrong.

"Pastor Holmes, Bill Rivers here. Just wanted to check in and see how things were going."

Jonathan's heart sank. Had Charles Angus heard about the trouble at the mission?

"Pastor Holmes? Did I catch you at a bad time?"

"No. Sorry. I was in the middle of a pile of papers."

"I've called several times. I was surprised when I didn't get a call back."

Jonathan groaned. Between the attempt on Cynthia's life and Stubby in critical condition, he had responded to few of his calls. "Things have been hectic here. I'm afraid I'm a little behind."

"Mr. Angus likes to keep abreast of things."

He knows. He knows what happened. He knows about Cynthia and Stubby.

"I appreciate his interest. We're all grateful for his generosity."

"Yes, well . . . Mr. Angus *is* a generous man. But like I said, he wants to be kept in the loop. And there are a few things that need clearing up."

Please God, don't let him close the mission.

"He's troubled that you've departed from Reverend Gates' policy by allowing women to stay at the mission. He sees potential problems."

"There are so many more homeless women now I felt I had no choice."

"I'm not criticizing. Not at all. Please don't think that. Mr. Angus just wants to be sure the new arrangements are working. But he also hopes you are sheltering more men in your mission than women."

"Yes, twice the number."

"Because the homeless men are his priority."

Jonathan wrinkled his forehead. "I don't understand. Do I or do I not have full control over this mission and that includes the allocation of beds?"

"Pastor, there's nothing to understand. This is just a check-up call. Nothing more. There'll be others from time to time. I thought that was understood. I believe Mr. Angus spelled it out quite clearly."

"Of course and I've no problem with it. It's just that . . . ."

"I'll report there'll be no further cutbacks on men. That you will continue to allow the same number to stay at the facility in the future."

"Yes. Two floors of men, one floor of women. I've no plans to change that at this time. But should it become necessary in the . . . ."

"It's been a pleasure talking with you."

When the phone went dead, Jonathan held it and shook his head.

After leaving the hospital and Stubby, Cynthia wasn't certain she was up to meeting Jonathan. Maybe she'd cancel and make it for another night. She had entertained that thought the entire ride home. Even after she made her customary juice drink and relaxed on her floral couch for twenty minutes, she still opted for a no-show. It wasn't until she thought of Miss Emily's words that she changed her mind.

After people have opened their hearts to you, you have to give them their proper due.

Cynthia swirled the remainder of her carrot juice in the glass and watched it coat the sides orange. Okay . . . she'd see this through. She'd meet Jonathan and explain things, make the proper apologies. She'd do the decent thing . . . up close and personal, just how Miss Emily liked it. When she thought of Stubby, when she pictured his gray face and lifeless body, she hesitated.

Up close and personal wasn't all it was cracked up to be.

But neither were letters.

She drained her juice, then carried her empty glass into the kitchen, rinsed it and placed it in the dishwasher. Then she wiped down the counter, even though it was spotless. Already her mind was on what she would wear—something casual but not flirty, something tasteful but not frumpy. Something that wouldn't embarrass a preacher.

A preacher.

Wouldn't her co-workers have a good laugh over that one? She was glad Bernie was tightlipped.

She rummaged through her closet for ten minutes, then settled on a simple broadcloth skirt that fell below her knees, and a hyacinth-colored square-neck tank, over which she'd wear a hyacinth-colored crewneck cardigan with three-quarter sleeves and turn-back cuffs. And her only jewelry would be a pair of pearl earrings. She tried to ignore Steve Bradley's voice in her head—the comment he'd make every time he saw her wear this. *"That getup really shows off your curves!"* Well, what was she supposed to do? Wear a muumuu?

As she stepped into the shower, Cynthia couldn't help feeling a sense of wonder. It had been a long time since she dressed for a man. And now she was making all this fuss over one she had no interest in whatsoever.

Or did she?

As Cynthia walked into the packed dining room of the Beef and Brew, she was glad she had made reservations. She had never seen it so crowded. She glanced back at the man following her and smiled. He seemed comfortable and relaxed.

Cynthia was glad when the waitress directed them to a corner table, away from the hustle and bustle. It would make talking easier. They each took their seat and a menu.

"It just struck me, when I was here last it was also a woman who bought me dinner." Jonathan flashed a cheerful smile. "Guess this must be my restaurant."

"Who treated you? Your saintly grandmother?"

"My saintly aunt."

Cynthia laughed. "Tonight it's compliments of a heathen. I hope the food will taste just as good."

They spent a few quiet moments searching the menu, then gave the waitress their order. It wasn't until she returned with a glass of water with lemon for each of them that Cynthia noticed a change in Jonathan's face.

"You're wondering why I went to this length to make my apology?"

"No, I'm wondering who you are. After seeing you with Detective Bradley, my guess is an undercover cop."

"Cop? Then Miss Emily didn't tell you." Cynthia laughed and drew a stick man on her frosted water glass. "No, not a cop; a reporter for the *Oberon Tribune*. My name is Cynthia Wells."

"*Wells?* As in Nanny Scam Wells?"

"The one and only."

Jonathan took a sip of water. "You sure had me fooled."

"I know . . . and I'm sorry. And that's why I wanted you to come tonight. So I could explain." Cynthia watched Jonathan put down his glass, watched his hair fall over one eye, watched his jaw clench. "I wish now that I had come to you, in the beginning, and told you the truth. But I didn't know you then and I couldn't trust that you'd let me come as an undercover reporter."

Jonathan's cheerful smile reappeared. "You might have been right. In some ways I'm a little green. I might not have seen the wisdom of your disguise."

"No one would talk to me as a reporter. I tried. I realized if I didn't disguise myself I'd never get anywhere. Over the years, I've developed good instincts. There's a story here. I know it."

Cynthia squirmed in her chair when she saw the look on Jonathan's face. His expression was too much like that of a preacher getting ready to deliver a sermon. "I know that sounds callous—me just thinking about getting my story. But there's more to it. Three people have been killed on Skid Row, all within two months of each other. And the police aren't motivated to dig into any of them. I figured if I could piece together what happened, then, in a way, justice would be served."

"Was that your motive? Justice?"

"Partly . . . that and sensing a story and wanting to report it."

"What part was more important? Justice or your story?"

Cynthia focused her eyes on her glass and drew another stick man. "My story." When she looked up, she was shocked by the tender understanding that radiated from Jonathan's eyes. "But that was before, before I got to know you and Miss Emily, Effie and . . . Stubby. Now I want to write something that will help, that will do some good. Maybe my story will make Skid Row a little safer."

"I'm glad you've come to care about us, somewhat, anyway. It's amazing how a place can grip you. When the Lord first directed me there, I was sure I had heard wrong. After I realized I hadn't, I was devastated."

Cynthia's eyes widened.

"Now, I'd be devastated if the Lord told me to leave."

As the waitress placed their heaping plates of steak and potatoes before them, Cynthia studied Jonathan. "You seem to care so deeply for the people at the mission. I had no idea that it had been a struggle for you."

"You think preachers don't struggle like everyone else?"

"But you love these people."

Jonathan nodded. "Yes. Now. But not at first. God had to soften my heart. I still struggle with one thing, though. I find it hard to accept the fact that some homeless won't even try to help themselves or won't work. I guess that was what made me notice you right away. You had a work ethic." Jonathan laughed. "Now, I know why. *Cynthia Wells.* How unbelievable is that?"

Cynthia felt her face flush. "I guess I am a bit of a workaholic. But if God sent you to the mission, won't He also give you the necessary ability and patience?"

"I could use more patience for sure." Jonathan smiled. "You know, for a heathen, you've got a lot of Godly insight."

Cynthia picked up the wooden-handled steak knife and cut into her prime rib, surprised at how pleased she felt by his compliment.

Cynthia pulled into a parking space next to her apartment still thinking about her "date" with Jonathan. After her explanation, the rest of the evening was spent in discussing the mission and some of Jonathan's ideas, in talking about her story angle, and about some of the people they had come to know, especially Stubby. They had even managed a few jokes, had a few laughs. She was pleased she went. Miss Emily was right. It was more gratifying saying things in person.

Her dashboard clock told her she had been out a lot longer than planned. She'd head straight to bed. She locked the car, then strolled toward the sidewalk. That's when she saw him, leering at her from the front seat of a beat-up, blue Ford.

Skinner.

What was he doing here? It seemed he had purposely parked under one of the high-mast lights so she could see his face. She hadn't noticed anyone following her, which meant he knew where she lived and had been waiting. Her hand went to her throat. It was still tender and discolored. Her heart raced as he rolled down the window and stuck out his head.

"You've been causing a lot of trouble. The people I work for don't appreciate that. The cops are all over the place. Like maggots. They think something's rotten at the shelter, all on account of you. But they ain't gonna find anything. They never find anything. And when the dust settles, I'm gonna be paying you a visit. Count on it. From now on, wherever you are, I won't be far behind. And when

I'm finished doing what I plan to do, nobody's gonna recognize you." Skinner laughed as he turned on the ignition.

Cynthia could still hear him laughing as the Ford sped away.

CHAPTER 14

"Are you out of your mind?"

Cynthia sat next to Detective Steve Bradley's desk watching him turn various shades of purple.

"Why did you wait 'til this morning to come in? Suppose he had come back and made good his threat?"

Cynthia's hands were folded on her lap. She had taken pains with her hair that fell in soft yellow waves around her face, and in choosing her navy-blue Armani suit—all in an effort to look more composed than she was.

"You took some chance," Steve mumbled, his face still crimson.

"Last night was just meant to scare, and it worked. I hardly slept."

"Next time, don't wait!"

Cynthia nodded. "What can you do?"

"Get a restraining order. Maybe lean on him a little. First, let's make sure we're talking about the same guy. There's only one person I know named Skinner. But I need you to ID him."

Steve left the room and came back carrying a large album of mug shots. He flipped through it and stopped. "This the guy?" His finger stabbed the photo of a hollow-cheeked man with a scar running down the right side of his face.

The hair on Cynthia's arms bristled. "Yes. That's him."

Steve slammed the book shut, then shoved a form across his desk. "File a complaint. Then you'll have to go before a judge to get a restraining order. I'll do my best to rush it through."

"Who is he? Really."

"A punk."

"Steve, I want to know."

Steve toyed with his ball-point pen. Click-click, click-click, click-click. "Okay . . . he's a killer. Someone we've never been able to pin anything on. But he has a bad rep, and is supposed to be good with a knife. He's connected with the local drug trade."

"That's just what Stubby said. Do you think it was Skinner who tried to strangle me?" Her hand traveled to her throat. The bruising was nearly gone and it barely hurt when she swallowed. But since returning to her apartment, she had started sleeping with a light on. "Was it Skinner, you think?"

"No."

"Why not?"

Steve leaned across his desk and squinted the way he did when he was all business. "Because it was an inside job—someone living at the mission. Same with Stubby."

"So now you don't think it was an overdose?"

"No."

"Since when?

"Since we got the doctor's report. You said to look for bruises, signs of a struggle and we did."

Cynthia felt the beginning of a tension headache working its way up her neck. "Thanks, Steve. I just couldn't believe Stubby had gone back to drugging."

"You know what this means—the mission is a dangerous place. And Pastor Holmes has a killer on his hands."

"Will you warn Jonathan? He needs to know." Her temples began to pound.

Steve nodded.

"What have you found at the Men's Shelter?"

"Nothing. The shelter's clean."

Cynthia sat on the edge of her seat, squared her shoulders and pulled on her suit jacket—transitioning from victim to reporter. "You're not going to quit are you? You're not going to let it drop, not after what happened to me and Stubby, not after Skinner's threat?"

"If I could prove there's a connection between what happened to you and Stubby and the Men's Shelter, then the answer would be 'no.' But I can't. I'm not saying there isn't one; I'm just saying that right now, I can't prove it. On the other hand, this could be a simple case of a crazed homeless guy who's flipped and hurts people."

"Come on, Steve, you don't believe that."

"It doesn't matter what I believe. I'm a cop and I need to build a case on evidence. So far, I've got nothing so I have to drop the investigation."

"Drop it!"

"Harassment. Ever heard of it? I can't continue to pursue a case without a reason, not unless I'm willing to be accused of harassment. Which I'm not."

"And what about Skinner? Doesn't his threat mean there's something very wrong at that shelter?"

"Probably. But the only thing I can legitimately pursue is your complaint and your request for an order of protection. That doesn't mean I can't keep my eyes open, or keep asking questions. It just means that the official investigation of the Angus Avenue Men's Shelter is closed."

"Ever hear the expression, 'where there's smoke there's fire?'"

"Sure, Wells, but in my world if I want a conviction, I need to see the fire."

Jonathan entered the main room of the mission in time to see a man flying through the air. Another man followed—then a tangle of arms and legs, as fists and feet connected. There was the sound of fabric ripping as the sleeve of a shirt was torn off. Then a chair was kicked over. Jonathan looked around for help and saw Willie Tanner slouching in a corner. He motioned for him to come, then the two of them separated the brawlers.

"What's the problem?" Jonathan said, smelling alcohol.

"This guy's hand was in my pocket!"

"No it wasn't!" Came the denial, as the man used his sleeve to wipe the blood from his nose.

"Fighting's not allowed in here." Jonathan eyed the first man, the one who didn't look like he was able to stand on his own.

"They already know that," Willie Tanner said, grabbing the man with the bloody shirt. "Cause it's the same everywhere. All the shelters throw out their troublemakers otherwise there'd be chaos."

Jonathan studied the battered men. "How long have you two been staying here?"

"Less than a week," said the one who didn't seem so drunk.

"But long enough to know the rules." Jonathan picked up the overturned chair and settled the staggering man on it. "What Willie says is true. Fighting is grounds for expulsion. We can't maintain order without accountability. So here's what I'll do. I'll let you pick the punishment. You two can leave now, or you can unload the shipment of groceries that just came in. Which is it?"

The man with the bloody nose glared at Jonathan. "I was leaving anyhow. Can't stomach the thought of having to sit through another one of your Bible sermons you make us listen to."

Jonathan watched the man walk out. Then he looked at the one in the chair. "What about you? Will it be black coffee and a few hours of labor or . . . ."

"Coffee . . . coffee and work." The man flopped backward like a rag doll. "I've got nowhere else to go."

When Jonathan headed for the kitchen, Willie Tanner followed. "He's a troublemaker, that one. I've seen him before. In other shelters. You've made a bad bargain."

Jonathan poured coffee into a white ceramic mug. "Thanks for helping back there." Out of the corner of his eye, he studied Willie. His shirttail was out, his greasy hair formed spikes on his head, his blackened hands looked like they hadn't been washed in days. And yet, it was unmistakable what the Lord was directing him to do.

"You know, Willie, it's been hard with Stubby in the hospital. I could use an assistant. The pay's not much, minimum wage, but steady, and you'd be on the first floor with staff which means access to the refrigerator and all Miss Emily's goodies. I'm afraid those are the only incentives I can offer. Think you'd be interested?" He watched Willie shift his weight, then pull on one ear.

"I . . . don't know. Suppose I get one of my urges?"

"Suppose you do. Would you try to hurt anyone?"

"No. Just myself."

"Then that settles it. You help me out and I'll help you out. Whenever you get an urge, you come to me and we'll see it through together."

Willie let go of his ear and grinned. "It's been a long time since I've been on the clock."

Jonathan handed him the mug. "Consider yourself hired. Now, give this to our friend out there, then help him unload the truck."

Willie took the mug, turned to leave and stopped. "We'll do it on a trial basis. Give it a few days and see. No guarantees, okay?"

"Okay." Jonathan watched Willie walk out of the kitchen hoping he had heard the Lord correctly.

"I want you to come stay with Roberta and me. And no argument, Cynthia. This is serious."

Cynthia Wells sat facing Bernie's desk, thinking how little she had appreciated his friendship before—how much she had taken it for granted. "I'm touched. But it's not necessary. The judge has granted the restraining order and Steve will lean on Skinner. I don't think Skinner will be stupid enough to try anything, now."

"And what if he does?"

"My news feature said nothing incriminating about the Shelter. And Steve told me the investigation was over. What is there to be gained by hurting me?"

"Didn't you tell me Skinner *enjoys* hurting people? That's reason enough."

"I have to admit that at first I was scared . . . okay, make that *terrified,* but I've had time to think. I can't allow some creep to rearrange my life. I've been threatened before. You know that. It comes with the territory. I can't start cowering, now. And I can't live with you forever."

"I . . . suppose not." The corpulent editor drummed his fingers on the desk, his cheeks bulging from a mouthful of jellybeans. "I just thought it would be a good idea if you stayed with us a few days, that's all."

Cynthia smiled, He looked like a big Saint Bernard with his floppy hair and large brown eyes and sweet manner. "Did I ever thank you for all your kindness? For always being there? For being my . . . friend?" She leaned over and covered Bernie's hand with hers.

"The offer was for our spare room." Bernie squeezed her hand before pulling away. "Don't make it sound like some kind of adoption."

"I'm just trying to say that I appreciate you, that's all."

"Okay, you said it, now back to work."

As Cynthia walked out of Bernie's office, she saw a Cheshire-cat-like smile on his face.

Jonathan rose from his desk when Detective Bradley entered.

"Thanks for seeing me on such short notice."

Jonathan shook Steve's hand then gestured for him to take the vacant chair. "You said you had news. I'm guessing it has something to do with Stubby White."

The detective's muscular body filled the seat. "Actually, there are a few things I need to discuss, and yeah, Stubby White's one of them. I hear he's still in a coma."

Jonathan frowned. "Yes."

"Too bad. He could tell us who tried to kill him."

"Then it was attempted murder, like Cynthia said?"

Steve nodded.

"Any idea why someone would want him dead?"

"A man with a past has enemies. Especially a man whose past involved drugs. But the thing you need to know is that whoever did it is living at the mission."

Jonathan frowned. "How did you arrive at that conclusion?"

"We suspected it right from the start. For one thing, none of the windows and doors showed signs of forced entry, and considering that at night you lock your place up tighter than a vault, it would be impossible for anyone to get in, meaning the killer was already inside."

"Yes . . . that makes sense."

"We think it's likely that the same person who tried to kill Stubby White also tried to kill Cynthia Wells."

Jonathan tensed. "Any clue who that might be?"

Steve pulled a photo from his jacket pocket. "Ever see this character?"

Jonathan took the picture and studied it. "Looks like the man Stubby threw out of the mission for carrying a weapon."

"A knife?"

"Yes, come to think of it. And Stubby called him, Skinner."

"Yeah, that's one of his street names. He's got others. Seems he was waiting in the parking lot for Cynthia when she got home last night after she left you."

Jonathan's heart jumped. "Is she all right?" He saw a strange look cross the detective's face.

"Yeah. He only threatened her. And you know Cynthia. Won't admit he almost scared the dinner out of her. But other than that, she's fine."

Jonathan leaned his elbows on the desk. "You'll give her protection, won't you? Stubby said this man was dangerous."

"He's a lunatic, but not the lunatic we're looking for in connection with what happened at the mission. Cynthia said he never slept there."

"No, he never did."

"Any other candidates come to mind?"

"Sixty-five percent of the men in shelters or missions test positive for drugs. Others have drinking and gambling problems. Still others are mentally ill. There are no lack of candidates here, Detective."

Steve's lips pursed. "I don't know why you bother with any of them."

Jonathan thought of Stubby. "Ever hear of Divine Appointment?"

"No, and I don't want to. I'd rather hear about you and Cynthia. Is there something going on between you two?"

Jonathan was shocked into silence and just shook his head.

"Good. Then you won't mind if I play in that yard?"

Again Jonathan shook his head

Steve rose. "Okay. That's about it. I just wanted to let you know what's going on, and to tell you to watch your back. You've got a killer living at the mission, Preacher."

Cynthia was having difficulty retrieving the bulk of Part Two from her head. It had sounded so smooth and poignant when she first conceived it. Now, it came out in fits and starts like artist's oils from a clogged tube. Her plan was to focus on Stubby's life, with Manny and Turtle as shadow characters. Then pull the three threads together to show the trials, dangers and often tragic ending to a homeless life.

Trouble was, Stubby's life had turned into an open-ended promise, at least until someone tried to terminate it. Day after day, she had watched him, seen a joy that defied understanding and the kind of hope that often eluded even the young. The pieces were not fitting together. And the only way she could make them fit was if she included what Stubby called his "Divine Appointment." But how could she when she didn't believe in such things? Maybe it didn't matter, as long as *he* did. Didn't children sleep better at night when they went to bed believing in fairy tales and that everything always ended "happily ever after?"

Not always. Fairy tales were also full of monsters and giants.

Cynthia picked up her pen and began drawing stick figures. She wasn't ready to write this. She needed to do more thinking. She threw down her pen. Thinking was always easier behind the wheel of her car. And it would be good to get away from the noise and confusion of the newsroom . . . away from the watchful eyes of Bernie Hobbs. He had been behaving like a mother hen, stopping by her desk in regular intervals as if to make sure Skinner had not somehow penetrated the building. No, what she needed now was not a babysitter, but an open highway. She grabbed her purse just as the phone rang.

"*Oberon Tribune*, Cynthia Wells speaking."

"Well, Praise God, you don't sound like someone who's been terrorized."

"Jonathan?"

"Detective Bradley just left. He told me about Skinner. Not exactly the way to end the evening on a high note. Now it looks like our little 'date' will be memorable for the wrong reason."

Cynthia laughed. "I'm glad Steve came. I asked him to warn you."

"Well, he did. I'm still having a hard time adjusting, though. I guess I don't want to believe that someone here is a . . . ."

"I know. Are you looking at everyone differently, now, trying to guess who it is?"

"No. I've been asking God to show me."

Cynthia was quiet.

"Keep me in prayer and the mission, too, okay?"

"*Me?* You're the preacher. You should be praying for me."

"I am, Cynthia. From the moment I met you."

"Well . . . thanks . . . I'll try to . . . say a prayer for you, too."

"Listen, if you ever need to talk, if you get lonely or scared, call me, okay?"

"Nobody wants to listen to someone bellyaching."

"I do. I'm serious, Cynthia. You call me anytime. You've been through a lot these last few weeks. You've seen a lot and I know God has stirred your heart in ways you never expected, especially with Stubby. This is not an empty invitation."

"Thanks." Cynthia took a moment to clear her throat. "By the way, how is Stubby?"

"No change. I plan on going there later. Will I see you?"

Cynthia felt her color drain. "No . . . I'm busy . . . it's not a good time."

"That's okay. Stubby would understand."

"I appreciate the call, Jonathan. Thank you." She could hear soft breathing on the other end. "Was there anything else?"

"I just wanted to tell you, it's not your fault what happened to Stubby. You can't blame yourself."

Cynthia swallowed hard. She had been too cowardly to return to the hospital after her partial confession. She still couldn't believe she had admitted so much. What was she thinking? What if he actually *heard* her? Some claim people in comas hear what is said around them. It was seeing all those tubes and machines, seeing Stubby so gray and rubbery that dismantled her defenses. She couldn't let that happen again.

"It's okay, Cynthia."

"I think about it a lot—about being responsible for what happened. But that's not why I won't go see him. It's something else. Something that happened long ago." *Now, why had she said that?*

"You want to talk about it?"

"I don't think so."

"Okay. When you do, call me. Anytime."

Jonathan sat next to the hospital bed watching Stubby's chest rise and fall. Tubes were everywhere, going in and out of machines that filled the room with a low, steady noise. *Lord, you were wounded for our transgressions, You were bruised for our iniquities; the chastisement of our peace was upon You; and with Your stripes we are healed.*

Jonathan thought he saw Stubby's hand move, then decided it was his imagination. He had been here for over an hour. He leaned back in the chair and closed his eyes. He was tired, but he'd sit, just a while longer, and continue praying.

Cynthia leaned over the kitchen table carefully painting diagonal marks of raw sienna with a small brush. She stepped back and looked at the mirror frame. So far so good. Another half hour and she'd start with the burnt sienna and then move on to the burnt umber. Within two hours she'd be using her pasting brush to blend the colors together. Then she'd use a natural sea sponge dipped in turpentine to create a grain, a grain she would soften by once again applying her pasting brush. She doubted she'd have time to deepen the tortoiseshelling, to coat a toothbrush with black oil paint, thinned slightly with turpentine, then spatter the frame. The other processes would keep her busy all night. With any luck she'd finish them before the Eleven O'clock News.

Instead of spending the evening with Stubby.

Jonathan tossed his shirt and trousers in the hamper and yawned. It was late. He needed to get some sleep. As he went to the sink to wash he thought of Stubby. The burden to continue praying was still there. But Jonathan also wanted to seek the Lord about the information Detective Bradley had given him today. Maybe he'd try to stay up another hour.

He was getting ready to brush his teeth when the phone rang. Reluctantly, he answered it.

"Aunt Adel, what are you doing up? It's nearly midnight."

"Well, dearest love, you're impossible to get a hold of. During the day you're doing Bible studies, counseling, loading and unloading trucks, and at night, more of the same I imagine. Except for last night. That's why I called."

Jonathan put down his toothbrush. "What about last night?"

"I heard all about it from Gertie."

"Gertie?"

"She heard all about it from a friend who saw you. At the Beef and Brew. Gertie said you were with *Cynthia Wells* and she was in quite an excitable state."

"Who? Cynthia Wells?"

"No! Gertie. Gertie said her friend told her you were dressed and shaved and looked . . . *wonderful.* Gertie said that all her prayers and those of the prayer chain must be working, because it seems like you've turned yourself around."

Jonathan headed for the bed and stretched out. "I thought you were through caring about what Gertie said. I thought that was all over."

"Well . . . nearly, Dearest. I've been praying about it and asking God for help, and I'm getting better. When was the last time I called and talked about Gertie?"

"Ah . . . ."

"Exactly! It's been so long you can't even remember. So you must admit I've been quite self-controlled and mature."

"If you say so."

"That's why I think I'm entitled to ask a favor. One small teensy-weensy favor."

"Anything I can do, Aunt Adel, you know I'll do it." He heard what sounded like a sigh of relief.

"Well, that's what I was hoping you'd say. Because you know I don't ask for many favors. In fact, I can't remember the last time I did ask."

Jonathan smiled. "Stop with the guilt trip, Aunt Adel. Just tell me what it is."

"Gertie said her absolute favorite reporter in the world is Cynthia Wells, and she was hoping you could introduce her, maybe even have dinner together, the three of you . . . or I could come, too, if that would make you more comfortable."

"Out of the question."

"Why!"

"Because . . . I don't know her well enough . . . and because it's totally inappropriate. I can't ask someone like her to come to dinner with my aunt and ex-secretary."

"Why!"

"Because . . . it's going to put me in an awkward position."

"Like you've put me in these past few months?"

Jonathan sat up. "I know it's been rough on you, and I'm sorry."

"I'll never ask you for anything, again, I promise, but please Jonathan, grant me this one little indulgence."

"I want you to ask me for things. That's not the issue. We're family and should be able to count on each other."

"Exactly. I knew you'd understand."

"Has it really been that bad?"

"Worse, dearest love. Much worse. She's been an absolute beast. God forgive me for saying it. I know I shouldn't look to justify myself, that I should let God justify me, but I'm flesh and blood, Jonathan, not a plaster saint. Meeting Cynthia Wells, going out to dinner with you and her, well . . . it will stop Gertie in her tracks. She wouldn't dare say anything more about you. She'd stop all her nasty remarks and snide comments and . . . ."

"No she wouldn't. This isn't going to change Gertie. It's just going to slow her down a bit."

"So, you're saying you won't do it?"

"I'm saying you're looking for comfort in the wrong place."

"I know you're right." Aunt Adel's voice deflated. "But somehow that doesn't help. Thank you anyway, Dearest. I'm sorry to have troubled you. Kisses and hugs. Good night."

"When?"

"When what?"

"When do you and Gertie want to go to dinner with Cynthia Wells?"

"You're not joking are you? No, of course not. You'd never be so cruel. Well . . . anytime . . . anytime at all. Oh, my goodness! Wait 'til I tell Gertie."

"I can't promise anything. Remember that. But I'll see what I can do."

CHAPTER 15

Cynthia had been sitting at her keyboard for three hours and had exactly eight words to show for it: **You can't spell bum without *u* in it.**

Mentally, she had switched her lead three times, but when she committed each to paper they sounded wrong. She wasn't sure about this one, either. She stared at her monitor, mesmerized by the nearly blank screen. How was she ever going to fill it? Any minute, Bernie was going to come bounding over and ask, for the millionth time, how it was going.

Well, it wasn't.

Her phone rang, and Cynthia let it go on her machine. She half listened to her own voice as it spit out the automatic salutation. But when she heard Jonathan, she lunged for the receiver.

"I'm here," she shouted over the machine's message. "Don't hang up." When the recorder stopped, she heard Jonathan sigh. "Sorry about that. I'm screening calls today. I'm way behind with my article."

"Then I wouldn't keep you. I wanted to let you know that the hospital just called. Stubby's taken a turn for the worse. I'm not trying to make you feel guilty. You don't have to come. I just thought you should know, that's all."

Cynthia's throat tightened. "Thank you for telling me." Her palms dampened and the brow over her left eye twitched. "Of course I'll be there. I'll leave in a few minutes." She bit her tongue. *Why had she said that?* She no more wanted to go to the hospital than she wanted to continue sitting in front of a blank screen. But it was too late, now. If she didn't go, she'd lose all credibility with Jonathan.

She hung up, then sat staring at her monitor like a zombie. *Her prayers hadn't worked for her sister, either.* And now Stubby. How was she going to face it? The dying part, the burying part, the crying part, the *guilt* part? She shuddered when she felt a chill. Someone once told her you could feel death as it passed. But that was ridiculous. *Wasn't it?*

"How's it going, Wells?"

When she glanced up, Bernie's pleasant expression changed to one of concern.

"You look like you've just seen a ghost. What's wrong? That creep, Skinner, didn't call here, did he?"

Cynthia shook her head. "It's Stubby White. I think we're going to lose him." She felt Bernie's hand rest on her shoulder. With a shy, awkward movement, she reached up and covered it with hers.

All the way to the hospital, Cynthia tried thinking of viable reasons for turning around and heading back to the office, but couldn't. When she saw the huge brick and stucco building on the hill, her mouth went dry. As she pulled into the parking space, her head began to pound. And when she walked into the large, tiled entrance, her stomach felt like it had been given a-once-over by a bulldozer.

People die, Wells, and there's nothing you can do about it.

She headed for ICU and recognized the nurse from her first visit.

"You're Mr. White's granddaughter." The nurse winked. "Go right in." Her voice lowered. "I don't know how long he has left."

Cynthia mumbled, "thank you," and headed for Stubby's room. She stopped at the door when she saw Jonathan sitting by the bed. She was glad he was already here. It would make things easier. She avoided looking at Stubby, and crept in. When Jonathan glanced up with tear-filled eyes, she took a deep breath.

This was it.

"Is he . . . has he . . . ."

Jonathan rose and pushed his chair back so she could get closer to the bed. When she hesitated, he took her arm and drew her to him.

"Is he . . . dead?" she whispered.

Jonathan shook his head and smiled. "Something wonderful has happened. God has just told me He's going to heal Stubby. He reminded me that 'these signs will follow them that believe . . . they will lay hands on the sick, and they shall recover.' And I've just laid hands on Stubby and prayed for God to fulfill His word."

Cynthia was wedged between the bed and Jonathan, and having no avenue of escape, finally looked at Stubby. He appeared worse than the last time she saw him. His face was sunken and even grayer, his breathing labored and shallow. She glanced at the heart monitor and saw the irregular blips on the screen. Even her untrained eyes knew distress when they saw it. She twisted around to look at Jonathan, her insides knotted by both anger and fear.

"That's a cruel, crazy thing to say. Just look at him! He couldn't get closer to death without being there."

"When God tells me something, He's faithful to perform it. I'm called to walk by faith, Cynthia, not by sight."

"Well, I'm not!" She tried to get by him but couldn't, so she just eased herself onto the nearby chair and began massaging her temples. "I know you're not cruel, Jonathan. And I know you believe in what you say. But I don't understand your faith. And what's more, I don't want to. It . . . scares me."

"Why?"

"Because . . . it's irrational. I'm a reporter. I believe in what I can see, and I believe in my instincts."

Jonathan squatted by the chair, bringing his face level with hers. Concern and kindness filled his eyes. "I've come to learn you have good instincts. You knew there was a story at the mission and you were right, even if you may never prove it."

Cynthia felt herself relax. "You think my instincts are good?"

"I think God has given you a gift, a talent if you will, for keen insight and sharp deductive reasoning."

"Thank you . . . I think."

"Don't thank me, thank God."

A slow smile spread over Cynthia's face. "You're the most persistent man I've ever met. And you're mulish, too. Like me. You won't rest until you get your point across. I can respect that." Cynthia folded her hands on her lap and felt the perspiration between her fingers. "I don't know if you're right about Stubby, but I can tell you when I first walked into this hospital I was a wreck and now . . . I feel peace. I know that doesn't make sense, but it's a fact." She glanced at the bed, then looked away. "I can't explain it, just like, I suppose, you can't explain why you believe Stubby's going to be alright. But if it doesn't happen the way you say, I think I'll be able to handle it."

Jonathan took her hand. "You know you have a friend who's always ready and willing to help you handle your problems."

"Thank you, Jonathan. That's kind of . . . ."

"I was talking about Jesus. But you can include me, too." He took her by the arm and helped her to her feet. "There's no need to stay any longer. Let me walk you to your car."

All the way to the parking lot, Cynthia felt strangely lighthearted. It was irrational. But oddly enough, she loved it; loved the feeling she was a leaf the wind had taken up and was now twirling in the air. And for once she didn't want to analyze. She just wanted to revel in the fact that she no longer felt afraid or burdened. Maybe later she'd examine it. Pull it apart and ask the tough questions. But for now, she'd just let it be. She allowed Jonathan to do all the talking, to fill the space with small talk about Miss Emily and Effie. She barely listened.

Before she knew it, Cynthia found herself by her car. She unlocked it and let Jonathan open the door. She slipped in and was surprised to see him linger, almost hanging on the door, and staring at her like a little boy facing a trip to the principal's office.

"What's wrong?"

"This is awkward, but, do you think you could stand going out with a preacher just one more time?"

Cynthia's heart jumped. *He was asking for a date.* The thought pleased her. "I suppose so. If you could stand going out with an older woman."

Relief washed over his face. "Aunt Adel is going to owe me big time."

"Aunt Adel?"

"She has a friend, not a friend exactly; it's the church secretary, Gertie Eldridge. Anyway, she . . . they . . . found out we went to dinner together and now are pestering me for an introduction."

"Oh . . . well . . . sure." *Pestering?*

"They had hoped it would be for dinner or maybe lunch. Whatever you prefer."

"Dinner's easier. Sometimes I work through lunch."

"Okay. How about tonight? This way we can get it over with."

"Oh . . . well . . . sure." *Get it over with?* Cynthia rummaged in her purse and pulled out a business card. She turned it over and wrote down her home phone number. "Let me know the time and place. If I'm not home, put it on my machine."

"Should I pick you up?"

"No. I'll meet you. It's easier." She thought he looked relieved.

"Okay. And thanks for being such a good sport."

After starting her car, Cynthia peeled out, leaving Jonathan standing in a cloud of fumes. She could hardly keep from laughing because of what she had been thinking. *A date?* He hadn't wanted a date. He just wanted to fulfill, as quickly as possible, something he had obviously been pressured into doing. She hadn't gone half a mile when she realized how terribly disappointed she was.

Cynthia pounded her keyboard, filling her monitor with three lines of Ds for deadline. She wasn't going to make hers. Bernie asked to see her piece no later than tomorrow to determine if he wanted to do a simultaneous photo essay. But if tomorrow was a hundred hours away instead of twenty-four, she still wouldn't have it ready. She tapped out two lines of Cs for can't, can't, can't. Then she filled five lines with Ms. *Mad.* That's what Bernie was going to be.

"How's it going, Wells?"

Cynthia shrank in her seat. If Bernie asked her that one more time she was going to scream. When he leaned over her shoulder she minimized the screen.

"What's all that gobbledygook I saw?"

"You know I hate it when you try to see my work before it's finished."

Bernie plopped on her desk, not even bothering to move the folders scattered over the top. She wondered how he could possibly be comfortable, then saw him wiggle his bottom like a chicken getting ready to brood over an egg.

"So what have you got for me?"

"Be patient. You can't rush a masterpiece."

"A masterpiece? Now, you've got my interest. Every time you come up with a great story, circulation jumps. The front office will love that."

"Speaking of the front office, how *are* the sharks, Bernie?" Cynthia saw a worried look come over his face and tried not to smile.

"All they've been talking about lately is the Hunter News Corp. Did you know Hunter just unloaded their Canadian papers?"

"Not surprised. Last year they sold all forty-nine of their U.S. papers. The year before that, their UK interests. Everywhere you turn, it's consolidation madness run amuck."

"The front office keeps reminding me that's the only way to survive. They keep telling me it's all about profit opportunities, long-term situations, accessible markets, economies of scale. It seems that the newspaper game has become synonymous with capital chasing."

Cynthia laughed, then stopped when she saw the look on Bernie's face. "Sorry. But that's why *you* get the big bucks. Somebody has to deal with them."

"They're all bean counters. Not a reporter among them as far as I'm concerned. Journalism graduates who defected to business. Oh, my mistake. One of them did a few side-bars twenty years ago."

"Side-bars?" Cynthia burst out laughing.

"Keep it up, Wells, and you'll be chum. The sharks are always looking for extraneous salaries to cut, then regurgitate to their bottom line.

"You saying I'm expendable?"

"Everyone's expendable, including me. And you know when money stops pouring into the cash register, the front office starts pouring into our backyard. Sniffing under computers and desks and wherever else they think they can find a dollar to cut."

"You've always been the voice of reason. So reason with them." Cynthia noticed how tired Bernie looked. "You've done a great job so far. Nobody will ever know the number of jobs you've saved over the years. But I bet it's enough to fill half this press room."

Bernie slid off the desk and Cynthia watched him rub an obviously sore posterior.

"Did they bloody you this time?"

Bernie sighed. "Just make sure you get that story in on time. Make me look good. I don't want to end up at the copy desk. And like I said, Wells, everyone's expendable. I hear they are looking for someone in archives, so watch out. A transfer to the basement might be in your future."

Cynthia gave him one of her superior smiles and waited until he was half way back to his office before maximizing her screen. Then she began typing several lines of Es.

For *expendable*.

By the time Cynthia got home, she was in no mood to go out with what's-her-name, Aunt Adie? Maybe there'd be a message from Jonathan telling her the whole thing was off.

She was still nowhere on her story. She should've told Bernie the truth. Better now than later, and just let him explode and get it over with. His anger didn't bother her as much as the feeling she was letting him down. But if she went with her story the way it was now, it would only be half a story. She wanted more. She wanted to give Bernie something he'd be proud of.

She poked her head in the refrigerator and pulled out a wedge of Gouda. After cutting a few slices, she carried them to the bedroom. She nibbled them while listening to her messages: someone wanted to repaint her apartment, someone else wanted to shampoo her carpets—three rooms for the price of two; another wanted a contribution for their "Save the Park Fund," then Jonathan's.

"Meet me at the Pink Parasol, 6:30. I hope this isn't too much of a hardship. I know it's early and that you'll have to rush. Sorry about that, but Gertie Eldridge says eating late gives her indigestion. Oh . . . the address, in case you don't know, is—210 Main Street, right next to the North Oberon Bank. See you. Oh . . . in case something comes up and you can't make it, call me: 554-9876. See you. Oh . . . and this is my treat. No arguments."

Cynthia erased the messages, then went to her closet and flipped through her clothes. She pulled out a short sleeve denim A-line which came to her calf. She didn't feel like fussing. This would be perfect: simple, casual and suitable for entertaining someone's addled aunt and her nervous friend.

Why had she let herself get talked into this?

The clock on the nightstand told Cynthia if she rushed she'd have just enough time for a quick shower. The debate lasted a full minute. Then Cynthia stripped off her clothes and turned on the water. Maybe a shower would improve her mood. At least it would help her look fresh. Right now, she felt as wilted as yesterday's salad.

By the time she washed and dressed, Cynthia felt better, at least physically. By the time she drove to the Pink Parasol, Cynthia's spirits began to lift. Maybe eating with two Alzheimer patients and one preacher wouldn't be so bad after all. Besides, she had always wanted to go to the Pink Parasol, try it out.

As soon as she entered the restaurant she knew her outfit was all wrong. Men were dressed in suits. Women in evening wear. She had heard the Pink Parasol was on the pricey side, but she had not heard that people dressed to the nines for it, especially for a 6:30 seating. She saw Jonathan in the corner, towering over most of the other people who stood waiting. She cringed when she saw his suit and tie. One woman, standing near him, came close to his height. She wore a cream, raw-silk dress and matching blazer. Cynthia thought she saw a resemblance. Another woman, much shorter and also dressed in silk, seemed to be monopolizing the conversation. She guessed it was the woman with the nervous stomach.

With a forced smile plastered across her face, Cynthia walked up to the threesome. "Hi!"

Jonathan looked both relieved and pleased. He made the introductions while the taller lady smiled sweetly and the shorter one looked Cynthia up and down.

"You look taller on TV . . . and better dressed," Gertie Eldridge said. "And not as skinny. We better make sure this girl gets enough to eat tonight, eh Adel?"

Jonathan gave Cynthia a distressed look as the maître d' directed them to a lavishly-arranged, square table. A short, pale pink linen covered a white tablecloth that brushed the floor. Large pale pink napkins spiraled out of crystal goblets. In the center of the table a half-dozen pink roses floated in a crystal bowl. A large fern, in the corner, gave the illusion of privacy by blocking their table from those nearby.

Cynthia fingered the buttons of her denim dress and hoped that the maître d' would put her next to the fern. *You really fit in, Wells.*

The maître d' seated the two elderly ladies first, then Cynthia. And it wasn't next to the fern, but in the seat most exposed to the rest of the room. She took it without comment and made up her mind she'd forget about her outfit and try to enjoy the evening.

When everyone was comfortable and handed menus, Cynthia smiled and looked at her companions. Jonathan had taken the seat to her right, Aunt Adel, her left. That meant Gertie Eldridge sat across from her and would be harder to ignore.

Maybe this wasn't going to be that enjoyable after all.

"Have you ever been here?" Gertie asked.

Cynthia shook her head and tried to disappear behind the large, leather-covered menu.

"Well, you're in for a treat. The food is Divine. Should I say Divine? I suppose not, but it's scrumptious. Outrageously expensive, too. I came here once with my husband and another couple and we dropped over five hundred dollars. Can you believe it?"

Cynthia glanced anxiously at Jonathan and wondered how he could afford this.

"We only had one glass of wine apiece, an appetizer, a salad, an entrée, a small desert and coffee. That may sound like a lot but the portions were practically microscopic. If you're a big eater," Gertie squinted at Cynthia, "which I can see you're not . . . you might leave here hungry. I suppose we could order you a double entrée. I wouldn't want it said that we invited Cynthia Wells to dinner and she went home with an empty stomach. And nobody should worry. I came with plenty of money."

"I'm sure one entrée will be sufficient." Cynthia slid lower in her chair so she couldn't see Gertie over her menu.

"I don't know . . . what do you say, Adel? Since we're paying, we should make the decision, don't you think?"

"I was planning to pay," Jonathan said in a soft voice, but Cynthia detected strain.

"Not on your life!" Gertie snapped. "I don't want to be responsible for you sliding back onto dangerous ground, not with you pulling yourself up by your bootstraps and all. Of course I've been praying for you every minute. I know that helped."

Cynthia peeked around the menu at Jonathan and saw that his face resembled a strawberry. *What was going on?*

"For awhile there we were really worried about Pastor Jonathan. Yes sir, the prayer chair has been busy storming heaven. And you can see the results for yourself."

Cynthia continued studying Jonathan from behind her leather barrier. His face was still red and his jaw made a grinding motion, but when he glanced her way, his eyes were not full of anger, as she had expected, rather, they brimmed with kindness.

"Thank you for your prayers, Gertie. A pastor can't have too many people praying for him."

"Well, naturally. It's a hard job. Everyone knows that. Say . . . I think this is new. This wasn't here last time. At least I don't remember seeing it before. Filet De Boeuf `a la Tapenade. I *love* poached beef. And *tapenade* . . . well, you haven't lived until you've eaten tapenade. Why don't we get a double portion for Cynthia and I'll get a regular portion, but I'd also want an appetizer . . . let's see . . . ."

Cynthia felt a soft, warm hand cover hers. When she looked up, she saw the kind face of Aunt Adel smiling at her. "I think our guest is quite capable of ordering her own meal, so let's have no more talk about what we should get her . . . or about money . . . or about

Jonathan. And let's give our guest a chance to talk, too. Shall we, Gertie?"

"Well . . . of course . . . I was just trying to help."

After saying "good night" to Gertie and getting a hug and kiss from Aunt Adel, Cynthia and Jonathan walked together in the parking lot.

"Thanks for being such a good sport. I know how hard Gertie is to take. But you've given her an evening she can talk about for weeks. And I'm grateful."

Cynthia shrugged. "Sure. Anytime. Your aunt was nice. I liked her."

"She liked you, too. As a matter of fact, I think you made a big hit. She always mothers—defends and protects—those she really likes."

"She seems the type who likes everyone."

Jonathan chuckled. "I think that's pretty accurate, except maybe for . . . ."

"Gertie Eldridge?"

"Yeah. My aunt needs to work on that a little more."

"And you? I saw how you controlled yourself when Gertie mentioned your past. But once, just once, I noticed your jaw tighten. What was that all about?"

Jonathan's eyes danced, making him look mischievous. "Just a misunderstanding." He quickly told her the story.

After Cynthia stopped laughing, she slipped her arm through Jonathan's. "You are remarkably kind. I think I would have told her to . . . well never mind what I would have told her."

When they reached Cynthia's car, she unlocked it. "But she isn't what she should be, what I would think a church secretary should be, I mean."

"I guess none of us are. We're all a work in progress."

Cynthia studied him. "I find you very strange."

"Peculiar?"

"Yes, that's it . . . peculiar." Cynthia was surprised to see that her remark pleased him. "But I also find you sincere. It's been a long time since I've met anyone as sincere. I don't see how someone like Gertie, who knows you, who's worked with you, could ever think those horrible things about you." Cynthia watched Jonathan shuffle his feet. "But Gertie was right about one thing. Tapenade is wonderful."

"I'm not a fan, but I'm glad you liked it. I'm also glad you came. I had a good time."

"So did I."

"I was thinking, if you're not too tired, maybe you'd like to go back to the hospital with me and see Stubby?"

Cynthia glanced at her watch, nine-thirty. "I don't know. I'm beat." When she looked up she saw a strange expression on Jonathan's face. It was kind and tender, but also full of power. She felt drawn by it, as though sensing something important was happening. She also sensed a dare, a dare that pricked her reporter's interest. "But, okay. I guess it's still early enough."

"I'll meet you there," he said, flashing a smile.

She watched him walk away, then got into her car. Maybe she was the one who was peculiar, for allowing him to lead her around by the nose.

All the way to the hospital Cynthia mumbled under her breath, calling herself names. *Why did she let him talk her into this?* How was it he could get her to do things she didn't want to do? Suppose Stubby was still at death's door? Supposed he had already died? How was she going to handle her disappointment and . . . Jonathan's? Jonathan believed so completely in God. What if God didn't deliver? And she so wanted Him to. Not just for Stubby's sake or Jonathan's but for her own. Maybe it would help her believe in something.

She pulled into a parking space and waited until Jonathan pulled into his, then waited until he walked over to her car. She got out and together they ambled silently through the dark lot.

She eyed him nervously. "What if . . . ."

"You know, the best part about walking in faith is not having to worry about how God is going to do a thing, or even when."

He seemed relaxed and Cynthia thought she detected a slight smile, though it was too dark to be sure. "If this doesn't end up like you planned, you're not going to go to pieces on me, are you?"

Jonathan turned to her just as they passed under a light. He stopped and reached for her hand and held it. "I know how hard this is for you. Not only the believing part, but just being here at the hospital. I felt God prompting me to bring you tonight. And He's not a sadist out to hurt you. He has a plan for you, and it's for good and not evil. No matter what you see, will you try to remember that?"

Cynthia nodded and curled her fingers around his hand. She continued holding it as they walked the rest of the way through the parking lot then into the large, tiled foyer. And she didn't let go until they reached the entrance to Stubby's room.

Cynthia closed her eyes. *Oh, please let there be a miracle.* Maybe he'd be sitting up and eating. Would he be able to talk? She heard the creak of the door as it swung open, then heard Jonathan walk to Stubby's bed. She took a deep breath before opening her eyes. Even from her place by the door, Cynthia could tell that Stubby was still unconscious. The only change was that he was no longer hooked to a respirator but breathing on his own. It took all her willpower to enter the room.

She stood next to Jonathan studying the prone body. "He looks a little better, don't you think? Not so gray. And he's breathing easier." She glanced at Jonathan. "It's not my imagination, is it?"

Jonathan gave her a bright smile. "No, he *is* better."

"He still looks pretty bad, though, with all those tubes. You think it'll be . . . ."

"Miss . . . Cynthia? Is . . . that you?"

Cynthia's jaw dropped when she looked down and saw Stubby's eyes open and look up at her. "Stubby! You're awake."

"I heard voices." He tried reaching for Cynthia's hand, then gave up. "I was dreamin' and didn't wanna wake up."

Cynthia bent over the thin, aging man, and with her fingers, swept the fringe of white hair away from one ear. "When you're feeling better, you can tell me all about your dream."

"Yeah. I'm tired." He closed his eyes. "I'll tell you tomorrow."

"I'll be here."

CHAPTER 16

"I'm going back to the Mission, Bernie."

"Have you lost your marbles? There's a killer there. What are you trying to do? Save Skinner the trouble and just hand yourself over to this other guy?"

"I can't finish Part Two."

Bernie leaned across his desk as though trying to invade her resolve. His normal pleasant face looked as tight as a bowstring. "I thought you said it was all in your head and ready to write."

"That's what I thought, but when I tried putting it on paper it came out hollow, dry. It's got no *life*. Miss Emily was right, I haven't learned enough."

"You're talking crazy. There's nothing more for you to learn. If Steve couldn't find anything, what makes you think you can?"

Cynthia crossed her legs, brushing the bottom of Bernie's desk with her beige, linen pantsuit. "It's not about trying to get a scoop on a drug ring anymore."

"What is it, then?"

"It's about trying to find out what happens to people like Manny, Turtle and Stubby, people who get so beaten down by life they give up. I think I've got that part. I know I can give you a good piece on that. But it's the other part I can't put my finger on. It's the redemption aspect I can't work out."

"Redemption?"

"Yes. What makes some people and not others get back up on their feet and start all over. It's like something gets inside them and gives them hope; gives them the strength to stand up when everything around them tells them to lay down and quit."

"Are you talking religion here, Wells?"

Cynthia thought of Stubby and the miracle at the hospital. "Maybe. I don't know. I just know I've seen it in Effie's eyes, in Stubby's, too. And what I see makes me *know* they're going to make it. And I need to understand why that is. What power can change lives and make them . . . well . . . like new?"

Bernie dipped his hand in the jar of jellybeans, scooped up several then began popping them, one by one, into his mouth. "Have you thought of the consequences? You'll be looking over your shoulder every second. The risk will be enormous. And even if you're willing to take it, what guarantee do you have you'll find this elusive missing piece of your story?"

Cynthia shook her head. "None. No guarantee at all. And that's what I'm discovering, Bernie. That's what I'm beginning to understand. There are no guarantees, for any of us. Only choices . . . choices we have to make each day. But what I need to know is do the choices we make save us or is there something else, something else entirely, like a higher power? Or is it a combination of the two? See what I mean? How can I write this piece when I can't even answer these basic questions?"

Bernie held his last jellybean—a black one—between his fingers and studied it. "Half the population of North Oberon couldn't answer those questions. Why should you be any different?"

"Because they don't have a story to write. And for that story to have teeth, I need those answers." Cynthia shifted in the wooden chair. It was impossible to get comfortable. She didn't know why she tried. "Trust me on this. I can make this a great story. One that will sell papers."

Bernie popped the black jellybean into his mouth and picked up the folder in front of him. "Two weeks. That's all you've got. After two weeks you hand in your piece—without excuses, without whining. In the meantime, we'll do a photo essay of Skid Row, make that Part Two, and your new story will be Part Three, and end it. Is that a deal?"

"Deal."

"And get a new cell phone—that's an order. I don't want you at the mission without one. You need to be able to call anytime. Got it?"

Cynthia nodded.

Bernie threw the folder back onto the desk and reached into his jellybean jar, again. "Maybe I'm the one who's lost his marbles."

Cynthia's hand trembled as she punched in numbers on her new cell phone. A strange man's voice answered, and for a second she thought she had dialed the wrong number.

"Is this the Beacon Mission?"

"Yeah."

"I'd like to speak to Pastor Holmes, please."

"He's busy."

"This is important. Can you tell him Cynthia needs to talk to him?"

"Does he know you?"

"Of course he knows me!" Cynthia looked at her speedometer and slowed the car. Her impatience was finding an outlet through the gas pedal. She had to slow twice more before Jonathan got on the phone.

"Cynthia? What's up?"

"Sorry if I pulled you away from something important."

"Nothing important. I was checking inventory in the back."

"Whoever answered the phone made it sound like my intrusion was a capital offense."

Jonathan chuckled. "That's Willie Tanner. Stubby's temporary replacement. He has trouble distinguishing between busy and can't-disturb-busy. I keep telling him to let the calls go on the answering machine, but he forgets."

Cynthia slowed to a crawl when she saw the school sign. "Listen, Jonathan, I won't beat around the bush. I'll tell you straight out, I'd like to come back to the mission so I can finish my story." She held her breath.

"That's not a good idea. Not until we find out who tried to kill you. Besides, I thought you reached a dead end on your drug piece. Has Detective Bradley found something new?"

"No, and this has nothing to do with drugs. This has to do with Stubby and last night, and Effie and Miss Emily. This is about miracles and changed lives. I don't know anything about things like that, Jonathan, so I need to come back and find out. And when I do, I'll have my story."

"It's still all about your story, isn't it? No matter how you word it or how high-minded you make it sound, it's still just about your story."

"That's all I know, Jonathan." Cynthia passed the school zone. "If there's more, then you'll have to help me find it, only please tell me I can come back." During the long silence, she floored the pedal.

"All right," Jonathan finally said. "You want your old job back?"

"You bet!"

"There'll be at least one person happy to see you. Miss Emily's been lost without you. I was thinking of putting an ad in the paper, but now . . . well, welcome aboard. Again."

"Thanks. I'll be there later this afternoon, after I see Stubby."

The periphery whizzed by in a blur as Cynthia sped down the road. He could have said he'd be happy to have her back, too, even if he didn't mean it. He could have lied.

Preachers don't lie, Wells, only reporters.

Cynthia tiptoed through the doorway, trying not to disturb Stubby who looked asleep. She got halfway to the bed when he opened his eyes.

"Miss Cynthia . . . I feel awful. What happened?"

Cynthia pulled the brown vinyl armchair closer to the bed and sat down. "You've had us all worried. But you're going to be fine, now."

"The nurse said the cops are comin' later to ask questions. What for?"

"You don't remember?"

Stubby shook his head. "I had a dream, and didn't wanna wake up."

Cynthia covered his bruised hand with hers. "Last night you promised that today you'd tell me about it."

"Last night?" Stubby closed his eyes and Cynthia thought he had drifted back to sleep. When he opened them, the look on his face startled her. It was as though he was looking past her, at something far away. "Jesus is beautiful, you know that? *Beautiful.* His hands and feet . . . they got scars. I didn't wanna come back. Not after lookin' Him in the eye. Not after seein' all that love."

"Was that your dream? That you saw Jesus?"

"He was real. As real as you sittin' here, only we was in heaven."

Cynthia frowned. "That sounds nice, Stubby." She watched him close his eyes again. "Maybe you should rest. I'll try to come back tomorrow."

When she rose, Stubby's hand caught her fingers and held them. "You was in my dream." Stubby opened his eyes and stared at her. "Not *in* it exactly. Jesus told me I gotta come back . . . so I could take care of you . . . so I could be your friend. He said you needed a friend."

How was she to respond to that? It was irrational—Stubby thinking he had gone to heaven, thinking he had a mandate from God to protect her. She didn't know whether to laugh or be insulted that Stubby would think she'd believe such a story. But when she realized *he* believed it, she bent down and kissed his forehead. Jonathan had told her God would heal Stubby, and it looked like He was in the process of doing just that. Now, Stubby was telling her he had seen Jesus and that Jesus had given him instructions concerning her. This was too much of a stretch.

"Get some rest. We can talk more another time." Cynthia got as far as the door when Stubby called her name.

"What happened to me? No one round here'll tell me."

Cynthia turned and studied the aging man on the bed, still hooked up to tubes and machines, still looking like any minor thing could tip the scales against him. "Someone tried to kill you."

His face crinkled like foil as tears glided down his cheeks. "I'm glad . . . I'm glad it weren't me that started up again with them drugs."

Jonathan Holmes didn't look up when he heard someone walk into his office. "Have a seat, I'll be right with you," he said, tallying the column of figures and feeling pleased with what he saw. At this rate, if he was careful, he could last a year on the funds left in his bank account. There was a smile on his face when he raised his eyes, but it was quickly replaced by a look of surprise. A man, dressed in an expensive-looking three-piece suit, sat in the nearby chair. Although he looked familiar, Jonathan couldn't place him.

The man must have sensed this because he flushed, then extended his hand. "Bill Rivers. Charles Angus introduced us, remember? I'm the liaison between Angus Enterprises and the mission."

Jonathan gave Bill's hand a vigorous shake. "Yes, we spoke the other day. But I have to say I'm surprised to see you here. Nothing wrong, I hope?"

"No. Nothing at all." Bill Rivers straightened his silk tie that needed no straightening. "Like I told you on the phone, I'll be checking in from time to time."

Jonathan suffocated a rising fear that Angus had finally heard what had happened at the mission and was going to pull the plug. "I hardly expected a personal visit, especially so soon after your call, but I'm delighted. Was there something in particular you wanted to discuss?"

Bill shook his head. "No. I think we covered it all on the phone."

"What then?"

Bill's hand moved to his tie again. "Maybe a tour. I thought I'd check the place out—see your operation first hand."

The smile returned to Jonathan's face. "Sure. I'd be happy to oblige." He rose to his feet. "We'll start on the first floor and work our way up."

For over thirty minutes Jonathan paraded Bill Rivers through one room after another, explaining what they already had in place, as well as his vision for the future. At first Jonathan thought he was imagining it, but by the middle of the tour he was sure that his guest had no interest in what he was saying. The man barely listened. Instead, he stared at everyone that passed, turned his head at every sound, wandered away in the middle of a sentence. By the time Bill Rivers left, Jonathan was relieved to see him go.

He just didn't get this guy.

Jonathan tapped the fingers of one hand against the desktop. The other hand held the phone. "I'm fine, Aunt Adel. Just fine." Bill Rivers had left moments before and Jonathan still had to prepare his Bible study for tomorrow, plus return calls to several local merchants. In between, he had three counseling appointments.

"You sound distracted. Is this a bad time, Dearest?"

"I'm busy, but never too busy for you." He forced his fingers to be still. "What's up?"

"Nothing. I just wanted to thank you for that lovely evening at the Pink Parasol. Gertie is still flying high. Of course the entire congregation knows all about it, now. And they're all happy for you."

"Happy for me? Why?"

"Gertie has been telling everyone that you're seeing Cynthia Wells; that you two are an item."

"She *what!*" Jonathan bolted out of his seat.

"Why Jonathan, I do believe I hear irritation in your voice."

"This time Gertie's gone too far. I *can't* believe her gall! How dare she spread such rumors! When her gossip was just about me, that was one thing, but now she's involving someone else, and I don't like it."

"You don't? You mean Gertie has finally pushed *your* buttons?"

Jonathan sat down. "Can you stop the talk? Before it gets out of hand? Before it ends up in the church bulletin or something?"

"I can try."

Jonathan thought he heard his aunt giggle.

"She is quite lovely you know, your friend, Cynthia. And I've been praying for God to send you a wife. You could do worse."

Jonathan rose to his feet again. "Cynthia doesn't know the Lord." He felt his irritation rise to a level he seldom experienced. He paced the floor, trying to calm down. "And since when have you gone into the matchmaking business?"

"Since you turned thirty."

Jonathan sighed. "Please, Aunt Adel, stay out of this."

"Well . . . if you insist. But surely you won't mind if I continue praying for Cynthia? If I ask the Lord to bring her into the saving knowledge of Jesus?"

"Of course not."

"Good. Then we shall see what we shall see. I really like her, Jonathan."

"Aunt Adel!" Jonathan heard the phone go dead.

For several minutes Jonathan just stood, like a mannequin, holding the dead receiver in his hand. He hardly noticed it droning. His mind was busy beating out its own drone. *Cynthia Wells. Cynthia Wells. Cynthia Wells.* She had become a distraction. But what to do? That was the question. Finally, he placed the phone on its cradle and went to the door, locked it, then went back to his desk and sat down. He was drawn to her, no use pretending otherwise. She had even stirred something in him, a feeling of wanting to protect her and . . . yes, strong affection, too. But Cynthia couldn't be the woman for him. She had no knowledge of God, and from what he could see, only a superficial desire to know Him. And even that desire was fueled by an obsession to get her story. Jonathan closed his eyes. "Oh, God, help me keep focused on You and the mission, and not on Cynthia Wells."

All the way to her apartment, Cynthia kept thinking about what Stubby had said.

"Jesus told me I gotta come back . . . so I could take care of you. . . so I could be your friend. He said you needed a friend."

He better not try telling others that or they'd start fitting him for a straitjacket. In spite of herself, Cynthia smiled.

But what if it were true?

She shook her head. No. There was no great big God in the sky looking down on little Cynthia Wells and caring one hoot what happened to her. She thought of Jonathan, and Stubby's miracle. She remembered how wonderful she felt the evening they had visited Stubby—the peace, the joy. Even now a residue remained. Had God touched her that day? She had yet to ask the hard questions. But even her natural cynicism had begun showing signs of cracking, like a windshield that gets dinged from a flying pebble then fractures, and eventually shatters. Surely, there had to be someone . . . something. An overseer maybe? How else could she explain what happened to Stubby? No one, not even the nurses and doctors, expected him to live. There had to be a higher power. And maybe sometimes prayers really were answered.

She parked her car and felt her head pound like Miss Emily's fist when she'd knead her dough. That's what she got for taking on the mysteries of the universe. Maybe it was faith, faith in anything—it didn't matter—that made things happen. But that was as ridiculous as believing in nothing. No, there was an answer. At least to the missing half of her story, and she was going to find it.

Once in the apartment, she wasted no time in digging out an old backpack from her closet. This time she'd take a few items, underwear, some toiletries, a nightgown. Her clothes she'd get from the mission, like last time, so she'd blend in, make others feel comfortable around her. She removed her suit and put on the jeans and T-shirt Miss Emily had let her keep. Then she looked around her clean, tidy apartment. She was going from the lap of luxury back into a small, austere room with few possessions, and the thought filled her with unexpected joy.

Cynthia slipped into her old room, unnoticed. She put her few things away, then headed straight for the kitchen. When Miss Emily saw her, she dropped the large soup ladle she was holding, scooped Cynthia up in her arms and gave her a hug that almost hurt.

"My, it's good to see you! I can't tell you how much I missed you."

"Me, too. Did Jonathan tell you I was coming back?"

"Coming back? You mean for good?"

"I mean for two weeks, so I can finish my story."

"Your story? Pooh. I've been praying that the Lord draws you back here so He can finish the job. I told you you hadn't learned enough. "

"Well, my editor's only giving me two weeks so I better learn fast."

"Pfff. You're in the Lord's timing now. You might as well just kick back and relax, because He's in control, not your editor."

"Seems like the Good Lord is controlling a lot of things lately. Have you seen Stubby?"

"No, but I heard. A lot of people have been praying, you know."

Cynthia followed Miss Emily to the stove and watched her stir the soup. "Smells good. What is it?"

"My specialty. Chicken soup."

"May I taste?"

"Sure. But you need some of my fresh baked bread with it." Miss Emily picked up a loaf from the cooling rack and broke off a piece, then dipped it into the pot. Then she put the sopping bread on a small plate and handed it to Cynthia. "Welcome home, child."

Cynthia didn't want Effie to find out through the grapevine that she was back, so after she finished eating a huge chunk of Miss Emily's homemade bread and a small bowl of soup, she left the kitchen and headed for Day Care. She didn't bother knocking, but opened the door part way and peeked in. Effie was in the middle of handing out large, oval cookies that looked like they had come straight from Miss Emily's kitchen. Cynthia noticed the group had increased. Seven children now sat on blankets.

"Hey, Effie. How's it going?"

Effie turned, and her smile made Cynthia happy she had made this effort. She waited while Effie finished passing out cookies and instructing the children to sit quietly. Finally, Effie walked over.

"I knew you'd be back. I been prayin' and here you are!" The two women hugged. "I just knew it was gonna be you that helped me get my boy back."

Cynthia gave Effie a stern look. "Don't make this into something it's not. I'm here to finish my story. That doesn't mean I don't want to help. But to be fair, I don't know if I can."

"God'll show you. You'll see. God'll show you."

Cynthia was relieved when Daisy walked over and ended the conversation. "My, don't you look pretty!" She noticed the little girl's head was free of sores. She also noticed that her brown hair, which was combed and tied-back by a bright green ribbon, had luster.

Daisy smiled, then tugged on Cynthia's hand. Cynthia looked at Effie. "What does she want?"

"She's still a little shy, but praise God, she's startin' to come around. I think she wants to tell you somethin'."

Cynthia bent down far enough so the little girl could whisper in her ear. When the child was finished, she skipped away, leaving Cynthia frowning.

"What did she say?"

"She said she had asked God to bring me back."

Cynthia splashed water on her face, then combed her hair. She, Miss Emily, and Effie were going to the hospital to see Stubby. But before returning to the mission, the three of them planned to make a detour to Favorite Flavors, the best ice cream parlor in North Oberon. Effie had gotten one of the mothers of the Day Care children to watch Daisy for the evening. And while Cynthia and Miss Emily had sped around the kitchen getting all the dinner dishes done, Effie had given Daisy an early bath.

Cynthia was almost embarrassed by her excitement. When her cell phone rang, she tried ignoring it, then gave in on the fourth ring. "Cynthia Wells."

"Hi! This is Pamela Harmon, you know, the girl from Social Services? The one you asked to check and see if I could get information on those two guys who died in Skid Row?"

"Yes, of course, how are you?"

"I'm fine. Your editor gave me this number so I hope it's okay that I called."

"I'm glad you did. Do you have news?"

"I'm dating a real nice guy—a dentist. I never thought I'd go for a dentist. Can you believe it? Liking a guy who does root canals?"

Cynthia laughed. "Well, I hope it works out."

"Of course I didn't call to tell you about my love life. I called to tell you that I saw Andy last night. You know, that caseworker I told you about? The one who handled both Turtle and Manny? I bumped into him at the S&S Market. You could have knocked me over with a feather when I saw him there, big as life.

"At first he didn't want to talk, but when I wouldn't stop following him around, he told me he was in town for only a few days so he could finalize the sale of his house and get his things moved out. I asked why he retired early and left without a word to anyone. He said for health reasons. Well, he looked pretty healthy to me, so I pressed and asked him what was wrong, did he have cancer or something? And he said no, it was nothing like that.

"Then I asked him whatever happened with his investigation of those two men, and he turned green. I kid you not! As green as the pepper I was holding. Then he clammed up. I knew something was wrong. He was leaving clues around like breadcrumbs and I wasn't going to let him off that easily. So I asked him point blank, was he running away from something? Had he stumbled upon some dangerous information? I thought he was going to faint! And for the longest time he just stood there staring at me, not saying a word. I told him I wasn't going to let him go until he told me.

"He finally admitted he had learned something that made it 'unhealthy' to remain in town. And he told me if I knew what was good for me, I'd just forget the whole thing and go off and get married and have lots of babies. I told him I wasn't even engaged and that we were civil servants and had a duty to the public, and if he knew something he needed to speak up. That's when he laughed. Not the kind of funny haha laugh, but more sarcastic like. It scared me a little because it was so unlike Andy—meek, mild Andy. I couldn't believe it."

"Did he tell you what he found out?"

"No. He just said if I wanted to solve a puzzle do the crosswords."

Cynthia sat on the edge of her bed. "We already know we're dealing with drugs; that the Angus Avenue Men's Shelter is involved, and that they use some of the homeless to run the drugs to the crack houses."

"Wow! That's . . . criminal!"

"Trouble is, we can't prove it. The police have tried, but they've run into a brick wall. So we're going to need a lot more information. Keep your ears open. If you hear anything, let me know."

"Count on it! After what you said I couldn't turn a blind eye even if I wanted to." Pamela paused to take a breath. "One more thing. I did some checking today. I figured I owed the taxpayers that much. I was able to retrace some of Andy's steps without drawing attention to myself. I checked out his computer and the last thing he worked on—the files have those dates next to them, you know— well the last thing he did the day before he quit was to compile a list of vendors."

"What kind of vendors?"

"Suppliers the city use to stock their shelters with food, bedding, toilet articles. You know, things like that. It doesn't make sense. I mean, why would Andy waste time doing that?"

"You think you can get me that list?"

"Sure, if you think it's important. But you can't tell anyone you got it from me. I know I can trust you because reporters never reveal their sources. They'd go to jail rather than reveal their sources. Right?"

Cynthia dropped her head into her hand. "Don't worry, Pamela, I won't tell. Just fax that list to me when you get it, okay?" She gave Pamela her office fax number. "But be careful. Be very careful."

When Cynthia, Miss Emily and Effie entered Stubby's room, they found him sitting up in bed. For ten minutes, the place was bedlam as everyone tried to kiss and hug and talk at once. It took the intervention of a stern looking nurse to quiet them all down.

"You sure had us worried," Effie said.

"Speak for yourself. I always knew God would heal him. Why do you think I stocked up on all that butter? For his baloney and butter sandwiches, that's why." Miss Emily fluffed Stubby's covers, then began tidying his nightstand.

"How long before you can come back to work?" Cynthia said, noticing how much Stubby's face beamed as he watched Miss Emily fuss.

Stubby shrugged. "I'd go right now, but the doc said I gotta stay a few more days."

"You're feeling that good?" Cynthia thought he still looked drawn and tired.

"Well, after bein' with the police all afternoon, I gotta admit I'm done in. But after I get me some rest, I'll be fine."

"Did you remember anything?" Cynthia took out a mental pencil, preparing to inscribe every word Stubby said onto her brain. "Were you able to give them any information?"

"They kept askin' if I knew who tried to kill me. And all afternoon I tried and tried, but the only thing I remember is that I was in the men's room, gettin' ready to wash when someone came up behind me and threw somethin' over my head . . . a towel maybe . . . I ain't sure. Then my head smashed against somethin'. And that's the last I remember, 'til I saw you and Pastor Jonathan standin' over my bed."

"You never saw who it was?" Cynthia said.

"No. But one thing I do remember. It's kinda weird. Probably don't mean nothin'. But I remember smellin' fruit."

Cynthia's heart jumped. "Fruit? You mean like a fruity smell?"

Stubby nodded.

"That's just what I smelled when . . . . It's the same man, Stubby. Don't you see? That proves it's the same man who tried to kill us both!"

Favorite Flavors was nothing to look at. Vinyl booths lined both sides of a large room, forming a monotonous gray line. In the middle, small gray and pink vinyl covered tables left little space for walking. Grey and pink checked curtains covered the only two windows and did nothing to enhance the drab camel-colored walls.

In spite of the lackluster décor, the place was always packed, and patrons believed themselves fortunate when they were able to get a seat after only a twenty-minute wait.

Cynthia craned her neck to survey the room and spotted an empty corner booth. Without waiting for the waitress to seat them, she led her small band to the cubicle and settled in—Miss Emily on one side, then she and Effie on the other.

"Reporters are used to barging into places," Cynthia said, picking up one of the menus lodged between the napkin dispenser and wall. She could tell Miss Emily was displeased.

"Suppose someone else was ahead of us, waiting?"

Cynthia smiled sheepishly. "I don't always think about things like that."

"I know." Miss Emily folded her hands on her lap, not taking a menu. "Perhaps that's one of the things you can learn, this time around. Thinking of others."

Cynthia nodded and looked into Miss Emily's kind eyes. She loved that about this white-haired woman . . . her ability to be honest without being cruel. "I'll work on it," Cynthia said, as a waitress sauntered over. "Have we taken someone else's table?"

"No, it's slow tonight. Nobody's had to wait more than five minutes. So, you're okay."

Cynthia winked at Miss Emily. "Give us a second, will you? We need time to decide what we want."

"Sure. Just signal when you're ready," the waitress said before bouncing off.

Cynthia watched Miss Emily finally pick up a menu, then she scanned her own. "The banana split sounds good. So does the hot fudge sundae. Did you know that all the ice cream is homemade? They make it right in back, with real cream and fruit and . . . ."

"You have a teachable spirit," Miss Emily said. "That's a good thing."

Cynthia felt uncomfortable by the compliment, but pleased, too. "I also have something else." She replaced her menu behind the napkin holder. "A BIG yen for nuts and whipped cream and syrup. Tonight I'm tackling the El Grande."

"Make that two," Effie said with a laugh, looking younger and prettier, even with her damaged teeth, than Cynthia had ever seen her.

"I guess I'll have the Cookie-Dough Sundae Supreme," Miss Emily added, leaning over the table and tapping first Cynthia's then Effie's hand with her menu. "And while we're eating I'll tell you the secret of finding true love."

Effie whaled with laughter. "I just got rid of one man. I ain't interested in gettin' another."

Miss Emily folded her arms across her chest and arched her eyebrows. "You just take notes, Effie. No telling what God will do with your marriage once you give it to Him. And you," Miss Emily turned to Cynthia, "You take notes, too, because it's obvious you've never found any man who remotely interested you."

Cynthia bit back laughter and slumped against the seat. For one night it was going to be wonderful not worrying about her story, or Stubby's assailant, or the mission. For one night it was going to be wonderful just to be silly and talk girl-talk.

"Effie, I think we should let Miss Emily have the floor. You know what they say, give someone enough rope and *she'll* hang herself."

Effie's head bobbed up and down. "That's right. We'll let her eat, let all that cookie dough loosen her tongue."

"Right, and we *will* take notes. Maybe we'll get enough on her tonight to ensure extra cookies for Daisy and second helpings on desert for both of us, and maybe even some of that fresh fruit she hides way back in the refrigerator whenever she thinks no one's looking."

"I save that for some of the sicker ones, who need it," Miss Emily said, unmoved by the fact that both women had ganged up on her.

Effie leaned closer to Cynthia. "So she says."

"Okay, tell us all about true love," Cynthia said, settling back in the booth and knowing there was no other place she'd rather be tonight than right here.

Cold air slapped Cynthia's face as she studied the outline of her new Holly Hobbie kitchen. The little oven door hung on one hinge, the cabinets open and empty, her beautiful china tea set that Grammy had given her—gone.

Julia!

Julia wasn't supposed to touch it. But Julia won't be punished. She was never punished no matter what she did. She could wreck all of Cynthia's things and get away with it.

But not this time. This time Cynthia was going to get that little terrorist and make her pay.

The swish of denim and smell of Blossom Eau de Toilette made Cynthia turn her head. Oh, not her new toilet water! Julia must have used the whole bottle. Out of the corner of Cynthia's eye, she spotted the wisp carrying a small china tea cup and creamer.

"You give that back!" Cynthia demanded as she ran after the wisp. "You give that . . . ." Suddenly she remembered the window. "Stop!" Cynthia shouted as the imp headed straight for it, looking backward at her and giggling.

"Stop!" Cynthia shouted again, and was answered by one more giggle just before it turned into a scream.

Cynthia jerked up in bed. Perspiration soaked her nightgown. She looked around the semi-dark room, remembering she was at the mission. Had she cried out? She was sure she had and sure she had woken someone up. She listened for sounds and heard only silence.

She sank back onto her pillow. She hadn't had her dream in a while. Why now? Hadn't she and Miss Emily and Effie had a wonderful time at the ice-cream parlor? Yes, after they left *Stubby*. And he would be returning to the mission soon. Was that it? Was that what she was worried about? How to continue keeping her secret from him? How much longer could she go on like this? The strain was too much. She closed her eyes. When she did she saw her little toy oven, saw the window, saw the wisp. She blinked. There would be no more sleeping tonight. That was certain. And as she lay in bed, staring up at a black ceiling, she thought of all the so-called miracles happening around her, and found herself whispering, "*Oh, God, I need a miracle, too.*"

CHAPTER 17

Cynthia tied back her shiny blonde hair with a black scrunchy then applied more mascara.

Why was she fussing?

She tossed the mascara into her make-up bag and zipped it. She ran her hands down her T-shirt, smoothing it out, then glanced one last time at the mirror. The reflection pleased her. Even the washed out T-shirt and faded jeans didn't detract. But why go to all this trouble?

Primping like a schoolgirl. Honestly, Wells.

It was only Jonathan.

She had cornered him at breakfast and told him she wanted to talk. They had made an appointment for two-thirty, when all the lunch madness was over.

She grabbed her room key and jammed it into her pocket, then filled a paper cup with water and drank. Her mouth was as dry as dust. As she tossed the cup into the small corner pail, her stomach flipped.

Why was she so nervous?

She locked her door then scooted down the hall and around the corner. She stopped when she saw Jonathan's door ajar, when she saw his head bent as in prayer. She wondered if he was praying for her. He always prayed before his counseling sessions.

Counseling?

She hoped he didn't think that's what this was. She just wanted to talk. Get something off her chest. She smoothed her T-shirt one more time, then took a deep breath.

Ready or not, here I come.

A series of loud raps on the heavy maple door raised Jonathan's head. His face told her he had been deep in thought. "If I've caught you in the middle of something, I can come later." She backed away from the door.

"No, I've been waiting for you." Jonathan rose and gestured for her to enter. "Take a seat."

Cynthia noticed that the empty chair, which was usually stationed by the side of the desk, had been moved to the front, opposite Jonathan. She wondered why he felt the need to put such a large object between them. It only added to her suspicions. She sat, then leaned against the desk, one elbow propping her chin as she watched Jonathan ease his tall, muscular frame onto his chair. No point in beating around the bush. "Are you mad at me?" she blurted.

A look of surprise rearranged his face. "No . . . why?"

"I've been here three days and seen little of you. It's as if you're avoiding me."

Jonathan's face colored. He spent time brushing hair away from his eyes before clearing his throat. "You sure are blunt."

"I just wondered if you resented me for being here. I hope not, because it makes my task harder and . . . ."

"I don't resent you."

"Then why, when you see me coming, do you go the other way?"

"I've been busy . . . and you've been busy, looking for your story. I wanted to give you plenty of space to find it."

"You sure that's it?"

"Cynthia, I don't know what it is you want me to say."

"Say you like me even though I don't know the Lord, even though I don't believe what you believe. Say you'll help me understand the mission and what you see in it and why. Say we can be friends."

Jonathan seemed to relax. "That I can say without hesitation."

"Well . . . that's a relief." Cynthia rose from her chair, a smile on her face. "All this time I thought you held it against me for forcing myself on the mission . . . on you. I won't get in the way, I promise. I have a lot to learn and hope to learn it right here."

As Cynthia rounded the corner heading away from Jonathan's office she noticed Willie Tanner lurking in the hall. He scowled at her as she passed. His black, brooding eyes were still fixed on her when she turned back to look.

The man gave her the creeps.

It was silly. There wasn't one tangible thing she could put her finger on to explain her uneasiness. His face was always dirty; his black greasy hair uncombed and hanging in his eyes, but that wasn't it. Nor was it the way he looked at everyone. She had seen that look on some of the boys she'd grown up with. A look that told her to keep her cat indoors so its tail wouldn't be set on fire or its little body hung from a rafter. No, it was something deep and ominous, right behind his eyes. And it was this thing Cynthia couldn't quite make out that scared her.

How did Jonathan put up with him?

He rarely did his job and when he did, it was poorly done. Everyone, including Miss Emily, who never complained about anyone, was counting the days for Stubby to come back and relieve Willie.

"What were you talking to Pastor Jonathan about?"

Cynthia heard Willie's shoes scrape along the floor, and resisted the urge to turn around. She continued walking.

"You're so stuck-up! You think you're better than the rest of us?"

Cynthia sidestepped a puddle of dirty water that Willie had failed to mop up. "You ask inappropriate questions, Willie. You need to learn some manners." She kept walking and heard his footsteps keeping pace behind her.

"I don't think you're the one to teach me." He caught up and slipped in front of her, all hunched over and smelling like he hadn't bathed in a week, his hands jammed in his pockets. "I see you asking everyone all sorts of questions. How come you can ask questions but I can't?"

Cynthia studied his dark eyes, eyes that looked like black reflecting coals. It was pointless to argue with someone like him. "Forget it," she said, turning away.

"Yeah . . . well I don't forget that easily."

The phone rang just before Jonathan was able to take it off the hook. He had planned to disconnect himself from everything so he could spend time with the Lord, praying about something that troubled him. But after the fifth ring, he gave in and picked it up.

"Hello."

"Bill Rivers here. I wanted to thank you for the tour."

Jonathan stifled a groan and tried to keep impatience from seeping into his voice. "You're welcome." The last thing he wanted to do was waste more time with this man.

"Yes, it was interesting . . . very interesting."

Jonathan rubbed his forehead. "Okay, maybe we'll do it again some time."

"Oh, count on it. But in the meantime, I was wondering if you could send me a list of all your male residents, past and present."

"Why? For what purpose?"

"Pastor Jonathan, I don't think I need to remind you that you have this mission because of the benevolence of Mr. Angus. One would think you'd be willing to bend backwards in order to satisfy any requests made by his appointed liaison."

"And Mr. Rivers, I don't think I need to remind you of the limited staff at my disposal. If Mr. Angus cares to loan me his secretary for a day, so she can compile a list of all those who have come and gone since we've opened, then I'd be happy to oblige."

"You needn't be curt. It's a simple request. A list of names. Is that so hard? How long would it take you?"

"Like I said, Mr. Rivers, if Mr. Angus would like to loan me his secretary . . . ."

"Forget it!" Bill Rivers snapped before slamming down the phone.

Cynthia's hands were wrist-deep in meatloaf fixings when Bernie's call came. She quickly rinsed them off. "Sorry," she mouthed when she took the phone from Miss Emily. This was hardly the time for a phone call. They were swamped with work, trying to get the dinner together. But Miss Emily didn't seem to mind. She smiled and patted Cynthia on the shoulder as though saying it was okay, then returned to dicing onions.

"Hello. Hello!" Bernie's voice bellowed over the receiver.

She brought the phone to her ear and walked to the other end of the kitchen. "I'm here, Bernie, stop shouting."

"You're one hard lady to reach! I've had to jump through more hoops than a dog at Ringling Brothers. First I get the pastor and he transfers me to the kitchen." Cynthia heard Bernie chuckle. "I still can't believe anyone would want you in their kitchen . . . anyway, then I get this sweet lady . . . ."

"Miss Emily."

"Yeah, I figured that's who it was . . . anyway, why can't I get you on your new cell phone, the phone I had to buy because you lost your last one?"

"I didn't lose it. It was stolen, remember?"

"Yeah, well, all I know is that I've bought you two phones in the past year and I still can't get you when I want to."

"Bernie, I'm supposed to be homeless, remember? The staff know who I am, but how would it look to the others if I walked around with a phone sticking out of my pocket? I keep it in my room."

"But you're never *in* your room!"

"That's because I have cooking to do." Cynthia shifted her feet and glanced at the mound of meatloaf fixings. She needed to get back to work. "And Bernie, you may not believe this, but people are starting to like my cooking."

"You're right, I don't believe it. Anyway are you going to let me tell you why I called? Because I wasn't going to call since I think this is some kind of joke, on the other hand, since it was for you and no telling what you're into now, I thought I'd better, just in case. Anyway, I just got a fax addressed to you from someone named Agatha Christie. Does that do anything for you?"

Cynthia's attention peaked. "Yes. What does it say?"

"Nothing. It's just a list of vendors. Fifteen of them. What's it all about?"

"Remember I told you about that guy who retired suddenly from Social Services, the one who was going to do some checking on our two homeless men?"

"Yeah."

"This was the last thing he worked on before quitting. Give me the names, Bernie." Cynthia scurried for paper and pencil, then scribbled the names as Bernie read them. "I'll hand this over to Steve. Maybe he can do something with it because I can't."

"What do you mean you can't?"

"I told you I'm going after a different angle, now, and you agreed."

"Yeah. That was before you got your hands on this."

Cynthia walked over to the mound of chopped meat and sprinkled the top with dried parsley flakes. "What was all that talk about my safety? Just talk?"

"I figured as a reporter you'd want to follow up your own leads, that's all. What could happen at a food store?"

"If Steve comes up with something interesting, I'll check it out." Cynthia put down the parsley and began lining up her loaf pans.

"What's all that clanking noise?"

"I have to go, Bernie. I've got to get my meatloaf in the oven or there'll be no dinner tonight."

"Now, that would be a shame."

"Sarcasm doesn't become you. I'm on the front lines here, working hard to get this story. Think about the climb in circulation. Think about all those happy faces in the front office."

"Right now I'm thinking about your dinner. It's got to be tough enough being homeless without having to eat your meatloaf."

Before molding the chopped meat in the loaf pans, Cynthia decided she needed to make her own phone call—to Detective Steve Bradley. By the time her meatloaf was cooked, Detective Bradley was there to watch them all come out of the oven.

"I'll never, as long as I live, I'll *never* understand you, Cynthia! Just what are you trying to prove?"

"Nothing." Cynthia, wearing heavy oven mitts, carried her loaf pans, one by one, to the cooling racks. "That's why I'm giving you this list. You follow up."

"Whose bright idea was it to have you come back here? Bernie's?"

"No, mine."

"Do you have a death wish or something?"

Cynthia bent over the pans and inhaled the steamy vapor. "Can you smell the basil? I tried a new recipe. I hope it's good."

"I get paid to put my life on the line. What's your excuse?"

"It's not what you think, Steve. I'm not digging for that drug story. I just want to finish my story about the mission and how sometimes people get a new lease on life."

"Maybe so, but does Skinner know that? And how about the killer who may still be here at the mission? Did you send them memos with your change of plans?"

Cynthia stripped off the oven mitts and placed them on the counter next to the hot pans. "I'll be more careful this time with my questions. It won't be long before interested parties understand that I'm looking for something totally different."

Steve squinted at her. "You willing to take that chance? To do what? Some sob-sister piece? Did you get religion or something?"

"I guess I got the 'or something' but don't ask me to explain what that is."

Steve moved closer and put his hands on her waist. "I can't say I approve." He eyed the pans on the counter. "Although I find this new domestic side of you sexy. You were never this good in the kitchen when we played house."

Cynthia pushed him away. "Let me know what you find after you've checked out that list."

"Okay, okay." He tried to nuzzle her ear but she stepped to the side. "It sure would be nice if you'd make meatloaf for me sometime."

"Don't hold your breath."

"Is that what you tell your preacher friend?"

"You don't usually say stupid things, Steve, so what makes you say something stupid now? Why bring Jonathan into this? He's not my type at all. And I'm certainly not his. Besides, he's a pastor with his mind always on higher things."

"He's a man, Cynthia. Just a man, like the rest of us."

Jonathan sat at his desk staring at his open Bible. *Her princes in the midst thereof are like wolves ravening the prey to shed blood, and to destroy souls, to get dishonest gain.*

Two days ago, when he was reading Ezekiel 22, this verse jumped out. And for the past forty-eight hours he had been asking the Lord what it meant. He still had no answer; only an uneasy feeling that continued to linger.

He thought of Cynthia and felt fear slide over him like a shirt. He rose from his desk and walked to the maple door and locked it. Then he returned to his seat and began praying. Even after several minutes of doing spiritual warfare he still sensed a force so hostile, so foreboding that he felt compelled to continue. He also felt something else—the assurance that God was going to expose the wolves.

Cynthia's lips formed a wide smile as she carried a tray of dishes into the kitchen. Three people had stopped and complimented her on her meatloaf.

She breezed past Miss Emily and tried to read her face. Miss Emily had not said one word about her masterpiece. Cynthia had promised herself she wouldn't ask, but Miss Emily's silence was driving her mad. "Well, are you going to tell me if you liked my handiwork or not?" she finally blurted.

"The basil was a nice touch," Miss Emily said, already washing down the stovetop with Clorox. "I'll have to remember that for next time."

"Then you liked it?"

"Rivaled mine." Miss Emily winked. "It makes you feel good, doesn't it?"

Cynthia shrugged. "It's a trivial accomplishment. Nothing that will ever earn me a Pulitzer."

"But it gives you pleasure."

"Actually . . . yes." Cynthia placed the tray on the counter, her face beaming. "But for the life of me I don't understand why."

"It's because you've given others pleasure. It's the law of reciprocity . . . the law of sowing and reaping. In other words, you're getting what you have given. Understand?"

Cynthia wiped her hands on a towel then walked over to Miss Emily and hugged her. "Yes. I believe I do."

Cynthia finished washing down the last of the tables and looked around for Willie Tanner. He was supposed to mop up after each meal but she could tell by how her shoes stuck to the floor when she walked that he had missed doing it today. Maybe she'd just mop it herself. It was a good time. Aside from a few stragglers, the place was empty. Almost everyone had gone to his room. She headed for the corner closet which housed the mop and large, yellow pail on wheels, but stopped when she saw a man step from the shadows.

"I'm glad to see you, Willie. This floor's in bad shape."

When the man got closer and Cynthia saw it wasn't Willie, her heart raced. "What are you doing here?"

"No need to ask you that 'cause I already know. You're meddling. You just can't stop meddling, can you?"

"I'm doing a story, on the mission and how lives are transformed here."

"Is this why your cop friend was here?" Skinner's eyes glowed like magma.

"You need to leave. There's a restraining order that says you can't be here."

"That's not gonna do you any good. That's what I wanted you to know. Before, I was only going to cut you up a little, alter your face—give you a new look. But now, I'm turning you into bait."

Cynthia walked away. "I'm calling the police, Skinner."

"It don't matter. They won't find me. But I can find you. Anytime I want. You think on that. And count yourself among the dead. You hear? You're dead!"

CHAPTER 18

"I want you out of there! Pronto! I should have my head examined for listening to you; for letting you convince me to send you back."

"If I leave, Bernie, my story won't have clout."

"I don't care. You get your tail back here. Skinner doesn't sound like the kind of man you can reason with. Let the police handle it. You *did* report Skinner's threat to the police?"

"Yes, Bernie, of course. I suppose I could try to salvage what I can of the story and maybe write it along some other angle. I'll have to play with it a bit."

"Just do your playing back here in North Oberon."

"Okay, okay. But it'll have to wait for another twenty-four hours because Stubby's getting out of the hospital tomorrow and I want to pick him up."

"Fine, but after that, no more excuses. Not if you still want to work for the *Trib*."

Cynthia laughed. "Ooooh . . . I think I'm scared."

"You should be. Yesterday, some hotshot reporter came into my office with her resume. Impressive, too. She was looking for your job."

"You don't say? Mind if I ask who?"

"You'll find out pretty quick if you're not here at your desk in two days."

Cynthia's palms felt clammy and her stomach wouldn't stop doing flips as she walked toward Stubby's hospital room. She blinked several times hoping to relieve the heaviness in her eyes. She hadn't slept well because of her nightmare. It was the same haunting dream where she couldn't get to the window in time, and ended with Julia lying on the concrete patio, as lifeless as a rag doll; and blood splattered everywhere, painting the concrete, red.

She couldn't go on like this. She felt as if she was trapped on some weird board game where she'd take one step forward, then two back, and all the while the object was to keep from sliding downward into what resembled Dante's Inferno.

One thing she had learned at the mission was that your secret sins always find you out. Even if they were never made public, they'd eat you alive. There was no escape. She was sure that's why so many homeless had drinking or drug problems because they couldn't run from their sins, either. She had come to believe there was wisdom in confession. Would it bring her peace? Get rid of those nightly demons? No way of knowing. But she was finally willing to find out.

Even so, there would be a price.

There was always a price. Stubby would hate her. So would everyone at the mission when they found out, and they were sure to find out. Maybe it wouldn't be so bad, because she was leaving anyway. Bernie had forced that issue. And that would make everyone's disgust, bearable. She wouldn't be around long enough to let it beat her down.

Still . . . she hated the thought of disappointing them. But their contempt would be well deserved. And payment was long overdue.

She wondered if Stubby could ever forgive her. She wouldn't hold her breath. Then there was Jonathan. Wouldn't Steve Bradley have a good laugh if he knew how much she liked that man? She could almost see the derision on Steve's face. Now, Jonathan would hate her, too. And though she had hardly dared think it or admit it, a part of her had wanted, had hoped, there would be more than friendship between them. She could forget that, now.

And what of Miss Emily and Effie? She couldn't bear the thought of losing their friendship, especially Miss Emily's. But she would after they found out she was a coward, a killer.

Her chest tightened. And for a moment she couldn't breathe— the pain of it all was too great. But this time she'd see it through. She had to. No matter what. Because she could live with people hating her. But she couldn't live with the lie. Not anymore.

It was killing her.

"You sure are quiet, Miss Cynthia. You ain't said two words since pickin' me up. I hope this weren't a big inconvenience for you."

Cynthia's knuckles were white from clutching the steering wheel. She looked over at her passenger and forced a smile. "No inconvenience, Stubby. I was happy to do it. And Jonathan didn't mind loaning me his car."

"Well, I appreciate it. You sure are good to me."

Cynthia slammed on the brakes, making the tires squeal and causing Stubby to grab the arm rest. Then she pulled into a small park containing a plastic slide set, and stopped the car.

"You okay, Miss Cynthia? You ain't lookin' so good. If I didn't know better, I'd say you'd been on a binger. An all-nighter."

Cynthia took a deep breath. "No binger, but I didn't sleep well last night."

"Miss Emily says hot milk can cure that along with a little . . . ."

"Only the truth will cure it, Stubby." She unhooked her seat belt because she was having trouble breathing again, then turned to the elderly man beside her. "You're going to hate me and I can't bear the thought of that, but it can't be helped because I have to tell you something. Something important. Something I should have told years ago."

"I could never hate you, Miss Cynthia. Never."

Tears filled Cynthia's eyes. "Oh, yes you can. And that's okay. I want you to know that. I don't expect you to forgive me, and that's okay."

"You're startin' to scare me. You got a crazy look in your eyes. I ain't never seen that look in 'em before. You sure you don't just want to go to the mission and lie down?"

"Years ago, you came to a house in North Oberon's Spring Terrace and installed a large casement window in the upstairs playroom—a playroom belonging to two little girls. Remember?"

Stubby's face whitened as he nodded.

"What you don't know is that one of the girls removed the screen, to see if she could fly her kite out that window. It never did fly. But the trouble was she couldn't get the screen back on, so she just leaned it against the edges. Later, when that girl saw her sister taking her things she chased after her, only she had forgotten about that screen until it was too late, until that sister, who wasn't looking where she was going, ran straight for it and . . . out. I was that girl, Stubby. I was the one who removed the screen. Everyone thought you had been careless, that you had installed it improperly. Everyone blamed you. And I never said a word. Not one word. I let you take the blame. And I'm so very very sorry." Tears streaked

Cynthia's face. "I was a coward. And I ruined your life. I hope that someday . . . maybe someday, a long time from now, you'll be able to forgive me."

Stubby's mouth was open, his bottom lip quivering. "You the big sister of that . . . ?"

Cynthia sat sobbing into her hands unable to speak.

"You mean, it weren't my fault? It weren't my fault that that little girl died? All these years . . . I was thinkin' I killed her. That I . . . ."

Cynthia felt a hand patting her shoulder.

"There. There. No need to cry. That was mighty kind of you tellin' me, lettin' me know. It takes a load off my heart. So don't cry no more, Miss Cynthia. Please don't cry. It's okay."

Cynthia looked up. "You don't understand. *I'm* the one who ruined your life, Stubby. If I had told the truth you would have kept your business. You would have been successful and lived a happy life."

"Maybe . . . maybe not. Who can say? I was still the old Stubby, the sinner. But I was a growd man, while you was a wee bit of a thing no more than five. I coulda handled it better, me bein' the adult and all. I coulda pressed through, continued tryin'. But at the first sign of trouble, what did I do? Cut and run. That's what. So if you expect me to blame a five-year old for my troubles, you'd be wrong. 'Course it woulda been better for you if you had come clean. It woulda made you happier. Made you sleep good at night."

Cynthia used her fingertips to blot her tears. "Why are you being so kind? Why don't you yell or curse or something?"

"'Cause I ain't mad."

"Are you saying you . . . forgive me?"

"'Course I forgive you. So, no more cryin', okay?"

"But how? I don't understand? I . . . ."

"It's that simple, Miss Cynthia. I gotta forgive you. After all them things Jesus forgave me for, if I don't forgive you how am I ever gonna look Him in the eye again?"

Cynthia scrambled over the center console and gave Stubby an awkward hug, then kissed him on the cheek. "Thank you," she whispered, her voice catching.

"Now, Miss Cynthia, you're embarrassin' me. Quit that."

"There's one more favor I'd like to ask."

"Sure Miss Cynthia. Anythin'."

Cynthia settled back in her seat and buckled in. "From now on, just call me Cynthia."

"Well . . . I don't know. Seems kinda disrespectful."

"We're friends, Stubby, and should call each other by our first names."

"Well . . . I . . . ."

"Okay, if you can't do it then I'll start calling you *Mr.* Stubby. How's that?"

"Don't sound right. In fact it sounds downright silly. So . . . okay, Cynthia, I'll do it."

As she started the engine she turned and saw a smile spreading across Stubby's face.

Stubby White walked around his room at the mission touching the bed frame, the dresser, the sink as though assuring himself this was not a dream.

The past two and a half weeks in the hospital were foggy, like a bad drug trip. Sometimes he thought he remembered. A word here . . . a word there . . . would pop into his head. *Fruit* was one of them. But there were others—none of them made sense—*striped shirt sleeve, winded breathing and a snake . . . no . . . not a snake, some-thin' else . . . somethin' familiar.* He'd have to trust God to put those words together and make sense of them.

But trusting God seemed easier now. He had seen Jesus. And ever since he woke up from what doctors called a coma, Stubby had felt the Presence. It warmed him. It held him. It filled him with joy. It made it easy to forgive Cynthia when she told him who she was and what she had done. Even now, the Presence was strong enough for Stubby to feel without any effort at all. He wondered how long before the filth of the world would spoil it—how long before he'd lose it altogether.

At times, he still hated being here. Hated the idea that he had been pulled away from his beautiful Jesus. But Jesus said he had to come back, so here he was. And to Stubby's way of thinking, there was nothing left for him to do but live all out for the Master. Only he wasn't the old Stubby anymore, little and worm-like. A big God loved him and that made Stubby big. Maybe he'd write a poem about it—a praise poem—when he got the chance.

Stubby pulled a clean pullover from his drawer. Cynthia had brought him fresh clothes when she picked him up, but they had absorbed that nasty hospital smell. Even his skin, his hair smelled like the hospital. He stripped off his shirt and pants, and redressed.

It was good of Cynthia to come. He had planned on taking a cab. But there she was, without being asked. *Cynthia.* He smiled when he thought of her. He loved her like he imagined he would a daughter if he had one. He could never hate her no matter what she did. He pictured her spinning on a wheel, a clay pot being molded and pressed into shape. But the enemy would try to mess things up; keep her feeling guilty over her past and maybe even use Skinner or someone else to hurt her. He'd have to watch, keep a good lookout, just like Jesus told him to. Cynthia was his responsibility now, and he didn't mind a bit. Only . . . he didn't want to lose the Presence. Not yet.

"Stubby?" There was a loud rap at the door. "Can I come in?"

He tried to ignore it. It seemed to make the Presence fade, seemed to pull him further into the mud of the earth.

"Stubby! You in there?"

He hesitated, then shuffled to the door and opened it. Jonathan's kind, concerned face made Stubby smile in spite of himself. This must be where God wanted him, now.

"Stubby, are you okay?"

Stubby nodded and gestured for Jonathan to come in. "I'm fine, Pastor Jonathan. Just sorta in a fog, I guess. But I'm comin' around."

"Well, it's good to have you back." Jonathan gave Stubby a hearty hug, then a pat on the back. "We missed you around here."

"That's nice of you to say." Stubby glanced shyly at his dirty sneakers. The leather was scuffed and cracked around the toes, and imbedded grime outlined the stitching. Laces, once white, now gray and frayed, hung loosely. Dirty shoes from walking in a dirty world.

"Anyway . . . I wanted to welcome you back. That and to ask a favor, but only if you're up to it. While you were in the hospital, Willie Tanner helped us out."

"Yeah, I was glad to hear you got someone. This place is too big for you to run alone. But I ain't never heard of this Tanner. Least I don't think so—the name don't ring any bells." Stubby noticed that Jonathan looked troubled. "Hope he kept the place ship-shape the way you like it."

"I hate to say it, but he didn't do well. He's got problems and needs someone to show him how things should be done. And that's what I wanted to ask—if you're feeling up to it, that is. I want you to take him under your wing. Train him, as an assistant. God knows there's plenty of work for two. He doesn't have your skills, though. Sometimes he oversleeps and starts late. Sometimes he doesn't show up at all. Sometimes he'll start a job and not finish it. But you can whip him into shape, teach him what to do. It may be a challenge, but you'll be doing him a favor and helping the mission as well. What do you say?"

Stubby scratched his head. "Is that all? You had me worried, with your face so troubled-lookin'. 'Course I'll do it. You were there when I needed a helpin' hand. I'd like to be there when someone else needs one. Might as well be this Willie Tanner."

Jonathan sighed. "I can't tell you how good it is to have you back. I have to admit, it's been somewhat of a strain around here without you."

"Now you gotta quit braggin' on me like that or I might get a swelled up head." Stubby glanced at his sneakers again. "Then I might ask for a raise and that ain't gonna make you happy. You let me see what I can do with Tanner. One thing I know—if God can change someone like me, He can change anybody."

"Stubby's back!" Cynthia said, bouncing into Day Care just in time to see Effie drying her eyes. Before Cynthia could ask what was wrong, Daisy ran up and gave her a hug.

"Read story!" Daisy said, pushing a book, with a large, red dog on the cover, into Cynthia's hand.

Cynthia planted a kiss on the child's forehead, then stole a worried glance at Effie. "Okay, but let me talk to your mother first."

"Mommy's sick. We gotta play by ourselves." Daisy put a finger to her lips. "We gotta be *quiet*."

By now, Effie had finished blotting her eyes and shooed Daisy away. "Go look at them pictures and if you don't pester Cynthia and me, maybe she'll come over and read to you."

Cynthia watched Daisy skip away. "She's not the same little girl. She's becoming quite a chatterbox. She's even smiling!"

"Yes, praise be to God. Everyday, she's gettin' better."

Cynthia turned back to Effie and noticed the deep circles, the sunken eyes.

"I haven't been sleepin' so good," Effie said, as if apologizing for her appearance.

"What's wrong?"

"It's my boy, Jeff." Effie pulled a tissue from her pocket and twisted it in her hands. "He got in a knife fight with someone in a rival gang. Cut the other guy pretty good. Now, the cops are lookin' for him." Effie swiped her eyes with the tissue. "Cynthia, I just gotta find him, talk some sense into him before it's too late. If he's with them Salamanders much longer he's gonna go to reform school for sure. Then what? Prison?" Effie broke down and wept. "I been prayin' and prayin'. I don't know what else to do. I'm at my wits end. And time's runnin' out. I just know it. I gotta do somethin' quick."

Cynthia saw that the children were beginning to look frightened so she smiled and waved at them, then turned Effie and herself so they faced the wall. "Calm down. Just take a deep breath and calm down."

Instead of calming down, Effie grabbed Cynthia and shook her. "You gotta help me. You promised, remember? You promised you'd help find my boy."

"I said I'd *try*. But I'm not sure there's anything I can do."

"You're a reporter. I always knew there was somethin' different about you the minute I laid eyes on you. You got education and you been to more of the world than South Oberon. I met educated before, even eaten out of the same garbage pail with 'em. But I knew you was different. You know how to get things done. You got sources. You can ask questions. People will talk to you. People always talk to reporters."

"I can try. That's all I can do. I can't make any promises. But I'll try. Okay?" What could she say? What words were adequate enough to soothe the heartache of a lifetime of poverty and struggle, disappointment and pain? As she put her arms around Effie, felt her heartbreak, Cynthia understood why she had cultivated so few friendships. And for a fleeting moment, she wished it were still so.

Cynthia watched Steve Bradley nibble on the bologna sandwich she had made him. Other than the crumbs he was leaving all over the counter, the kitchen was spotless . . . and quiet. Miss Emily had discreetly disappeared when Steve arrived. From time to time, a man's voice or muffled laughter floated from the main room and through the double doors of the kitchen. Cynthia could tell by the low volume that most of the residents had gone to their rooms. She poured hot coffee into two empty mugs and handed one to Steve.

"No sign of Skinner. We've got an APB out but we're not holding our breath. Too many places to hide around here. Places even the police won't search." Steve sipped his coffee and frowned. "Should I bother saying, 'I told you so'?"

Cynthia shook her head. "You warned me. I didn't listen. You were right. I was wrong. Simple as that."

"It's not about being right or wrong. It's about being *stupid*."

"If you think you're going to get me to admit I was stupid, then you've got another think coming. Let's just say I'm learning . . . the hard way."

Steve placed his cup on the counter, accidently knocking it against the sandwich plate. "How long do you intend staying here?"

"I'm leaving tomorrow. Bernie's pulled the plug. Ordered me out. So I'm stuck writing an un-writeable story."

"If that's so, why wait? Why not leave tonight? I could drive you home. Maybe stay at your place, give you a little police protection." He tried moving closer to Cynthia but she stopped him.

"What I need right now is not protection, but information. I need to find someone. How would I go about that?"

"Depends on who it is."

"A Salamander." Cynthia watched as a disapproving look crawled over Steve's face.

"Forget it. Most of them don't want to be found. And they're a nasty bunch. Imagine a whole gang of Skinners running around with knives and you'll get an idea of what they're like."

The analogy made Cynthia shudder. "But . . . if someone had to find one of them, how would he go about it?"

"Is this for your story?"

Cynthia shook her head.

"For what then?"

"For a mother who's sick with worry about her son."

"I swear, Cynthia, you're losing your edge. Where's that famous Wells instinct? Are you going to make me call you stupid all over again?"

Cynthia picked up his cup and poured out the remaining coffee, then put it into the sink.

"Hey! I wasn't finished!"

"Yes you were. Good night, Steve."

"Now, wait a second. I know I was insulting, but it's because I want you to think. Okay? Think about what you're doing, Cynthia. Will you do that?"

"Good night, Steve."

"You haven't even given me a chance to tell you the reason I'm here." He pulled a paper from his jacket pocket. "The list you asked me to check out—you know, the food stores and other vendors.

Well, I did and nothing, nada, zilch. They're all legitimate businesses. No red flags, nothing amiss."

Cynthia took the paper from Steve's hand and stared at it. "What's this asterisk next to Alliance Bakery Supplies?"

"It's nothing. I only marked it because I was surprised and wanted to check it further."

"Why? I thought you said there were no red flags."

"There weren't. When we looked into Alliance Bakery we found it was owned by Charles Angus, or rather it's a wholly owned subsidiary of Angus Enterprises. Nothing wrong with it. Like I said, it just surprised me because I thought Angus was into computers and software now."

"What exactly is Alliance Bakery?"

"A wholesaler that supplies local bakeries, as well as the men's shelter, with flour, sugar, that sort of thing. Come to think of it, I even saw Beacon Mission on their list."

Cynthia paced the kitchen, glancing, from time to time, at the paper in her hand. "Doesn't Angus own the glass factory?"

"Yeah, and Nationwide Distributors. But he keeps these open to help employ the Skid Row crowd. A sort of civic duty thing."

Cynthia wadded up the list and threw it into the garbage. "You're right, Steve, there's nothing here. It all seems hopeless. If we could just catch a break, get a real lead. Anyway, thanks for trying. I appreciate it."

"Sure . . . anytime. I could also try to help, with that other matter, if you really want me to. You know, finding that Salamander, that kid for his mother."

Cynthia gave Steve's hand a squeeze. "Well, aren't you a dear?" Then she pulled a clean cup from the cabinet and poured fresh coffee into it. She handed the steaming cup to Steve and smiled. "What's the plan?"

"There's this informant who knows the area. It's going to cost you. I don't know how much, yet. I'll shell out the money, but you'll have to reimburse me since it's not police business and I can't very well charge it to the department."

"Sure, I'm good for it. You know that. Just see if you can get your snitch on it right away. The boy's name is Jeff Watson. Now, tell me the plan."

"It's simple. You're going to pay an informant to set up a meeting with Jeff."

"What am I going to pay this informant to say? That Jeff's mother wants to see him?"

"No, we're going to tell him that a reporter wants to write a story on gang life and will make it worth his while to do an interview."

"More cash?"

"Yes. This isn't going to be cheap."

"Okay, so I don't go to Bermuda this year. What reason does the informant give for me signaling Jeff out?"

Steve scratched his head. "I can't do all the thinking. Help me out here."

"I don't know much about him. Effie . . . that's Jeff's mother . . . told me Jeff is new to the gang and that he just had a knife fight. Maybe I could say I wanted to get the slant on gang life from a new member, and that I heard about him on the street, heard about his recent fight."

"That could scare him off. Make him think it's a trap. Especially if the police are looking for him."

"They are." Cynthia ignored the irritated look on Steve's face.

"On the other hand, it may appeal to his machismo, his masculinity. Anyway, if Jeff has a need to prove himself, a need to have his ego stroked, he may show. Fifty-fifty. That's the odds I'd give."

"All right. Set it up. For tomorrow."

"*Tomorrow?*"

"I know a little about human nature, too. If I give him a narrow window and make him think I'll go elsewhere for the interview, it might tip the odds in my favor."

"Speaking of odds. You want to tell me the chance of us getting back together?"

"Zero-zero."

Cynthia sat with her ankles crossed, studying the dark paneled room. Her shiny, blonde hair was pulled into a ponytail, and she swiped it, self-consciously. When she did interviews, she always dressed the part, but this morning all she could find in the storeroom, where Miss Emily kept the donated clothes, was a sleeveless blue jumper and white cotton, short sleeve tank top. She put the two together to create the ensemble she now wore. It obviously didn't serve her well because the secretary, after giving her the once over, refused to believe Cynthia actually had an appointment.

She should have gone home and gotten decent clothes. But it was only after Steve left that Cynthia had come up with the idea of interviewing Charles Angus for a possible ending to her un-writable story, and it was far too late then to head home. And when she called the Angus headquarters this morning and was allowed to speak with the man himself, he had agreed to an interview if she could get to his office by nine. He promised to give her fifteen minutes.

Now, looking at the Picasso hanging on the wall behind the desk, Cynthia felt embarrassed. She'd have to get over it or it would hamper the interview. *Clothes don't make the man . . . or woman, Wells.* She twirled her hair around her finger. *But people do judge a book by its cover.*

When the door opened behind her, Cynthia smelled cigar smoke. She turned and saw a large, imposing man enter, holding what looked like a knockwurst in his hand. He brought it to his lips, making the tip glow.

She rose, out of respect or awe . . . she couldn't tell which . . . and extended her hand. She saw an amused look on his face as he glanced at her outfit. *Don't apologize, Wells. Don't you dare apologize.* "Forgive my appearance, but it was rather short notice and I didn't have a chance to change." She bit the inside of her lip as she watched Charles Angus smirk, then descend onto his chair as if it were a throne.

"I must confess I was taken back by your call, and curious. You said you wanted to discuss Alliance Bakery Supplies and what was going on in Skid Row. Of course you didn't mention what exactly was going on there or the relationship to Alliance."

"I've been working on a drug story involving Skid Row." Cynthia almost gagged on the cloud of cigar smoke that streamed from Charles Angus' mouth like one of the chimneys at his glass factory. Unconsciously, she fanned the air with her hand. "Anyway, I've had to table the story because of lack of evidence. But it seems that homeless men are being recruited to run drugs in and out of Skid Row."

Charles Angus rested his cigar on the long, marble ashtray and leaned his elbows on the desk. "Interesting and unfortunate, but I still don't see the connection."

Cynthia watched as he placed the fingertips of one hand to the corresponding tips of the other hand and bounced them together.

"What exactly do you want from me, Miss Wells?"

"Everyone knows how civic-minded you are. I was hoping you could use your influence and resources to put a stop to this kind of thing, to help clean up Skid Row."

"I've been trying to do that for years, in one way or another. I operate my glass factory and distribution house at a loss. A lot of those people have no trade, no skills. What else could they do if I were to close down these enterprises?" Charles Angus stopped bouncing his fingers and smiled. "Of course I prefer you didn't print that part. I'd hate my competitors to learn I operate *anything* at a loss."

"You can count on me leaving that part out. I don't think anyone would believe me, anyway. But I'd like to end my story more hopeful than it currently is, and since I can't deliver what I had planned, I'd like to at least deliver a promise from one of Oberon's most prominent citizens, a promise that our city will do all it can to clean up this problem."

"Which problem is that, Miss Wells? The drugs or the homelessness? Or . . . the problem of ending your story?"

Cynthia smiled. She may look like a country bumpkin in this outfit, but Angus was certainly not treating her like one. "Actually, I'd like you to help me with all three."

"In any particular order?"

Cynthia shook her head.

"Well, let's see. Drugs. I'm a member of the Chamber of Commerce, and the chief of police and I play golf once a month. It won't be difficult to convince other businessmen that a drug-free North and South Oberon would be good for everyone. We could raise funds for adding private security and patrols; use our influence, unofficially of course, with the police to see that more manpower is directed in that area. Start a Clean-Up-the-City campaign. If Giuliani can clean up New York City, we should be able to cleanup Oberon. How am I doing so far?"

Cynthia grinned. "Great."

"Okay, next one—homelessness. Now that's a tough one. Aside from providing jobs, and building the mission and . . . ."

"The mission is yours?"

"That's right. I built it fifteen years ago at Reverend Gates' request. Okay, aside from the jobs, the mission, and donating free supplies through Alliance, I don't see how I can do much more, do you?"

"Your efforts and contributions are impressive, Mr. Angus. But there is one thing more that may prove helpful—and here's where Alliance comes into the picture. Allow Alliance delivery trucks going to the men's shelter to be manned by an undercover cop. Maybe, just maybe, he'll see something and . . . ."

"Now we're talking drugs again. I thought we covered that?"

"More than a third of the homeless use drugs. You can't discuss one without the other."

"You have an interesting way about you, Miss Wells, similar to a tenacious predator or, dare I say it, a true reporter?"

Cynthia unlocked her ankles and settled in the chair. Her outfit was no longer an issue.

"Now, suppose I agree, which I don't right now, but suppose I do agree to this scheme of yours, have you cleared it with the police? Are they willing to do what you suggest?"

"The investigation is over, but at your request perhaps the police will be willing to reopen the case and to utilize Alliance."

"So, this plan is all without police approval or even knowledge?"

"Correct. It's just the appeal of one citizen to another, for the good of our city."

Charles Angus fingered his cigar. In the silence, Cynthia heard the desk clock tick loudly as though pacing the executive—keeping him on track. "I must excuse myself. My meeting has started. But I'll leave you with this: Regarding the use of my trucks as an undercover vehicle, I'll think about it. And as for your story, my gift to you is this statement, which you can quote verbatim, 'Charles Angus declares war on drugs and homelessness in Oberon.'"

From the door of his office, Jonathan watched Willie Tanner wipe his nose on the sleeve of his dingy, blue-striped shirt, then resume pushing his mop across the hall floor. The mop dragged dirty water from one spot to another, streaking the beige linoleum and making it look more like gray marble. Willie looked surlier than Jonathan had ever seen him. The perpetual scowl was obliterated only when Willie's greasy black hair fell across his face. This happened when Willie bent down, which Jonathan had only seen him do twice— once, when Willie grudgingly moved the yellow industrial pail for a passerby, and the other, to pick up what Jonathan thought looked like a quarter.

Jonathan felt an overwhelming urge to grab the mop from Willie, give it a good rinsing, then rewash the entire hall himself. Instead, he backed into his office and closed the door. He had seen Stubby talk to Willie earlier, had heard Stubby explain the art of using a string mop, apparently with little success. He'd have to be patient. Willie wasn't going to change overnight. If Stubby kept at it, maybe— somewhere down the road—Willie would catch on. But not without the Lord's help. From several of his own encounters, Jonathan knew Willie didn't take instruction well. Didn't like authority. Didn't seem to want to change. Stubby must have sensed this too, because after his instructions, he disappeared and hadn't returned.

Jonathan walked to his desk and sat down. He had a list of calls, as long as the Great Wall of China, to make. When he was finished, maybe he'd have another talk with Willie. See if he couldn't make a few things clearer. He'd also have another talk with Stubby. It wouldn't do to have Stubby giving up so easily.

Jonathan ran his finger down his planner and began dialing the first number but stopped when he heard a gentle tap on the door accompanied by a familiar voice.

"Jonathan?"

He slammed the receiver down on his hand. "Come in, Cynthia." He rubbed his fingers as he suppressed a smile at seeing her outfit. She looked silly and beautiful all at once. When she pulled a chair next to his, his first reflex was to push backward and roll further away but the wheel of his chair caught on one of the desk legs and he could only move two inches. From where he sat he saw the mole, or was it a freckle, dotting the side of her right eye.

"What's up with Willie?"

Jonathan shrugged.

"When I passed him he growled. He actually growled! He told me I was messing up his clean floor. The man needs glasses if he thinks *that* floor's clean."

"Sometimes the Lord sends someone into our lives, someone He uses as sandpaper—to smooth and polish us. It's painful, but that's how He removes those rough edges. I think Willie's our sandpaper."

Cynthia folded her arms across her chest and slid further down in her chair. "I know this is unkind, but to me, Willie symbolizes the worst of what I've seen in some of the homeless. He's dirty, lacks ambition, has no work ethic, can't relate to others and doesn't even try, and has no apparent desire to improve himself."

"You're not going to hear me contradict anything you've said."

"But now you're telling me he's sandpaper and I've got to like being irritated by him. I wonder if I'll ever understand you, Jonathan." Cynthia straightened then leaned forward. "But that's why I like you. You're refreshing and you're honest. I can respect that. I don't have to understand or agree, but I can respect it." She slipped her hand over his. "That's why I value your friendship—why I need a friend like you."

Jonathan placed his other hand over hers and was surprised by how small it was, how it disappeared under his own large-knuckled paw. He hadn't noticed that before or realized how petite she was. She always seemed to fill a room. "You have my friendship."

"Then you'll keep in touch when I leave?"

Jonathan felt a sinking sensation. "When are you leaving?"

"Today. I have an . . . errand . . . to do with Effie. She's asked me not to talk about it with anyone—except Stubby, he knows—but maybe you can keep us in prayer? Okay?"

Jonathan nodded.

"Anyway, right after that, I'm leaving. Going back to North Oberon."

"I expected as much, after Skinner's last threat. And I've seen your detective friend coming and going. I was sure he'd convince you to leave. And it's for the best. It's too dangerous here for you."

"I wanted to stay, to go the distance this time. For the story and myself."

"Were you able to get what you needed? For your article, I mean?"

Cynthia shook her head. "Maybe you and I could have lunch sometime. Maybe you could give me the perspective I'm looking for."

"I don't think Detective Bradley would like that." Jonathan noticed his hand was still over Cynthia's and removed it.

"He's just a friend, Jonathan. Nothing more. As a matter of fact, I'm not dating right now, so I don't have to answer to anyone. Will you? Have to answer to anyone, I mean?"

Jonathan shook his head. His temples pounded. For years he had prayed for the Lord to send him a Godly wife. So how was it possible that he was so attracted . . . so utterly attracted to and actually falling in love with someone who didn't know God at all?

"Well, if you're not dating anyone and I'm not dating anyone, then who's to object if we have lunch from time to time?"

"No one." Jonathan scribbled down a number on a Post-it and handed it to Cynthia. You can reach me on my cell."

"How many other women have you given this to?" Cynthia asked, with a smile.

"Only one." Jonathan thought he saw a flicker of disappointment cross her face. "My Aunt Adel."

Jonathan almost fell off the chair when he saw Aunt Adel walk through the door of his office.

"Well, Dearest, I couldn't bear another one of your refusals for dinner, so I decided to come here in person. We can eat at the mission or I can take you out. Your choice."

Jonathan rose and gave his aunt a hug. He waited until she was settled in the nearby chair before retaking his own. Then he glanced at his desk clock. "Since when has three o'clock become your dinner hour?"

Aunt Adel giggled. "I know it's early, but I don't mind waiting until you're free. I thought I'd look around. See where my nephew spends his days and nights. Then I thought I'd pay that delightful Cynthia Wells a visit. You said she was staying here, collecting information for a story."

"I'd be happy to show you around, introduce you to my staff. But you won't be seeing Cynthia. She left."

"Oh . . . will she be coming back?"

"No."

"Never?"

Jonathan saw his aunt studying him like she used to when he was a little boy and had done something wrong. "She's finished here. Her boss wanted her to wrap things up and go home."

"Really? That's a shame. I mean . . . I'm sure everyone is going to miss her. You are going to miss her, aren't you?"

Jonathan shuffled the papers on his desk. "So what's going on in my favorite aunt's life?"

"I've been busy, with the church ladies—you know, the usual thing. By the way, Gertie sends her love. She told me to tell you to be sure to invite her to the party."

"What party?"

"The engagement party. Yours and Cynthia's. She's sure you'll be getting engaged any day now."

Jonathan felt his face flush. "Sometimes that woman is beyond ridiculous! I hope you set her straight. I hope you stopped her from spreading yet another one of her outrageous rumors."

"How was I to know it was outrageous? You never tell me anything anymore. You're always busy. That's why I came. To touch base with my nephew. See what God is doing in his life."

Aunt Adel's sweet smile stopped Jonathan from exploding outright. Instead, he banged drawers and pushed papers from one side to another until Aunt Adel tapped on the desktop with her knuckles.

"Have I said something wrong?"

"Wrong? You don't see anything wrong with hoping a pastor marries an unsaved woman?"

"Well of course, Dearest. Gertie understands that you can't marry Cynthia until she comes to the Lord. And she said she was taking care of things. She and the prayer chain."

Jonathan sighed and pushed his chair away from the desk. "It pains me to say this, Aunt Adel, but you're sounding more like Gertie every time we talk."

"Oh, dear, are her traits rubbing off?"

Jonathan thought he heard his aunt giggle.

"Still, give me enough credit to know there's no way you'd ever look at someone like Cynthia. After all, she's a reporter. And you know how they are."

"That's unkind."

"What I mean is, God would never choose someone like *her* as a wife for you. She's too . . . too . . . well, for one thing she smiles too much and she talks a lot. And she doesn't seem that serious either, about serious things, like homelessness for instance. I bet it's all about the story. Right? I bet she doesn't even care about any of the people she's met here. I bet they don't mean anything to her at all."

"That's not true. She's really tender hearted. Stubby told me she's had great loss in her life—a sister died when they were both young. He wouldn't go into details but I can see how this makes her distant at times, makes her try to protect herself from being hurt again. I think she wants to reach out and love others and have them love her back and . . . ." Jonathan stopped when he saw the smug look on his aunt's face.

"So, when are you going to see her again?"

"She said she'd like to have lunch sometime."

Aunt Adel reached over and tapped Jonathan's arm. "She needs a friend, Dearest. I believe God wants you to introduce her to our Jesus, to the best friend she'll ever have. Are you up to it?"

"I don't know. It's become personal. You know?"

"Yes. I saw it . . . the beginning of it anyway . . . when we were all together at the restaurant."

"I can't be unequally yoked, Aunt Adel. You know that. And I can't go through the heartbreak of another Lydia. I can't afford to fall for someone who isn't interested in being a pastor's wife. Someone who has little concern for the things of God. You know how long it took me to get over Lydia. I can't . . . I *won't* go through that again."

CHAPTER 19

Cynthia walked beside Effie, holding her hand as if she were a child. She felt the quiver of Effie's arm, heard the faltering steps of her feet. When she looked at Effie's face, Cynthia saw a mix of anticipation and fear. She wished she knew this God Effie and Jonathan were always invoking. They'd need a protector where they were going.

She had called Bernie earlier to tell him she wouldn't be in today, that she was still in South Oberon, and his response made her fear he was going to pop a blood vessel. She'd have plenty of fence-mending to do when she returned to work and hoped this adventure with Effie was going to be worth it.

As she walked, she formed a rushed prayer, like a voice mail, and sent it heavenward to some giant answering machine in the sky. She figured God could play it whenever He wished. There was always that chance He'd just hit the delete button without listening. But since it included Effie, maybe it gave her an edge.

As they got closer to the meeting place, Cynthia's own arm quivered, her own footsteps faltered. She squeezed Effie's hand and noticed she made Effie's fingernails turn white. Effie didn't seem to notice at all.

When Cynthia had gotten the call from Steve telling her the informant had come through, his last words of advice were, "Don't go." Now, she was sorry she hadn't listened. All she knew was that they were heading for a laundromat several blocks inside the infamous South Oberon Projects. Effie said she knew the area well. It was where she grew up.

As Cynthia maneuvered the sidewalk, trying not to trip over the large cracks in the concrete, she wondered how anyone could live here. Instead of flowerpots lining the walk, empty beer bottles and crumpled newspapers formed random clusters. Overturned garbage cans created barriers; and bicycle parts and radios, tires and even broken-down furniture produced odd-looking collages against the sides of buildings.

But it was the graffiti that caught Cynthia's attention. It was everywhere: on signs, doors, buildings, garbage cans. Some of it Cynthia found beautiful—pictures of two children playing under a tree, an eagle in flight, a flower garden behind a white picket fence. But most of it was ugly and violent—scenes of murder and abuse. It was on these canvases of hate and frustration that Cynthia saw drawings of salamanders—a warning, no doubt, of who's territory this was and the consequences of trespassing.

She half expected to see totems or tribal markers rising from the abandoned lots as boundary definers. Instead, she saw silhouettes darting among the shadows. "We're being followed."

"Just keep movin'. The laundromat's only another block."

"What do they want?"

"They're checkin' to see who's comin' into their neighborhood. If they think we're from a rival gang, they'll sound the alarm."

Cynthia laughed in spite of herself. "They wouldn't mistake us for members of a gang. We're practically middle aged!"

"Round here, you can't tell a woman's age just by lookin'. When I was growin' up, I knew sixteen year olds with two or three babies that looked older than you."

Cynthia glanced back at the silhouettes. "Let's make sure we're out of here before dark."

Effie nodded, and the two continued in silence. When they spotted the laundromat, Effie broke free and started jogging. Cynthia followed with her own sprint and when she caught up she grabbed Effie's arm and pulled her to a stop.

"Think about what you're doing. You can't go rushing in like a mama bear. They are expecting a reporter. We have to go in together. So take a deep breath and calm down."

Effie closed her eyes and nodded. "Okay . . . we do it your way. But first, you gotta let me pray."

"Effie, this is not the time or place . . . ."

Effie opened her eyes. "I ain't lettin' you go in there without prayer cover. You gotta have your wits, think fast on your feet. I ain't takin' no chances you'll mess up. No offense, Cynthia, but my boy's future's at stake. Maybe even his life. And you ain't got what it takes to pull this off, not without the Lord." She grabbed Cynthia's hand and began praying. She spoke as though talking to a friend. She asked God to give Cynthia courage and wisdom. Then she asked what Cynthia considered a strange request—she asked God to put His own thoughts and words into Cynthia, and to guide and direct all the upcoming conversations and events, to *use* Cynthia for His purpose.

Strange how Cynthia never considered herself useable by God. Stranger still, that someone else did. As Cynthia looked into Effie's dark, anxious eyes, she realized Effie wasn't trusting her at all. Rather, it was God she was trusting.

Please God, for Effie's sake, don't let me mess this up.

Inside, a large, buxom woman in jeans and a V-neck T-shirt stopped folding clothes when Cynthia and Effie entered. Even from where Cynthia stood, the salamander tattoo scrolled across the top of the woman's breasts was unmistakable.

"You lookin' for someone?" the woman said, strutting up to them, her hips bouncing from side to side. Her arms were muscular and Cynthia guessed they could press a hundred pounds or more; strong enough to toss both Cynthia and Effie out if need be.

Cynthia met the woman's gaze and hoped she didn't look intimidated. "I have an appointment with Jeff Watson."

The woman rested her hand on her hip. The way she looked Cynthia up and down made Cynthia happy she had changed from the hideous blue jumper into a pair of jeans. "Jeff said he was expectin' one woman. Not two. Who's she?"

Cynthia followed the buxom blonde's gaze to Effie. "She's with me."

"That's not what I asked. I asked you who she was."

"I don't see how that's any of your business." Cynthia tried pushing past her but the blonde proved to be a brick wall. "Jeff said we were to meet him in the office."

The woman hesitated, then tossed her stringy, bleached hair. "Yeah . . . okay . . . follow me."

Machines on both sides of the aisle whirled and sloshed as the three women walked to the tiny office in back. Without saying another word, the blonde gestured for the two to go in, then closed the door, leaving them alone.

Cynthia looked around. One corner housed a small safe, the other, a door to a tiny bathroom. A small, cluttered desk took up the center of the room. Next to that, an overflowing garbage pail. There was barely enough space to walk.

On the far wall, a calendar and map partially obscured a giant, talon-like crack. To the side of that were pinned what appeared to be schedules and phone numbers. The next two walls were bare except for a little furniture—a two-drawer filing cabinet and a small, brown vinyl chair. It was the fourth wall that grabbed Cynthia's attention. A huge painted salamander stretched end to end, and reminded Cynthia of the other salamanders she had seen among the graffiti. Did this small office serve as their headquarters? She shuddered at the thought and glanced at Effie who was inspecting the miniscule bathroom.

Any minute Jeff would be coming through that door. Without a word, Effie stepped into the bathroom and closed the door. A few seconds later, a thin, tired-looking boy with burning, frightened eyes walked in. He seemed so young, so vulnerable—not at all what Cynthia expected. It took a few seconds for her to recognize him as the Salamander who had come to her defense the day she went shopping for Daisy and the other children.

"Hey, I know you," Jeff said, strutting like a rooster over to her and stopping just short of her face. "You were that lady on the street, with all them bundles—toys and things for the mission—the cook. Hey! What you doin' here? Huh? You ain't no reporter."

Cynthia stood her ground, feeling moved by this young, frightened boy who would be a man, a boy brave enough to stand up to his leader on her behalf. "I *am* a reporter. I've been working undercover." Cynthia could tell she had said something Jeff didn't like.

"So, *you* are that lady. That reporter lady who's been causin' all the trouble. Maggot said you were the one."

"Maggot? What's a maggot?"

"You watch your mouth! In case you ain't noticed, you're on our turf, now. So you better show some respect."

"I thought you agreed to do an interview."

"This ain't no interview, lady. Wise up. I was sent to check you out. And if you were that troublemaker, then you weren't never gonna get outta here. Know what I mean?"

Cynthia shook her head. "Why would you go to all this trouble to check me out? Why would you care that I was writing a story about two homeless men? Skid Row isn't even your territory."

"Don't go tellin' me what's my territory. You just sit down and shut up. I'll be the one askin' the questions."

Cynthia took the small vinyl chair, leaving the chair behind the desk for Jeff. She wondered how much of this conversation Effie was hearing and what was going through her mind. "If you kill me, you might as well kiss the rest of your life goodbye, because you'll be spending it in jail."

"There you go again, poppin' off your mouth. Did you hear me askin' you anythin'? And don't pretend you'd care where I spend the rest of my life." Jeff dropped into the chair like a flour sack and hung his arms over the sides.

"I do care. Because I care about your mother, and she's sad that you're here with the Salamanders and that you could destroy your life if you're not careful."

Jeff jumped to his feet and did what looked like a belly flop on the desktop. "You keep my Mama out of this. You hear? Don't you even mention her! What right you got, anyway? Talkin' about her? Bringin' her up like that?"

"She's my friend."

"Yeah . . . so? You think that's gonna cut you some slack?" Jeff straightened and pulled out a switchblade then snapped it open. "You think that'll keep me from usin' this? Besides, I don't believe you."

"Then ask her yourself. Effie. Effie!"

Jeff dropped the switchblade when he saw his mother step out of the bathroom. "You brought her here? You crazy? Do you know what you did? You got any idea what you . . . ?"

Effie was all over him, hugging and kissing and squeezing. And Cynthia watched as Jeff yielded to her love, as he softened and warmed, and for a fleeting instant, looked like a little boy. Then she watched as he pushed Effie away. But his face was no longer hard or menacing. It was fear-filled.

"They'll kill you, Mama, if they even think you're mixed up in this. And they won't think twice about it, neither." He looked at the door and frowned. "Did you tell anyone out there who you were?"

Effie shook her head.

"What did you say?"

"Nothin'. Cynthia did all the talkin'. And she said nothin'."

Jeff glared at Cynthia. "I oughta kill you right now for doin' this to my Mama."

"She didn't do nothin' except be a friend. I was the one who begged her to arrange this meetin'. *I was the one.* If you're gonna be mad, be mad at me."

"I could never be mad at you, Mama." His tone softened. "You're my best girl, remember? You'll always be my best girl. You know that." Jeff put his cheek against his mother's, lingered there a moment, then broke away. "But you don't understand how it is. You don't understand what's happenin' here."

Cynthia rose and made Effie take the small vinyl chair. She could see by Effie's face she was about to cry. When she had Effie settled, Cynthia turned to Jeff. "Why don't you tell us what's going on?"

"Somebody wants you dead." Jeff pointed a finger at her as though accusing Cynthia of this all being her fault. "The order's been given. That's all I know. I was supposed to play along with you, pretend to do an interview and try and find out how much you knew, what your angle was. Then I was supposed to give a signal— and some guys in one of them alleys would be watchin' for you. You were never gonna make it out of the Projects alive."

"Because of my article? There's nothing in it that would hurt anyone."

"Well, you ticked somebody off. The contract's big—fifty grand. Maggot said earnin' it would be like takin' candy from a baby. And when a contract comes down, you don't ask 'why' you just do it. It's nothin' personal." Jeff shot a worried glance at his mother. "But I didn't get the contract on account of I'm new and Maggot said it wouldn't be fair to the guys with more seniority."

"I just wish I knew why," Cynthia said with a frown. "It doesn't make sense."

"You already know, lady. You already said the reason. It's your story. Somebody don't want you diggin' around."

Effie rose from her chair and walked over to her son, then cupped his chin between her hands and looked hard into his eyes. "You can't do this, Jeff. You can't let 'em kill Cynthia. You gotta help her."

There was a wild, frantic look on his face before he broke free. "You don't understand, Mama. It don't matter what I want or don't want. It's outta my hands. I don't even know how I'm gonna help *you*! Don't you see the fix you're in? If you're with her, you're goin' down. And there ain't a thing I can do to stop it."

"Then pray with me. We'll ask the Lord to protect us. He's our only hope, now." Effie reached for Jeff's hands, but he pulled away.

"If I don't give that signal, Mama, I'm a dead man."

"And if you give it, you're a different kind of dead man." Effie poked her chest. "In here. That's where you'll start dyin'. Piece by piece. Just like your daddy."

"Don't go talkin' about him! Him and me, we're miles apart! I ain't never gonna be like him!" Jeff cursed loudly. "He's a loser . . . a loser, Mama, and I'm gonna be somebody. People are gonna pick up their heads when I walk by. They're gonna know who I am."

"Yes, boy. They're gonna say there goes that punk the police are after; there goes that boy who's headin' for jail. If you keep with this crowd, there's only two endin's for you—bars or bullets."

"I can't believe what I'm hearin' from my own Mama. My own Mama!"

"You're hearing love words, Jeff. Love words. I love you, baby, and want what's best. You stay with the Salamanders and they'll eat you up, and leave you nothin' for yourself. No life, no future. You gotta come back with me."

"And live in a homeless shelter? No way. I got dreams, places I wanna see. You think I'm gonna be a bum like my old man, a drunkard who beats the stuffin' out of his wife and kids so he feels bigger than he is? So he feels like he's got some power over his life? No, I'm gonna have money in my pocket. I'm gonna get outta this hellhole and be somebody. Get me some respect."

"How? With that?" Effie pointed to the switchblade on the floor.

"If I have to." Jeff picked it up, closed it, and slipped it into his back pocket.

"Then I've come for nothin'."

"What . . . what you mean, for nothin'?"

"For weeks I've known, in here," Effie placed her hand on her chest, "in my spirit, that Satan had his hooks in you and that if I didn't see you soon, that you . . . that it would be too late."

"You're talkin' crazy, Mama. I'm my own man. Nobody's got their hooks in me. Nobody."

"Then prove it by walkin' out of here right now and comin' back to the mission with me. Prove that the Salamanders don't own you."

Jeff looked over Effie's shoulder and glared at Cynthia. "This is all your fault. Things were fine 'til you came around and started ed meddlin'—started stirrin' things up. Now look at the mess you made! You're just what they say—a troublemaker. And you got me in a real fix. If I don't help you, they'll kill my Mama. And if I help you, they'll kill me."

Stubby leaned into the shadow of the building wondering why Cynthia and Effie were taking so long. He tucked his frayed shirt into his dirty khaki pants and almost gagged from the odor. It seemed like ages since he had smelled this bad. But this time, it didn't come naturally; it came by way of hard work. He had found the shirt in the dumpster behind the mission, had put it on, then smeared garbage all over himself, including the fringe of hair around his bald head. That was the worst part, having his hair clumped and sticky with this tonic of rotten fish and curdled milk. No matter which way he turned, he couldn't get away from the smell.

He clutched a small paper bag-covered bottle of gin and took a swig, swished, then spit it out. It smelled and tasted like rubbing alcohol, and Stubby wondered if the liquor store hadn't cheated him. He capped the bottle and stuck it in his shirt, all the while keeping an eye on the laundromat across the street.

Where were they?

Above the tall buildings, Stubby saw a reddish glow telling him the sun was setting. There was still time to get out of the Projects before dark.

But not much.

He wished he had gotten to Cynthia before she left, to tell her about the striped shirt . . . about that tattoo. It was news she'd want to hear. But earlier, when Effie told him her plans, he knew he'd follow because what she and Cynthia were planning was just plain crazy. He'd be their backup in case anything went wrong, though he didn't tell them because he hadn't wanted Effie to say, 'no'. And now something *had* gone wrong. He was sure of it. Effie had promised she'd be back before dark. He looked up at the sky again.

Where were they?

Three youths in red bandanas walked by without giving Stubby a glance. A dirty, drunken man leaning against a building in the mouth of an alley was a common sight in the Projects. And that was an advantage. It made Stubby invisible. But that would change soon enough. He glanced upward again. He couldn't wait much longer. He closed his eyes and prayed, then stepped out of the alley.

As he staggered across the street, Stubby took note of everyone on the sidewalk. It looked like the Salamanders were keeping their distance. No stakeout, no surveillance, and no trace of the three thugs who passed him earlier. He edged his way around the side of the laundromat and toward the back. Then he pulled out his bottle and pretended to take a swig before rounding the corner of the building. From there, he saw one small window. He inched toward it and peered into a bathroom the size of a closet. The door was open and through it Stubby could see into the other room. He squinted, waiting for his eyes to adjust to the different light. A woman stood against the wall talking to a skinny kid. *Cynthia*. Thank God!

He studied the window and decided it was too small to crawl through. He'd have to find another way. He backtracked until he stood by the front door, said another quick prayer, then entered. Half a dozen women were loading or folding clothes. He headed for the back, but was stopped before he got half way.

"You lookin' for someone?" said a buxom blonde with a tattoo across her chest.

Stubby pretended to teeter on his feet and noticed the look of nausea on the woman's face when she got a whiff of him.

She cursed, then grabbed him by the arm. "You got no business here." She began pulling him towards the front door. "I won't have you upsettin' my customers."

"Wait! Now just hold on." Stubby said, slurring his words. "You don't understand. I got big trouble. The old battle-ax is gonna skin me alive if I come back without 'em."

"Make sense, old man."

"I been out with some business . . . associates," Stubby pulled the bottle from his shirt. "Been gone three . . . maybe five days, and she's plenty mad." He removed the cap and offered the bottle to her. "Want some?"

The blonde slapped his hand away, almost knocking the bottle to the floor.

"Hey. I'm just tryin' to be friendly."

"You're smellin' up the place. Get out." She clamped onto Stubby's arm again, but this time he was ready. In a flash, he shoved a ten dollar bill into her other hand.

"If I don't come home with that laundry the witch ain't gonna let me in. See?" He reeled back and forth so his hair brushed against the woman's face. Finally, she let go and backed off.

"Which stuff is yours?"

Stubby shrugged. "Search me. You think I know? Maybe you remember where she put it. She was here a while ago. About five feet, gray hair, walks with a limp." Stubby was describing a woman he had seen coming out of the laundromat earlier. "If you find it, that ten in your hand is yours. And if you fold it up real nice like, I'll give you another just like it."

"Now, where did an old drunk like you get so much money?"

"I told you. My friends and I were doin' business. And I was real lucky. I keep tellin' the battle-ax that five-card stud's my game."

Stubby lurched forward, clutching his stomach. "I'm gonna be sick. I need to puke and get me to a bathroom, quick."

The blonde eyed the ten-dollar bill in her hand then pointed behind her. "Down the hall and to the right. You'll see the sign on the door. And don't miss the bowl. Otherwise, you clean up. Understand?"

Stubby staggered down the hall. When he turned his head, he saw the blonde open a dryer door and pull out some clothes. *He wouldn't have much time.* Instead of going right, Stubby went left, opened the door and quickly closed it behind him. Both Cynthia and Effie's mouth dropped when they saw him.

Jeff pulled his knife.

"Put that away," Stubby said. "I'm a friend."

Effie went to Stubby, as though verifying his statement, and gave him a hug. "We got trouble here, and if you don't get out now, you're gonna be in the middle of it."

"Listen and listen good," Stubby said. "I got Jonathan's car. It's parked right outside the Projects, about a fifteen-minute walk from here. I can be back in twenty. You be outside and waitin'. I'll come and pick you all up."

"Jeff won't stop us," Effie said, looking sadly at her son. "But he won't go with us, neither. Tell him he's got no chance if he stays."

Stubby glanced at the knife in Jeff's hand. "I'm glad you ain't intendin' on usin' that. I bet you're pretty good with it."

"You got that right," Jeff said, his chin jutting. He ejected and retracted the blade several times, then twirled it between his fingers and ejected it again. Even so, Stubby could see the fear behind the young boy's eyes.

"I lived your life. I been where you are." Stubby unbuttoned the top buttons of his shirt. On his chest was a tattoo of a salamander.

"When I was your age, I woulda given anythin' for someone to have told me there was a way outta all this. That I could have a life that meant somethin'. Well, I'm tellin' you that, now. Only, you gotta come with us if you wanna live it. Otherwise, take a good look. Take a good whiff. If you don't leave and if you live long enough, this is gonna be you."

Suddenly, the door flew open. "Hey, what's goin' on? What are you doin' in here, old man?"

Stubby turned to see the buxom blonde filling the doorway. There was fire in her eyes. He swayed and pointed to the tiny bathroom on the opposite wall. "What kind a place you runnin' here, anyway? I gotta throw up and you send me to wait in line? Then this punk pulls a knife. What did he think I was gonna do? Cut the line?" Stubby followed the blonde's eyes to Jeff's knife.

"You drunken fool! The public restroom is across the hall. This one here's private."

Before she could move toward Stubby, he covered his mouth and made gagging sounds. "Oh . . . I'm gonna be sick," he said, and ran out of the office, down the hall, and straight out the front door.

Stubby walked as fast as he dared, stopping from time to time to pull the bottle from his shirt and fake a drink. As he pitched and stumbled down the street, he took every opportunity to get the lay of the land, to see who was where and why. He spotted two Salamanders coming out of Tulio's Bar, and slowed down. During one of his pretended swigs, he had bumped into three others. The five now converged and were talking. They looked agitated and on edge. Stubby guessed they were high. He would have to get past these five . . . twice more. Like running a gauntlet. And if they uttered a cry of alarm, Stubby had no doubt that more of them would come pouring out of the woodwork.

Stubby tried to picture Jesus' face, not because he was afraid, but to remind himself that no matter what was going to happen here, God was in control.

Jonathan paced the floor of his office, staring at the clock. Three times he had reached for the phone and three times he had thought better of it. He had been wrestling with this ever since Stubby had come and told him about Willie Tanner. *But what if Stubby was wrong?* Then Jonathan's phone call could destroy a life. Set Willie back so far it would take months, perhaps years, for him to trust anyone, again. And where was Stubby anyway? He had asked to borrow Jonathan's car. Said he'd be back in an hour. That was two hours ago, around the time Jonathan had sent Aunt Adel home with the promise they'd do dinner another night. She had understood the emergency and left. But Jonathan had yet to act. He wanted to talk to Stubby one more time before involving the police.

Jonathan stopped in the middle of the floor and watched the large, black hand of the desk clock tick off more time. He was getting an uneasy feeling. Not only about this whole Willie Tanner thing but about where Stubby had gone, and why. He suspected it had something to do with Cynthia and Effie. Stubby had seemed worried about them when he left. Now, that he thought of it, Jonathan had never seen Effie so distracted, either. Twice she dropped a dish at lunch and when he talked to her about the increase in the Day Care budget, something she had been hounding him about for weeks, she stammered "that's nice," and walked away. And hadn't Cynthia been rather cryptic when she talked about an errand she and Effie were going on? She had even asked for prayer. She never did that. For all Jonathan knew, the three of them were in danger. His stomach turned at the thought of something happening to Cynthia. It made him pick up the phone and finally call Detective Steve Bradley.

Then he began praying.

Out of the corner of her eye, Cynthia watched Effie mouthing prayers. She hoped they were getting through, penetrating the heavenlies and finding their way to the holy in-box because one mistake, one cry of alarm, and all three of them would be dead. She glanced at her watch and nodded to Jeff. "It's time."

Perspiration poured down Jeff's face as he gnawed his lip so hard Cynthia thought he was going to bite it off. "This ain't gonna work. I'm telling you, this ain't gonna work."

Effie walked over to her son and stroked his wet hair. "No matter what happens, I love you. You hear? You remember that."

Jeff nodded and fingered his back pocket where he had put his switchblade. "Okay. Let's go."

They walked silently down the hall, the two women in back, Jeff in front. They had barely gone ten feet when the tattooed blonde approached. "You finished with the office?"

"Yeah." Jeff made a slicing motion across his neck. "Give Tulio's Bar a call, will you?" It was Jeff's prearranged signal that would alert the gang the interview was over.

The blonde nodded. "Sure thing." Then she gave Cynthia a dirty look and walked away.

"Keep praying," Cynthia whispered as she slipped her arm through Effie's. She held onto Effie until they got outside, then released her and looked around. The streets were emptying. People were going home. Twilight was not far away. Perhaps God would use this to their advantage. That, and the element of surprise. The waiting gang was expecting the women on foot. Maybe by the time they figured it out, it would be too late.

Cynthia checked her watch. Stubby should be here any minute. That is if he was on schedule—if nothing had happened. She felt exposed on the sidewalk, and huddled closer to Effie. She could see by Effie's face, by the way Effie kept glancing at her son, that all of Effie's thoughts were on him.

Jeff was clearly agitated. He jerked when he moved and kept running his tongue over his mouth. For a minute he looked like he was going to bolt. But then Stubby showed up in Jonathan's old black Toyota and Jeff pulled open the door and shoved the ladies inside. Then he ran around the front and slipped in beside Stubby.

"Step on it, man!"

Stubby didn't have to be told twice. He did a quick U-ie, then sped back the way he came. Cynthia looked out the window in time to see the buxom blonde scream and shake her fist, then run inside, no doubt to call Tulio's Bar, again.

The Salamanders would be waiting.

Jonathan opened the door of his office to admit Detective Steve Bradley. He was amazed at how fast the detective had gotten here.

"So, where is he now?" Steve asked, taking large strides around the office, touching objects as he went.

"I assume you mean Willie Tanner. The last time I saw him he was in the TV room."

Steve stopped by a wall plaque. "'Blessed is he who considers the poor . . . the Lord will deliver him in time of trouble.' You still believe that? I mean, with you almost having two homicides right here. Where was the Lord in time of trouble? Huh?"

Jonathan sat down. "I'd say He was right here. Neither of them died, remember?"

"Yeah, I guess you could twist it that way. But I think it's a lot of hooey. And I've got to be honest. I consider people like you pretty useless. You flutter two inches off the ground spouting platitudes and looking for paradise, while the rest of us try to deal with the real world and make it a little better. That's why I can't understand what Cynthia sees in you."

Jonathan's heart jumped. It hadn't occurred to him that Cynthia considered him more than a friend.

Steve finally took the empty seat and stretched his legs. "I'll need to talk to Stubby before I do anything about Tanner."

Jonathan nodded. "I thought he'd be back by now . . . actually I'm a little worried. He said he'd be back within . . . ."

"Where did he go?"

"I'm not sure. But after Effie and Cynthia, I think. Wherever that is."

Steve cursed under his breath. "I had hoped Cynthia would just send the mother. Guess I should have known better. She's a reporter and can't help herself. No more than I could help it if . . . ."

"Where *is* she?"

"The Projects to meet with Effie's son."

"Isn't he a gang member? One of those . . . ."

"Salamanders. Yeah."

"And you let her go?"

Steve's eyebrows arched. "You can't stop Cynthia from doing anything she sets her mind on. You better understand that if you ever think you're going to have a chance with her. But for the record, I did try to stop her. And Cynthia isn't stupid. Even though I sometimes accuse her of acting like she is. She knew what she was getting into."

Jonathan closed his eyes. All day the Lord had kept an image of a reptile before him. Jonathan knew it was the symbol of one of the gangs and had believed it was a call to pray for them. But he had also sensed an evil that was stronger than anything Jonathan had ever experienced. Now, he understood.

No, Cynthia had no clue what she was getting into.

"Where's your car?" Jonathan said, leaping out of his chair.

"Out front, why?"

"We're going to the Projects."

Even before they reached Tulio's, Cynthia could see that a large group had gathered around the bar and were fanning out onto the street. *A human blockade.* They were forming a human blockade. "Stubby . . . ."

"Yeah, I see 'em."

"You gotta plow through, man. Just plow through. If you slow down, we're all dead." Jeff vibrated in his seat, his head jerking this way and that to see out both sides of the car.

"What are you going to do, Stubby?" Cynthia said, unable to keep the panic from her voice.

"Jeff's right. I ain't slowin' down. I gotta make 'em think I'll run 'em over."

Cynthia felt the car accelerate. She closed her eyes. They were really moving now—faster, faster. She heard that swishing noise a car makes when it whizzes past something. When she heard shouting, she opened her eyes in time to see a young man raise a gun and point it at her. A bullet shattered her window on entry and Effie's on exit. She saw bodies running in all directions trying to get away from the car. She heard sporadic gunfire. A ping, then a clanking sound told Cynthia a bullet had pierced one of the doors. When the car skidded, she knew a tire had been shot out.

"Keep going! Keep going!" Jeff shouted. "Whatever you do, man, don't stop."

"Front tire's flat!" Stubby said, clutching the vibrating steering wheel. A heavy chain came crashing down on the hood, then another one landed on top of the car. A third caught the rear bumper, making Stubby lose control. He swerved and almost hit one of the gang members. Cynthia saw terror on the young face as they passed, heard a loud clank as their bumper dropped off.

They were out of the worst of it. They had passed Tulio's Bar, but from the back window, Cynthia saw several of the youths firing their guns. She pulled Effie lower onto the seat, then felt the car skid again.

"They hit the back tire!" Stubby shouted. "We ain't gonna be able to go much further."

"You got to!" Jeff's hand was on the vibrating wheel, trying to help Stubby straighten it. "Ride the rims. Just don't stop. Don't stop!"

Cynthia could feel the car slowing, could see the crowd of young men shouting and running behind them, could see with every passing second that the Salamanders were gaining ground.

"I got lights goin' on all over the dash. They must've hit somethin'," Stubby shouted.

The car made a strange death-rattle-type shudder and conked out. Jeff threw open his door and jumped into the street. "Come on, run for it!" he shouted as he struggled to open his mother's door.

Cynthia glanced through the back window. It wouldn't be long before the gang reached them. Could they get away? Jeff might. He was young, fast. But Stubby? He wouldn't get twenty yards. Neither would Effie. Should she try it on her own? But how could she run away and leave her friends? And how many more Salamanders waited up ahead? She watched, as if it were a movie: Jeff opening the back door and trying to pull his mother out.

"Come on, run for it!" he shouted. But Effie was having trouble unfastening her seatbelt and pleaded with her son to go and save himself.

Cynthia didn't move. It was partly fear, partly a reluctance to leave the others. But mostly it was because she felt safer in the car, safer in this cocoon of metal that could grant her some protection of what was to come; perhaps add a few precious seconds of life to her account. Through the back window she could clearly see faces, now. Young, angry faces. She heard shouts, like war cries, rise to a deafening pitch. She closed her eyes. Only God could save them now. She heard the sound of stampeding feet, the sound of gun fire, the sound of cursing, and way off in the distance . . . the sound of a police siren. Cynthia opened her eyes and watched in disbelief as the Salamanders scattered to the four winds. But it wasn't until the unmarked car, with its pulsating light, pulled up next to them and Cynthia saw Jonathan and Steve's face, that she actually believed she'd live to see her thirty-first birthday.

In a flash, Jonathan and Steve opened their doors and jumped onto the deserted street. Steve's gun was drawn. Then Stubby, Cynthia and Effie tumbled out of their car. Effie went up to Jeff, weeping and laughing at the same time, and running her hands over her son as though making sure no bullet had found its mark. Stubby walked in a circle around the car, shaking his head.

Cynthia stood still, watching Jonathan approach her. When he was close enough, she threw her arms around him and buried her face in his chest. When she felt his arms encircle her, she began to cry.

"It's okay," he whispered. "It's okay."

Cynthia shook her head. "No it isn't. Look what we've done to your car." She felt Jonathan's chest heave as he laughed.

"I never liked it anyway. Now, I have an excuse to get another one."

CHAPTER 20

"This wasn't necessary," Cynthia said, bouncing in the back of a cab with Jonathan.

"Maybe not, but I wanted to come."

Cynthia rested her head against the seat back. "Well, I appreciate it." She closed her eyes. It had been a long day . . . and night.

"Of course I would have driven you myself . . . ."

"Don't even go there," Cynthia said, laughing. She opened her eyes and turned to him. "But this has made a believer out of me. I can't deny the existence of God anymore. By all rights I shouldn't be here. Stubby, Effie and Jeff—none of us should be alive. When I saw Steve's car pull up, with that red light flashing, I knew, right then and there, only God could have orchestrated something like that. Or . . . Cecil B. DeMille."

Jonathan chuckled and slipped his hand over hers. "No denying that God was with you today."

"My head's still reeling over all of it, including Willie Tanner. I always found him scary, but I never thought . . . never imagined Willie was the one. I can't get over how Willie's striped shirt triggered Stubby's memory. Or that Willie could be foolish enough to wear it again. He must have been pretty cocky, pretty sure that Stubby wouldn't remember."

"It wasn't just the striped shirt. It was also that tattoo of a reptile. But the police are going to need more if they want a conviction."

"Steve told me that since Stubby and I both claim our attacker smelled like fruit, the Medical Examiner's advice was to look for a type-1 diabetic. According to the ME, a type-1 diabetic can develop ketoacidosis from sudden physical stress. One of the warning signs is *fruity-smelling* breath." Cynthia felt his warm, strong hands cradle hers.

"So, if Willie Tanner is a type-1 diabetic, that might be all the proof the police need to charge him." He turned toward Cynthia. "I wonder why he did it, supposing it was Willie."

"I guess we'll have to let Steve figure that out." The car went over a large bump, causing Cynthia's head to roll onto Jonathan's shoulder. She left it there.

Jonathan draped one arm around her and adjusted his position to make her more comfortable. "You know, I had all I could do to keep Stubby from coming tonight. He wanted to stay with you. He thinks you need a bodyguard. He says this isn't over."

"It's over for me. I'll take a few days to get all my facts together and then write the piece. But once I've turned it in to Bernie, I don't want to hear the words Salamander, homeless or Skid Row ever again."

"Oh . . . ."

Cynthia squeezed Jonathan's hand. "Naturally, I want to continue hearing about the mission and Effie and Jeff. What do you think will happen to Jeff?"

"It's complicated. Effie told me about Jeff's knife fight. It's possible the rival gang member won't press charges. After all, he'll be implicating himself, too. We'll see. If nothing happens with that and Jeff isn't facing charges, then he and Effie and I will have to sit down and talk about his future. One of the things God has been showing me is that there are no quick fixes for these people. And that if I want to make a difference, I need to start a mentoring program, take those individuals who are interested, under my wing, in a manner of speaking. Some of these people don't even know how to go on an interview. What's more, when they get a job, they don't have the discipline to get up morning after morning and show up, never mind show up on time."

"When you talk like that, it makes it sound so hopeless." Cynthia watched Jonathan turn her hand over in his. Just his touch, just having him close, gave her a feeling of security.

"It's not hopeless. Just hard. I've been toying with this idea for some time. Maybe now would be the right time to implement it."

Cynthia lifted her head from Jonathan's shoulder and saw, by the street lights, the excitement on his face.

"The mentor program would stick with a guy from beginning to end—from the time he comes in for help to the time he's able to stand on his own two feet and support himself. One entire floor of the mission would house those in the program. And it would be tailored to individual needs, whatever they were—encouraging them to get a high school diploma, job training or drug rehab. Teaching them how to go on an interview, how to handle finances and a check book, etc. And it goes without saying, there would be plenty of Bible studies and prayer time."

Cynthia sighed. "Sounds like you're going to need more staff. It might even work. But regarding Jeff, I don't know. He's bitter and angry, and discipline's the last thing he's interested in. And that's the dilemma, isn't it? You can lead a horse to water but you can't make him drink."

"No, *I* can't. If Jeff doesn't want to do it, I can't make him. I've got to leave that to God. He can change any heart."

Cynthia leaned closer to the window as they passed the Starbucks where she got her coffee everyday. In less than five minutes she'd be home. She glanced at Jonathan and wished it would take another hour. She leaned back in the seat, her shoulder touching his. "I've never known anyone like you. When you thought I was a homeless nobody, you were willing to pay a lawyer for me and now, Jeff. He's nothing to you. Just a kid with a chip on his shoulder who got the raw end of the stick. Why would you go out of your way to help him?"

"I guess that's the part of your story you haven't gotten down. The part that covers forgiveness and mercy. I've been praying for you to understand it."

The cab rolled to a stop and Cynthia looked past Jonathan to her apartment. "You want to come in and explain?"

Jonathan shook his head. "No, but I'll walk you to the door." He helped her out, then took her arm as they strolled up the sidewalk.

Cynthia pulled the apartment key from her pocket. "You sure?"

"We're both exhausted."

She nodded and smiled then put her arms around his neck and kissed him, a long lingering kiss on the lips. When she parted, she saw a look of surprise on his face but sensed, too, that if she kissed him again, he wouldn't mind. Then, without turning back, she entered her apartment and closed the door.

Cynthia sat in front of the computer blocking out the noise of the busy newsroom and banging out her piece for Bernie. The words seemed to flow faster than her fingers. She put it all in, snippets from interviews she had done with more than three dozen homeless men and women, the drug connection, the two attempted murders, the early retirement of the Social Service worker. She even threw in the questionable and untimely death of Reverend Gates, and she ended by quoting Charles Angus and his declaration of war. Let Bernie cut what he wanted. She wasn't going to hold anything back.

The phone rang and she ignored it until she heard Steve's voice, then picked it up.

"What was that you were saying?"

"I was saying it turns out that our boy, Willie, has got type-1 diabetes. And you'll never guess who Willie worked for, on those rare occasions when he did work."

"Ah . . . I give up." Cynthia squinted at her monitor. *Five pages.* The word count was going to be a problem. *Let Bernie worry about it. Let him cut.*

"Alliance Bakery."

Cynthia almost dropped the phone. "Say that again."

"Alliance Bakery. He was one of their drivers."

Cynthia's mind began running a marathon as she grabbed a pad and pen. "What's the connection, Steve? My gut's telling me there's a connection. Now, what is it?"

"My gut told me the same thing. And the only thing I come up with is drugs."

"You thinking what I'm thinking?"

"Yup. Drugs are being moved into the Angus Avenue Men's Shelter via Alliance delivery trucks."

"On the other hand, it could be a coincidence."

"Sure, Wells. And there really could be a tooth fairy."

"We've got to slow down. Think this through. We're handling dynamite here, and we've got to be careful. Just remember, Steve, Charles Angus employs a lot of homeless. The reason he keeps his distribution and glass factory open is to provide employment for those who come to Skid Row. Maybe he views Alliance in the same vein."

"Maybe."

"And even if you find that Alliance is delivering drugs to the shelters, it doesn't mean Angus knows about it. It could all be happening behind his back. The man's a leading citizen, for crying out loud. He's promised to combat the drug problem. He's someone who believes in giving back."

"I guess now we have to determine who he believes in giving back to—others or himself."

"What will you do?"

"We'll stake out the bakery and the shelters, and we'll follow every one of those trucks until we're satisfied that their deliveries are only sugar and flour."

"If Angus gets wind of this . . . ."

"He wouldn't. There's just one person at the Department who knows Angus is connected to Alliance, and it's someone I trust. In addition to that, I'm keeping Tanner on ice. I figure we've got forty-eight hours—seventy-two at most—to come up with something before the lid comes off. After that, I'll need compelling evidence to continue."

"You're forgetting one thing. If Angus's hands are dirty, then he'll have friends at the station who are on the payroll. He could have a legion of people who'll try to cover up . . . who may have been covering for him for years. That means . . . ."

"That means my window will be more like twenty-four to forty-eight hours."

"It means you've got to be very careful."

"Wells, I thought we established you no longer care for me, that the odds of us getting back together were zero-zero and . . . ."

"And don't forget, I get the story. Before you throw any of those hounds at the station your bones, I want them first."

"Your *Trib* reporter at the precinct isn't going to like that."

"Don't worry. I'll square it with Bernie."

"Okay. And thanks."

"For what?"

"For smacking me between the eyes that it's really over between us."

After Cynthia told Bernie about Steve's phone call, she went back to her desk and called Jonathan. It took five full minutes for someone to find him, then another five minutes to convince him to have lunch with her. Then Cynthia hung up and flew out of the office.

Cynthia sat in the clean, well-worn booth of the South Oberon Diner staring at the handsome man across from her.

"I'm glad you came," Cynthia said softly.

"And I'm glad you asked. Although I've left a ton of work behind. I've been thinking about you all morning. But then I suppose that kiss last night was meant to keep you in my thoughts."

"Yup. A little like ginkgo biloba—to stimulate the memory cells."

"It succeeded."

Cynthia looked at her watch, then eyed the approaching waitress. "I know you have a counseling appointment and I promised I wouldn't make you miss it, so just order me something quick. A burger will do fine." She sat quietly while Jonathan ordered two burgers and two iced teas.

When the waitress left, Cynthia leaned over the table. "I wanted to see you because I got a disturbing call from Steve Bradley." She filled Jonathan in on the details then waited for his reaction. He just sat and stared.

"Well? What do you think?"

"I'm not sure. Maybe it's not Angus at all. Maybe it's someone in his organization who's behind all this."

"Any ideas?"

"That would explain Bill Rivers." He told her of the frustrating encounters he had had with Bill. "I don't think we should rush to judgment. We need to wait and see what Steve comes up with. But I find it disturbing."

"Yeah. Me, too."

"You have a spare couch?"

"*What?*"

"Do you have a spare couch? Big enough for someone to sleep on?"

"Yes. Why?"

"Because Stubby's still bugging me about staying with you until this thing is over. And now, all things considered, I think it's a good idea."

Cynthia pulled a napkin from the chrome dispenser and shook her head. "I don't think so."

"Why not?"

"I'm a private person, Jonathan. I'm not used to having people in and out of my apartment."

"You managed okay at the mission. And if you can eat and sleep with a building full of strangers, this shouldn't be difficult. Besides, it would just be for a little while. And it would mean a lot to me . . . knowing that Stubby was there looking out for you. I'd feel better."

"Would you?" Cynthia pressed the napkin between her palms and remembered the feeling of security she had had in the cab when he held her hand between his. But this overly zealous concern for her was out of character, even for him.

She leaned against the orange, vinyl seat, trying to think of what to say, trying to understand his motives. She had noticed how his eyes got soft when he spoke to people, and animated when he talked about God. But there was a new look she had never seen in them before and it took a moment to recognize.

Fear.

He was afraid for her.

"Why don't *you* come and stay on that couch yourself?"

Jonathan shook his head. "I think, for obvious reasons, it would be best that Stubby went."

Cynthia put the napkin on her lap, then reached over and took Jonathan's hand. "What happens with people like us? I mean, I don't date pastors and you don't date older women."

"I've been praying about it . . . about us."

"Well, thank you for that, anyway."

"You do know . . . naturally you would know . . . that I'm looking for a woman who is like-minded."

Cynthia smiled and squeezed his hand. "Of course I know that. So have there been many like-minded women who interested you?"

"No."

"But surely you've had girlfriends or lovers?"

"Girlfriends, yes. Lovers no—not in the sense you mean. I'm a pastor, remember?"

"But surely there's been someone special?"

Jonathan frowned and looked uncomfortable. "There was someone . . . once," he said, slowly. "Lydia . . . she was the daughter of a prominent pastor."

"Sounds like a perfect match."

"As it turned out, it wasn't."

"What happened?"

"She didn't want to be a preacher's wife. She said she had spent her entire life living in church, and now she wanted to find out what it would be like to live in the world. Sometimes this happens to preacher's kids."

"You mean they go out and slop pigs?"

Jonathan looked surprised. "You know that parable?"

"Well, you've preached it often enough."

"And you listened?"

Cynthia felt annoyed when the waitress came with their food and she had to release his hand. She watched him pick up the large sesame bun on his plate and take a man-sized bite. Everything he did, he did totally and with gusto. It would never be halfway with him. She wondered if she was ready for that. It took only a second to realize the answer was yes. It took another second to realize she had been waiting for someone like Jonathan for a long time.

I'm looking for a woman who is like-minded.

Would she ever be like-minded? Jonathan was far too committed to God and had far too much integrity to settle for less. And she had enough integrity to keep from faking it, even for someone like Jonathan.

"Tell Stubby I'll be home around seven. I'll leave a spare key under the mat. If he gets there before I do, he can let himself in." Cynthia picked up her burger and took a bite. She saw a look of relief wash over Jonathan's face. Yes, she had been waiting a long time for someone like Jonathan. And now that she found him, she didn't know how it was ever going to work out.

After freshening up the bathroom, Cynthia laid out clean sheets and towels for Stubby. She chose her best ones: Her Antoinette Blue sateen sheets and matching Azure ringspun towels. She glanced at the wall clock. Not quite seven. She had come home earlier than expected because she wanted to do a few things before Stubby got there. She couldn't believe how nervous and . . . excited she was. She still hadn't gotten over his generosity . . . his forgiveness of her great sin. She knew he would never mention it again. And though her nightmares had stopped, she had yet to feel any real peace over the matter.

She fluttered around her apartment wondering how she was going to entertain Stubby. Should she cook dinner? And what about breakfast? She rarely shared her home with anyone. She thought there was irony in the fact that she was doing so now with a homeless man, a man who, a few months ago, wouldn't have gotten the time of day.

Now, he was so dear.

The doorbell rang and Cynthia raced to answer it. Within seconds, she ushered in a short, smiling man holding a pizza box in one hand and an overnight bag in the other.

"Hope you like mushrooms and pepperoni," Stubby said, following Cynthia into the kitchen.

"Love them. That was kind of you to bring dinner. I was just thinking about what I should cook."

"That's the point. You ain't supposed to be cookin'." Stubby put the pie on the table. "I didn't bring nothin' to drink, but water's fine with me."

Cynthia laughed. "Me, too." She watched Stubby wander into the living room, then heard him whistle.

"You got a real swanky place here. I ain't never stayed in a place as nice as this." When Cynthia entered, he turned and smiled. "An earthly place, that is. 'Cause heaven's beyond anythin' we got down here."

"Maybe you can tell me more about it—your heavenly adventure—over dinner," Cynthia said as she walked back into the kitchen. She pulled dishes and glasses from one of the cabinets and set the table. When she finished she stepped back. To one side was her Edelstein made-in-Germany white china with its delicate green and brown pattern. Lenox crystal water goblets stood, like sentries, next to the plates. Centered in the middle of the table was a crystal bud vase containing the single yellow rose she had cut from her small flower garden that morning. Next to that was the pizza box.

A study in the ridiculous.

Cynthia laughed to herself and pulled out green linen napkins, then placed one next to each plate.

Might as well complete the folly.

She walked to the hutch and retrieved two sterling silver knives and forks from the drawer and placed them on the table. She may not enjoy cooking, but she loved setting a handsome table.

When she was done, she glanced at Stubby who had been watching the whole comedy from the doorway.

"I hope you ain't gonna fuss like this every time we eat."

Cynthia laughed and shook her head. "Our first dinner together should be special. After that, it's paper plates."

"You even own a paper plate?"

Cynthia walked up to Stubby and gave him a hug. "Of course not."

Jonathan had been sitting in his office for hours. Even when Miss Emily came and tried to get him to go to dinner, he had refused. Ever since coming back from lunch with Cynthia he had been disturbed—on two counts. First, his attraction to Cynthia was becoming overwhelming. The second point was even more troubling. Cynthia's revelation about Alliance caused him to think about something he had been mulling over for a long time. Stubby had told him about the death of Reverend Gates, including his suspicion that it wasn't accidental. Now, for the first time, Jonathan was beginning to wonder if there might be something to it. Between the mammoth laundry room and the rooms used as classrooms, the basement saw its share of traffic. But since coming to Beacon Mission, Jonathan had yet to find a reason for visiting it late at night. According to Stubby, the Medical Examiner believed Gates had fallen down the stairs and died between one and two a.m.. Why would Gates go down to the basement so late?

Why would anyone?

Jonathan rolled a pencil between the palms of his hands. For more than an hour he had been mulling that question over in his mind. Along with the Angus Avenue Men's Shelter, Alliance Bakery supplied the mission as well. And that's what kept sticking in his mind. If Alliance was running drugs to the men's shelter, had they also been running drugs to the mission? And if the answer was yes, that could explain what Reverend Gates was doing on those cellar stairs at one in the morning. Because if Gates found out about it and was trying to discover where the drugs were stored, and waited until there was no one to disturb him in order to investigate, then a one o'clock trip to the basement made perfect sense. And if someone caught him going down and thought Gates suspected something, then a push, a shove, a murder, also made sense.

Jonathan rose to his feet. Maybe it was time to check out the basement.

Cynthia watched Stubby wipe his mouth with the linen napkin then wad it into a ball next to his plate. Throughout their meal she had observed that Stubby was a man with little polish. He chewed with his mouth open, talked with his mouth full, used his knife like a fork, burped without apology, and preferred to wipe his mouth on his sleeve rather than a napkin. She looked at his deeply lined face, his large kind eyes, his sweet smile. She couldn't remember when she enjoyed a meal more, that is if she didn't count lunch with Jonathan today.

"Did you ever think you'd have a bum stayin' in your house?"

Cynthia got up and filled his goblet with more filtered water from the refrigerator, then sat back down. "You're not a bum, Stubby."

"Well . . . not no more. Not since the Lord got hold of me. But when I seen Jeff, I swear Cynthia, it was like I was lookin' at myself in the mirror, you know? I grew up like him. My dad would come home drunk as a skunk, and beat the tar out of everyone. Yeah . . . Effie told me all about Jeff's dad. And everythin' she said, it was like she was describin' my own father. I hated that man. And that's what drives you—all that hate, all that rejection and hurt. You wanna strike out and hurt somebody, too. That's why I joined the Salamanders. Even then, they was around. Nothin' changes. Now, I understand why. We got this here adversary, the devil, who's lookin' to see who he can mess up. 'Course you probably don't believe in the devil. But he's real and he'll use anythin', even gangs to destroy kids, to kill their dreams, their future."

Cynthia absently traced stick men on the table with her finger. "Life isn't fair, is it?"

Stubby took a giant bite of his fourth slice of pizza, chewed it quickly, then swallowed. "It ain't about fair or unfair. It's about winnin' a prize. A prize the devil don't want us to win. I seen Jesus' face,

Cynthia. And when He looked into my eyes, I knew, I *knew* that all I had gone through was nothin' compared with what I had to look forward to with Him for all eternity. That's the prize. This life—you blink and it's over. The real prize—it's Him, God Himself. And it's forever."

Cynthia put down her glass and rose to clean up the dishes. Stubby was talking crazy. She didn't believe a word he said. At least not the last part. She pulled a large Ziploc bag from the drawer and stuffed the leftover pizza in it. But if it was true, if there was any possibility it was true, then she wanted that prize, too. But the thing about prizes was that only a few got them. And if that was the case, what made her think she'd qualify? What made her think Jesus would want her?

Jonathan spent a good ten minutes trying to find a flashlight. He finally found one in Miss Emily's kitchen junk drawer. The basement was well lit for ordinary use, but Jonathan planned to poke into spaces where the overhead lighting didn't reach. He checked his watch. A few minutes past ten. He heard voices coming from the vicinity of the TV. By eleven everyone had to be in their rooms. There was no way he could check out the basement before then. He'd have to wait.

Cynthia spread her sateen sheets over the couch, then a light blanket over that. She slipped a pillowcase over her spare pillow, fluffed it and positioned it at one end. "Hope you'll be comfortable."

"Don't worry about me. I slept on things you wouldn't believe!"

"Well, okay then, goodnight. I'm hitting the hay." Cynthia gave him a hug. "Maybe tomorrow night you can tell me more about heaven."

Stubby looked like he was going to say something. Instead, he just smiled and nodded.

Jonathan crept from his room into the hall, stopped and listened. It was after twelve and all was quiet. He tiptoed down the hall, through the kitchen, then down another hall towards the supply room. Opposite the supply room was the door leading to the basement. He opened it, then stopped again and listened for sound. Nothing. He flipped the light switch.

From the top of the stairs he could see the first two dryers in a row of twenty. Nothing looked amiss. He tucked his flashlight into the waist of his slacks and began his descent. As he went he scanned the ceiling, steps, and walls. He didn't know what he was looking for. He supposed he wouldn't know until he found it.

When he got to the bottom of the stairs, he flipped on another light, illuminating the entire laundry room. Starting at one end, he checked the walls, ceiling, floor and all the machines. He checked for any sign that something had been moved or was out of place. When he got to the corner, he pulled out his flashlight and turned it on. He inspected every nook and cranny. When he was satisfied, he moved down the hall and began the procedure all over again.

Then one by one, he inspected the classrooms. There were three in all. By the time he finished the last room, he was convinced he had let his imagination run wild. There was nothing here. Reverend Gates had slipped and fallen. Pure and simple.

He placed his hand on the light switch and was about to turn it off when his eyes happened to glance at the metal bookshelf. It resembled the other bookshelves in the two previous rooms: gray, four shelved and approximately five feet by four feet, with a metal backing. He had already checked it out and found nothing amiss. Only . . . it wasn't overflowing with material like the shelves in the other two rooms. It just held about twenty books and two stacks of magazines.

Odd.

Jonathan walked over and scanned it from top to bottom. After staring at it for another minute, he began to feel foolish. The only odd thing was that he was thinking it was odd. It was late. He was tired. It was time to tuck his overactive imagination into bed and call it a night.

He gave it one last look, then stepped back. When he did, he noticed the industrial carpeting in front of the bookcase was more worn than it should be. He bent down and ran his fingers over the short pile. The rug was crushed and worn in an arching pattern. It made no sense. He squatted on his heels, and stared at it. It reminded him of something. Then it came to him. His mother's improperly hung pantry door had made this same kind of pattern on the kitchen linoleum floor. This bookcase had been dragged across the rug.

Repeatedly.

Jonathan rose to his feet and pulled the bookcase forward. It was heavy, impossible to move if it were full. When it was several inches from the wall Jonathan stopped and glanced behind it. His heart flipped. There, about a foot off the ground, a large opening was cut into the sheetrock.

He pulled the bookcase further, until there was enough space for him to get behind it, then he retrieved his flashlight from the floor, turned it on, and inspected the opening. Strewn between the studs were drug paraphernalia, a small scale and a residue of whitish-looking powder—all covered in cobwebs. Obviously, no one had been here in a while.

He scanned the opening again and noticed a torn wrapper wedged in one of the corners. Carefully, so he wouldn't disturb anything else, he reached in and pulled it out. It looked like part of a paper bag, the kind sugar or flour came in. He read the lettering: ALLIAN. The rest of it had been ripped off.

He flashed his light again into the opening. There was nothing else. But he didn't need anything else. It all made sense, now. This was where the drugs must have been hidden after being delivered to the mission. Hidden until they could be distributed by their inside man. Apparently, operations had stopped since Reverend Gates' death. But now that the mission was open again, had a new inside man been installed? *Willie Tanner?* Unlikely. He didn't have what it took to be head of maintenance. It was reasonable to think it was the head of maintenance that ran the drug operation. A head maintenance man could come and go without suspicion; would have access to the entire building. It would be important to have the right man in place. Was that why Stubby had to be removed? Was Willie the advance man? Someone sent to remove Stubby and create a vacancy until a new inside man could fill the spot?

Jonathan pushed the bookcase back into place, then picked up his flashlight. The police would have to unravel this mess. But one thing was certain. Cynthia was right. Alliance Bakery was delivering drugs to the shelters.

Cynthia.

Jonathan flicked off the light and bolted down the hall and up the cellar stairs. He had to call the police. It was after one o'clock, but maybe someone at the station could get hold of

Steve. He couldn't take the chance of telling anyone else what he found here. If Bill Rivers or Charles Angus was involved, no telling who could be trusted. After Jonathan contacted Steve, he'd call Cynthia.

She was in real danger.

Cynthia rushed around the apartment stepping over couch pillows and bedding. She was late. And she had promised Bernie she'd be in early or at least on time so she could wrap up her story.

Just wait till he read the ending!

Last night, Jonathan had woken her and Stubby out of a sound sleep, then made their heads spin with his discovery. He had made Detective Steve Bradley's head spin too, so much so that Steve planned to immediately send his forensic team to the mission and gather enough evidence on Alliance so he could move on them first thing this morning. Jonathan had made Cynthia promise not to step foot outside her apartment without Stubby, and not to let anyone in. Then Jonathan had spoken to Stubby and given him the same information and instructions.

It had taken Cynthia hours to fall asleep again, but when the alarm went off, she bolted out of bed, not even allowing the snooze feature to go through its usual paces. So, by all rights she shouldn't be rushing. But she was, thanks to having one bathroom and two people who wanted to use it. She wasn't accustomed to sharing it. Her timing was off and so was Stubby's. They had spent most of the morning bumping into each other.

She glanced around the apartment. It looked like a bomb had gone off. She had never left it like this. She smiled because it didn't matter one bit.

"Get the lead out, Stubby. I'm late!" she shouted toward the kitchen. She could hear the refrigerator door close. Within seconds, Stubby walked out carrying two slices of buttered toast.

"I made us breakfast."

Even from where Cynthia stood, she saw the inch-thick layer of butter on each piece. "Thanks." She blew Stubby a kiss then ushered him out of the apartment, locked the door, and headed for her car, leaving him to carry the toast.

"Great day, ain't it, Cynthia? Just look at them colors on that bush, and over there at them flowers."

Cynthia hurried to her silver Jeep Cherokee, not bothering to look at the scenery. "If I don't get to work on time, the only color I'll be seeing is red, when Bernie starts breathing fire." She pressed her remote and unlocked her car.

"Oh, no!" Cynthia said, standing behind her Jeep. "Some people don't know how to park!" She squeezed past the truck that had pulled too close to her driver's side, and opened her door. "For heaven's sake! How am I supposed to get in?" No matter which way she turned she couldn't open her door wide enough to slip through. She looked over the hood at Stubby. "Don't get in. I'll have to use your side." Cynthia tried walking toward the front of her car so she could cross over to Stubby's side, but the truck was angled in front and passage was impossible. She turned and walked toward the rear.

She squeezed past the white paneled truck and noticed that the large company letters which had once blazed across its side, was now scrapped off, leaving a faint outline. She scanned it as she passed. A-L-L-I-A. She turned to Stubby in panic. "ALLIANCE!" she croaked.

"What?"

"ALLIANCE!" she repeated, pointing to the truck. Before Stubby could move, the rear of the truck rolled up like a garage door and a man, the size of a gorilla, jumped out, landing a foot from Cynthia. By the time Cynthia or Stubby realized what was happening, the man grabbed Cynthia and jerked her towards the back of the truck. Another pair of hands, belonging to someone inside, pulled her upward and onto the truck bed.

"Stubby!" Cynthia screamed as she saw the door of the truck close. She tried to scramble out, but somebody held her back then threw her to the floor. Then the interior of the truck became black. "Stubby!" Cynthia screamed again.

"That little runt can't help you now," a voice said in the darkness. "My friend'll make sure of that. Then he'll drive us some place nice and quiet."

Cynthia's heart melted with terror when she recognized the voice.

"Yeah, we'll go to a nice quiet place where I can keep my promise. And I'm gonna take my time. I'm gonna enjoy it."

Perspiration streamed down Cynthia's face. She could barely breathe. Outside, she heard Stubby shouting and the sound of bodies crashing against the truck.

What if that man killed Stubby?

Oh God. What was she going to do? She couldn't count on Stubby's help. She found herself praying . . . begging God to protect her and Stubby . . . to help them both out of this. She looked around wide-eyed. She had grown accustomed to the dark and could see Skinner standing close by. It didn't look like he had a weapon, but she couldn't be sure. What was she going to do? How was she going to get out of this? Oh God . . . *help me!*

"You're gonna see what happens to troublemakers. And it ain't gonna be pretty."

Frantically, she scanned the walls for anything hanging, anything she could use as a weapon.

Nothing.

"I've been looking forward to this. I would've done it for nothing. But I don't mind telling you I'll be getting a nice piece of change for my pleasure. Looks like you really pushed somebody's buttons."

Cynthia, who was still sprawled on the truck bed, pulled herself up on one elbow. From this position she noticed a coiled rope not far from her left hand. If she knocked him away then got to the door and open it, she could escape.

Oh God, give me strength.

"And where we're going, you can scream and cry all you want. In fact, I'd like you to."

Cynthia sat up and inched backward until her left hand felt the rope. Then she brought her feet up under her so she could spring forward.

"I'll start with your face."

Now, Cynthia. Now. Cynthia swallowed hard. *Do it now.* It was as if a voice whispered in her ear. Her fingers tightened around the rope. In one quick motion she was on her feet. Then in blind, savage fury, Cynthia swung the coiled rope in the air and heard it connect. She raised her hand again and again, swung blindly. Skinner groaned as she scrambled for the door.

She was inches from the lever now. All she had to do was pull and the door would roll up. With a strength that surprised her, she smashed the rope against Skinner one last time and saw him reel backward. Her hand was on the lever now and she pulled with all her might. As daylight entered, she saw Skinner remove the knife from his sheath and lunge toward her. Without thinking, Cynthia threw the coiled rope causing it to uncoil and entangle him like a dozen lassos. Then she dove out of the truck and on top of Stubby. He was panting, and at his feet the gorilla-like man lay rubbing his eyes.

"How . . . what . . . ?" she stammered, feeling her elbow and left ankle throb with pain.

Stubby bent over and pulled the gun from the sprawled man's waist and turned toward Cynthia. His gaze remained fixed on the prone man. "'God has chosen the foolish things of the world to confound the wise.' That's scripture, case you don't know. Before he took one punch or got his gun out, I nailed him with my toast, one in each eye. It was the butter that done it, made it where he couldn't see. Then I knocked him to the ground. How'd you get out?"

Cynthia glanced at the truck and watched Skinner stagger toward the opening. "Same as you. God."

"You're learnin', kiddo. Now, go call Steve."

While Stubby covered the gorilla and Skinner with his gun, Cynthia retrieved her bag from the asphalt where it had fallen and pulled out her cell then punched in the familiar number. As she listened to the phone ringing on the other end, she felt the sun warming her head. Behind her, she heard footsteps. People were gathering. Someone shouted "What's going on?" then someone else yelled, "Call the police." Cynthia took a deep breath and smelled wisteria. It was good to be alive.

Thank you God.

CHAPTER 21

"I'm telling you, it's the best story you've ever done. People are eating it up. They just can't get enough. The *Trib*'s selling like hot cakes. Circulation says their phones are ringing off the hook." Bernie sat with his feet on his desk, a big grin on his face.

"That's because people like to read about giants who get knocked on their tails. And Steve gave me plenty of good inside info when he cracked the Skid Row drug ring along with the Angus Empire."

"False modesty doesn't become you, Wells. Let's face it, you aced this in spite of me or Angus or anyone else."

Cynthia picked up her pen and began drawing stick men down the length of her yellow pad. Steve's investigation had turned up nothing incriminating on Bill Rivers—only the fact that Bill had a younger brother on drugs who had dropped out of sight and who Bill hoped would turn up at the mission. But Cynthia was still having trouble digesting Steve's other discovery—that in addition to using Alliance Bakery to run his drugs, locally, Charles Angus used his glass factory to package drugs, and his distribution company to ship them to seven different states.

"I know the Angus Empire got hurt when many manufacturers were no longer competitive on U.S. soil, but Charles Angus, with all his millions, didn't need to do this, to get involved in drugs. So why did he? It still baffles me."

"Greed? Power? Maybe fear that his empire was slipping away. Who knows? He's not the first rich man to dip his beak into a poisoned well."

"I checked his financials. His corporations are doing well. It's not like he was desperate or needed money. I can't figure it out. There was no reason for this."

Bernie repositioned his feet. "Some things can't be figured out, Wells. Just chalk this up to a bad seed, a bad apple, whatever you want to call it. You can't explain people. Just when you think you've got a handle on them, when you think you've seen it all, another surprise comes down the chute."

"I suppose."

"Look, you did a terrific job. You should be proud of that. It's a great story. Even if you don't win a Pulitzer, you've won yourself a raise. And you know I don't give those often. You can round out the story with something on that young woman, what's-her-name from Social Service . . . ."

"Pamela Harmon. But she must remain anonymous. I promised her that."

"Fine. Fine. Do a story on her—without revealing her identity—then maybe a piece on Social Services and another on the South Oberon gangs. We've got enough here to milk this thing for another few weeks." Bernie chuckled as he removed his feet from the desk and plunged his hand into the jellybean jar. "The other papers are fuming. They want to know why none of their reporters got wind of this story. I told them because they didn't have Cynthia Wells on their payroll."

Cynthia noticed how comfortable Bernie looked in his massive leather chair. It made her hard wooden one feel all the more uncomfortable. "Didn't you promise to buy a new chair if I got this story?"

"Chairs, shmairs. You've bigger fish to fry. You finish up with that Pamela person and see what else you can dig up on Social Services and those gangs. The longer we keep this going, the better Circulation will like it."

Jonathan was about to sprawl across his bed with a good book when the phone rang. His heart jumped. Maybe it was Cynthia.

"Hello, Dearest!"

"Oh . . . hi Aunt Adel."

"You sound disappointed that it's me."

"I'm not. I'm just tired."

"I won't keep you. I just wanted to tell you that everyone, absolutely everyone at church is buzzing about Cynthia's articles. Of course you came out quite well, too. Especially in that piece about your keen instincts and how you checked out the entire cellar looking for clues. You're a hero."

"Aunt Adel . . . ."

"You two make a good team—you and Cynthia, I mean."

"Aunt Adel . . . ."

"So when will you be seeing her again?"

"I don't know. It's hard to say."

"Just take a guess."

"Probably never. She doesn't even return my calls. Now, that the story's finished, I'm sure she's already onto something else. You know how it is."

"No, not really. But just so you know where I stand—if the two of you do get married, that's okay, even if there will be no living with Gertie."

"Aunt Adel, *please* stop talking nonsense."

"Gertie's convinced that your relationship with Cynthia . . . ."

"I have no relationship with Cynthia. Not the kind you mean."

"Gertie's convinced that this is all her doing, getting you and Cynthia together, since it was, according to Gertie, her prayers that turned you around. All week she's been telling everyone she's sure you'll announce your wedding soon. And she wants you to know she expects an invitation."

"Aunt Adel!"

"And if you do, marry Cynthia that is, then there'll be no end of hearing her say, "I told you so.""

"Aunt Adel that's not going to happen because . . . ."

"Anyway, I just wanted you to know that if you did marry Cynthia, I could live with all that. I could live with Gertie's remarks."

Cynthia couldn't sleep and wandering around the apartment. Everything was spotless. She ran one hand over the back of the sofa, then strolled to her desk. She glanced at her reflection in the polished top. The past week was a blur, like a merry-go-round whizzing out of control and going in one endless circle. But it had stopped.

Finally.

And her life was coming back together. No more looking over her shoulder, worrying if Skinner or someone else was there.

So why couldn't she sleep?

She headed for the kitchen. Maybe warm milk would help. She filled a mug, then put it in the microwave. While it heated, she scanned the pile of papers next to the phone. She saw a note with the name, Jonathan, scribbled across it, then another one and another one. She sighed. How could she have gone so long without returning his calls? She remembered the merry-go-round. It could happen. But would he understand?

The microwave beeped and as she removed the mug, she glanced at the clock. It was too late to call him, now. She sipped the milk, nearly burning her tongue. If the milk didn't work, maybe she'd finish her project. She glanced at the mirror propped in the corner. There were still areas that needed to be enhanced with black paint. She walked in the opposite direction. The thought of working on the mirror left her cold.

She paced the kitchen, then pulled out one of the chairs and sat down. Why did she feel so antsy, so wired as though she had eaten a dozen candy bars?

Why couldn't she sleep?

She should be as happy as a clam, back in her safe nest, her life under control, again. And things couldn't be better at the paper. She had never seen Bernie so delirious—talking of Pulitzers and raises. He'd give her carte blanche, now, at least for the next few months.

The milk steamed in the mug and Cynthia raised it to her lips. This feeling of being out of sorts, this depression, didn't make sense. She took a few sips, then put it down. On the other hand, maybe it did. Because unlike most people, Cynthia *didn't* like to see the giant land on his tail. She preferred to see him tall and strong and bearing up the weak, strengthening all those around him with his power and goodness. The truth was, the fall of Charles Angus had saddened her. A lot.

She tried putting him out of her mind, but couldn't. As a reporter, she didn't like unanswered questions, and the one that kept popping in her mind was *why*? Why had a man like Charles Angus, a man who had everything, do what he did?

Jonathan had often talked about fallen man; how we were all sinners. No shock there. No bursting of a bubble. In her line of work she had seen plenty of corruption—sinful men living sinful lives. And she well knew the cornucopia of her own sins. But if that was what all mankind was, where was the hope? But there was hope. She had seen that, too. Stubby, Effie, Miss Emily all testified to it.

Stubby had tried to tell her about it, had tried to tell her about Jesus, but she had been too afraid of rejection. Or . . . was she too afraid of what it would cost?

Cynthia swirled her milk and watched it pitch from side to side. When it settled, she brought it to her lips then stopped. A cup of hot milk wasn't going to cut it. After a brief hesitation, she put it down, picked up the phone and dialed.

"Hi, Jonathan."

"Cynthia? Is everything alright? Are you okay?"

"I'm fine. I just wanted to talk."

"Now?"

Cynthia squinted at the clock. "I know, it's indecent to call at this hour."

"I called three times last week. You never returned one of them. I was worried. I haven't talked to you or heard from you since the night I told you about what I found in the mission basement."

"I know, I'm sorry."

"I thought we were friends."

"We are."

"Well, friends don't treat each other like that."

"I know. *I know.* But it's been crazy. Really crazy. Between all the paperwork at the police station and their questions, then working to get my story out . . . then the sequel . . . ."

"I've been reading them. You did a great job."

"Yeah, that's what Bernie said, but Jonathan, in my heart I know the story isn't finished." She heard him groan.

"With you, it's always the story, isn't it?"

"A good reporter digs until she gets the *whole* story. And there's so much I still need to find out . . . to understand. Like Stubby's changed life. Like Effie and Daisy and Miss Emily. I really need to understand."

"Cynthia, you can't come back to the mission. It's too disruptive."

"To whom?"

"To me."

Silence.

"This isn't about you and me—although I'd like it to be . . . want it to be. But first I've got to get this settled."

"Get what settled?"

"Once, you did a sermon about someone who was on a journey and stops at his friend's house because he was hurt or in trouble or was searching for answers. And even though it wasn't convenient, the friend didn't turn him away.

"What is it you want, Cynthia?"

"Some answers . . . some hope . . . some faith. Some . . . mercy."

AUTHOR'S NOTE

I so enjoyed writing **Mercy at Midnight** because I love stories of redemption. I'm constantly taken back by the great love of our God and how He desires none to perish. There is no life too damaged, too broken, too lowly to escape His attention or love. That should be a comfort to us all, for that means no one is disqualified.

If you are one who has yet to experience the love and acceptance of God now is a good time to change that. Jesus said in John 14:6, "I am the way, the truth, and the life: no man cometh unto the Father, but by me." That's the starting point and there's no getting around it. And it's simple, too. Just ask Jesus, our sin bearer, to forgive you for all your sins. Tell Him you want Him to come into your life, leading it, directing it, in short, to take control. Then be prepared to be blessed and changed, and to come into a vibrant new life with Him.

I can think of no greater wish for you than this.

Love and blessings,
Sylvia Bambola

http://www.sylviabambola.com
sylviabambola45@gmail.com

Made in the USA
Middletown, DE
10 July 2016